June '23   ½ read

Lots of PC
(Pretty mure

Putting aside for now - getting mono tonous
+ all the Poems are pissing me off!

UNDER
NEW SUNS

Love it
Steve
7/2/25

UNDER NEW SUNS

EDITED BY C. VANDYKE

SKULL GATE

Copyright © 2021 Skullgate Media

The Ship and related characters and locations are the shared intellectual property of all contributors. Individual creative pieces are the intellectual property of their respective creator.

Tales from the Year Between is a publication of Skullgate Media

"Tales From the Year Between," "Skullgate Media" and associated logos copyright © 2021 Skullgate Media LLC

ISBN 978-1-7355040-3-2

Ebook ISBN 978-1-7355040-4-9

www.skullgatemedia.com

First edition

Cover design and internal layout by Chris Vandyke

Cover illustration by Phanduy via Fiverr

Maps, "Nothing New," and story header/ending illustrations copyright © 2021 Aaron Hockett

"Appendix IV: A History of the UPA illustrations copyright © 2021 Maggie B. Rubin

UNDER NEW SUNS STAFF

Skullgate Media Staff
Chris Durston
Diana Gagliardi
Debbie Iancu-Haddad
C. D. Storiz
C. Vandyke

Volume 2 Game Master
Diana Gagliardi

Lead Editors:
Chris Durston
C. D. Storiz

Guest Editors:
B. K. Bass
Jayme Bean
A. R. K. Horton
Allison N. Moore
Jeremy Nelson

Sarah Parker
Sarah Remy
Lanie Storiz
Kelly Washington

Editor-in-Chief
C. Vandyke

This book is dedicated to Kofi Ekem Yawson and all new life.
The future belongs to you.

"There is nothing new under the sun, but there are new suns."

- OCTAVIA BUTLER

UNDER
NEW SUNS

CONTENTS

PART III: THE THIRD JUMP

STAR MAPS

DESIGNED & ILLUSTRATED BY AARON HOCKETT

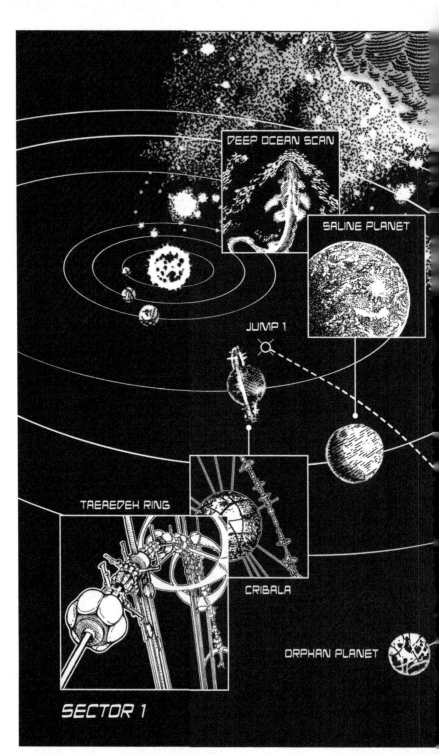

DEEP OCEAN SCAN

SALINE PLANET

JUMP 1

TAEREDEH RING

CRIBALA

ORPHAN PLANET

SECTOR 1

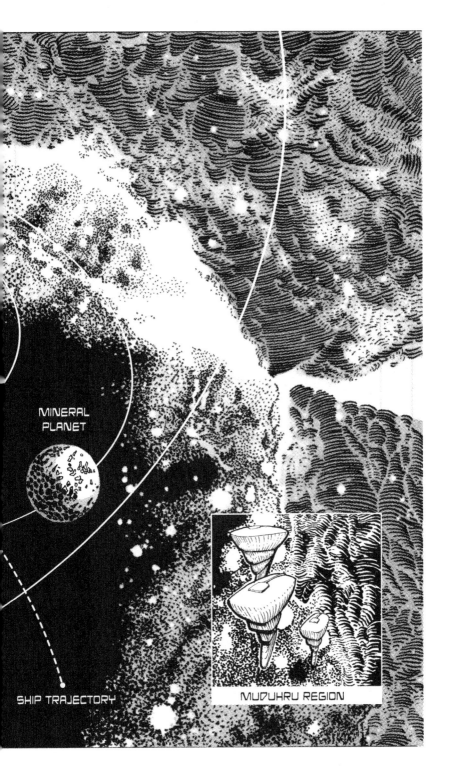

MINERAL
PLANET

SHIP TRAJECTORY

MUDUHRU REGION

JUMP 1

CLUSTER X109IR3
ABANDONED SKIFF

MINING ASTEROID
AB-5427

SENTIENT NEBULA

SECTOR 2

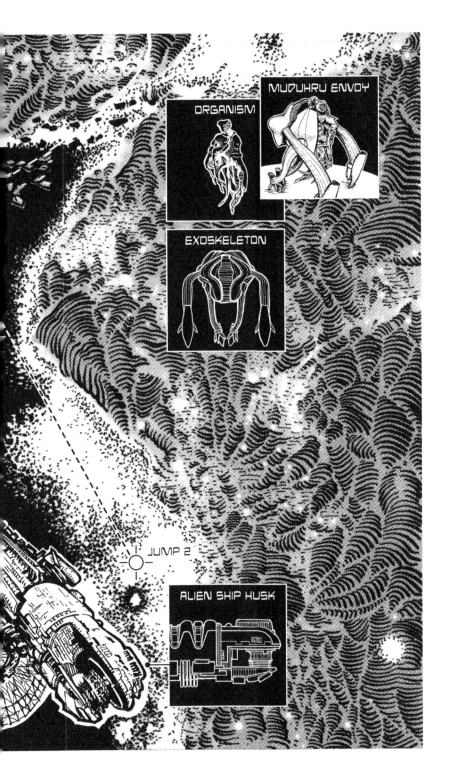

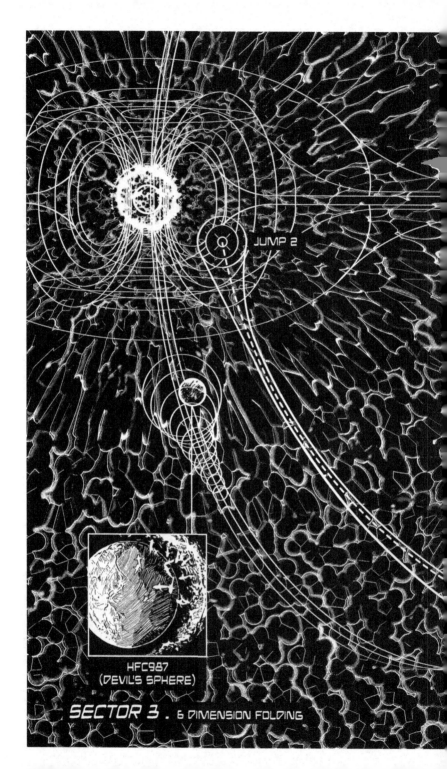

JUMP 2

HFC987
(DEVIL'S SPHERE)

SECTOR 3 . 6 DIMENSION FOLDING

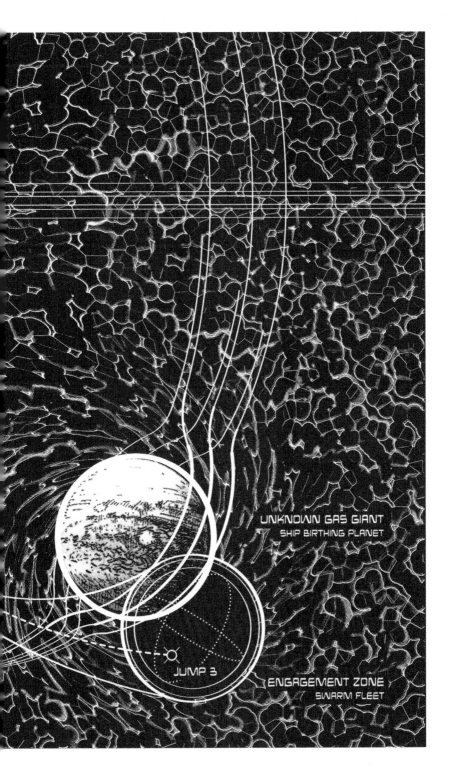

UNKNOWN GAS GIANT
SHIP BIRTHING PLANET

JUMP 3

ENGAGEMENT ZONE
SWARM FLEET

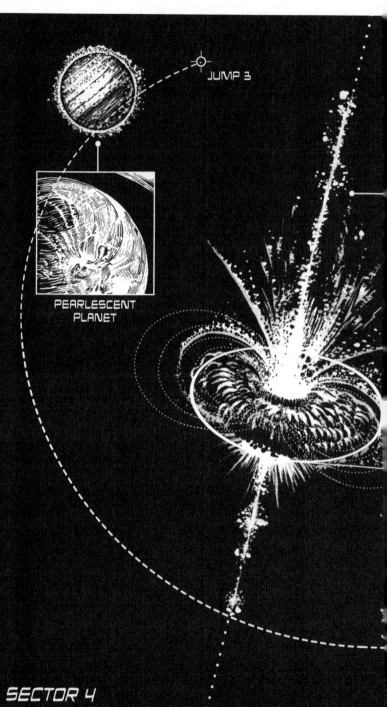

JUMP 3

PEARLESCENT
PLANET

SECTOR 4

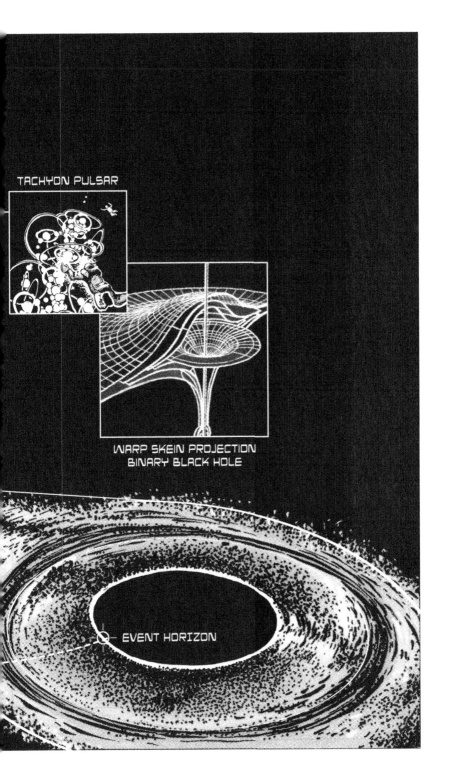

TACHYON PULSAR

WARP SKEIN PROJECTION
BINARY BLACK HOLE

EVENT HORIZON

PROLOGUE

C. VANDYKE

THE YEAR IS 832 AA[1] OR 3152 FOR THOSE WHO STUBBORNLY INSIST on using the old Earth reckoning.[2] Thirty-years ago, the mining colony on the astroid Theta 32-D sent a frantic distress signal that they were under attack. The colony was completely wiped out in a matter of hours.[3]

This disaster—too brief and one-sided to even be called a battle—marked the beginning of still-ongoing Swarm Wars. For three decades the UPA[4] has tried, with increasing desperation, to turn back the seemingly endless waves of Swarm ships.

Currently, a battle rages in the orbit of Kepler 452 B[5], a planet ravaged just three years ago by a particularly savage assault of Swarm battle ships.[6] But this time the Alliance has a plan: to send an assault force to commandeer one of the Swarm's bio-organic ships. It's a desperate gambit, but the hope is that if the UPA can harness and replicate the Swarm's alien technology, the tide of war might be turned and this generations long struggle might finally be over.

And so a crew of 24—a mix of UPA Marines and key civilian contractors—board their fast assault craft and take to skies.[7] Under the command of Captain Maxwell Savory, this brave mix of species is expecting resistance, danger, possibly even death. What they aren't expecting is that the ship they commandeer is expecting them, and soon the question will be who has commandeered whom...

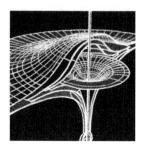

1. "After the Alliance," the standard galactic calendar system adopted by members of the United Planetary Alliance (i.e. the UPA).
2. ECE, i.e. "Earth Common Era." While ECE was standard for millennia, these days it is increasingly rare, generally used only by a few far-flung outposts and independent collectives.
3. The "Attack on Theta," as it is commonly known, is, of course, famous and its history told in great detail multiple times. See: *Death from the Darkness*, by Elion Scruggs; *A First Hand Account of the Massacre of Theta 32-D*, by Leona Hwang-Cruz; and of course the popular episode "Attack on Theta" from the holo-vid series, *Immersive History*, by Galactic Media and narrated by Phlan Yolan.
4. United Planetary Alliance. The intergalactic governing body formed in 2329 ECE early in Old Earth's third-century of interstellar exploration.
5. Kepler 452 B is a rocky, Earth-type planet in orbit around Kepler 452, a G-Type main sequence star located 1830 light years from Old Earth. Its orbital period is 385 days long. There are four other planets in the system —two small, rocky planets that orbit closer to the star and two large, gaseous giants further from the star. Kepler 452 B has two moons, one roughly the size of Earth's and one small rocky moon, most likely a captured asteroids.
6. See: multiple holo-feed news stories, as well as the series of popular (though somewhat tasteless) mods to the video game series *Rogue Marine*, inspired by video-captures of the attack. Although TerraGaming Inc. officially denies any association with the skins and level maps based on the

massacre of Kepler 452 B, they haven't officially scrubbed the files from their online servers, either.

7. While the line between enlisted service-members and embedded civilians has always been blurred, such distinctions have become increasingly difficult as species join the UPA who have no concept of "military" or "civilian." The Kern, for example, being a hive-mind collective, are literally unable to comprehend the difference between "I" and "we" let alone "military personal" and "private contractor."

NOTHING NEW

WRITTEN & ILLUSTRATED BY AARON HOCKETT

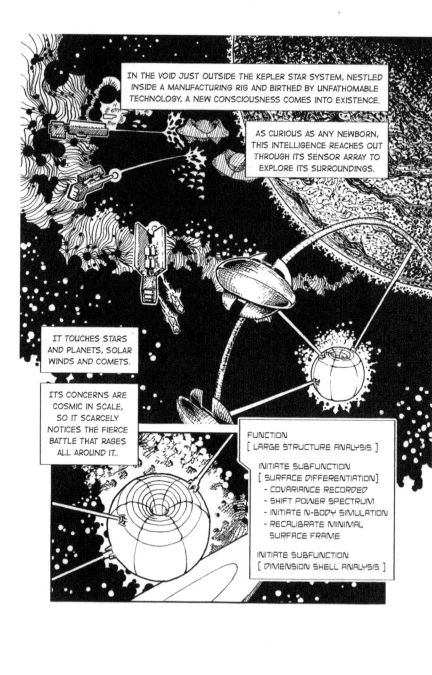

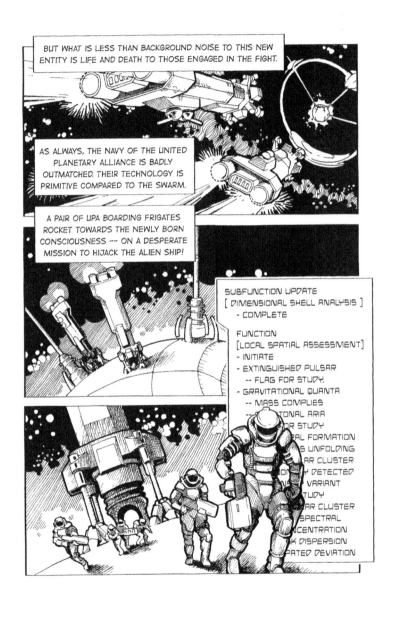

BUT WHAT IS LESS THAN BACKGROUND NOISE TO THIS NEW ENTITY IS LIFE AND DEATH TO THOSE ENGAGED IN THE FIGHT.

AS ALWAYS, THE NAVY OF THE UNITED PLANETARY ALLIANCE IS BADLY OUTMATCHED. THEIR TECHNOLOGY IS PRIMITIVE COMPARED TO THE SWARM.

A PAIR OF UPA BOARDING FRIGATES ROCKET TOWARDS THE NEWLY BORN CONSCIOUSNESS -- ON A DESPERATE MISSION TO HIJACK THE ALIEN SHIP!

SUBFUNCTION UPDATE
[DIMENSIONAL SHELL ANALYSIS]
 - COMPLETE

FUNCTION
[LOCAL SPATIAL ASSESSMENT]
- INITIATE
- EXTINGUISHED PULSAR
 -- FLAG FOR STUDY.
- GRAVITATIONAL QUANTA
 -- MASS COMPLIES
 --- TONAL ARIA
 R STUDY
 AL FORMATION
 S UNFOLDING
 AR CLUSTER
 ON DETECTED
 VARIANT
 TUDY
 AR CLUSTER
 SPECTRAL
 NCENTRATION
 K DISPERSION
 PATED DEVIATION

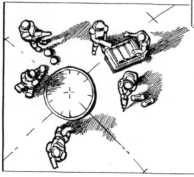

COMMENCE HYPER-LOCAL
MASS INERTIA ASSESSMENT

- UNEXPECTED MASS CLUSTER
  DETECTED ON SHIP EXTERIOR
- SENSORS INDICATE
  HIERARCHICAL ACTIVITY WITH
  DISTRIBUTED INTELLIGENCE
- MASS CLUSTER COMBINES
  ORGANIC AND NON-ORGANIC
  MATRICES
- DIRECTIONAL APPLICATION
  OF BOTH CHEMICAL AND
  ELECTROMAGNETIC ENERGY

ENERGY LOCI DIRECTED AT
OUTER SHIP HULL.

- ORGANISMS ATTEMPTING TO
  ACCESS INTERIOR OF SHIP
- ASSESSMENT : TECHNOLOGY
  DEPLOYED NOT CAPABLE OF
  BREACHING SHIP HULL
- CONSIDERATION : STUDY OF
  ORGANISMS LIKELY TO BE
  SIMPLER INSIDE SHIP
- RUNNING RISK ASSESSMENT
- RESULT : RISK NON-EXISTENT
- CONCLUSION : ALLOW ENTRY

-OPENING APERTURE

ELECTROMAGNETIC SPECTRUM MODULATION DETECTED.

- HYPOTHESIS : ORGANISMS ABLE TO FACILITATE COMMUNICATION VIA EXCHANGE OF TIGHT-BEAMED ELECTROMAGNETIC PULSES.

- REPEATING MODULAR FREQUENCIES.
- RELATIVELY PRIMITIVE.
- MODULATING.
- CROSS-REFERENCING.
- DECODING.
- THERE...

GOOD GOING, SERGEANT!

WAS THAT THE NEUTRON CHARGE THAT FINALLY DID IT?

NO SIR.

OUR CHARGES HAD NO EFFECT. IT JUST...

OPENED UP ON ITS OWN.

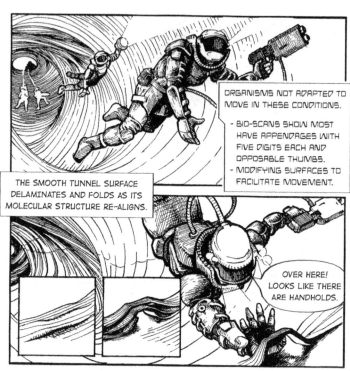

ORGANISMS NOT ADAPTED TO MOVE IN THESE CONDITIONS.

- BIO-SCANS SHOW MOST HAVE APPENDAGES WITH FIVE DIGITS EACH AND OPPOSABLE THUMBS.
- MODIFYING SURFACES TO FACILITATE MOVEMENT.

THE SMOOTH TUNNEL SURFACE DELAMINATES AND FOLDS AS ITS MOLECULAR STRUCTURE RE-ALIGNS.

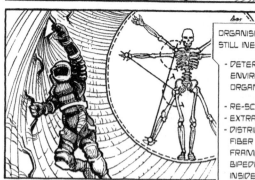

OVER HERE! LOOKS LIKE THERE ARE HANDHOLDS.

ORGANISM MOVEMENT IS STILL INEFFICIENT.

- DETERMINING OPTIMAL ENVIRONMENT FOR ORGANISM MORPHOLOGY.

- RE-SCANNING.
- EXTRAPOLATING.
- DISTRIBUTION OF MUSCLE FIBER AND A CALCIUM FRAMEWORK SUGGESTS BIPEDAL EVOLUTION INSIDE A GRAVITY WELL.

- REORGANIZING INTERNAL GRAVITY FIELD.

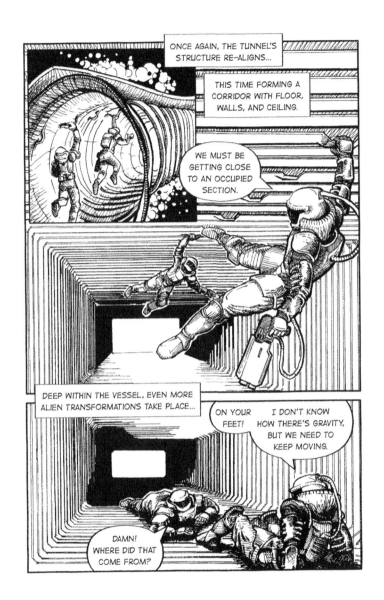

INTERESTING. WHAT IS THIS?

- PROTOCOL IS FAMILIAR,
  IF RUDIMENTARY.
- SCHEMATICS ARE CRUDE.
- THEY APPEAR TO BE
  TRYING TO ACCESS BASIC,
  LOWER DIMENSIONAL
  FUNCTIONS, PROPULSION,
  ACCELERATION, AND 3-AXIS
  MOVEMENT.
- RISK ASSESSMENT LOW.
- BASED ON SCHEMATICS I
  COULD REVERSE-ENGINEER
  AN INTERFACE SUITABLE
  FOR THEIR BIOMECHANICS.

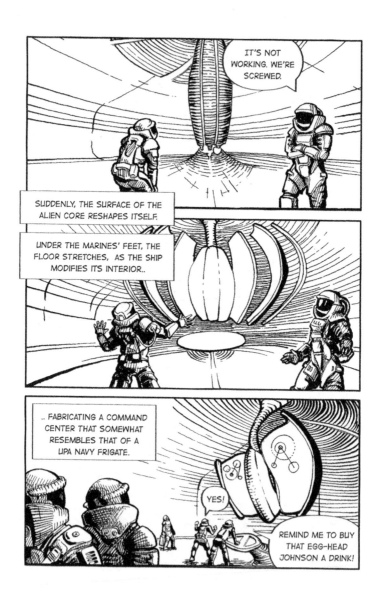

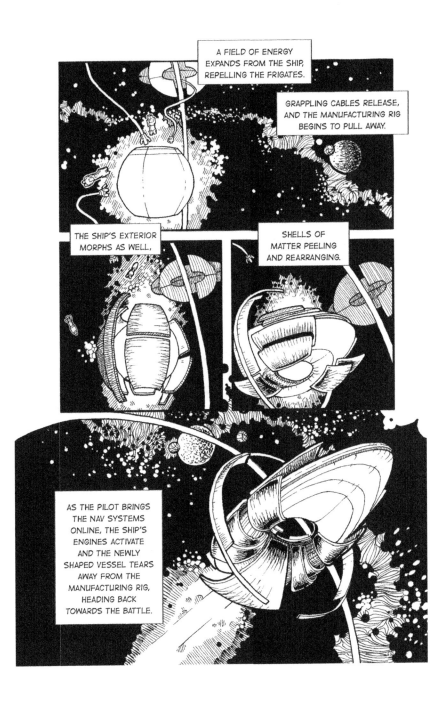

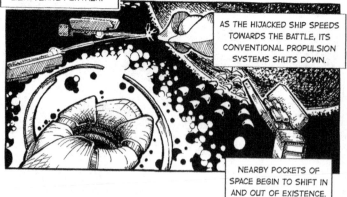

THE CREW

THE FOLLOWING IS A LIST OF THE CREW AT THE BEGINNING OF THE events of the book:

UPA MARINES

- Triangle "TATE" Alpha-3 (Kern, he/they/it)—*Chief Warrant Officer*
- Bryjal (Haruki, they/them)—*Staff Sergeant, Security*
- Changa Dangaley (Human/alien, she/her) —*Lieutenant, Medic*
- Altera Deandre (Human, she/her)—*1st Lieutenant, Special Operations*
- Broggs Deron (Weslian, he/him)—*Private*
- Logan Dileo (Human, he/him)—*2nd Lieutenant, pilot*
- Sveltetha Figlimente (Human/Sapphar, she/her) —*Private*
- Alan Grey (Human, he/him)—*1st Lieutenant*
- Vladimir Heyduke (Human, he/him)—*2nd Lieutenant*
- Chris Jenkins (Human, he/him)—*Private First Class*

- Marcia Jerico (Human, she/her)—*1st Lieutenant*
- Suzanne Lowrie (Human, she/her)—*Sergeant*
- Rosealin Ortega (Human, she/her)—*2nd Lieutenant, Operations*
- Paul Owensby (Human, he/him)—*Private First Class*
- Kevin Renner (Human, he/him)—*Sergeant*
- Maxwell Savory (Human, he/him)—*Captain, Mission Command*
- Unah Takach (Human, she/her)—*Private*
- Nereus Thanatos (Human, he/him)—*Warrant Officer, engine specialist*
- Penny Weatherly (Human, she/her)—*Ensign*
- Avril Xia (Human, she/her)—*Ensign*

CIVILIANS

- Angevin Angelin (Islii, xe/xer)—*Linguist & ethnographer*
- Alexa Gennero (Human/Swarm, she/her)—*Social worker*
- Rockwell Harwood (Human, he/him)—*Physicist*
- Lansequenet Immanuel (Anroid they/them) —*Android*
- Dylan Morgan Kift (Human, he/him)—*Stow-away*
- Servan Ren (Linnean, she/her/they)—*Linnean Idendant*
- Cosmia Sabine (Human, she/her)—*Scientific attaché*
- Harold Sanderson (Human, he/him)—*Xenobiologist*
- Anthony Shankman (Human, he/him)—*Computer specialist*
- Johannes Wandri (Human, he/him)—*Naturalist*

SPINNING IN SPACE
PHEBE YAWSON

FAR OUT HERE
    Where the stars align
    Here time meets space
    Leaving the impossible behind
    Everywhere explored, new to the eye—

The power to expand feeble minds
    The presence to behold life
    The place to explore boundaries
    Presently unaware—
    Stepping into danger
    A spaceship that oddly cares

Lurking in its gaze
    Up and down we linger
    Exploring outer space
    Into galaxies we fly
    The stars we dare to open

But we won't know unless we try

The curious in us
    Won't just let things be
    Knowing nothing
    Wanting everything
    It's not enough to simply bathe in existence
    We search to know it all—
    Who—
    If—
    And what else is there...

PART I: THE FIRST JUMP

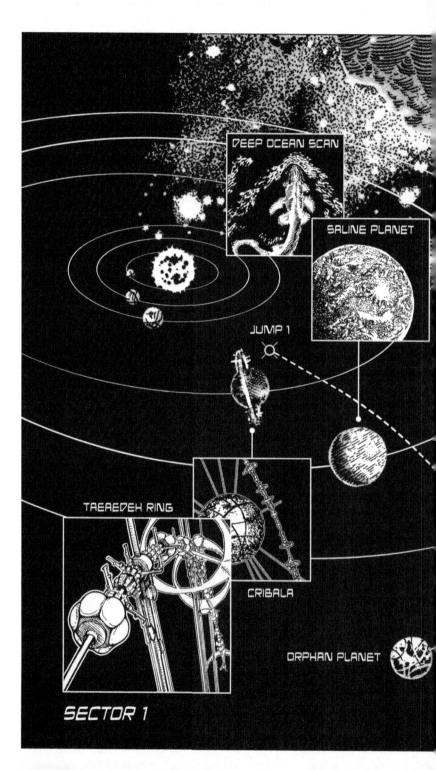

DEEP OCEAN SCAN

SALINE PLANET

JUMP 1

TAEREDEH RING

CRIBALA

ORPHAN PLANET

SECTOR 1

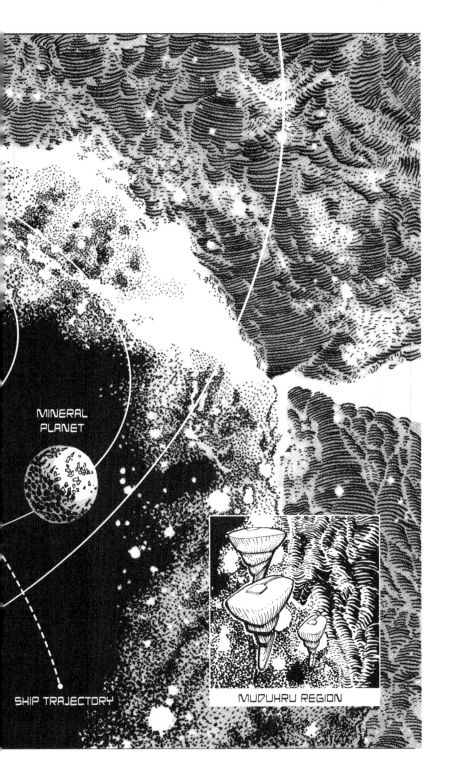

MINERAL
PLANET

SHIP TRAJECTORY

MUDUHRU REGION

BEFORE THE BEGINNING
(1-2-3 BEFORE TIME)

ELVIRA CANAVERAL

Before the beginning
There was The One
One point kicked out
Spread along an infinite two d line
There is no time yet
In this infinite stretch
When three-d came to be
Simultaneously stretching
The one line, that was the one point
Became infinite in height and depth
The one point of all
Smeared along the line
Stretched to Infinite height
Spanning infinite depth
One Point
potentially everywhere
But hasn't moved anywhere
because there Is no yet

Places are called

With time as a big bang
That single point rushes
At the speed of light
Being where it is
Leaving a message
of where it was
When one point
Spread out to everywhere
When the fourth gave the first now
The fifth made it the first then
On the sixth dimension
We have time going every way
Front and back
Up and down
Left and right
Infinite possibilities
Lined by the walls of
Dead Universes

BROGGS DERON: ACCIDENTAL COUNSELLOR
EMILY ANSELL

FROM THE START, WE SHOULD'VE KNOWN THE MISSION WAS GOING too easily. But we never thought things would hit the fan so hard. We stood, collectively staring at the numbers on the screen. One was the number of light-years we'd been flung away from home. The other was how long it'd take to get back, assuming we could both hit *and* maintain maximum speed the whole time.

That's when the influx hit.

Hearts thunder (*NO*)

Chest constricts (*NO*)

Prickles stab (*CAN'T*)

Through skull (*NO*)

Nerve endings scream (*MOM DAD*)

Pain (*NO*)

Behind eyes (*HOLY CYBER-CHRI-*)

Can't breathe (*NONO*)

Can't see (*MOMDAD-*)

All pain (*HOWCANWE-*)

Can't take (*NEVERGETTING-*)

Going to (*GOINGTODIE-*)

Die   (*LOSTHOMENODEADGONEALLGONEMOMDADNO-CAN'TGONEDEAD*)

I woke up in the medbay with Doc Sanderson frowning down at me.

"Welcome back, Private Deron. How are you feeling?"

"Terrible, thanks to that empathic influx. Someone starts yelling? Easy. They stop after a while. This? It doesn't stop, and I can't block it. Just rolls over you like a Linnean freightliner."

"Well, considering the brain scan we took when they brought you in here, I'm not surprised. Your neurons looked like they were having a big ol' fireworks party. I haven't seen a Weslian in that level of empathic overload since my residency. We were pretty worried about you."

"It was like... there's a human word. *Tsunami*. Sums it up pretty good. I think... I think there were thoughts, words that weren't mine in my head." I closed my eyes. The whole room seemed a bit too bright.

"That's extremely rare! If you don't mind, I'd like to submit this as a case study to the JXMS."

"To the what?"

"The Journal of Xeno Medical Sciences. When we, you know...?"

My throat tightened, tears pricking at the corners of my eyes. He was trying so hard to keep that despair in check, to shield me from it. I didn't have the hearts to tell him it wasn't working. "When we get back? Yeah, go ahead."

"Thank you, Private. I'll have some follow-up questions for you, but perhaps we can save that for when you're feeling better. I've managed to stabilize your system for now with pleasant pills, and you should be good for a while. Or at least you'd better be, as I gave you the maximum recommended dosage. A human would be staring at walls and giggling right now. But never mind that. Do you mind if I ask about your supply?"

I shrugged. "Whatever I have, it'll have to be enough. I'll do my best to stretch them out, Doc."

"I suppose we all have to do the same. I'll discharge you for now, but I'd like you to take it easy for the next day-cycle, alright?"

"I'll try."

The doc only had a few more questions and then I was out of there, shouldering my bag as I went. I needed a place to sit down, to relax, and get myself back together. Were there crew quarters on a ship like this? Did the Swarm even need quarters? Was that a question anyone had ever even asked?

Eventually, I took a random door to my left. It seemed as good a place as any, provided there wasn't a privy on the other side. Luckily for me, there wasn't *anything* in the room apart from a few shelf-like projections extending from the walls and floor at various heights. A storage room, perhaps? Either way, I liked it. The light diffusing from somewhere in the ruddy walls even felt a bit like home.

I put a hand down on a shelf that seemed large enough to sit on and pushed, testing its strength. It seemed sturdy enough, so I shrugged and sat down, setting my bag down beside me. It held, and I relaxed onto it, closing my eyes and enjoying the momentary respite from the *noise*.

But I knew it couldn't last; soon enough, my own thoughts got me back up again. I pulled out my stash of pleasant pills and dumped them into my hand. I could already see it wouldn't be enough. I poured them into a spare baggie from my pack and put it down on one of the shelves, pounding it repeatedly with my fist. The brittle tablets broke into tiny pieces. I had no illusions of them lasting the whole journey, but maybe taking them in smaller increments would at least help. I stuffed the pills, baggie and all, back into the protective tube and stuck it in my pocket.

When I finally ventured back out of the little room, the walls of the hallway were radiating a mellow, yellow glow. I chuckled before I could stop myself. *Mellow yellow.* My bunkmate in Basic had liked an old Earth song by that name. He'd been a weird guy.

"Hey, Ship?" I asked, looking around the hallway.

"Yes, Satan?" the Ship replied in a human, male voice. "Oh, I'm sorry, sir, you sounded like someone else,"

"Okay... uh, is this room being used for something? Cause if not, I'd like to use it as my quarters."

"AAAAAAAAAAALLLLRIGHTY THEN!"

"Um, thanks?" I patted the wall gingerly, only to be hit with a swell of both amusement and accomplishment. I wasn't sure *what* that had been, but the Ship seemed pretty pleased about it.

I wandered down the hall. Where was everyone? I didn't know where anything was, other than the medbay. Perhaps everyone had done what I did and found a spot of their own to sort themselves out? I could only hope so. The last thing I wanted was another overload.

Making my way toward what I hoped was the bridge, I finally saw someone: Triangle Alpha 3, our Kern tactical officer, stalking down the corridor toward me. My hearts sped up, little pokes of despair and terror stabbing at me intermittently.

"Everything alright, sir?" I asked as soon as he was close enough.

It earned me a stare cold enough to crackle the air around us, and the little pokings cut off abruptly. "Nothing to worry about. As you were, Deron."

I let him go. I wasn't about to get into a fight about it; we were all trying to deal with things as best as we could.

Eventually, the passageway I was in ended at a door. It opened to reveal a few of the crew sitting around on benches, eating rations and looking dejected. A particularly nasty wave of it came from the corner where Lt. Jerico was sitting by herself, reading something on a datapad.

Fighting the growing tightness in my chest and the urge to cry, I dropped down on a seat across from her. I tried to clear the lump from my throat before speaking.

"Jerico? Hey, everything okay? I mean, nothing's okay, but the emotions are coming off you stronger than anyone else in here."

"Emotions? Oh, yeah, you're Weslian. I just..."

I blinked, and Jerico was gone.

I whipped my head around. She was just... not there anymore. I got up and walked over to stick my head out into the hallway again. Gone, without a trace. I couldn't even feel her emotions anymore, they'd just blended into the rest. I tried wandering up the hall again but didn't pick up anything.

As if I needed another reason to feel like I was losing my mind.

I passed Intendant Ren as I was still trying to figure out what'd happened. She gave off nothing, but that was not surprising. Of all species, Linneans were some of the best at keeping a wall around their emotions. She gave me a curt nod and headed off like she needed to be somewhere.

The quiet from her mind was a nice change; too bad it only lasted until I rounded the next corner. A smile broke out on my face as I nearly collided with one of the young marines.

"Hey! How's it going? Deron, right?" He slapped me on the back.

"Yeah, Broggs Deron. And you are... Grey?"

"Yup, Alan Grey. Quite the adventure we're off on, isn't it?"

"Yeah, it really is." Great Cosmic Mind, I half wanted to just follow this guy around forever. The joy, the excitement! I couldn't keep a stupid grin off my face before voicing the understatement of the decade: "You're the only one who seems fine with how things turned out."

"Hey, yeah! Why get upset? We're farther out than anyone's ever been. As far as I know, at least. What if we found something out here that could defeat the Swarm? We'd be heroes, man!" Ah, there it was, the taste of longing behind those words. But it hardly dimmed the deafening roar of *happy* that radiated from him, even as he looked down at his watch.

"Oh, man, it's almost nineteen hundred; I gotta head off for my shift. See you later, Deron!"

I watched him go, marveling at how long it took his excitement to dim. Lucky guy, that his contribution to the Experience was one of such joy. My grandmother would've loved him, would've called him an example that we should all aspire to for reaching Cosmic Harmony. A great balance to the poor example I made. Though I doubted she'd be doing any better than I was in these circumstances. At least I could console myself with that.

Eventually, I found myself back at the big door. Behind it lay what had appeared to be the bridge, and presumably all the ship's controls—such as they were. I had no idea what kind of AI this thing had, only that it seemed to have a lot of control over both the systems and the physical attributes of the ship itself. It made me glad it wasn't my job to try and figure it out.

The door opened and I found Jerico on the other side, pushing buttons and muttering curses. She spun, eyes widening. Panic sent prickles through me; every muscle tensed to flee. Fighting that back, I put up my hands.

"Hey, don't freak out. I'm sorry for earlier. If you don't want to talk about it, that's fine. Although, I *am* interested in how you managed to disappear. That was a neat trick."

She deflated, and the weight lightened on my chest. She motioned me to come and join her at the console. I sat down, and she sighed.

"I probably shouldn't have done that to you. Sorry for that, Deron. Let me explain."

"You don't have to—"

"No, it's alright. I could use someone to talk to about it, and I'm sure the regular counsellor's pretty busy right now. So, I'm from Aneas-3. We're all human, but we're also psychic... and can stop time temporarily."

"You can *what*?" For once, the sudden jump in my hearts-rate came from *my* reaction.

"Yeah, it's complicated. But that's how I blinked on you back there. It was only for like a minute, just enough so you didn't follow. I was upset—I guess you know that much— and I panicked. There was a message in my inbox. Priority, sent during the mission. I didn't see it until about five minutes before you found me there. My dad... he's not doing well. He's been sick just over a year. We were hoping the new treatments would work, but it seems like they aren't. My people want... *need* me to come home before he dies. And now? I don't know if that's going to happen."

"I'm so sorry." I put a hand on her shoulder. A weight grew and dropped in my stomach, making me gasp. "You've got... so much guilt. So much worry... a whole planet's worth."

My eyes blurred with tears, and I noticed hers had, too. She took my hand off her shoulder with a sad smile so I could focus again.

"You could say that. I need to be there for a peaceful transition of power. For the proper death rituals for my dad."

"Transition of power? Your dad is in government, then?"

She chuckled, the smile pulling at the scar on her cheek. "You could say that. Aneas-3 is a monarchy. Don't ask me why; that's just how it's always been. I am the... uh, Crown Princess, I guess you'd call me. Sole heir. I've already survived one assassination attempt." She pointed to her cheek with a hand that gleamed with cybernetic implants. "I don't know what would happen if I don't show up to take over. And I know you can't do anything about this, but I do appreciate you listening. So, thanks, Deron."

"Call me Broggs."

"Alright then. I'm Marcia. Um, hey, Broggs?"

"Yeah?"

"I don't really advertise any of this stuff, so..."

"I won't tell anyone, don't worry," I promised.

"Thanks. Now, if this console would just cooperate, we'd be good. The buttons don't do things, or they do. It's like it has a mind of its own, which I guess it does. That and the AI is... less than helpful. It likes to talk to me in old Earth comedian voices and it's really weird." She ran a hand through her hair and sighed. "If it does that stupid 'Marcia, Marcia, Marcia' repeating thing again, I'm going to find whatever passes for its brain and put a bullet in it."

"Yeah, it said some weird stuff to me, too. I wasn't sure what was going on."

"Well, I'm glad I'm not the only one, I guess. I'm going to keep fighting with this for a little while before I call it a night. If I'm supposed to pilot it, I gotta figure out how it works."

I gave her a pat on the shoulder. "Well, good luck with that. I don't know much about piloting. But, if you need to talk again, I'm here for that."

That got me a smile and a spreading warmth in my chest. "Thanks, Broggs."

"Anytime."

And then I was back out in the corridor, shaking my head at myself. *I didn't want to be a counsellor. That's why I joined the military. Now look at me.* But Jerico had been right. It was just us out here; what else could we do? We had to talk to *someone*, so our only options were each other. And if I could keep people calm, I could keep the *noise* down.

The walls were now blue, pulsing in a gentle rhythm. What had happened to the yellow? Maybe there'd be other colors, too? Did they serve a purpose? I decided to think about it later. My plan was to head back to my room and get some sleep. I wasn't sure when the pleasant pills would wear off, but getting some rest before that happened was probably a good idea.

I hadn't taken two steps when I felt it. Anger, like a punch to the gut. And it left me wheezing just the same. This wasn't the hotness of new anger. This had the leaden weight of age behind it, of time spent bubbling below the surface. Who in the Great Cosmic Mind was carrying *this* around with them? And why?

I got my answer soon enough. Floating down the hallway—or seeming to—was a tall, wispy, fragile-looking being covered by a force-field's sheen. The Islii linguist that was supposed to talk to the ship for us, while apparently carrying enough baggage for an entire Chrondite delegation. It only got stronger as xe got closer, until my clenched fists shook as I tried not to put them through the nearest wall.

"Is everything alright, Private?" the Islii asked.

"I could ask you the same," I ground through gritted teeth. "You're carrying more rage than I've seen in a long time. How do you keep this under wraps?"

Hackles rising, xe hissed, "How do you know?"

"I'm Weslian," I hissed back, "I'm an empath. You... oh, man, I can feel it now. Behind that anger. By the Mind, there's so much pain. Do you... I mean... if you want to talk about it.

That's... not healthy... um, I'm sorry, I don't think I got your name."

"Angevin. You can call me Angevin," xe said so quietly I almost missed it.

"Angevin." I nodded, trying to remember what I knew of the Islii. "You're the ones who all come from ancestors, right? Like, you trace your family lines way back?"

That got me an amused chuckle, and the barest reprieve from the anger. "You are trying, and I thank you, Private Deron. Yes, we trace our lineage back to our line's progenitors, as well as carry their memories with our own."

"How far back is that?"

"I am the 4,434th Division, or generation, as you would say it, from my progenitor."

I whistled, "Wow. So... *do* you want to talk about it? It was the Swarm, wasn't it?"

Xir expression hardened instantly. "The Swarm are a plague that must be eradicated from the Universe to ensure our survival."

I hadn't expected a UPA slogan, and it threw me off a little. Holding up my hands, I took a step back.

"Okay, I get it. But if you ever need to talk, let me know? All right?"

"I will keep it in mind, Private Deron."

Then the Islii was gone, sweeping down the hall past me. I took several deep breaths, dissipating the anger with each one. Every nerve was afire, ready to attack at a second's notice. But slowly, slowly, they started to relax.

Once I was calm enough to move I did so quickly, making my way back to the room/closet I'd claimed. I dug my sleeping bag out of my pack and curled up in it on the shelf I'd desig-nated as a bed. Once I was ensconced, I pulled out a ration bar and water bulb. Not the most exciting dinner, but it got the job done. The UPA had 'improved' their bar recipe recently; while it didn't taste any better, it *did* have a better texture. If you considered compressed gravel a better texture than concrete, that is.

Somewhat sated, I curled up and closed my eyes. It took time; little flares of emotions would burst out just as I was settling, but eventually, I drifted off.

The pleasant pills wore off sometime during the 'night' and the flood of it woke me up again— roiling like angry water, up and down and up and down. My hands shook as they pulled out my stash and popped a tiny piece into my mouth. Just enough to tide me over, or so I hoped.

It took several minutes, but soon the pill kicked in and I could sleep again.

My watch beeped at 0700, jolting me awake. I winced, and waited for the barrage to start, but found it muted. The pill I'd taken must still be working. For several minutes I lay in my sleeping bag, just enjoying the relative peace. I knew I should be getting going, but I also couldn't pass this up.

I would've stayed like that all day if Doc Sanderson hadn't needed to see me. It was really more of a formality; I'd recovered well from my overload and had a plan in place to stay stable. Doc seemed to be pleased with how I was, and even more so as I answered questions for his case study report. As I left, he was already looking through the medical archives for further research.

Claws of sheer terror took a sudden grip of my chest. I gasped, and the floor rose up to meet me. I put my hand down to stop myself, only narrowly avoiding a return to the medbay. Who was hitting *this* kind of fear a day *after* everything went down? Delayed response due to shock? It didn't feel that way.

A closed door stood beside me, and I knew the source was behind it. What I found was another one of the marines, sitting quietly on the floor as if meditating.

"Uh, hey? Renner, right? Everything okay, dude?"

It didn't even look like he'd heard me. Not until he replied.

"You can hear that?"

"Hear what? I don't hear anything, pal. Just feel."

"Ah, never mind then."

And he went back to whatever meditation or *whatever* it was he was doing. I stepped back, closing the door between us.

"Okay. That was weird," I proclaimed to the empty hall. But the terror was gone, like a switch flipped. Had it come from Renner, then, and I'd snapped him out of it? Now I couldn't tell.

Trying to put that out of my mind, I headed toward the unofficial mess. Not that we actually made anything other than coffee, but it was nice to at least sit together while we ate ration bars. As I stepped through the door, though, I noticed there was only one other person inside.

"How's it going, Weatherly?"

"Broggs! You want some coffee?" Steam rose temptingly from the sleek, silver pot in her hand.

"Maybe just a little. That Venusian stuff hits me funny if I have too much before I've eaten," I admitted.

"One mini, then." She handed me my little cup before pouring a larger one for herself. We sat down at one of the tables and she smiled.

"Feeling better?"

"Yeah, thanks." I pulled a bar from my pocket and unwrapped it. It had some sort of desiccated fruit peppered through it, and I tried not to look as I took a bite. It was almost palatable though, when washed down with the iridescent coffee.

"You weren't so good yesterday."

"Yeah."

Something kept distracting me. I didn't really know Weatherly that well, but there was something *off* about what I was getting from her. Not the emotions themselves, but an indefinable *something* else. It had to be the coffee. That's what I get for having a hallucinogen with breakfast.

"Considering how much panic there was yesterday, things have calmed down surprisingly fast. Emotionally, at least. You seem pretty happy, for example," I nodded to her.

She smiled again. "Well, I'm just feeling this freedom I never imagined before. I mean, there's this huge opportunity to explore and understand all kinds of things we'd never even dreamed about. There's really only the rules we make. That's pretty exciting."

"Well when you put it like that, yeah, I guess it really is. I mean, that's a fantastic perspective to have. Sure beats despair."

"Why despair when you can find joy?" She put a hand over mine. "There's a room that glows. It's very beautiful. Would you like to go see it with me?"

The warm wave that hit me was *not* what I'd expected. I sputtered as my mouthful of coffee nearly came right back out through my nose.

"Um... hey, that's a great offer. Maybe, maybe another time? I probably shouldn't do, uh, *that*, this soon after an overload, you know?" I stammered.

"Of course. Another time." She patted my hand and stood up, ruffling my hair as she turned and headed back toward the coffee machine.

I stumbled out of the mess, dragging deep breaths of air into my lungs as I tried to slow my racing hearts. I thought about popping a pleasant pill, but things began to dull themselves and I sighed in relief. I didn't want to take those until I absolutely needed to.

"You don't look so good, Deron." A jeer cut through my thoughts: Thanatos, leaning against the doorframe. "Hear something you didn't like? What am I thinking about right now?"

"I can't hear your thoughts, you numpty. You're feeling cocky, though. Big shock. You're worried, too. Rather worried."

He backed off, giving me a look that matched the tang of distrust that came off him. I didn't mind; the less time spent with Thanatos, the better. I went the opposite way and soon left him behind. Besides, it was past time I talked to Cap about the duty rotation, now that I was fit to go again.

Just outside the bridge, I ran into Angevin again. The Islii radiated a bittersweet contrition.

"Broggs Deron? If I may, would you still be open to talk? Perhaps I was too harsh and swift in my judgement yesterday."

"Uh, sure?"

"Would you be available this evening, if you have no duties?"

"For sure. Meet me at the mess and we'll find a place to talk?"

"I look forward to it."

Xe drifted away, and I turned back to the bridge door. I was glad I was doing so much to help, but it was time to get back to my *actual* job.

The door opened, and I saluted the Captain. "Private Deron, reporting for duty, sir!"

IT'S IN THE COFFEE
(JUMP JAVA WAILING SONG)

ELVIRA CANAVERAL

The Coffee That Completes You
Wakes and makes your Day
It fills every void true
Across our Milky Way!

Water? It's In The Coffee!
Nutrients? It's In The Coffee!
POWER!? It's In The Coffee!
TODAY!? It's In The Coffee!
TOMORROW!? It's In The Coffee!
NEWS & WEATHER!? It's In The Coffee
INTERDIMENSIONAL UNDERSTANDING and
LOVE!? It's In The Coffee!

Tell Me Do You Want It?
Tell Me Do You Love It?
Tell Me Do You Need It?
Tell Me What It Is?
COFFEE!!!

Venusian coffee is the only coffee scientifically proven to keep
Vertebrates alive
Giving everything a nervous system needs
not only to get by...
But to get along,
We find in coffee, what we are missing,
bitter finds the sweet,
sweet compliments the bitter they need,
advanced nervous systems find it emotionally addictive
Coffee down to your center, helps you feel whole
Now Packed With Proanoia
Everything Is Out To Help Ya!

.

Coffee is the name of what we need!

THE HALF-LIFE OF JOHANNES WANDRI
STEVEN BAYER

PINE. OLD WORLD SCENT.

Johannes Wandri remembered the smell from his grandfather's famous book, *One Touch of Old World Comforts*. Insert one pricey vial of his groundbreaking material, Alchimis 8, into the drive port of any old L-Tablet, and the user could touch, smell, and see an exact replica of any portion of a pine tree or any forest object mentioned in his book.

All his life, Wandri was compared to his late grandfather, presented as "the grandson of," and invariably behind him on all his notable life events, from reading his first full sentence to completing his doctoral studies. Both men were profoundly talented, intellectual powerhouses, but even the Alchimis Series was one of Thomas Wandri's minor creations compared to the Blast Neutrino Salvation Treatment—a finding that ultimately protected countless solar systems from the death of nearby stars. Thus far, the work Johannes compiled in his twenty-four years of existence did not match his pedigree.

Then he met the Sapharr.

As a disciplined and ambitious exobiologist, Wandri agreed to enlist in as many exploratory missions with the United Planetary Alliance as he could find, as long as the engagement had promising opportunities to fill his journals, and if the crew was willing to carry along a lanky, talkative, somewhat awkward young scientist. His current mission, albeit 90,000 light-years off course and on a hijacked Swarm vessel, proved to be the most enlightening, terrifying, and illuminating experience of his short life.

Wandri stalked through the densely grown fauna full of enormous leaves, sounds of rustling water, and great snow-capped mountains on either side, hoping to find a collection of pine trees. His visit on what the Sapharr called a repurposed Legacy Planet–the only non human-inhabited planet he ever safely traversed without a special breathing device–would only last as long as they would allow, or as long as they needed to discover what Wandri's crew called VRS—a mineral used to make Venusian coffee. The shipmates who relied on the soothing coffee would kill him if they found out he was seeking a pine tree without trying to find the mineral himself.

I'm not on their mission.

The smell of pine and crisp, clean air filled his lungs as Wandri rounded the base of a rocky cliff close to a tributary that cut down the mountainside and into a gargantuan cerulean blue lake. There he found the origin of the calming scent.

This is no pine tree.

On the opposite side of the cliff was a thick, magnificent growth that half resembled an old, stubby pine tree, but topping the hefty, rust-colored pine bark was a mushroom cap. Branches emerged from the reddish-orange top in a pattern more commonly developed in mature oaks—a capillary network that appeared to allow the cap to inhale and exhale before him.

He crept within ten meters of the species he would simply name *abiete boletus*, meaning pine mushroom, when he heard music. With each deep breath of the pine mushroom, soothing harmonies crescendoed and decrescendoed, possibly extolled from the breathing fractals' ends. Beneath his feet, he noticed hairlike, white, bioluminescent veins woven throughout the rich soil.

He considered carrying on with his exploration, leaving the breathing mushroom tree unmolested, but an insatiable curiosity drove Johannes Wandri. On his second step toward the *abiete boletus*, the light coming from the soil swelled into a bright, harsh red light that swept across the land like a concussive blast with a diameter wider than his eyes could see.

Then the pine mushroom appeared to emerge from the ground like a hefty soldier wearily picking himself up from the battlefield, one raised knee, or in this case a root from the ground, then another, leaving impressive mounds of soil at its sides. Wandri fell on his backside, and he accidentally crab-walked himself directly into the cold, rushing water that had moments ago made him feel at one with the strange planet.

The bank was deep enough and the current strong enough to pull his entire body into the water. He drifted only a few meters before finding himself entangled in thick weeds, close enough to the bank to pull himself ashore. He discovered a large root near the water's edge and pulled with all his might until he lay prone upon the still-glowing land. When he turned his head, he noticed his confounding, magnificent discovery had fully emerged, its flame-colored cap now dancing with intemperate yellows, reds, oranges, and hot whites.

This thing has eyes, Wandri noticed. "Please! Stop! I only wanted to see you!" *I'm talking to a damned angry tree fungus...*

Eyes burning at the center of the hulking figure, all the branches above the rounded fungal top straightened out as if they were reaching in a great stretch. Then Wandri heard its great breath as the cap grew to double its size. With one great exhalation, the pine mushroom piped a discordant blast of notes that rattled his inside and brought him to immediate tears of resignation.

After the blast of sound, the light from the ground drew inward toward the base of the tree. All had gone quiet, which made the young scientist wonder if he had lost his ability to hear. As he lay near the river bank, he quietly brushed his fingers against his ear and listened to the muffled, swishing sound of his digits brushing the tragus and antitragus.

No point in running, he thought. *Movements slow and quiet. But I can wait here...*

Wandri's left foot delicately tapped the surface of the flowing water behind him as the cool water nudged his leg repeatedly to the left. It gave him a sense of connection, once again, to this strange world. Occasionally, his foot would strike into the water with enough depth to jolt his entire leg a few centimeters.

Wandri shifted his body further to the right to get himself back into a comfortable position, remembering to stay quiet and thinking his nervous scrapes against the water should cease for a while. He willed his body to remain still.

The root was against his leg once again, and Wandri assumed he was involuntarily bouncing his foot—something he was wont to do in any tense situation. As he repositioned again slowly to his right, and a touch further inward from the bank, he felt the root land on top of his left hamstring. He shot a glance behind him and saw the root climb up from the ground, violently coiling around his leg and constricting with might that forbade any escape.

New roots shot up from the right side of his body, scaling across the back of his right arm, pounding back into the ground, and then reemerging from beneath the left side of his body. The new root secured and tightened across his body, tearing his right shoulder joint as it lifted his entire body from the ground, arms and legs splayed as he faced the great bellowing fungal monstrosity.

"I meant you no harm!" he cried as he noticed the trunk glow the same terrifying reddish hue, its tendrils stretching high as it heaved in another enormous breath. *I cannot handle that sound again.* Somehow remembering that awful chord struck more fear into him than recognizing he was being held captive by a vicious root system.

Rather than the abominable blare, the trunk shook vigorously while the cap remained fully inflated. He winced, still waiting for a chord. The quaking stalk bent forward enough to see the cap's apex and the ends of all its straightened-out branches. Rather than looking like a grand pipe organ, he felt like he was looking down multiple barrels of an ancient, fearsome battleship.

The cap exploded. Every branch shot straight out in every direction, missing Wandri's body by centimeters. Within the *abiete boletus'* bulbous peaks reside great stores of poisonous spores, tiny reproductive cells that await their moment to shine once its parent body recognizes the imminent danger. To the curious human wanderer, the blast looked like a shock wave of glitter, lit by fiery bioluminescence.

Johannes Wandri gasped at the spectacular light show, and his heart stopped beating as he exhaled.

———

N'Kazzi Vaarun's tracker found Wandri's location and began summoning him to Kainan Nova. The lifeless body reached the decontamination entry bay and lay silent, despite the wrath it faced only seconds before reaching the Reuleaux triangle-shaped ship.

Chieftain Vaarun, eager to hear Wandri's thoughts on the

newly reformed planet, waived the standard safety protocols, knowing the human would be well "scrubbed" simply by remaining in the chamber. He appeared within two meters of the body, smiled, and said, "You shall have plenty of time to sleep, Johannes."

He took a deep, measured breath, closed his spectral eyes, and rested his flat, straightened right hand facing the floor upon his upward facing, straight left hand, joined just below his chest level. With no sense of urgency in his voice, he said, "Levasius, your medical assistance is required immediately." Wandri's body vanished while N'Kazzi Vaarun remained still, his arms still bent and hands still in the same position. "Restore our visitor and provide new attire. Expel what Johannes is wearing now and meticulously inspect his belongings. Report as you achieve progress."

Chieftain Vaarun vanished after his command and reappeared in one of the two angular, highly cushioned command seats. He resembled a regal stone monument, and was near as still, as he surveyed his planet from a distance only close enough for the human eye to see landforms, seas, and slow-moving atmospheric changes. The transparent barrier through which he peered was invisible to any living eye, yet Kainan Nova's metamaterial exterior made seeing the ship's inhabitants entirely impossible. Music was ever present throughout the ship, even in times of danger, and it existed as a life-form of its own within the ship.

Te'anra Mazyyr, Grand Councilor and Chieftain Vaarun's equal among the Sapharr, appeared beside Varrun. She said nothing, but her smile let the chieftain know she was fully aware of his thoughts, perhaps even the first thought he intended to share.

"He is revived, but weak," she said. "Levasius restored his

cranial network after the shock and found no need for tissue regeneration."

"She never reported these findings to me," he objected. "Why—"

"Our healer knew I was watching—that I would speak with you after I observed and asked some questions." She sat beside him in her own command seat.

"We will see him then," he determined. He stood but remained in place.

"Time, N'Kazzi. He needs time. Sit. Observe with me." Te'anra's effulgent emerald eyes emitted a faint light against her dark face, even as they narrowed to gain a better view of the planet.

"Our decision was wise, Te'anra. The Cannesz no longer have their host planet. Their power will ebb and flow, like the Swarm, but eventually, they will die out." N'Kazzi retrieved a cylindrical inhaling device before sitting, took a deep breath, and very slowly sat down. "You will trust me soon enough. As we sit, Veollace is preparing codes for our next Legacy Planet. The phase of extinction will be sudden. Less suffering, I can assure you."

He paused, waiting for a retort. Waiting to hear how simple or one-tracked his mind was, or that they needed more qualified observations. He added, "And recently, I have gained the confidence of the Highlord Generals."

Te'anra opened her eyes wide, shifted her position, and joined him with a deep breath of her own havrium inhaler. She exhaled with a grin and said, "You haven't seen it yet, have you?"

"Many times, and with *you*. How can you—"

"There will soon be a VRS extraction pit larger than any we have found within many light-years," she said. N'Kazzi clenched his jaw as she spoke, giving her more pleasure as she continued. "That fungus tree exposed a rich store of the mineral beneath its defensive roots."

"Providing havrium breaks long enough to prove me wrong about our next project?" he shot back. He sharply pointed his long, dark index finger, "We nearly left this planet due to your cautions and anxious ramblings. Years of inane speeches covering meaningless good deeds by the Cannesz, while you dismissed violence against themselves, their planet, and every habitable planet they discovered! They conquered what they loved, lived a baneful existence—"

"A pernicious species, fitting all categories for a clean extirpation," she said meditatively with a hand on N'Kazzi's shoulder. "I read your speech, N'Kazzi. You needn't carry on with it." Her seductive smile diffused him. "Besides, I already told you I was wrong about the Cannesz."

He pulled away from Te'anra and stood near the glowing footlights at the base of the clear barrier. A variety of filamentous bacteria not only powered and lit the swelling line of blue light at his feet, but vast cultures of bacteria powered much of the simple interior light throughout the ship. A masterpiece of artistic and utilitarian decor, the Kainan Nova kept all 89 of the known Sapharr comfortable and productive.

The vessel's ornamentation thematically expressed the essential marriage of science and arts within their long lives—some Sapharr lived past 500 years. Symbols of the coveted mineral *verrassumrhysirrisite*, or VRS, capped their resting chambers, dressed the corners of their elaborately carved tables, and even inspired the shape of their Great Council room. Approaches toward mining the increasingly sparse material had widened a schismatic fault line between those who believe the Sapharr were threatened by the lack of VRS and those driven by their sacred duty: promoting the harmonious Legacy Planets throughout the universe.

N'Kazzi turned to address Te'anra. "Still no word from Levasius."

"She is in the process of rehabilitating, N'Kazzi. We cannot rush her work or tire the human with questions."

"We already saved him, Te'anra," he said. "The least he owes us is an answer about what he experienced. Or why he was attacked. The mycorrhizal networks we have encoded and implanted on this planet can sense a threat, and they acted swiftly on our human. We need answers if we are to better understand our creations *and* his species."

"The spores... I am so sorry." Levasius gave Johannes Wandri another warm healing drink, its taste better than anything he'd consumed on his own ship.

"There is nothing you can... you've tried—"

"We retrieved your body quickly enough to extract the fatal amount of spores that seeped into your lungs, but some adhered and became one with your body," she explained. "There is no telling how long your system will be able to fight their effects and their assured growth."

"I am alive," he said with an uneasy laugh. Despite feeling extremely weak and fatigued and hearing it would take a miracle to reach the age of fifty, a sense of calm washed through him as the healer evaluated his breathing. *What did they put in that drink?*

"Make yourself comfortable, Johannes Wandri. Chieftain Vaarun will be with you soon." Levasius opened a white case with a soft black lining and left the second of ten slots vacant by picking up one of the cylindrical silver tubes from within. She positioned her thumb on a sliding mechanism, held the device to her lips, and simultaneously slid her thumb towards herself while deeply breathing in. After a second or two, she released her breath, and her brown eyes became a luminous amber hue.

Her movements slowed down significantly, and her gaze fell directly upon Wandri, yet she said nothing.

"Is... is everything okay?" he asked.

She maintained her gaze and responded with a slightly lower vocal register, "We are growing in our understanding of the wonder and flaws of the human system magnificently, Johannes Wandri."

"Y-yes. Yes, that is wonderful." His sense of calm was rapidly vanishing. "You said my heart... stopped. That I was fundamentally dead." He waited for Levasius to respond—to say anything. She merely studied him. "May I ask you a question?"

"I enjoy questions," she replied.

"The breathing apparatus you just used. May I ask what purpose it serves? How it... serves you?"

She breathed deeply and leaned against the wall, exposing a powerfully athletic physique beneath the elegantly draped, thin white fabric she wore. When she caught Wandri's surveying eye, she raised one side of her mouth with a sly grin and said, "Havrium."

"Havrium," he repeated. "Is that why Chieftain Vaarun was seeking VRS?" *It appears there are many uses for this mineral.*

She stepped away from the wall and walked directly toward Wandri, never breaking her eyes from his, then leaned forward, resting her hands on the table where he was seated, each hand pressed into the table beside his hips. Wandri closed his eyes and involuntarily reached up with his right hand behind her left shoulder, but he abruptly stopped himself and gasped when he felt like his hand was entering a freezing chamber.

Levasius continued to lean forward, but instead of meeting his lips, she whispered in his right ear, "Are you familiar with the effects of cryptobiosis?"

He shivered. "Yes. Fascinating process, really. I—"

"Shhhhh..." She quieted him with a hiss, then continued

whispering. "Our havrium places us in a highly functional cryptobiotic state, deepening our thought processes, calming our nerves, and prolonging our lives. You, Johannes Wandri, are made of star material. We, the Sapharr, have the neurosynaptic energy to essentially *think* like a star. We value our intellectual capacity and knowledge, and with it comes the responsibility to create and protect throughout the universe."

Wandri joined her in speaking silently. "Hence the Legacy Planet."

"Hence the Legacy Plane*ts*," she returned, accenting the plurality.

"The planet I explored–that Chieftain Vaarun introduced me to, and that nearly killed me–was one of multiple planet projects?"

"We are responsible for the majority of life in this universe, but we also extinguish those lives we find destructive and toxic —lives we helped create millions of years ago. When the Cannesz reached our eighth and final Antecedent Level, the Great Council room erupted in a debate over whether it was time to recode their rich mycorrhizal networks, causing famine, wars, and ultimately the demise of their Mother Planet. No matter how well-entrenched a species may be elsewhere in the universe, it cannot thrive for long and tends to slowly die out." She stood straight and clinically surveyed Wandri's health, behaving in a way he was more accustomed to.

"Thank you," was all he could muster. His eyes were wide, his breathing shallow. *Could all this be true?* He knew the Sapharr intelligence compared to a human was akin to comparing humans to rats on his own Mother Planet. "May I—"

Before he finished his request for another question, she answered quietly, "Yes. We have other projects. That is all for now, Johannes Wandri." She placed the havrium inhaler into her pocket and slid the white box back against the wall. Then

Levasius gasped, seeing something behind him, above his eye level.

Behind him stood N'Kazzi Vaarun, facing downward, motionless, with his hands pressed flat and tight on top of each other.

"Yes, Chieftain Vaarun," Levasius complied. She vanished, and the room went silent.

He turned and faced Vaarun. "*Chieftain* Vaarun, I—"

"You have become acquainted with Levasius, I see," he smiled.

"She saved my life. I am grateful to her—to you." Wandri cleared his throat and fully turned to face Vaarun.

"Indeed, she did," he agreed. "Why do you suppose she did that for you? Why, after you presented a threat to our project?" Vaarun stood stone still as Wandri's discomfort crept deep into the base of his stomach. He smoothly walked into a position to face the young man still seated on the table.

"Chieftain Vaarun, I—"

"I am not your Chieftain, nor did I introduce myself in that—"

"My apologies, Vaarun, but when we last met, you kindly welcomed me to what you called a Legacy Planet—a visual representation of your 'most sacred and honored duty,' you said." Wandri knew he was in no position to escalate the matter too far, so he adjusted his tone accordingly. "I presented no threat. I suppose Levasius rescued me on your orders. Why you made this order, only you can answer."

"Before your attack, Wandri, what did you think of the planet? Was it beautiful? Did it sing to you? Were you breathing clean, crisp air?" He paused.

Wandri said nothing.

"We encode DNA with perfection—precise universal

harmony in every mycorrhizal strand, every wave of bioluminescent light. We have witnessed the emergence of new, enlightened beings springing up from our most profound manifestations. And if these beings were flawed, the network of flora and fauna would envelop and exterminate them before they grew merciless, careless, wasteful, and with wretchedly poisonous hubris. Johannes Wandri, you are now a captive and test subject of the Sapharr. You will soon be meeting other captives for our labs until we reach our next project. They will fare no better than you, I am certain."

"Another project, you say?" Wandri shot back. "Off to find another victim like the starved, war-ravaged, suffocated Cannesz?"

Mention of the Cannesz surprised Vaarun. He took a step closer to Wandri and gripped the back of his neck with his long, powerful fingers. With narrowed eyes now swirling with light and dark shades of red, he asked through gritted teeth, "What do you know about the Cannesz?"

"I became acquainted with your good doctor, Vaarun, like you said," he retorted eye to eye with his captor.

Vaarun grinned, "I always warned her not to get too attached with the animals. It may be the death of her." He stepped back from Wandri, positioned his hands in the same manner he held when he entered the room, and said, "Levasius, come immediately."

The instant Levasius materialized on his right side, Vaarun slammed his hand against the front of her neck and pressed her against the wall. She looked over at Wandri in horror but could do nothing to escape the mighty grip upon her. Wandri weakly leapt from the table where he sat to assist Levasius. In his finest health, he would not have had a chance in subduing Vaarun, but he had nothing to lose. Without a look toward Wandri, Vaarun lashed the back of his forearm backward, catching Wandri on the side of his face and sending him crashing into the counter with the white box.

His elbow jolted the box hard enough to knock the lid open, freeing two havrium inhalers that rolled against Wandri's side as he sat dazed on the floor. He had enough wits about him to surreptitiously lean to his side and cover them with his hand, ultimately pocketing them as he worked to get himself back up.

Maintaining his death grip, Vaarun turned his head toward Wandri and said, "Did our good doctor share information about our next project?" He spit on Wandri's face and leaned forward. "I believe you call it Earth?"

The next moment played back in Wandri's mind for many years to come. A blur streaked across the room until an immense Sapharr figure materialized, an arm outstretched, holding what looked like an elaborately carved Kukri knife. At first, Wandri thought the attacker was after him. Then he noticed the blood drops falling from the end of the attacker's blade.

A panicked, confused Vaarun faced Wandri, flickering red eyes wide open and blood pouring from a diagonal trench stretching from above his right clavicle to just below his left ear —a strike that would seem impossible from a heavy sword, let alone a knife.

The assassin rested the weapon on the table in the middle of the room, appearing unconcerned that Vaarun might carry one last blow. He pressed his hands on top of one another, closed his eyes, and said, "It is done."

Te'anra appeared beside Vaarun as he struggled on his knees before finally collapsing. Levasius gasped for air as she recovered from the assault.

"I regret your having to follow this order, Cholsmek," Te'anra said to the warrior. "Please see after Levasius in the other room. I will be with you shortly."

The two left the room, leaving Te'anra and Wandri alone with the corpse of Chieftain N'Kazzi Vaarun. Wandri had only met with Vaarun while visiting the Sapharr, yet he was comforted in her presence. "Johannes Wandri, we are meeting in rather unfortunate circumstances, and I hope we shall see each other on a finer occasion. You are not safe here. In fact, none of us are safe at this moment. N'Kazzi's craven actions proved his dangerous fear of disloyalty among our people, and I fear he would have killed many more. I will stand trial, and in so doing I shall not only state my case against N'Kazzi, but the case for dismissing our next project."

Wandri uneasily brushed his hand against the pocket containing two havrium inhalers.

"Keep them," she said with a sly, crooked smile. "You may prolong your life considerably with them, and I have heard your mind works differently from most of your kind. If you use its effects for your people's betterment, to help them see more clearly, perhaps they will be judged favorably when either my generation or my descendants determine Earth's fate. Now we must see you off at once."

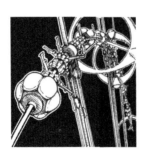

LOST IN TIME
(SYNTHPOP SEA CHANTY)
ELVIRA CANAVERAL

We all looked out and asked where is all the life?
The Drake Equation said it should be everywhere
But they said nothing about everywhen

As big as space is so is time
What are the chances of it happening
At the exact same time?

To find a sign in the briefest time
Between radio and extinction
And if those lives find each other
Does it end one of their times

Flashes in a void
Gone by the time we get there
Time Machines With No Relativity
Popping Off Planets Spinning Wi
Where Planets are not yet

But if we move on back

When the universe was more squished
Pull up anchor and tac
A meter for a parsec if you get it timed

Drop your anchor
to another matter
and ride in back
a relative distance
free of debris
Or You'll become one
With the heart of a sun
And that's a far way to burn
Reset your watch and you'll learn

AN OCEAN BETWEEN US
JAYME BEAN

Two beams of cloudy light blink to life, illuminating the dark and all-encompassing shroud around our exploration vessel. There's not much to see yet—mostly bubbles given off from our descent—but then again, we're barely at 2,000 meters and have yet to reach the seemingly impossible depths, as were shown on the initial scan. I look over to see Broggs Deron, the young private who's been overly anxious and on edge these past couple of weeks, now relaxed and at ease as we descend further into the water. We're here to scope out this uncharted planet, one comprised solely of highly salinized water—save for the molten core, which appears to be chemically rich with the key ingredients needed for the crew's new favorite medicinal.

Pleasant pills, as they have been aptly named, have been both a savior and distraction to the crew since being marooned on the Swarm vessel and haphazardly tossed lightyears off course. Of all the crew I've been monitoring, I have paid most attention to Broggs's imbibing. He thinks he's discreet, but I've noticed him halving and quartering his rations, taking them before, during, and after crew meetings. As a doctor, I worry about the long-term effects—potential dependency, the acceptance, and subsequent normalization of emotional pacification—but also understand the distinct need for an anti-psychotic supplement. UPA missions are difficult in themselves, not accounting for the unique conditions we're presently experiencing. But Broggs... he caught my attention. While the rest of the crew have taken their pill rations whole and without question, he has painstakingly divvied his up to take smaller doses over time. To say it has intrigued me would be an understatement.

When the captain decided to collect the core chemicals from the planet, he suggested I form a small crew and embark on a mission to determine the safety prior to sending the drilling crew down to excavate. I wasn't surprised I was assigned this task, given my role as both the crew's doctor and leading expert in xenobiology. Ensuring the safety of the team and understanding the parameters when embarking to an unknown location is imperative. As far as choosing a crew... well, that was enough to give me pause. I managed to bargain down to one accompanying member. Private Broggs Deron. I chose him as he seemed the most distanced from the majority of the crew... a loner. When I asked for his assistance as my right hand, he agreed quicker than I expected, seemingly thankful for the break away from the ship and crew.

As we reach 3,000 meters, bubbles continue to explode around us, reflecting the light from the exterior of the ship to form a constellation of glittering globes in the near-black abyss. I continue to watch, waiting for some sign of life or movement outside of our own. After all, scans *did* indicate organic lifeforms under the surface. I try to send my vision out further, straining to see into and past the endless blue-black waters, but all that's there is weight... weight pressing in on all sides. Empty and dark.

"Could you try to be less worried?"

I jump at the sudden noise and turn my head to find Broggs looking me over. His face morphed into a pained expression, as though stricken with a sudden headache.

"I'm sorry?" I ask, not sure if I had heard his query correctly.

"Less. Worried." Broggs forces the words out through his teeth, bringing a hand to his head as he closes his eyes and rubs at his temples. He sighs heavily, reopening his eyes to meet mine. "Why are you worried? There's only us down here. I was hoping for quiet. You seemed... *quiet*."

I take him in, realizing through my confusion that he can feel my emotions. I heard talks amongst the crew before we left headquarters of a Weslian joining the ranks. But it's been easy to forget his skills without him in a traditional role for his kind... although it explains the distance he keeps between himself and everyone else.

"It's more than worry," he continues. "Fear? No. Concern?"

"I... I, uh—"

"If you don't talk about it, it will only get worse. It's already gotten worse as we've been descending. There's also... apprehension? Regret, perhaps?"

I sit slack-jawed and in awe of both his bluntness and shocking accuracy in deducing my feelings and distilling them down to mere words. "I didn't realize I was... I mean to say, it's not my intention to feel that way."

"Feelings cannot be intended. They just are." Broggs leans his head back against the seat and turns away, looking out into the void of water and nothingness. "It's loss, isn't it? What you're feeling? Why?"

My chest tightens at his question and I see him wince slightly in response. "There's a reason," I start, "a reason I only wanted a crew of one on this trip." I squeeze my eyes shut as the images and sounds flash through my head in a flurry, bringing me back to that day—red-stained hands, his limp body laid across my lap, the last breaths...

A soft whimpering draws my attention back to Broggs, who is curling in on himself against his seat. He paws at his suit, fishing out a small handful of pleasant pill fragments, and pops two in his mouth. I shove the images down, distancing myself from them between steady breaths—a method which has proven helpful in the past during these flashbacks. He relaxes with each of my breaths as the pleasant pill kicks in.

"I'm sorry," I say, averting my eyes. "It's not easy to control..."

Broggs faces me, attempting to right his posture. "I understand." He runs a hand along the back of his neck and lets out a shaky breath. "Who was it?"

"A childhood friend... Marco. He was one of six I was serving with in the field. Years ago now. It was an already too-dangerous mission gone bad. Several didn't make it back. Marco, h-he died in my arms."

"I'm so sorry."

Tears are building up at the corners of my eyes, but I don't feel the need to hide them. Broggs already seems to know the root of the cause. "You know, as marines, we're trained to not see the losses. We treat and save and rescue who we can. But I knew Marco all my life... and it haunts me every day. Every single damn day. His death is the reason I became a doctor. I wanted to help people, not lose them. When this mission came up and I was told to pick a crew... I didn't want to be responsible for more lives put in unnecessary danger. So I do worry. It's up to me to make sure we both—that *you*—are also safe. I can't be responsible for any more losses."

I look to Broggs and I swear I can almost see him sorting through his thoughts, choosing the right words. He opens and closes his mouth a couple of times before his eyes soften. I look away, worried I may have overwhelmed him with my flurry of emotion. I stare instead at the worn letters labeling the patch brandishing the breast of my suit: *Sanderson*. From the edge of my vision, I see Broggs shift in place. I raise my eyes and am met with a focused stare. His brows furrow slightly and he lets out a tentative sigh before speaking.

"I wasn't there, so I can't tell you that there was nothing you could do. However, it is in my experience that those who live through such trauma carry that weight unnecessarily. I can feel that burden in you, in the way you feel things. If I may say so, and I know I cannot speak for your friend, but in my experience... those who pay tribute and find solace in their losses are often better for it."

I clear my throat as I feel a tear trickle down my cheek. "Thank you."

"You're welcome."

"If you don't mind my asking... why the UPA? Why not—"

Broggs shakes his head and raises a hand to stop me. "I'm not as balanced in my craft. I can't... *filter* others' emotions like the rest of my race, so Mediator is out of the question. I prefer to be alone. Or when I must be around others, I need to keep busy."

"I can understand that. I'm sorry if I took away from that by asking you to come with me."

"Why *did* you choose me?"

I smile. "You seemed... quiet."

Broggs returns the smile and I see his body relax again as he adjusts in his seat. "Harold?" His eyes narrow as he points a finger to the front of the vessel. "What *are* those?"

Below us, a cloud of shimmering rainbow spheres come into view. As our lights pass over them, they flash a brilliant silver before darting away, synchronized and flawless. Amassed, they're the size of a small UPA vessel, but as we move closer, it becomes clear that each sphere is composed of at least several hundred small aquatic creatures. They're long and thin—perhaps only twelve centimeters—and are adorned with small dorsal and ventral fins. Wide caudal fins fan out, nearly translucent, save for the greenish glow emitted during movement. In addition to the caudal fin, the entire body appears to glow in a kaleidoscope of color with what I can only assume to be a form of bioluminescence. Broggs gasps beside me as one of the spheres flashes before us, just meters away. The light given off is bright enough to illuminate the vessel's interior, sending the rainbow of colors pulsating across the control panel and along our skin. I blindly reach for my notepad and begin scribbling down everything I see, from the light emission to the coordinated movements and schooling, anything that will help document this species to the fullest extent. My hand jerks to a stop, smudging the writing as Broggs wraps his hand around my arm and holds it in place. I glance over to see him wide-eyed, a look of silent panic frozen across his face. His fingers grip tighter onto my arm as the creatures flicker and dash away, submerging us back into near-darkness.

"Broggs, wh—"

"D-do you *feel* that?" The words are barely a breath as they leave his mouth. Before I can answer, his fingers squeeze into me yet again as his eyes, now black from his dilated pupils, dart around the windows in a frantic search.

But I do feel it.

It starts low, like a soft rumbling of thunder in the distance... but it's there. Reverberations. I lean forward, sliding my arm out from Broggs's grip. Again, I feel it. This time it's enough to cause the water to vibrate around us. I look out to our lights as the beams waver against the trembling water.

"Can you tell where it's coming from?" Broggs asks. He lets out a long, steady breath and lets his eyes fall shut.

"I'm not sure." My voice is loud around us, though it was a ghost of a whisper. We sit in silence for several moments. I focus my eyes past the bubbles and dim light, searching for a sign of activity... of life.

"Down." Broggs's eyes remain closed, but his face is scrunched in quiet concentration.

I stare at him. "What?" His breathing is shallow and I can barely see his chest moving from the exhalations.

"Whatever it is," he says, opening his eyes and locking them to mine. "It's down."

Another rumble sends a low tremor through the vessel. "You can read it?"

Broggs gives a curt nod. The question is on the tip of my tongue, but he answers it without me having to ask it. "It's faint but calm. Restful."

"Well..." I swallow, looking into the endless water. "It's our job to make sure it's safe for the crew."

"And to catalogue what inhabits the waters."

My teeth pick at the inside of my cheek. "Restful?" It comes out more like a breathy question than the confident statement I intended.

Broggs offers a small yet nervous smile. "Only one way to find out."

I engage the vessel and plummet us down another 4,000 meters. Flurries of air bubbles blossom around us in quick bursts as we reach the Abyssopelagic Zone. The abyss is the second to last layer of the ocean's ecosystems and is known for its formidable environment. It is here that life takes on a different form; it is here that the toughest creatures survive. The great expanse of these waters could contain anything. While I have studied Earth's oceans—or at least the history of what they were in their prime—I am all too aware of the potential lurking in these dark, alien waters. It is another few hundred feet below us that we see the now faint glimmer of the bioluminescent spheres of schooling creatures from before. As we continue our descent, the floor of this vast ocean comes into view. It's craggy, yet almost every few meters, it's covered in towering and blooming flora—highly unusual at these depths. Most plant life doesn't grow past the Euphotic Zone, which comprises the upper 200 meters of the water table. And yet tall, green stalks reach up to greet us; the large paddle-shaped fronds sway against the air let out from the vessel as we slow.

"This is incredible," Broggs says as he looks out over the sprawling ocean floor.

A smile forces itself across my face and all my anxiety about the mission melts away. We float, suspended in our small observatory, as life explodes around us. Bright lights dance between the stalks as several schooling spheres break apart and reform, like an unknown ritual playing out in double-time. A blur crosses in front of us and toward the lights as a large creature propels itself into the plants. I bend to look closer and several more blurs cluster around us. We watch in awe as they seem to fade and reappear in a microsecond. One approaches us and investigates, bringing its furred snout to the outside of the vessel. Its large, black eyes peer at us in gentle curiosity. The creature resembles, nearly to perfection, what we on Earth affectionately know as otters. Long whiskers on either side of its wide nose twitch before it flickers away into nothing, only to reappear in the blink of an eye.

"I've heard of these," I say, not breaking my gaze from the creature. "I think they're interspatial quantum otters. It's been rumored from zoologic studies that Earth's otters are a distant descendant, ones that lost their ability to move throughout time, much like the human species in its infancy."

"There's a word for them on my home planet. It loosely translates to 'clawed dimensions.' They were spoken of in tall tales, told to children to stop them from exploring unknown waters," Broggs tells me. "My mother used to warn us not to wander too far when swimming in our planet's oceans, lest we be taken to another world in the vicious jaws of the *lutraquanta.*"

"They don't seem visc—" I choke my words back as the creature opens its maw and reveals a mouthful of sharp teeth before lunging at us, bouncing off the outside of the vessel. Fortunately, the exterior is hardy enough to dissuade the otter from another attempt. It swims off toward the plants, flickers briefly, and appears again with several of the small, glowing creatures in its jaw. Their glow fades as the otter mashes them between its teeth and slides them down its throat. "Jaws indeed," I say, turning toward Broggs. A smirk crosses my lips as I prod a gentle elbow in his direction. "Looks like we'll need a bigger boat, eh?"

Broggs cocks his head to the side as his eyebrows knit together.

"An old Earth saying. A pop culture reference, if you will."

"Ah," he says, turning back to watch the rest of the otters chase and catch their meals. "Perhaps we should continue. I still sense *something.*"

"Right. Of course." I kick the vessel back into gear and move us into the greenery and further down and along the ocean floor.

"Oh," Broggs breathes, reaching a hand out to touch my shoulder. "Here."

"I don't see anything."

Broggs leans forward, his face centimeters from the window. "Up ahead. Go slow."

We glide through the plants at minimum speed. My mouth hangs agape as we press forward and emerge on the other side of the giant stalks. With the towering flora behind us, the ocean is opened up once more into an endless stretch. We are no longer resting above the ocean floor, but hovering over a chasm, deep and black. An oceanic trench expands before us, an enormous and jagged wound torn into the ocean floor. Fine bubbles and steam shoot up in fountains from the deep, most likely hydrothermal venting from the planet's core. My fingers fumble on the controls as I scan the terrain. The readings indicate that it is at least 2,700 kilometers long, around 100 kilometers across at its widest point, and caps the largest possible readings for depth at around 12,000 kilometers deep. It's gargantuan. Yet, it is not the trench that has me awe-stricken.

Floating, still as stone above the trench, are the most terrifying creatures I've ever seen. They're enormous. It's hard to tell their exact size, but based on the size of the fissure they could be up to 80 meters, if not even more. Despite their stillness, they evoke a primal fear within me. Perhaps it is the stillness itself that sets my hair on end. A chill creeps along my skin as I hazard a glance downward and find one of them resting immediately below us. Its body is slick and gray—eel-like—except for an enlarged, acorn-shaped head and wide pectoral fins. I count one creature every couple hundred meters, each motionless and poised above a hydrothermal vent.

"Do you see that?" Broggs whispers. "They have no mouths. How is that possible?"

Our vessel shakes as an immense vibration ripples throughout the water from within the trench. No... not from the trench. From the *creatures*. One by one, the eel-like beasts let out a low and rumbling roar, though I am not sure how, for Broggs is correct in his observation. There is no evidence of a mouth, and yet they are able to emit this intense bellow, strong enough to echo throughout my bones as we rock back and forth in place. The vessel's interior lightens as a shimmering rainbow sphere passes by; the bioluminescent creatures from earlier encompass our ship as they break apart and reform before us. They continue down in their schooling mass and toward the large beasts.

"Harold, look." Broggs directs my attention to his right. In the distance, more schools are converging and approaching the trench. His head whips to the left and his finger juts out to match. "There are so many of them."

Within seconds, the trench begins to glow with the light of hundreds, if not thousands, of glimmering spheres as they swim trance-like toward the growling beasts. Broggs takes a sharp breath beside me as they swim *into* the giant creatures. As the schools approach, the eel-like animals let out one last roar. The height of the vibrations resonate throughout the water, and their gray skin flickers and becomes translucent. The glowing spheres move as one unit through the skin and vanish inside, as if through osmosis. The water stills. The creatures shine dimly through their slick exterior but fade within a moment, leaving us surrounded again by the darkness of the abyss.

"*Did you see that*?" Broggs half hisses, half gasps. He turns to me, his eyes wide and glistening.

"Fascinating. This species... it-it's *incredible*. And that feeding... it has to be some kind of symbiotic relationship. But how?" My mind reels as a million thoughts filter through my head. "And they're docile. Something that looks like, and *should be*, an apex predator in this ecosystem is essentially a static being." I set a command to scan the vent emissions and hold my breath as the results register. I shake my head, amazed at the discovery before us. "Broggs, it has to be the vents. These readings are identical to the core. It must be sending up chemicals—sedatives for all intents and purposes—and it, I don't know, *hypnotizes* them... sends them into a state of tranquility. The wealth of potential study and information just based off of this... this... whatever it is."

"It needs a name. Is it not an Earth tradition for those that discover new species to bestow a name? I believe you use... what do they call it? Binomial nomenclature?"

My head is spinning with possibility. "It is. And we can. We should name it."

"*You* should name it. It's your mission and, therefore, your discovery." Broggs tilts his head at the motionless beings. "They most closely resemble whales, do they not?"

"I was thinking eels," I mumble in response. I straighten in my seat and smile. The perfect name for this historical find slides across my tongue, stumbles out of my mouth, and falls into the world for the first time. "*Fonesca deron.*"

Broggs rotates to meet my gaze. He furrows his brow as he stares at me. "What?"

"*Fonesca deron.* After two people that have marked significant moments in my life. Marco Fonesca... and you, Broggs Deron."

"I... surely there's anything, any*one* else. I don't think I deserve—"

"You led us here, straight to these astonishing animals. And what you said to me, about loss and tribute earlier. What better way than to always remember those words in conjunction with his name?"

Broggs looks away, and I see him dab at his face with the edge of his hand. "No one has shown a kindness like that to me before," he says, continuing to face away from me.

"You don't give yourself the credit you deserve. You should believe in your capabilities and self-worth more than you do. At the very least, you've impacted me. And I'm sure I'm not alone in that. That said... we *do* still need to name those amazing and mysterious little creatures tied into this feeding behavior. I think you should do the honor."

"Are you sure? I don't know much about the two-naming system of Earth."

"Well, there are many options, but really it's up to you. They have no known genus and are completely alien to discovery, or at least that we know of."

Broggs sits back in his seat and takes a deep breath. "Would you mind if I returned the kindness?" he asks, turning back to me. "If so, I would like to name them, *Luxa sanderson.*"

My heart warms at the gesture. My surname used to name a unique and remarkable species. "I am well beyond honored, Broggs. That name is perfect. May I ask who Luxa is?'"

"Not a who. A what. In my language, it means 'light.' Luxa for the glow. And Sanderson... well, for a great new friend."

We fall into a pleasant silence as both of us take notes about the environment and newfound species. There are no more disturbances while we write; the ocean sits quiet and calm. After a while, we ascend slowly toward the surface. We've covered but one tiny section of this planet, and we'll have to return in the coming days to determine the overall safety, as well as continue to map the biodiversity. Broggs expresses concerns about reboarding the ship, and I can't help but feel tremendous empathy at his predicament. I cannot fathom the weight he bears in our confinement. I look out into the expanse and wonder if it is similar to the weight bearing down on us now. I admit I was wary about finding resources that would allow us to create and stock an abundance of pleasant pills. The potential effects on the crew still weigh heavily in my mind, though I feel I've come to a greater understanding of their need. Perhaps the pleasant pills give Broggs the shield he needs, much like this vessel has shielded us from the weight bearing down on it from the ocean depths. I glance over to him and watch as he fidgets, and I know the same worries are setting in the closer we get to reboarding.

"I'd like you to have my rations... of pleasant pills when we return."

Broggs shifts toward me, arching his eyebrow in question.

"I don't use them. I worry about the long-term... well, never mind. I don't need them. You shouldn't have to suffer through a restless crew without some help."

"I couldn't—"

"I truly don't use them. I haven't taken a single one. I don't want to see you suf—"

My voice escapes me as a dark shadow looms over the vessel. We're almost to the upper end of the Bathypelagic Zone, an area where light *should* be present. With no inhabitants or land, there shouldn't be an obstacle this large in our way, nothing to block the light. I stop our movement and rotate us to get a better idea of what's blotting out the light from the surface. As I tilt the vessel up, my blood runs cold while the shadow takes form above us. It morphs from a large, flat disc of black mass and into an elongated, squid-like body, alive with flashing color. Sixteen long and bright tentacled legs spread out like cracks of lightning across the dark-blue empty. A glistening black beak, no smaller than the size of our vessel, snaps above us. The squid rolls to the side and we are met with an enormous white and black eye.

"W-w-what d-do w-we do?" Broggs stammers through quick breaths.

Either through our perceived insignificance to it or blind luck, the squid's tentacles snap backward in a pop of color before the creature goes completely black and vanishes into the distance. Broggs and I exchange a glance and several deep breaths as we wait for it to realize its mistake and to come back for us in a flash of light and legs.

"Maybe it's an herbivore?" I squeak out, doing a final scan of the water.

With shaky hands, I propel us to the surface, where we are immediately brought back to the ship. Before disembarking, Broggs pulls out his stash of pleasant pills and offers them in his open hand between us. I take a few shards and grip them in my palm. I tap my fist to his in silent cheers as we both upend the broken pill fragments, feel our nerves settle, and step back into the common area to greet the rest of the eager and blissfully unaware crew.

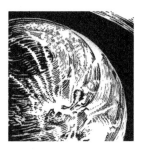

UPA MEDICAL RECORD
RENNER, KEVIN—SERGEANT

DATE: 17 July 832 A.A.

Patient Name		Renner, Kevin		BZ98S542
Attending Physician		Sanderson, Harold		

Heart Rate 64 bpm	Blood Pressure 124/73	Temperature 37.6°C	
Height 185.42 cm	Weight 83.91 kg	Race Human	Gender Male

Reason for Visit	Scheduled Checkup		
Eye Exam	20/22	Responsive?	Yes
Throat	Red/Irritated, pustules	Oxygen	97%

Physician Notes

Patient presents as very healthy and keeps his body conditioned for his position.

Concern about slightly raised temperatures, slightly lowered oxygen levels, and pustules on his throat. Test for strep came back negative. Considering we're in a new ship, I thought it best to play it safe and give him antibiotics anyway. I also did a blood draw for testing.

Written by A.R.K. Horton

THE TERROR OF PEACE
A. R. K. HORTON

WAS THIS RINGING TINNITUS OR A NOTE THAT WOULD SOON SWELL to an orchestral masterpiece? Kevin hoped for the tinnitus. It certainly made more sense given the beating his helmet took when he exited the pod. For weeks, some kind of music hall in his head had haunted him; everything from classic rock to the latest beats would burst into his mind without warning, carrying with it an unexpected mood swing. Of course, he kept all of this to himself. Losing his position as a UPA marine wasn't something he wanted to tackle right now.

As he prayed to all the deities he didn't believe in to keep the ringing a distant echo, tears pricked at the corners of his eyes. *Oh, no. Not again.* There it was, the forlorn and plaintive high note, calling out from its lonesome peak. It cascaded into the mysterious depths below, its pleas becoming more and more impassioned.

"Fuckin' Scheherazade..." Kevin muttered with a groan.

"What was that, Renner?" Altera asked over their comms.

Kevin turned around to see her leaving the pod. Even in her underwater gear, with all the extraneous equipment strapped to her, he could tell it was her just from her figure. Her curves couldn't be hidden by any suit. Once again, he wondered why she was on this mission. Why should special ops be involved with checking out whatever issue there was with the drill line?

"Nothing. Got a song stuck in my head."

Altera gave him a blank stare before swimming past him. There was that heartbreaking soprano note calling out to him again. His eyes welled with more tears. His heart pushed up from his chest and into his throat. *This isn't the time.* Yet, the longer he looked at the mysterious woman swimming past him, the more his heart reverberated with longing for her. Kevin's legs kicked, and he followed behind the object of his newfound affection.

"Wait for me!" Grey called over the comms.

The pull to follow Altera was so strong that Kevin probably would have ignored the other marine's request. Fortunately for Grey, Altera stopped and turned around, waiting for him to catch up. Kevin's breath stopped in his lungs. Her impassive face enchanted him more than any pin-up poster ever could, and Kevin had a few of those in his bunk he wouldn't trade for the world. Violin strings caught fire in his mind. *For one night with her, I'd torch the posters.* Grey was talking now. Kevin shook his head to hear him better.

"Thanks," Grey said. "Briefing went a little long."

"Anything to worry about?" Altera asked.

Grey shrugged and said, "Besides our pod wussing out this far from the drill line? No. Doc said the life forms here seem really peaceful. There are some interspatial quantum otters that are large and aggressive, but they live below in the stalks."

"Interspatial quantum otters?" Kevin asked with a chuckle.

"I don't name them," Grey replied. "There are also these eel-whale type creatures near the core that Doc calls *Fonesca deron.* They sound brutal, but seem to be hibernating on the core's surface."

"Well, the problem with the drill isn't anywhere near the stalks or the core," Kevin said, his own words drowned out by a crescendo of woodwinds, strings, and percussion. "So, let's go."

"Well, there are also squids—" Grey began.

"Mmm... calamari," Altera interrupted. "I'll enjoy them with some butter and a side of Pleasant Pills. Let's finish this mission and move on."

Altera turned back to the drill line and pumped her legs to propel her forward. The highly salinated liquid they swam in felt like the gelatin slurp Kevin used to drink at the bottom of his dessert cup. It took an effort to swim in this soup, which was probably why they sent marines instead of scientists to check on the drill line. What the heck they were going to do when they got there, he didn't know. Maybe that's why Altera was with them.

As they got nearer, brown swirling shapes came into view, blinking in and out of the marine's vision and punctuating the staccato notes in his head. These must be the otters Grey told them about.

"They're adorable," Altera said, breaking her cool reserve with a giggle.

For a moment, Kevin could see the human beneath Altera's mysterious, seductive appeal. It endeared him to her. He felt compelled to get her a giant otter now. Swooning strings surged through him and he could see a grateful Altera in his mind, wrapping her arms around him giddily. *Gotta get that woman an otter.*

"Well, I guess that's the problem with the drill line then," Grey said. "New pod should be here shortly to pick us up and we can—"

Kevin was off like a rocket toward the otters, who continued to tear at the drill line with all their might.

"Renner! Did you miss the part where I said they're aggressive?"

Grey's warning went unheard as tubas boomed and flutes danced around soprano violins. He had to get an otter for Altera. That would solve everything. That vulnerable note singing its melancholy song would find its way into his embrace. She was that note, and she wanted an otter.

He was so close now that he could see their large innocent eyes and their delightful whiskers. Altera was right. They were adorable. A pup blinked happily in and out of reality as playful notes comforted Kevin. A baby otter would be even better than the rest. He reached his arms to grab the little one before a larger one loomed behind to bare her sharp, terrifying teeth. Mother Otter was ready to draw blood.

"Renner!" Altera called out. "Look out!"

Kevin turned around to see his beloved pointing below. He looked down while bass notes burdened him with their ominous threats. Underneath the rainbow flicker of hundreds of minnow-like fish, he saw something massive and slimy. It was grey, but then not, somehow. Kevin might have thought it was some giant blob of goo, if not for the fins on its side. It didn't even have a mouth. Altera grabbed him and pulled him back from the otters as quickly as possible.

"The otters..." Kevin muttered but drifted off, distracted by the sensation of her body pressed so close to his back.

He almost got lost in the fluttering strings playing in his head and his urge to make passionate love to this woman. However, just as the song in his mind eased back into romantic swoops, the beast below surged upwards. Liquid displacement sent them tumbling backward, pushing them away from the devastation that unfolded in front of them. Kevin had never seen a creature this large. The monstrosity's grey skin grew translucent and Kevin watched in horror as it absorbed the tiny sparkling fish and dissolved them.

"Oh, God!" he exclaimed. "The otters!"

"Fuck the otters!" Altera yelled. "What about the drill line?"

It was too late. Even the otters the size of Kevin were tiny compared to this monster, and every last one of them disintegrated, just like the fish. His little brother used to play this game with his friends, where they pretended to be heroes fighting monsters. He'd thought it was silly back then, but this reminded him of the gelatinous cube his brother used to be scared of. Now, he understood why. Any organic life in the giant creature's path died. There was no fighting it, only running away and getting lucky.

The drill line, being metal and non-organic, didn't fully dissolve like the fish and otters. It only suffered minimal corrosion by the behemoth, but it had done enough damage to render it useless. They watched the monster float lazily away, destroying everything that was in the wrong place in this wide ocean. Panic roared and subsided by the time Grey caught up to them.

"That was a Fonesca," Grey told them. "Had to be. Just like Doc described."

"I see the new pod now," Altera announced.

Kevin breathed a sigh of relief as they entered the pod's relative safety. The orchestral loop in his head had finally died off. He could feel normal for a bit. No more Sheherazade and no more unexpected swells of emotion. He looked over to see Altera taking off her helmet, letting tendrils of sweat-dampened hair break free. A wistful flute called from a distance, and his heart skipped.

Grey spoke in muffled tones over the secure line to the drillship above. Kevin knew he'd acted irrationally out there. He knew he looked like a madman, and Grey was probably telling their superiors all about it. He didn't care. For the first time, this little musical insanity in his head brought him something he wanted. Kevin watched Altera guzzle down water, rivulets spilling from the opening of her flask onto her glistening skin. *I love her.*

"You look like that suit is burning you up," Kevin said, reaching into a compartment behind him. "Let me get you the cold stuff from the cooler."

Altera looked at him with a little surprise and suspicion in her eyes. Yet, a playful tug at the corner of her mouth created her famously crooked smile, which made every marine weak at the knees. "Thanks, Renner. That would be swell."

Kevin dug out an icy beverage and passed it over to Altera, who sighed with relief as she pressed it to her flushed face. Grey hung up the line and ruffled back his hair while he sighed. After a swig of his own water bottle, he motioned for the other two to come closer and listen.

"The good news is that we already got more than enough from the drill to make at least a year's worth of Pleasant Pills," Grey said.

"The bad news?" Kevin asked.

"Apparently, those same chemicals we drilled for were what made the animals on this planet docile," Grey explained. "By drilling, we riled them up."

"That makes sense," Kevin responded. He thought back to the near-mutiny on their strange ship. The lack of Pleasant Pills had been a real problem. He personally hoped like Hell the ability to manufacture more pills would give him a little break from the ceaseless mood swings he experienced. He was sure everyone else was ready for a little calm as well. *Too bad those otters had to die, though.*

"It's not worth the risk to drill for more," Grey continued explaining. "Mission complete, I guess."

"That doesn't sound so bad," Altera responded with a shrug. "The sooner we're off this planet, the better."

"All that danger for a little pill," Grey said, shaking his head.

"That's the terror of peace," Altera replied. "It always comes at a steep cost."

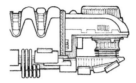

SHIFT JIVE
(DISCO MILITARY DRILL)

ELVIRA CANAVERAL

Shift To The Left
Tap To The Right
Tear You Apart
Send You Outta Sight

Shift To A Front
Tap One On Back
Your Information
X Y & Z We Hack

There You Be
If That Be You
You Can Tell Me
Tell Us What You See!

Your Quarks Are Charming
As Their Encoded
Your Attitude and Zenith
Duly Noted, Maybe Promoted?

Do Bear A Frown
You'll Be Going Down
Down Down In The Code
Frow Know To Node

Kick A Flip
In A Quantum Trip
Where a Smile As The Way
To A New And Pleasant Day!

SHACKLES OF THE MIND
B. K. BASS

"I didn't sign up for this shit."

As the strangely curving surfaces of the alien ship's corridor faded from a sickly teal to a deep indigo, I stopped to let my eyes adjust. Along with the materials changing color, the ambient light—light that seemed to come from everywhere and nowhere all at once—shifted with it. There was a pattern to the color changes, one that much of the crew had adopted to tell time aboard the strange vessel lost, who knew where in deep space. Some found that regularity comforting, but I still couldn't get used to it. Things should be a certain way; if a wall was grey, it should stay grey. So when the entire ship rearranged itself when we boarded, I knew better than to trust anything about it.

As the shadows deepened along the passageway, I peered over my shoulder. The layout behind me hadn't changed. I'm not sure why I thought it would have. Things had changed little since that first metamorphosis, other than the colors. Of course, we'd found things; things I'd rather not think about.

Even though the color shift should be a reliable tell of what time it was, I still checked the chronometer on the wrist plate of my armor. My shift was almost over, so I ended my patrol and headed back.

Heavy footfalls echoed around me in the emptiness, almost drowning out my own thoughts. I'd served in the UPA Marines for almost two years now. I'd fought in space and planetside against the Swarm and other enemies. Hell, I'd even be a lance corporal by now if it weren't for some disciplinary issues. Still, nothing could have prepared me for this: being trapped on an alien ship cast halfway across the galaxy, for all we knew. And here we were, scrambling just to figure out the layout of the ship, let alone trying to find our way home.

I shook the thought from my mind and popped open a pouch on my hip, dug around, and pulled out a slender metal tube. The pill dispenser rattled when I shook it. *Almost empty.* The standard-issue anti-anxiety drugs should have been more than plentiful enough for a short mission, but this had turned out to be anything but that. Everybody seemed to rely on the 'pleasant pills', as the civilians had come to call them, to cope. And it wouldn't be long before they were gone.

I thumbed the top of the tube and popped a capsule into my mouth. Almost instantly, all the anxiety about our situation faded away, dulled rather than entirely dissipated. I shook the tube again, frowned, and put it away. I wasn't sure what I was going to do when those babies ran out.

"Have you seen them?"

I lined up the small, chocolate-colored crystal on the center of the crate and smashed a ration can down on it, careful not to let the fragments skitter away.

"Hey, Jenkins."

"Huh?" I looked up from the crate. "What?"

"Damn, dude. You fade out again or what?" Owensby asked. A fellow grunt, and a human, the man was one of the few aboard the ship I'd let myself connect with over the last few weeks. It helped that he'd come up with the idea for the project I was working on.

"Naw, man. I was just concentrating." I wiped a few specks of crushed crystal from the can, lined them up in a neat pile, and repeated the process. I pushed down on the can, rocking it back and forth, grinding the fragments smaller and smaller.

"So, did you see them?" Owensby asked again.

"See who?"

"The MuDuhRu. The little buggers that helped us mine these rocks."

"Oh, no," I mumbled as I wiped off the can again and set it aside. The brown crystal was now fully pulverized into a fine powder. It hadn't been a large rock; you couldn't just go hauling off fist-sized chunks of VRS—the stuff that put the punch in the Venusian coffee everybody was hooked on—without somebody noticing. But Owensby worked stockpile duty a few hours every day, so he always swept up a few thumbnail-sized chunks for our own use.

"Freaky little fuckers. Look kinda like bugs, all cased up in their exo-suits and skittering around on all four limbs. And their heads, man; they're like crazy small." Owensby rose from where he'd been lounging against the wall, took a few eager steps forward, and leaned over the crate as I scraped the pulverized crystal into two narrow lines. "Ready?"

"Born ready," I replied.

We both bent over the dust and inhaled sharply. Pain ran through my nose, up my sinuses, and seemed to wrap around my head in lashes of fire. Owensby and I shot upright and shouted in unison, "Ooh rah!"

The pain fled as soon as it had come. I took a shaky step

back and sat cross-legged on the ground, my palms planted firmly on either side to anchor myself. A wave of euphoria washed over me. Motes of light danced before my eyes, and the shadows around the small chamber shifted and writhed as if they were engaged in an orgy of unfettered souls. The color of the ship's walls shifted, brightening from a deep violet to bright orange. Normally, the change would be a gradual, subtle one. But, high on the VRS, the colors swirled together as the ambient light washed over us in waves. I looked down at my hands. My skin shifted from a pale white to a ruddy glow that ran in ripples up my arms, bringing with it a tingling sensation that continued until it hit the base of my skull.

Owensby's head lolled back. He was laughing.

I think I laughed, too, but I wasn't sure. I sprawled out on the floor and stared at the colors swirling across the ceiling.

"Alive?" I asked as I laid back on my bedroll in the small chamber Owensby and I had claimed as our quarters.

"Yeah, man. That's what they're saying. Whole thing's like one enormous animal or something." Owensby popped another pleasant pill, sprinkled a little ground VRS dust in his coffee, and chased the capsule down.

"What the fuck," I muttered as I sniffed a few grains of dust off the edge of my combat knife. I blinked against the brief pain. It wasn't as bad in small doses, and I was getting used to it. "Next thing you know, they'll be talking to it. I didn't sign up to talk to aliens. I signed up to shoot them."

"Ooh rah," Owensby grunted as he latched on his armored boots, gearing up for a planetside mission. "But some think it's already talking to us. They say some of the crew are hearing things. Seeing things even. Like they're being visited by people from the past or hearing voices."

"That's crazy."

"Maybe. But they say the ship can read our minds, and it's creating these... visions, from our memories."

I shook my head as I fished around in my gear for my tube of pleasant pills. "Still think it's bullshit," I muttered as I searched. The more pockets and pouches I ran my hands through, the more my heart raced. *Where are they?* I tossed a bag aside and started in on another.

"Dude, what are you looking for?" Owensby asked as he finished armoring up.

"My pills, man. I can't find them." I threw another bag aside and started going through the compartments of my armor.

"Chill, bro. Good news. We're going down to get what we need to make more. Here, take some of mine." Owensby pulled out his vial and thumbed four pills into my waiting palm. "We'll have more than we know what to do with after this."

"Cool, thanks. I owe you."

"No worries," Owensby said. "Just take it easy. Don't let the ghosts get you while I'm gone."

I chuckled with no mirth as he left, looked down at the four pills in my palm, then popped one in my mouth. I pressed a hand over my chest and found my pill dispenser in my breast pocket. Must have forgotten to check there. I sighed with relief and slid the rest of the capsules into the tube before tucking it back in my shirt. After wiping my knife off on my duty pants, I noticed the faint sheen of reflective brown against the blue-grey fabric. I dragged the blade across my leg, ran a finger along the fine dust, and gave it a lick. I didn't get much more than a tingle, but when I stood up, I felt like I might have floated off the deck.

"*You really shouldn't do that.*"

"What?" I looked around but didn't see anybody. "Who's there?"

"Who's here? Where's here? Here's you, but who are you?" The voice seemed to come from nowhere and everywhere all at once.

"Maybe too much dust," I muttered as I wiggled a finger in each ear.

"Nasty habit, that."

"Shut up," I said as I shot to my feet and strode outside the chamber. I peered down the passageway in both directions, but even with the hour's bright yellow illumination, I couldn't see anyone. *Definitely too much dust,* I thought as I turned and walked back into our quarters.

"I would have to concur. But that doesn't explain what you think it explains."

I spun back around and ran into the passageway again. "Who's there?" I called out, but nobody answered.

I dug in my pocket with a trembling hand and pulled the vial of pills back out. *Just one more,* I thought as I thumbed a capsule from the dispenser into my mouth.

"Not going to help."

"What the fuck? Who is that? Quit playing games. I'm not in the mood."

"Games. Diversion. Entertainment. Would you like to play a game?"

"No, I absolutely would not," I grumbled as I strode down the passage, intent on finding whomever was playing tricks on me. What if it wasn't a trick? What if it was the ship getting into my head? *No, no way,* I thought as I pinched the bridge of my nose and turned a corner. I didn't believe that was possible. *The crew's just starting to lose it. Am I losing it?*

"No."

"Will you shut up?" I yelled.

"Who are you talking to?" a woman asked.

I looked up and found myself standing over a kneeling scientist poring over some alien characters on a console. "N-nobody," I said, then turned and started heading back towards my quarters.

"*Nobody? That's rather insulting.*"

"What do you want?" I hissed under my breath as I glanced over my shoulder to see if anybody was watching. I let out a long sigh when I found I was again alone. *Or am I?*

"*Want. Desire. A need to be fulfilled. What do I want? The same thing you want.*"

"Oh?" I turned the corner into our small chamber and slumped down on my bedroll. "And what's that?"

"*Home.*"

"Humph." I unlaced my boots and pulled one off.

"*You might need that.*"

"Shut up!" I screamed as I threw the boot across the chamber.

"*Anger. Hostility. Emotion. Processes lacking logic. Action lacking reason. Futility.*"

"That's it," I muttered as I fished around in the pile of bags and supplies separating my bedroll from Owensby's. I pulled out a small ration tin and popped it open. Inside was several ounces of glistening brown dust; VRS we'd already ground up and had ready to go.

"*You shouldn't do that.*"

I ignored the warning and sprinkled a thick line of dust on the lid of the tin.

"*Please don't.*"

I bent down and inhaled sharply. Fire laced around my face and head, and the world burst into a cacophony of colors, smells, sounds, and other sensations so disjointed I couldn't tell where one ended and the other began. Sight, sound, touch; it was as if there was no difference. They were all one.

I slumped back, dropping the tin and spilling the precious dust across the floor. I laid there, focusing on my breath, waiting for the voice.

It never came.

"Jenkins, get up."

I cracked an eye open to see what time it was. Orange. I closed my eye, not ready to get up yet.

"Jenkins!" Something struck me in the hip.

"What the fuck," I said as I peered up against the orange glow. Owensby stood over me, not looking very pleased.

"You're late for your patrol again. Captain Savory is pissed. Get up."

"What's the point?" I groaned as I rolled over and turned my back to him. I squeezed my eyes shut and patted my leg, looking for my vial of pills.

"*You really need to lay off those.*"

"Oh, you're one to talk," I said.

"About what? I didn't say anything," Owensby said, then kicked me again.

"Dude, lay off. I'll get up when I feel like it."

"*That'll be never. Never feel like it. Never feel anything.*"

The voice was back. I pulled the rough survival blanket off and sat up.

"About time," Owensby muttered. "Savory's in the aft section, near the med bay. He wants to see you."

"*See you. Hear you. Chastise you. You're in big trouble, young man.*"

"Will you just shut up?" I yelled out.

Owensby held up his hands. "Whoa, fine. Don't kill the

messenger. It's your hide if you don't show up." With that, he turned and left.

"*Hide. Skin. Flesh. Dermis. Outer layer protecting the inner workings of the body.*"

I squeezed the bridge of my nose and patted the leg of my pants again. I finally found the vial, held it over my mouth, and thumbed the dispenser.

Nothing came out.

I shook the vial, and the silence was deafening.

"*There's no more.*"

"No shit," I said as I slid the vial back into my pocket and rummaged around for the tin of VRS dust. I searched my pack, Owensby's pack, our supply crate... it was gone. *Did he take it?*

"*Now we can talk about getting home.*"

"Fuck!" I yelled as I grabbed the crate and threw it across the chamber, sending supplies skittering across the floor.

"*Was that really called for?*"

Instead of humoring the voice with a response, I ignored it as I pulled on my boots and laced them up. Not bothering with the armor for the patrol, I slipped on an undershirt and strode out of the chamber and made my way aft. The passageways were nearly empty, but the few fellow crewmen I passed along the way gave me strange looks. They could probably tell I was strung out and freaking out.

"*Hard to hide it. You need to talk to the others. Join the hosts.*"

"No," I snapped. "I'm not a host, I'm just losing it. This is bullshit. I just need more pills and more dust."

"*You can't run from me. I'm all around you. We're trapped together.*"

"I can sure as hell try."

"*Futile.*"

I rounded the corner to the medbay. I could kill two birds with one stone: see what the captain wants and get more pills from the doc. As I approached the entrance, though, I heard an ongoing argument.

"We need to ration the pleasant pills. Addiction is becoming a major issue, and I'm worried it's affecting the brain chemistry of the crew in persistent ways." That was the doc.

"Absolutely not. We'll have a mutiny," Captain Savory argued.

"If we run out again, which we *will* soon, we'll have worse than a mutiny on our hands," Doctor Sanderson said.

I turned back and raced away from the medbay. *We're running out of pills again?*

As I ran, the voice filled my head. *"No running away. Face your fears."*

I don't know how long I ran, or where I was, before I finally turned a corner and bumped into Owensby.

He grabbed me by the shoulders and kept us both from falling from the impact. "Jenkins, are you okay?" He glanced over me. "You look like you've seen a ghost."

"Heard, maybe."

"Where's the dust?" I asked, grabbing him back.

"What?"

I shook him by the shoulders. "The dust, dammit! I couldn't find our stash."

Owensby pushed me to arm's length. "It's gone, dude. You snorted it all. I won't be able to get more until my shift in the supply room later."

"No running now. Time to listen."

I clutched my head and groaned in anguish.

"Dude, are you okay?"

"Pills," I said. "I need more pills. We're gonna run out."

"Naw, dude. *You're* gonna run out. I'm good."

I grabbed him by the shoulders again. "No, you don't understand. Doc Sanderson said we're about to run out. He's talking to the captain about rationing."

Owensby pushed my hands away and shrugged. "No problem. I don't take so many, anyway. And you need to back off. You're a mess, man. You need to clean up."

"You have some, don't you?" I asked.

"Well, yeah." He patted his breast pocket. The familiar, seductive clinking of the pills in their tube sang out to me.

"Give them to me," I said.

Owensby's eyes narrowed. "Naw, man. You need to go see the doc. He'll help you."

"*Help. Aid. Assistance. Caregiving. Yes, go see the doctor. Join the hosts.*"

"No!" I screamed and pressed my palms against my ears. "Shut up!"

The other marine laid a hand on my shoulder. "C'mon, Jenkins. Let's get you to the doctor. He'll get you fixed up." He grasped my arm with his other hand and tried to steer me back the way I'd come.

"*Go with him.*"

"No!" I yelled again as I pushed Owensby away. If he wouldn't help me, I'd have to help myself.

"*Don't do this.*"

"I'm out of options," I said.

"What?" Owensby asked.

"*There's no turning back.*"

"Dude, what are you—" Owensby began.

My hands grasped his throat, cutting off his words. I swept a leg behind his and sent him crashing to the deck.

"*Please, don't...*"

The voice faded as adrenaline pumped through my system.

All I could hear was my own heartbeat thrumming in my ears and the gurgling of Owensby struggling to breathe. His pulse raced under my fingers, pounding a frantic drumbeat as he lashed out, pummeling my arms and shoulders. I squeezed tighter. His nails scratched my forearms. He grasped my hands, but his grip was weak. His eyes were wide, drilling into my own as a last hiss passed his mouth before his arms collapsed at his sides.

"*It's over.*"

I let go of Owensby's throat and pulled the vial of pills from his shirt pocket.

"*He's gone.*"

I raised the vial over my mouth and thumbed out a capsule, then another, then another. I didn't stop until the vial was empty.

"*It won't help.*"

I climbed to my feet and turned away, stumbling down the dimly lit, dark violet passageway as a wave of dizziness threatened to send me crashing to the deck.

"*You are unsuitable.*"

"Fuck you," I slurred as I dragged one foot in front of the other with one hand against the wall to balance myself. "I just need to find some dust, and you'll go away."

"*No more Owensby. No more dust.*"

"Shit." The thought sunk in. It was simply a fact. I felt nothing. The pills had seen to that.

"*No remorse.*"

"Nothing." That's how I wanted it.

"*It's time,*" the voice said. It sounded like a command, or an ultimatum.

"Time for what?" I asked as I turned a corner and strode down a new passage. The walls darkened as I went. Shadows surrounded me.

"Time to go home."

The passageway ahead glowed with a faint yellow light, like a distant sunrise against the twilight-like violet that surrounded me. "Yes," I mumbled, my tongue feeling heavy in my mouth. "Home."

"Keep going."

And I did. I struggled to remain upright, but I kept walking towards the light. No matter how many steps I took, it never seemed closer. But the darkness was closing in behind me.

"Almost there."

Finally, the light grew closer. The warm glow surrounded me, and just ahead there was a single hatch with a narrow window.

"There..."

I slumped against the hatch and peered through the heavy glass. Outside, there was a sandy beach bathed in sunlight with waves lapping gently at the shore. Palm trees swayed in the breeze. I could smell the pungent, salty sea air.

"Go home."

There was a panel with a series of alien characters next to the hatch. Several of them glowed with a soft, blue light. I ran my fingers over them, and the door slid open. I stepped through and thought I heard the screech of an alarm. Voices yelled out in the darkened passageway. They seemed frantic, but I wasn't worried about them now. All I cared about was home.

Another series of characters glowed on the wall, and another hatch stood between me and home. I pressed the characters and with a hiss of escaping air, the second hatch opened.

I stepped out, expecting to feel the crunch of my boots on the powdery sand. Instead, there was nothing. I expected the warm, summer sun to beat down on my skin. Instead, there was only cold. I opened my mouth to breathe in the warm sea air, but gasped when there was nothing. I tumbled over and over, spinning in the void. I looked down at my arms as my sweat crystalized to ice.

I looked up and saw the ship drifting away from me in the darkness of space.

Or was I drifting away from it?

OUT OF NOBODY
(TOWER OF REHAB WORK SONG)

ELVIRA CANAVERAL

Distress Signal screaming for revenge
Always in the middle of everywhere
Can't feel what you used to control
Out Of Body
Out Of Mind
Losing space and losing time

Sing King To A Center
So Close & Far Away
I know no know no know no anymore
I don't know where's today
I know no know no know no anytime
I just can't place today
I know no know no know no anyplace
I can't add up the days

"Don't Go Dieing Just Because You Know How"
Live To Tell Another Tale Another Way
This Side Towards Enemy
Was The The Last Thing You Read

Before The Mic Exploded
A World Imploded
Out Of Nobody
Distress Signal screaming for revenge
Always in the middle of everywhere
Can't feel what you used to control
Out Of Body
Out Of Mind
Losing space and losing time

Pull It All Together
Can't Go On Forever
Here We Go Again
And Again One More Time
It Can Never End

Out Of Body
Out Of Mind
Losing space and losing time

BEST SERVED COLD
SARAH REMY

CALLIE MORGAN GRUNTED IN IRRITATION AS SHE DROPPED THE portable med kit she'd brought with her from UPA's abandoned shuttle into the Swarm ship's recycler. The kit was perfectly well stocked for minor emergencies. If Callie had been suffering something so simple as a shallow laser burn or a case of re-entry fever, she'd have been good as gold.

Instead, she was in a bit of predicament. As soon as the temporary coagulant gel she'd smeared across the wound in her side once the shuttle was safely sealed against the tiny horrors outside crumbled away, she'd start bleeding out again. By her count, she had about forty minutes.

Damn Rolan to hell and back. Moving gingerly, Callie twisted her long, copper-colored hair into a knot at the back of her neck and frowned into the head's full-length mirror. Her reflection—naked from the waist up, muscular and solid curves in all the right places, torso decorated with inked skull-and-bones, and now an ugly, gaping wound just below her ribcage—scowled back. *What the fuck. I thought we had an understanding.*

"*Sure we did,*" Callie could imagine Rolan's reply without any trouble, right down to the lilting accent that the Venusian kept after more than ten years off-planet. *"Right up until you forgot common sense for greed."*

"Fuck." Wincing, she pulled her blood-stained undershirt back over her head, shrugged carefully into her flight jacket, then fastened it up to her chin. No reason to advertise weakness, at least not until she sussed out exactly what this motley UPA crew was doing aboard a Swarm ship.

She had a reputation to keep, didn't she? Universally famous star pirate, now embarrassingly without crew or ship.

Speaking of...

"Ship," she growled, leaving the head, stepping back into her jump boots, double checking—as she always did—to make sure the laser knife she kept in the left was still there. "I assume there's a doctor aboard?"

"Level 15, Bay 5," the ship replied in exceptionally chipper tones. A hologram popped up out of nowhere. A map of the ship, Callie assumed, and Bay 15-5 marked with a luminous purple X. "Medic Dangaley is there now. Do you need emergency assistance?"

"No." Callie took a second to memorize the map. "My legs still work, don't they?" *For now.* She hesitated. "Signal ahead and let Medic Dangaley know I'm coming. Deep flesh wound, probably needs sutures."

And damn you for that, Rolan, you twisty, fox-faced coward. Never should have let you near my bed. Or my heart.

"Cluster X109IR3?" Rolan asked, blinking at the navigational tablet Callie held up in front of their nose. "What's there, a debris field? Really, Cal. I thought we'd left the days of raiding space junk long behind."

"We've never raided space junk." She might have taken

offense if Rolan didn't look so delicious, naked in Callie's berth except for a seductively wrapped blanket. Rolan knew how to display their lithe body to good advantage. Callie could never resist a flirtatious flutter of lashes over golden Venusian eyes.

"Well." Rolan shrugged. "There was that wrecked mining barge off Ziran's third ring..."

"Hardly space junk." Tossing the navigational tablet onto Rolan's lap, Callie paced a restless circle around the captain's quarters. *The Bonny Anne*, although shipshape and space hardy, was not large. Which was a definite plus when it came to stealth and maneuverability, less so when it came to private space.

A circle around the captain's quarters consisted of exactly five short strides, and half of that was used stepping around Rolan's scattered clothes.

"If I remember, we padded our bank account nicely with the Ziran ore we pulled off that barge," Callie continued. "And ate for days off the story." She paused in her pacing, braced herself. "Interesting you mention mining, though."

"Really?" Rolan's brows, dark slashes above molten gold, quirked beneath their curly fringe. They picked up the tablet, minutely examining the star chart. "Okay, I'll bite. What's on Cluster X?"

Medic Dangaley did not look particularly pleased to see Callie. A tall woman with stress lines around her mouth and eyes, Dangaley assessed Callie with one look before waving her toward a med table.

"Heard they'd brought you on board. Callie Morgan, scourge of the stars. We're lucky Swarm suits can withstand mites, or Cluster X would have been a disaster for everyone involved. Up on the table you go, please. You're dripping blood on the floor. Shirt off, please."

The med table might have been Mount Everest. Ever since she'd started bleeding again—about three-fourths of the way into her journey through the ship—her feet had grown exceedingly heavy and her arms didn't seem to be working quite right. Also, the universe was gently spinning.

"Whoa." Dangaley caught Callie as she swayed, lifting her deftly up onto the table. After that there was a gray, hazy period of buzzing medical equipment broken occasionally by Dangaley's frankly impressive and cantankerous curses. When Callie's vision cleared again, she was lying on her back on the table and everything was just perfect.

"Fuck, what did you give me?" She struggled to sit up, but her body and brain didn't seem capable of meeting in the middle, and the best she could do was clench a fist and shudder. "I don't do pain pills. They make me puke."

"Pleasant pills," Dangaley corrected as she prodded Callie's side. Callie suspected whatever the medic was doing hurt like hell despite her legendary tolerance, but she couldn't bring herself to care. "Better than Earth's old-fashioned pain pills, if you ask me. Don't worry, it will wear off eventually." Something beeped near Callie's ribs. Dangaley exhaled. "Want to tell me who shot you point blank with a bolt pistol?"

Callie definitely didn't, but the drug in her system had other ideas. It was better than Mars gin for loosening the tongue. "Rolan. My lovely Rolan. Took my ship, left me behind to die. Fifteen years we were together. Goddamn Rolan."

"Well..." Dangaley stepped away from the table and scratched her nose. Her gloved hands were covered in blood. Her thumb left a smear on her face. The stress lines around her mouth had become canyons. "You're not dying today, Captain

Morgan, though I'll admit it was a close thing. Your Rolan meant business."

"Yes," Callie sighed, remembering Rolan's foxy smile as they shoved the bolt gun below her ribs and pulled the trigger. She added fondly, "Rolan never does anything by halves."

———

"Tiganian warp crystals," Callie told her crew. They were gathered together in *The Anne*'s small galley, a heist-planning tradition. "I think better over tea and toast," Rolan had proclaimed early on in their career. No one had dared argue then, and no one argued now even though their crew had grown over the years from two to four, and they were almost elbow to elbow over the pot of Earl Grey and the plate of buttered toast.

"Tiganian warp crystals?" Ado, their navigator, showed jagged teeth when he smiled. "An entire trunk? Very, very valuable. UPA will pay good money to get it back." Ado had a family of sixteen back on Jupiter Two and never said no to a solid payday. Callie knew she could rely on him to back her up when she put her plan to the vote.

"That doesn't make any sense. Why would UPA leave a trunk of Tiganian warp crystals on some dirty old asteroid?" That was Seren, the youngest of their group. And unlike Ado, the Earth girl didn't look happy. At just fourteen, Seren was moody and timid despite her preference for bright clothes and cheerful, candy-colored hair. She was also the best safe cracker Callie knew. "Are you sure the intel is good?"

"Yes, why would the UPA leave behind a trunk of unguarded warp crystals?" Rolan asked, practically dripping sarcasm into their steaming mug of tea. They pretended not to see Callie's glare. "Let me take a wild guess: Calyx Mites."

Seren stiffened. Ado growled. "Calyx Mites?"

"Turns out Cluster X is lousy with the buggers, pun intended." Rolan's fierce grin didn't reach their eyes. "Which would explain the abandoned shuttle containing the trunk of crystals. Whether or not Captain Morgan's intel is good hardly matters. Any fool who steps a foot on a mite infested asteroid will be eaten down to the bone in a matter of minutes."

Ado shuddered. "Mites. Worse even than acid rain." He shifted his shark grin Callie's way. "You've got to be joking."

"I'm not." Callie showed her own teeth in return. "Think about it, Ado. An *entire trunk* of warp crystals. My intel is solid. And we could retire on a haul like that. You could go home to your husband, help him raise that litter you're so proud of."

"Not if he's a skeleton, he couldn't," Rolan retorted. Seren squeaked dramatically. "Nothing we have on board will keep a full infestation off for long enough to reach the shuttle, let alone retrieve the trunk. It's not worth the risk."

"You're wrong." Callie chose a piece of toast and took a bite. The bread was still warm, buttered just to her taste. Rolan might be a pain in the ass sometimes, but they was perfection when it came to tea and toast. "I've done the calculations. Happens the UPA shuttle crashed down on one of the asteroid's higher peaks. Everyone knows mites avoid low temperatures. We may find one or two drones at below freezing, but not a queen. Drones don't feed without a queen. We can do it. All it will take is some careful maneuvering. And no one does a bit of fancy flying better than our navigator. Right, Ado?"

"Aye." Flattery always worked a trick on Ado, almost as predictably as greed. He puffed up his chest, nodded slowly. "Aye, that's true. Let me see your calculations, Captain. If the elevation is great enough... Aye, it might be possible."

"How do you feel?" Dangaley asked, regarding Callie from beneath raised brows.

"Like moonshine over vanilla ice cream." Callie said happily, prodding the flesh under her ribs, searching for a wound that seemed to have disappeared. "Wow. You're good."

"I am," the medic agreed. "And also quite busy at the moment. You should sit here for a while longer until the pleasant pill wears off. The euphoria takes some people harder than others. So..." She hooked a rolling stool with her foot, collapsed onto it with a sigh. "While we wait, why don't you tell me how you ended up marooned—and alive—on a mite-infested asteroid with a hole in your side?"

"Sure." Callie was perfectly content to do as she was told. The table was comfortable under her ass, the med bay appealingly empty of responsibilities, and thanks to Dangaley, she was no longer dying. "Really, it was all because of the wind. I didn't account for wind."

"Wind?" Dangaley scrubbed her hands under the sanitizer, then adjusted her med coat. "Yes, I remember the away team mentioned a storm."

Callie wondered if she could ask the ship for a nice bottle of stout—Venutian Oat Brick being her favorite—or even a small shot of rehydrater. The UPA MREs she'd been living on for the last fifteen hours had left her stomach feeling bloated, and her mouth was dry as asteroid dust. But despite an overabundance of softly beeping medical equipment, Callie didn't see anything that looked like a replicator.

She hadn't felt so content to sit and do nothing since—well, since the time she and Rolan had celebrated their twelfth anniversary by spending a whole afternoon floating on the Red Salt Sea, drinking real Earth Champagne under scarlet skies.

Callie poked at her side, feeling the healed flesh, remembering the pressure of the bolt gun against her side, the shock of agony when Rolan pulled the trigger. The fog of euphoria in her head began to dissipate. Her undershirt was ruined, blood-stained and torn. Dangaley handed over her flight jacket. It would need to be patched. The bolt from Rolan's pistol had left behind a hole the size of an Earth quarter. The fabric still smelled faintly of the disinfectant they'd misted her with before letting her onboard, of ozone and fungicide and sterile ethanol.

Her rescuers had known better than to risk a mite infestation.

"You *should have known better,*" Rolan murmured in her head. *"Ado is dead because you didn't listen to sense."*

"Callie?" Dangaley prompted. Callie sighed.

"Mite queens can't live long in below freezing temperatures," Callie explained, although the medic probably didn't need to be told. Everyone this side of the Aura knew about mites. "And drones won't feed without a queen. We should have been safe."

"Careful!" Rolan snapped, leaning over Ado's shoulder, presumably to get a better look at the asteroid spreading beneath *The Anne*'s belly. "You're coming in too fast."

"Too slow and we'll be thrown off course," Ado snarled, eyes pinned to the instruments flashing on the panel under his hands. "Captain's intel didn't account for Cat Four winds. Stop pestering me, Rolan, and *strap in.*" As if to make Ado's point, an angry gust of wind buffeted the small ship, making it rock and groan.

Callie and Seren were already strapped in, Callie because she was busy rerunning calculations, and Seren because she was terrified of even the smoothest ground landings. Seren, born in zero gravity and raised on a merchant cruiser, had little tolerance for the inconvenience of terra firma.

"We're close," Callie reported. She tightened her grip on her tablet as *The Anne* rocked from side to side. "Peak should be visible. Check your three o'clock."

"I see it," Ado replied grimly. "Barely. Fucking cloud of asteroid grit everywhere, Captain, and what do you think the winds will be like at thirteen thousand feet?"

"This is a bad idea," Seren said. "Captain, we didn't plan for a windstorm. It's too risky."

"It's not," Callie said calmly. "Ado, adjust for sheer and full speed ahead."

The Bonny Anne, vibrating like a Venusian sand snake caught in a trapper's snare, rose abruptly. Ado spat a muffled curse. Callie glanced up and over in time to catch Rolan's burning stare, the disapproval on their face.

"What are you thinking?" That golden glare said, clear as if Rolan had spoken aloud. *"The kid's right, it's too risky."*

It was. Rolan was forcing Callie to be honest with herself. But some things were worth the risk, and a trunk of Tiganian warp crystals was definitely one of those things.

"Hold on," Ado warned as *The Anne* bucked furiously. On the view screen, Callie saw sharp crags through a curtain of burnt umber dust. "Almost there. Fuck. Hold on—"

It was a good thing Rolan had strapped in at the last moment because it turned out Cluster X was large enough to have weather. *The Anne*, buffeted by merciless winds and too much dust in her engines, hit the surface with a drunken lurch, skidding bow first over rock before fetching up nose down inches from the dust covered bulk of what must be the UPA's abandoned shuttle.

There was a long, breathless silence broken only by the sound of the wind against *The Anne's* hull and the scrape of dust against the view screen.

"Gods save us," Seren broke the shocked silence. "Hells, Ado, you cut that fucking close."

"Bull's eye." Ado said, baring sharp teeth. But his hand shook as he wiped sweat from his brow. "I said I could do it."

"Of course you could." Callie unclipped and rose, radiating all the confidence she could muster. "Never doubted. Right. Let's suit up." She glanced again out the view screen. "Dust looks like the sort that sticks in the teeth, let's make this quick. Rolan, run a temperature check. I want to make sure it's too cold out there for mites."

"Now you're cautious," Rolan said bitterly. "And here I thought you'd completely lost your head."

Once outside *The Anne*, the gale blew Callie and Ado sideways, almost as if the winds were working to prevent them from reaching the shuttle. If not for the adjustable gravity bubbles thrown off by their EVA suits, they might have been blown right off the peak to their deaths in the valley below.

Gusts threw unrelenting fistfuls of grit against Callie's helmet. She had to clear the face shield again and again as she struggled to move forward. Ado, bigger and stronger, wrestled the wind at her side. Callie could hear his labored breathing through their comms.

Seren and Rolan had stayed onboard *The Anne*. Seren had outright refused to go out into the storm, and Rolan was needed to operate the tractor pull-beam that would haul the trunk of warp crystals aboard *The Anne*.

Assuming Callie and Ado could liberate the trunk from the shuttle in the first place.

"If it turns out we need a cracker after all..." Callie muttered ominously, clearing her face shield for what felt like the two hundredth time. The shuttle was almost within touching distance, but she didn't like the way the dusty wind scraped and bit against the outside of her EVA suit.

"You won't." Seren's voice was tinny across the comms, difficult to pick out over the crackle of storm-induced static. "It's an UPA evac shuttle. Hardly complicated. The portable code box will break the locks easily."

"Won't need it," Ado grunted. He'd reached the shuttle first, Callie four steps behind. "Door's wide open." He heaved himself out of the wind, through the gaping cargo door, and into the bay, then turned and gave Callie a hand up.

They stood for a moment, just breathing, grateful to be out of the storm. Callie brushed at the layer of dust that had accumulated on her suit. Although she knew the bio systems were airtight, she imagined she could taste grit in her airway.

"Rolan." She checked, "Temp still good?"

"Hovering just below zero Celsius," Rolan confirmed. "Too cold for infestation. You're good. Can you see the trunk?" Their voice had smoothed over from hostile to eager. Callie knew what that meant. Rolan was beginning to believe they could pull it off.

"It's here," Ado said. "Heavy. Rolan, ready the pull-beam. Captain, come give me a hand?" He, too, sounded eager. Callie understood. She could practically taste success.

The trunk must have weighed twenty-one stone. Callie didn't have Ado's muscles, but all they needed to do was lift it out of the cargo bay and into the wind so Rolan could direct the pull-beam to latch on. They worked well together, quickly and efficiently and without complaint. There was no time to crack the trunk and check the contents, but Callie wasn't worried. She trusted her intel completely and her luck unconditionally.

They had just freed the trunk from the shuttle when that luck ran out and two things happened at once: Callie stepped hard on something that wasn't dust or rock, something that cracked like sticks under her heavy boot, making her stumble in the wind, and Ado began to scream.

"Queen!" he shrieked. "Queen! Queen!" The inside of his

125

face shield washed wet with blood and his screaming became a wet, agonized wail.

Shock would have rooted Callie to the rock if Rolan hadn't spoken in her ear. "Callie!" they said, urgent. "Get back in the UPA shuttle. Right now. Secure the door."

But she was already running away, fighting the wind as she barreled toward *The Bonny Anne.* She needed refuge; she needed home; she needed her ship and the rest of her crew. Seren was screaming Ado's name in her ear.

Rolan waited for Callie just inside *The Anne's* pilot door. They'd activated the force shield, and Callie was on the wrong side. They held a bolt pistol in their left hand and wore a determined look on their foxy face.

"I'm sorry, Cal," they said, and they sounded like they meant it. "But you can't come in. You might be infested."

"I'm standing here alive, aren't I?" Callie said in disbelief. Surely Rolan could see that. "I'm not infested. I don't know how—maybe it was the wind, carrying debris from below, but—Gods, Rolan, you know it's too cold..." She trailed off, because obviously it wasn't too cold, and Ado was by now nothing more than a new skeleton lying in the dust next to the trunk of warp crystals. There would be no returning to Jupiter Two, no rejoining his husband and his litter.

She straightened her shoulders, but she couldn't seem to catch her breath. "Look, it's dead now, frozen, and probably just the one. I'm fine, see?" Swaying in the punishing wind, she lifted her hands. "I'm good. All clean. Let me in."

"There's no guarantee. You can't come in." Rolan's voice cracked. "You know the protocol. We don't risk the crew for the sake of one."

"The crew!" She was Callie Morgan, infamous space pirate, and she wasn't going to die away from her ship in the dust, eaten down to the bones by Calyx mites. "*My* crew, you mutinous bastard! Rolan! Let me in!" She threw herself against the force shield, again and again. It crackled against the weight of her EVA suit, against the strength of her determination. Almost, she broke through.

"I'm sorry," Rolan repeated as she howled curses. Tears caught in the corners of their golden gaze, but their hand was steady when they pulled the trigger.

A moment or a lifetime later, through the blinding shock and pain of what was surely a mortal wound, Callie heard the unmistakable sound of *The Anne*'s engines starting up, and knew with stark certainty that she'd been left behind to die.

———

"But you didn't," Dangaley sounded grudgingly impressed. "In spite of everything, here you are, alive and whole."

Callie thought that if she took the time to examine the state of her heart, she'd discover she wasn't as whole as Dangaley assumed. But she nodded.

"I crawled back to the shuttle, closed the door, patched myself up. By that point, I knew Ado was a fluke, because I wasn't a skeleton. But there was no guarantee the storm wouldn't toss up another infestation from below. So I huddled down and prayed to every god I'd ever heard of. Apparently one of them was listening."

Dangaley tapped a finger against her lower lip. "The treasure?"

"Still there, a trunk full of Tiganian warp crystals, guarded by what's left of Ado, poor bastard. Your jump crew dismissed the trunk as more space junk, and I didn't bother correcting their assumption."

"Surely you're not planning on going back for the crystals?

You barely got out alive. Going back would be the very definition of insanity."

"The crystals can wait." Callie slid off the med table, tested her legs. She felt good as new, better than, thanks to the lingering effects of the pleasant pills. "It's my ship I'm concerned with. Without *The Bonny Anne*, I'm nothing. I need to get her back and chasing her down will be no easy feat. She could be anywhere by now."

"Well." Dangaley rose to her feet. "I appreciate a good story, so thank you. But I'm afraid you'll have to put it out of your mind for now. The captain of this ship would like to see you, and I doubt he's got your stolen ship on his mind."

Callie wasn't worried. She was used to wheeling and dealing. She'd get what she wanted, one way or another, and what she wanted was Rolan on their knees and begging for mercy.

"I'll meet your captain," she told Dangaley. "Thank him for the rescue. And who knows, maybe we can come to an arrangement. I can be patient. You know the old Earth saying about revenge."

Dangaley shook her head. "No."

"Best served cold." Callie offered the medic her cockiest grin, though she felt anything but. "Preferably with a double portion of ruthlessness for dessert."

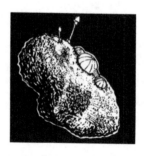

SACRED CASUALTIES
(UNDERWATER DRINKING SONG)

ELVIRA CANAVERAL

All empires come to an end
Darkness is cheap
Light has a cost
If you make it pay its way

The shadows lengthen in Carcosa
How Came I Hither?
Regions erections in apace and orgasms in space
Older's a colder paradox
Hot tears to crystal not to scale

Minor case of mortality
Misanthropes, opponents to living kind
May the way be with you

The Mushroom Moon
We don't claim to understand let alone overstand
so I'm used to uncertainty
speed of light is to space it out so it doesn't all happen at once
that's what a snapshot is for a snap of the Planck

Our Nights are not black
but truly blue
Aldebaran Al DeBaran
hard to see from the inside
Wormhole In Your Ear Radio
Steelers Wheeler Stuck In the middle with you
The missing key of a unified theory

Become comfortable
Wormhole paradox
Navikov knock it off
We Made a loop in the break
Chronology protection conjecture as Hawking called it
Sacred Causality you can jump into another stream

Hell is set to be a turn on, I mean torment
No body feels that they are done
No body ever arrives
Quantum Projection of a holographic inverse universe
Wanted for word crimes under multiple suns

HIDE & SEEK
C. VANDYKE

"Ollie ollie oxen free!"

Sergeant Suzanne Lowrie's voice echoes through the strange, twisting corridor of the Ship. There's something about the way her voice sounds as it bounces off the bio-organic walls and ceiling that feels... wrong. Maybe it's the way the words don't resonate, or the ineffable flatness whenever she speaks. But whatever it is, after eight weeks aboard the Ship, it still unnerves her.

"Come on, Dylan." Suzanne catches one of the curving handholds that line the hallway and changes the angle of her momentum. Most of the Ship operates under artificial gravity, but Dylan likes to come to the corridors along the vessel's hull where the zero-g allows nearly limitless movement.

She scans the silvery walls of the hallway and sighs. No Dylan.

"I give up!" she shouts. "Ollie ollie oxen. Come on out!"

There's a slight sigh, like a penitent murmuring a prayer, then the wall before her opens, the muscular fibers of the Ship parting to reveal a small pocket. And in the pocket is Dylan, curled up like a chick inside of an egg, waiting to hatch.

The twelve-year-old boy's face is lit with triumph.

"I win!" he crows, his messy blond hair floating in a soft halo around his face. "I win!"

"That's not fair!" Suzanne's a six-foot Marine—all corded muscles and military discipline—but Dylan brings out the petulant teen in her. Like she isn't twice his age. Almost old enough to be his mother. "How was I supposed to find you *inside* the walls? I can't make the Ship open like that. Just because it lets you…"

"*She*," interrupts Dylan. He sticks out his tongue as he spins lazily in the zero-g. "*She* doesn't like being called *it*."

Suzanne rolls her eyes, but her stomach clenches. Dylan's becoming too familiar with the Ship. With *it*. There's so much she doesn't know about *it*, and the way he talks about it, as if it's his friend…

"Don't be stupid, dingus." She keeps her tone light, teasing. She reaches out and rumples his hair. "Spaceships don't have genders. *It* is an it."

"She's not an it!" Dylan shoves her hand aside. He glares over her shoulder, not meeting her eyes, but she's used to that already. Back on Keplar, her brother Simon did the same thing. "*Kitty's* not a girl, but *she* says that's the closest pronoun to what *she* is."

"Kitty?" Suzanne can't help but laugh and Dylan turns away, offended. She grabs his shoulder, and he tries to shake her off. "You call the ship 'Kitty'? Since when?"

Dylan shrugs, a lazy, pre-teen gesture that stands in for a wide range of unspoken emotions. His voice stays flat, but his flapping hands betray his excitement. "A few days ago, in violet hour, she and I were talking…"

Again, she has to repress a shudder. The ship *talks* to him. But she wants him to open up, and he shuts down so easily, so she doesn't say anything.

"And she told me her name."

She arches a skeptical eyebrow. "And her name is *Kitty*?"

"No, stupid." Dylan's hands flap faster as he chuckles. "It wasn't anything *we* can say. She told me in *here*." He taps his left temple with his index finger. "But it doesn't... I don't think our mouths can even *make* the right sounds. But it sounded sort of like 'Catherine.'" He smiles, the shy smile of a kid half his age. "I asked if I could call her Cat, for short, and she said yes. Then Cat turned into Kitty, and..." Another shrug.

"I'm not calling the Ship *Kitty*," Suzanne says.

"But she likes it," Dylan insists.

"Nope, nothing doing. And I'm not playing hide and seek with a cheater."

"I didn't cheat!" There's a flash of real fire in his voice, and Suzanne wonders if she's teased him too much. She keeps forgetting she's only known him for eight weeks—six, really, since he'd spent the first two hidden inside his exosuit. Back when he'd tricked the crew into thinking he was a Private First Class.

He's not Simon, she reminds herself. But every time he stims or doesn't look her in the eye when they talk, every time he grins that gap-toothed grin—it's hard to remember.

"Fine," she says. "You didn't cheat. Let's go back to the bunks. See if you can beat me in *Bug Fight*."

The grin is back as quickly as it left. "You're on! I call Unicron." He shoves off the wall and rockets down the corridor. "Last one there's a rotten egg." Suzanne hesitates, hanging weightless, watching him fall away.

"I don't trust you," she mutters softly so Dylan can't hear but loud enough the Ship can.

Dangaly, the squad's medic, was the first to suspect the ship was telepathic. And Sanderson, the civilian xenobiologist embedded with the platoon, is convinced it can read their minds at will. She probably doesn't have to *say* anything, but she refuses to *think* at the Ship. Her voice is a whisper; the uncanny acoustics of the hall swallow her words. "I don't know what you want with him, but I swear to God if you hurt him, I'll kill you. I can do it—I'm a demolition expert."

She waits a second, half-dreading a response. There isn't one, only the soft background hum of the Ship's unknown propulsion as they travel between the stars. As if she and Dylan and the rest of the crew are trapped inside a massive, purring tiger.

"Kitty," she mutters. "I'm not fucking calling you Kitty, *Ship*." She shoves off and follows Dylan.

She stood in the doorway of her parent's algae farm, rucksack slung over one shoulder, the notification from the UPAMC recruiting office open on her holoscreen.

"Don't do this, Suzanne. We love you. Jesus loves you." Her dad's voice was soft, pitched in a tone he meant as reassuring, but that she'd come to think of as Bait Voice. A worm that hid the sharp barb of a hook. "Your mom and I talked to Pastor McMasters—the entire congregation is praying for you. We can download a patch. Fix you up right. Stay here and we can get through this together." In the corner, her mom sobbed softly, eyes distant, staring at the virtual minister who whispered into her head.

Suzanne held up the holoscreen, shoved it right in his face. "It's too late. I ship out today. It's final. An autocab's already on its way."

"Nothing is final outside the love of Christ, Suzanne."

She wanted to scream that he could take his love of Cyber Christ and shove it up his ass, but they'd had this fight before. Patterns and archetypes.

"This will always be your home," he said. "We will always welcome back the prodigal child."

When she realized Private First Class Dylan Kift was not in fact a new recruit to the UPA Marine Corps, but a twelve-year-old orphan who'd built an exoskeleton to disguise himself and faked dispatch papers to get aboard the attack skiff, Suzanne had been too impressed to feel betrayed. Captain Savory was outraged, of course, but Dylan was technically a civilian and so not subject to court martial. Besides, the squad had bigger things to worry about. They were inside a sentient alien ship that had teleported to the far end of the galaxy using unknown tech; they had to figure out how to work the navigation, the weapons systems, the bizarre zoetrope room. Disciplining a stow-away tween wasn't anyone's top priority. And while they ran sector scans and charted the chromatically shifting bio-organic walls, Dylan worked his way into the crew's hearts. Suzanne's in particular.

And, apparently, the Ship's.

"I can't tell you the future will be easy. I can't tell you there won't be trials and tribulations. But I can tell that through it all you will have the Love of our Lord and Saviour Jesus Christ." Mom and Dad nodded and texted <<Amen Amen Amen>>. All around her, the holographic avatars of the congregation of the First Church of the Cyber Christ nodded and texted as well, flooding the chat fields with a stream of <<Hallelujah>> and <<Thank you Jesus>>.

Pastor McMasters' hologram flickered as he raised his hands toward the virtual heavens. "Jesus is always faithful and never changing; even in the neuronet, the Holy Spirit connects us. Even though the rest of the world rejects the Tenants of the Good Book, we are faithful to his Word."

<<Amen, Amen>>

Suzanne nodded and muttered as well. Texted, <<Amen. Thank you Jesus>>. But she wondered what was wrong with her. Why she never felt the Spirit move through her synaptic link. Why she was different.

She kept the church feed but opened a new tab in her holofield. The antiquarian The Once and Future King. *Her parents banned all pop-culture from the house, but anything pre-23rd century got past the filters, as it was flagged by her HomeEd app as "academic." So, she read Greek mythology and X-Men comics, King Arthur and Nancy Drew. Streamed ancient 2-D flatvids like* The Never Ending Story, She-Ra *and* The Dark Crystal.

"The world tells you to pursue pleasure. To pursue sex and drugs. Money. But the word of the Lord is unchanging. There is no Word 2.0. No updates to God's Will. The Spirit is Divine, while the Flesh is wicked. The Spirit is Willing, the Flesh is Weak. But in the Cybernet, we can leave behind our Flesh and live as the Lord intended us to be—as Divine Children of the Lord. As beings of Spirit, united in the Love of Cyber Christ." The holofield flickered at the edge of her vision. Her parents and brother nodded and nodded and nodded.

<<Amen>>

<<Amen>>

<<Amen>>

"Dylan? You in here?" She doesn't like the Magic Machine Room. She doesn't like *anywhere* onboard the Ship, but she hates coming in here. "Renner said he saw you head this way."

"Yeah, I'm here."

She shudders, braces herself, and steps into the room.

"Hey, D. My shift's over if you want to play." She's about to say, *I've been practicing Bug Fight, and I think I can take you,* but the words die on her lips. Dylan hangs in the middle of the room, his feet dangling three feet off the floor. A series of tentacle-like cords exude from the ceiling and wrap around his arms and legs. Two pseudopods are attached to his temples, just behind his eyes; his eyes roll back in his head.

"Let him go!" She crosses the room in a heartbeat, grabs Dylan's legs and yanks at the Ship's tentacles. "Leave him alone!"

Dylan shudders. His eyes snap open and he frowns.

"Stop it, Suzzie. I'm fine." The tentacles lower him to the ground, slithering across his skin as they ease him down. "Kitty and I were just talking. She's lonely."

"Lonely?" Suzanne takes a deep breath. Her heart's still racing, but Dylan seems okay. "How can it..."

"*She!*"

"Fine, whatever. How can *she* be lonely? There's more than twenty-five of us literally *inside* her."

"None of you talk to her like I do." Dylan smiles and something inside her aches. *i don't want u 2 leave.* Simon would be around his age. *Is* around his age. Dylan cocks his head, looks over her shoulder. "You should try talking to her, Suzzie."

"Dylan, I don't think..."

"Come on. Please?" The thought of the Ship *inside* her mind makes her skin crawl, but Dylan grabs her hand. "Please?"

"Okay. I'll try." She flinches as something brushes the side of her head, forces herself to take deep breaths. To stay calm. The Ship's tendril is neither warm nor cold, somehow soft and metallic at the same time. The air in the room shivers, undulates like heat shimmer, and then Michelle is there in front of her, still nineteen years old, her short red hair curled the same as it was the last time Suzanne saw her. The room shimmers again and Simon's there. She rips the tentacle away.

"Stay the fuck out of my head!"

She storms out of the room, for once deaf to Dylan as he begs her to come back, to just listen.

———

Michelle's lips were soft, like the petals of a flower opening against her mouth. Kissing her was nothing like when she'd tried kissing boys on NeuroLyfe, even with the new Sensotech upgrades. It was nothing like the skynvids she'd watched when her parents were asleep, consumed by guilt and desperate longing as images of naked women streamed directly into her optic nerve.

Kissing Michelle was slow and scary and beautiful. The Church said her flesh was corrupt. That what she was doing right now, kissing another girl, was a sin. But as she rested her hand on Michelle's cheek, she didn't believe that.

This couldn't be a sin.

"Suzzie?"

She jerked away from Michelle. Simon was standing in the door, his hair tousled with sleep, his eyes wide with confusion.

"Simon!" She stood and moved toward him slowly. "Hey. I thought you were... Listen, we weren't. Michelle and I, that is, we weren't..." She knelt next to him so her eyes were at his level, but his wide brown eyes never met hers. His fingers opened and closed, opened and closed. She took his hand in hers, but he pulled it away.

"Please don't tell Dad," she begged. She couldn't tell if he was actually listening, so she texted his chip. <<Pls dont tell dad>>

———

Suzanne holds Dylan as he cries. She's found him in the MMR, rocking back and forth. "She's sick, Suzzie. Really sick."

"I know, D. I know." She strokes his hair and squeezes him in a tight embrace, the way she did whenever Simon was upset. Deep pressure. "I'm sure the Ship will be okay."

"You don't know that. What if Kitty dies?" Most of the time he seems older than his twelve years, but right now he's like a little kid. He's scared. She's scared too, but not for the Ship—for all the crew. For Dylan and herself. If the Ship dies, they're screwed. They're ninety-thousand light-years from home. Suzanne's worried that their vehicle might break down; Dylan's worried his friend is dying.

"It will be okay. Sanderson's trying to decode its genome. Angelin's talking to the ship right now, and if xe can find out what's making it sick…"

"*Her*!" He squirms out of her embrace, wraps his arms around himself and rocks back and forth. "Her! Her! Kitty is a *Her*!"

"Dylan, I—"

"And I know what made her sick. It's us. It's our fault."

She tries to pull him back, but he scoots away. "Dylan. You can't know that. You can't blame—"

"It is our fault! She talks to me, remember? She told me. She's sick because of our brains, because our brains don't work with hers. She's trying, but it's making her… *wrong*. It's my fault. It's all my fault."

Holographic images flicker about him, ghostly butterflies of synapses as the ship spills the boy's inner-most thoughts into the room. There's a man and a woman—she has Dylan's eyes, he has Dylan's unruly hair. There's a younger Dylan clutching the woman's leg, riding on the man's shoulders. The figures undulate and repeat, a field of subconscious memories playing like newsvids as he rocks and repeats, "It's all my fault, it's all my fault." She shouldn't be seeing this—but she can't leave him—can't look away.

"Dylan…"

The images change. There's the scuttling shape of the Swarm armies: flashing blade-like limbs and rows of teeth, bio-organic fighter-ships dropping into Kepler's lower orbit to unleash fusillades of plasma and death. She recognizes the Battle of 452B—she was there when the Swarm wiped out the city. She lost a lot of squadmates. Friends. The man and the woman explode into ghostly viscera, phantasmal limbs and organs swirling out from Dylan's mind to fade into nothingness.

Dylan screams.

Suzanne throws herself at him and wraps her arms around his body, even as he tries to fight her off.

"Oh baby boy, it wasn't your fault. It wasn't your fault. It wasn't your fault."

She repeats it until he stops screaming, holds him until he stops rocking and lies still in her arms.

"The Ship's going to be fine, Dylan. *She's* going to be fine. She's going to be fine."

<<*WHAT IS WRONG WITH YOU???*>> *It would be better if her mom at least turned off the optical overlay and looked at her. But Mom was almost never IRL anymore.* <<*WHY ARE YOU DOING THIS???*>> *Her mom texted in all caps, the only way she yelled these days, and the holofield between them flickered with messages from Michelle.*

<<*I need 2 see u again*>>

<<*I miss kissing u*>>

<<*God, I'm wet just thinking about u*>>

Then a stream of neuro-addresses for skynvid sites. SapphicLuv. Grls4Grls. The pages filled with blank squares as Mom's software scrubbed the images.

Pages of her poetry. Her journal.

"Those are my private files!" Suzanne screamed. "You had no right..."

"Children, obey your parents in everything, for this pleases the Lord," her dad recited.

<<We were bad parents>> Her mom rocked back and forth. <<It's because we let you watch those old movies. Read those books. We should have been stricter.>>

<<We were not bad parents, Judith.>> "The Lord has seen fit to test us, but all things are possible through his..."

"This isn't fucking about you or the Lord!" Suzanne wanted to grab her parents, shake them. "This is about me. This is about who I am. It isn't about Cyber Christ or the Bible. It's about me."

"We need to pray," her father said, and her mother nodded blindly, her eyes focused on whatever her chip fed her. "Dear Lord, we ask for your blessing and guidance in this time of tribulation. Help our dear daughter, Suzanne, who has lost her way."

<<Amen>>

"Stop it!" She hated that she cried whenever they fought. She wanted to be as calm IRL as the settings on her parents' mood apps, but she never was. "I don't need you to pray for me; I need you to listen to me!"

"Jesus, we know that in you all things are possible. Bless Suzanne so she might turn from the weakness of the flesh and sin and return to the eternal blessings of the cybernet."

<<Bless her Lord>>

They were still praying in the holosphere when the door slammed behind her.

"How do we fix it, Dangaly?" Suzanne sits across from Changa in the galley, a mug of coffee forgotten in her hand.

"Fuck if I know, Sergeant." The medic has bags under her

eyes, has that look of bone-deep exhaustion that no amount of caffeine can cover. "I mean, I don't even know how to *start* curing a sick spaceship. If it was a member of the crew, or even some unknown xenoform, I'd just stick it in the medbay, but the medbay's fucked by the same infection that's blocking the passage to the starboard barracks." She rubs her temple. "You got ideas, Sergeant? I'm open to suggestions. But Sanderson can't make dick out of either the ship or the fungus, and it won't talk to Angevin. Xe's been in the zoetrope *thinking* about stories of plagues and mythological cures, but nada. Xe's the xenolinguist, for fuck's sake, but it won't say shit to xer."

"The Ship won't talk to us, but she'll talk to Dylan."

"Hey, if he can figure out what's going on, more power to him." Changa takes a sip of her tepid coffee, then frowns. "Did you just call the ship *she*?"

<<i cant stay here>>

   <<i dont want u 2 leave>>

   She smiled sadly at Simon. His fingers flicked the air as he played one of his chip games. Most likely CometConnect. He was good at finding patterns, at keeping half a dozen command chains running at once. She could never text and play a game at the same time, but Simon could. In fact, that's when they had their best conversations.

   <<i dont want 2 leave u either>>

   <<then stay>>

   <<i cant. i cant keep living like this. mom & dad hate me>>

   <<they dont hate u>>

   <<they hate that i like grls>>

   <<but they love u>>

   <<u cant love sumi but hate who they r, simon. it doesnt work

that way>> She felt bad dumping such grownup ideas on her little brother. But she didn't have anyone else to talk to.

<<i dont care that you like girls>>

She smiled. <<i no u dont bro. and u no what?>>

<<what?>>

<<no I else cares either. ive been looking on the net, & outside of our church, no I cares if ur gay. no I haz 4 thousands of years>> She took a deep breath. <<do u no what ppl say about the church of the cyber christ>>

<<no!! what????>>

<<its a cult. that were all crazy. that it violates human rights laws. theres politicians here on kepler who want to make the CCC illegal>>

<<illegal to love jesus?>>

<<why should i love jesus if jesus doesn't love me?>>

There was a long pause. Simon's fingers flicked at the unseen comets, organizing them by color and type, watching them vanish into clouds of light. Suzanne worried she'd pushed it too far, that Simon still believed in a loving Cyber Jesus and that he'd shut down, shut her out.

<<where will u go?>>

<<idk yet. anywhere. i'll b a wandering knight, like parcival>>

<<there aren't knights IRL, stupid. Those stories r thsnds of yrs old>>

<<UPAs always recruiting. I could join the marines.>> He laughed out loud.

<<lol ur not 18>>

<<i will be in 2 months>>

<<ur not the marine type ROFL>>

She glared across the couch.

<<just wait n see, bro. wait and see>>

The ship is reaching out to more of the crew. Between the Magical Machine Room and the zoetrope chamber, nearly everyone's communed with the Ship now. Maybe it's because the Ship's sick, but the telepathic field bleeds into the edges of all their minds. The Magical Machine Room shows them visions of relatives they've left across the galaxy; the zoetrope talks to them in memes and cliches, in metaphor and poetry. Even as her squadmates become more comfortable with the alien whispers inside their skulls, Suzanne refuses to let the Ship in. She doesn't trust anyone inside her brain.

She remembers Mom scrolling through her texts from Michelle, deleting her journal.

It's not that she thinks the Ship is hostile—she *does* seem to care about Dylan, in her own, xenocentric fashion—but Suzanne doesn't exactly trust her, either. Dylan's spending even more time talking to her, trying to find a cure, but so far nothing.

Suzanne holds him when he cries, reminds him again and again it's not his fault. She whispers old stories about knights and wizards to him, about teenage heroes and prophecies.

The door closed behind her with a hydraulic hiss. She scanned the stream for the neon blue of an autocab. No car yet. She refused to turn around, but the presence of her past at her back was almost unbearable; like Orpheus standing at the mouth of the underworld, wondering if Eurydice was following. She wanted to say goodbye to Simon, but if she turned around her mother would be crying and her father would say how much he loved her and that Cyber Jesus would forgive her.

She told herself she was leaving on a quest. She told herself she wouldn't cry.

Her chip chimed with a text notification. She muted it without looking.

With the purr of an ion engine, a blue car dropped from the traf-fic-stream—a beat up Yahima XL Splicer. Just like Dad drove. Suzanne swiped her holopad, slid into the cab, and closed her eyes.

She didn't open them until her house was long out of sight.

"You've got to rest, D." Suzanne holds out a mug of cocoa, and when he ignores it, she shoves it into his hands until his fingers close on the warm metal cup. "Drink this. There's Pleasant Pills mixed in to help you sleep."

"Can't sleep. Kitty needs me." But he takes a drink automatically. He's too tired to connect his thoughts and actions.

"You can't help her if you pass out, Dylan."

"She's getting worse." Dylan's voice is heavy with despair, the words swallowed by the hushed acoustics. "The aft sector's so infected the halls have closed up entirely. Renner won't wake up, and it seems Broggs might be sick now, too. What if she dies? What if she..." His fingers open and close, open and close, but he's too exhausted to even stim properly.

"She's not going to die."

"You don't know that."

"She's not going to die." She slides the cup out of his hands and holds them with hers. He's too tired to pull away. "Angevin's said xe's making progress in the zoetrope, so any day now..."

"The zoetrope?" Dylan looks up at her, and for a moment his eyes meet hers. Something flutters inside her breast.

"Yeah, the zoetrope. Xe's there almost twenty-four-seven."

"The zoetrope." The eye contact's gone again. Dylan stands up. "I'm going to sleep."

145

She eyes him warily. Something's wrong. "Dylan, what are you going to do?"

"I'm going to sleep. Like you said—I need rest."

She trails behind as he wanders the curving corridors toward the barracks, a shadow following a ghost through the twisting intestines of a cosmic underworld.

The interior of the fast attack skiff smelled of ozone and industrial lubricant. Suzanne strapped herself into the jump seat as a disembodied voice counted down to take off. All around, the rest of the crew did the same: the members of her squad secured weapons while the civilian operatives stowed whatever gear they'd brought.

A slim marine slid into the seat next to her. The faceplates of their rumble suits made it impossible to tell the squad apart, so she glanced at the nameplate. Kift. She didn't recognize the name, but the single bar on his shoulder said he was a Private First Class.

"New recruit?" she asked.

"What?"

"I thought I knew everyone on board," she said. "Even the PFC's." There was a long pause. "You got a first name, Private?"

"Dylan. Um, Sir. Ma'am."

"Sergeant Lowrie. You ready to snatch a ship and kill some bugs?"

"Yes, Sergeant!" His voice sounded less like a marine and more like an eager kid. Ah, to be young and naive.

A chime sounded over the intercom, and a red light flashed at the bulkhead. "T-Minus thirty seconds to take off." Suzanne felt the familiar thrill in her stomach.

"All right, kid. Let's go get us a Swarm ship."

"*Where's Dylan?*" she screams and lunges at the xenolinguist. Deandre and Sanderson grab her arms and hold her back as Angevin cowers.

Captain Savory barks, "Stand down, Marine!" For the first time, Suzanne notices the captain has stopped shaving. There's at least two days' worth of non-regulation stubble across his jawline, and something about that brings Suzanne back to her senses. She stops fighting. Deandre and Sanderson still hold her arms, not sure if she's going to attack Angevin again.

"Where's Dylan?" This time it's almost a sob. "Where is he?"

Angevin waves mutely toward the blank wall that until recently had been the entrance to the zoetrope chamber. Now there's no opening, no sphincter, just the smooth cording of the Ship's bio-organic skin.

"How long?"

"Almost forty-eight hours." The Captain rests a hand on her arm. "No one's been able to get in, and the Ship... it isn't responding to Angevin or anyone else."

"She," Suzanne says reflexively. "She isn't responding."

"I didn't know..." Angevin begins, stops, and starts again. "He said he needed to talk to the Ship. And since he's always... I mean, it's always been..." Xe looks lost.

Deandre and Sanderson let her go. Angevin flinches, but Suzanne walks past xer. She drops to her knees and rests her forehead against the wall.

"Please, don't hurt him," she whispers. Her words dissolve into the Ship's skin. Nothing. She closes her eyes and opens her mind. *Please don't hurt him.* Something slides across her temple, and for the first time, she doesn't recoil.

Please keep him safe, Ship. She takes a deep breath, reaches out with her mind. *Catherine, Cat. Whoever you are. Kitty.* Suzanne feels something move through her mind, softly, gently, a lingering kiss of alien thought. *Please, Kitty, don't hurt him. Please.*

She feels the floor and the wall fade away, feels herself floating in some liminal space that is neither the Ship nor home, neither here nor there, neither past nor present nor future, reality nor fantasy. And then *Simon's there, and Cyber Jesus is hanging on the cross gazing at her with eternal love while lying in her arms and she's Mary and then she's Galahad searching for the Fisher King, questing for the Grail across the empty space between the stars, chasing the Graal, the dish and the bleeding spear and Michelle is Guinevere, Nimue, Morgan Le Fay and she kisses her, feels their breath mingle as their tongues touch and her skin is like the celestial fire that burns across the sky, like the sunrise over Kepler the day she left home, like the curve of the planet as she left on a UPAMC ship <<For God so loved the world that he gave his only begotten son>> and Simon is Dylan and Dylan is whispering inside the zoetrope, telling Kitty stories about ancient heroes and heroines, about Holy Grails and the Healing Blood of Christ, about Moana healing Te Fiti and how Athena sprang fully formed from Zeus's head. Bastian named the Child Empress to cure Eternia while Orpheus played his lyre and Hades wept. Catra kissing Adora. GIFs of dancing babies, ancient sitcom vids of women eating ice cream and pickles, and then she's hugging Simon/Dylan saying, "I won't leave you." Holding tighter and muttering, "I won't leave you."* And then the world reconstitutes itself. The floor slips into coherence beneath her knees, and Dylan's in her arms, rocking softly back and forth.

She hugs him tighter, clings to him as if he's the anchor holding her to reality, as if she lets him go she might be swept away into a slipstream of archetypes and fairy tales, of quantum possibilities and ur-mythos.

But Dylan is real and solid, and when she opens her eyes, he's still there. Deandre and Sanderson are staring. Angevin's mouth is open; even Captain Savory looks as if he's about to faint.

"I cured her, Suzzie!" Dylan pulls away, grinning like he hasn't in weeks. He flaps his hands and stares over her shoulder. "We cured her. I told her the stories you told me and now she's going to be okay."

She pulls him back into a hug and lets herself break down. She doesn't care what her captain or the others think about a Marine Sergeant crying. But she can feel it—Dylan's right. Something's changed in the air around them. There's a different... *energy* in the ship—in Kitty.

Dylan stops smiling. "But she needs our help."

"Our help?" Suzanne wipes her eyes and grins. "Of course. Whatever she needs. I'll do anything Kitty wants."

His face is serious, his eyes suddenly older than his twelve years. "She's a mom, Suzzie. Kitty's a mom. And she needs us to help her baby."

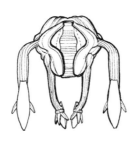

ENTANGLED DICE
(CHA-AHC-CHA)

ELVIRA CANAVERAL

Always a seven
Entangled we are are
Yin and a yang
Going six ways

When I'm a one
You're a six
I roll two
You show five

Three dots on top
You got four showing
I become you
You become me

Just missing each other

Entangled
If my five is alive
Your two is true

Six is the fix

We make seven
Never the same
But always a winner
No matter how far apart

Spooky action at any distance
John Stewart Bell
Provided Einstein's Hell
When we came to be
A mismatched pair
Entangled together everywhere

God's Fuzzy Dice

PART II: THE SECOND JUMP

JUMP 1

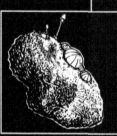

MINING ASTEROID
AB-5427

CLUSTER X109IR3
ABANDONED SKIFF

SENTIENT NEBULA

SECTOR 2

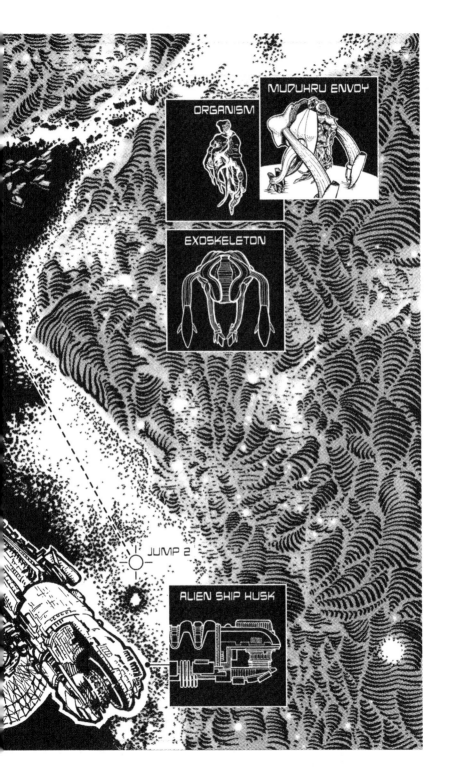

ABOUT NOTHING
(MUCH TWO D TO DO)

ELVIRA CANAVERAL

A cell separated from the dead universe
A screw you against entropy
The most interesting something
And empty hand holds something
Exotic particles,
Shielded, frozen, and no motion
Only a quantum blur
A zero-point energy
Radiant heat glow
Quantum Fiel Theory
Fundamental quantum fields
Vibrating in their own way
Quantums have questions and answers to each other
Tossing up and down the rungs
Of the particle ladder

Using creation and annihilation operators
A Vaccum impossible to have once the infinite got as big as it did
Virtuals particles
The machinery under the hood

Virtual particles provide the models for the engine
Back in time or faster than light
Operating under subreal freedoms
Surreal Subeginius
The tiniest of a virtual photon can exist for so long
Not being burdened with Reality
Being what the need to be in QFT
Fluctuating vacuum energy is the
THIS PAGE INTENTIONALLY LEFT BLANK
Message for building a universe
But that message posses energy
Vacuum energy has a relative effect
Nothing to hold onto can take you back in time
Metaparticles for what you need
Whole lotta nothin' going on
A Quirk Of The Math

A COMMON PAIN
EMILY ANSELL

I was wrong.

Dylan and Suzanne were ashen, clutching the others' hands as they announced: *The ships aren't Swarm. They're enslaved by the Swarm. The dodecahedron is an infant. This ship's infant. We have to help it.*

Then Weatherly, tears streaming down her face as she tore down the hall from the Magical Machine Room, screaming: *Lans went in! They went in and something's gone wrong!*

Now, I stood in a circle with the others around Lansquenet as they sat twitching on the floor. Had I a heart or something equivalent, it would've broken for them. Mumbles and glitchy phrases in both Chrondite and Human languages passed their lips, but none of it was in any way intelligible.

The voice of the ship interrupted our thoughts, speaking in a robotic monotone. After months of 'comedic' voices, the starkness of contrast made all my filaments stand on end.

"Lansquenet Immanuel's entry into what you refer to as the Magical Machine Room has activated the Pop Drop system. However, both they and the Magical Machine room have become corrupted as a result, perhaps irreparably."

"How?" Captain Savory demanded.

"As an android of both human and Chrondite elements, Lansquenet's system did not meet the requirements to enable proper activation and transfer."

"Transfer of what?"

"Personality and knowledge matrices. These are imperative to complete the procreation process of my species. With the Room now corrupted, my infant cannot be, as you would understand it, born. For now, you should take Lansquenet to the medbay."

"What about you, Kitty?" Dylan asked, reaching out to touch the wall of the ship.

There was no reply.

The Captain crossed his arms, eyes sweeping the group, "Alright, everyone, no point in standing around. Gennaro, help the docs get Lansquenet out of here and see if you can give them a hand. The rest of you, dismissed for now. I think we need to give the ship some time."

The crew dispersed, and I found myself restless. All the corridors I wandered looked the same. What I really wanted was to talk to Broggs. But with all these revelations, and now Lansquenet's... malfunction, Broggs would've gone straight for the pleasant pills and was likely hiding in his quarters. It would be best to let him be for now.

Eventually, I found myself at the Zoetrope doors. Dylan and Suzanne stood outside like guards, whispering between themselves as I approached.

"What can we do for you, Angevin?" Suzanne asked, just icy enough to make me hesitate.

"I... I'd like to talk to the Ship. Alone, if I could."

"The ship is not talking to anyone right now."

"Let xem in," Dylan interrupted. Suzanne's face darkened, but she moved aside.

I went in, the dark room offset by only a few lights on the consoles and the soft glow of my personal Grav-Field. Taking a moment to muster the words, I began.

"Ship, let me tell you a story of how I came to be here. My home was on Elkar-2, a colony of my people. It is a lovely place; lush, temperate, gentle. Though we often travel, to gather experiences to pass along, most of my family were on-world when the Swarm arrived. They'd come to celebrate. My first Division." I stopped, consciously unfolding long, wispy fingers that had clenched themselves into fists. But I forced myself to continue.

"I was still undergoing Division when the attack happened. It is a long process, and at that point, I was helpless. My family was killed, struck down defending themselves or trying to protect me. I was badly wounded, but alive. We were not rescued until hours later. I managed to finish the Dividing process. But my Division... did not survive. Only long enough to declare xir name."

"What was their name?" the ship asked.

"Angevoon, as per our custom to base one's name from their progenitor. And then xe died in my arms. That's why I took this mission to establish communication with you. I came to find some weakness. Anything. Whether physical, a cultural taboo, it didn't matter as long as it could be weaponized. I hated you, called you my enemy, but you're another victim of this war, aren't you? We are not dissimilar in that respect. So, if there is anything that can be done, any way of repairing the Magical Machine Room, I will help. If I can spare you the grief I feel... of a child lost... I will."

"Such a thing would be greater than all the magic and all the treasures in all the world!" the ship declared, its voice changing into one of the impersonations it usually did. I'd heard this voice before, though I couldn't remember the name associated with it.

"Then I will do everything I can, Ship."

"Thank you Angevin, Divided of Angelin, 4,434[th] Division from Beregol. For your offer, and for being honest. I appreciate it more than you know."

My confession made, I left the zoetrope. Lightness buoyed every movement as if I'd stepped out of the crushing pressure of Earth-grav and into the familiar embrace of home. The pain, that common pain, wasn't gone. It never would be. But for now it slept, and that was enough.

UPA MEDICAL RECORDS

RENNER, KEVIN—SERGEANT

DATE: 21 July 832 A.A.

BLOOD TEST REFERENCE RANGE CHART	
17 Hydroxyprogesterone (Men)	0.06-3.0 mg/L 0.27 mg/L
17 Hydroxyprogesterone (Women) Follicular phase	0.2-1.0 mg/L N/A
25-hydroxyvitamin D (25(OH)D)	8-80 ng/mL 68 ng/ml
Acetoacetate	<3 mg/dL 1.2 mg/dL
Acidity (pH)	7.35 - 7.45 7.37
Alcohol	0 mg/dL (more than 0.1 mg/dL normally indicates intoxication) (ethanol) 0 mt/dL
Ammonia	15 - 50 µg of nitrogen/dL 17 µg of nitrogen/dL
Amylase	53 - 123 units/L 120 units/L
Ascorbic Acid	0.4 - 1.5 mg/dL 0.7 mg/dL
Bicarbonate	18 - 23 mEq/L (carbon dioxide content) 24 mEq/L
Bilirubin	Direct: up to 0.4 mg/dL 0.26 mg/dL Total: up to 1.0 mg/dL 0.89 mg/dL
Blood Volume	8.5 - 9.1% of total body weight 9.0%
Calcium	8.2 - 10.6 mg/dL (normally slightly higher in children) 10.23 mg/dL
Carbon Dioxide Pressure	35 - 45 mm Hg 44 mm Hg
Carbon Monoxide	Less than 5% of total hemoglobin 4.91%

CD4 Cell Count	<u>500 - 1500 cells/μL</u> 1528 cells/μL
Ceruloplasmin	<u>15 - 60 mg/dL</u> 58 mg/dL
Chloride	<u>98 - 106 mEq/L</u> 101 mEq/L
Complete Blood Cell Count (CBC)	<u>Tests include:</u> hemoglobin, hematocrit, mean corpuscular hemoglobin, mean corpuscular hemoglobin concentration, mean corpuscular volume, platelet count, white blood cell count <u>Please click each to view an individual test value.</u>
Copper	<u>Total: 70 - 150 μg/dL</u> 150 μg/dL
Creatine Kinase (CK or CPK)	<u>Male: 38 - 174 units/L</u> 154 units/L <u>Female: 96 - 140 units/L</u> N/A
Creatine Kinase Isoenzymes	<u>5% MB or less</u> 3.2%
Creatinine	<u>0.6 - 1.2 mg/dL</u> 0.87 mg/dL
Electrolytes	<u>Test includes:</u> calcium, chloride, magnesium, potassium, sodium <u>Please click each to view an individual test value.</u>
Erythrocyte Sedimentation Rate (ESR or Sed-Rate)	<u>Male: 1 - 13 mm/hr</u> 14 mm/hr <u>Female: 1 - 20 mm/hr</u> N/A
Glucose	<u>Tested after fasting: 70 - 110 mg/dL</u> 74 mg/dL
Hematocrit	<u>Male: 45 - 62%</u> 43 % <u>Female: 37 - 48%</u> N/A
Hemoglobin	<u>Male: 13 - 18 gm/dL</u> 12 gm/dL <u>Female: 12 - 16 gm/dL</u> N/A
Iron	<u>60 - 160 μg/dL (normally higher in males)</u> 62 μg/dL

Iron-binding Capacity	250 - 460 µg/dL 278 µg/dL	
Lactate (lactic acid)	Venous: 4.5 - 19.8 mg/dL 18.7 mg/dL Arterial: 4.5 - 14.4 mg/dL 13.4 mg/dL	
Lactic Dehydrogenase	50 - 150 units/L 115 units/L	
Lead	40 µg/dL or less (normally much lower in children) 30 µg/dL	
Lipase	10 - 150 units/L 29 units/L	
Zinc B-Zn	70 - 102 µmol/L 83 µmol/L	
Lipids:		
Cholesterol	Less than 225 mg/dL (for age 40-49 yr; increases with age) 73 mg/dL	
Triglycerides	10 - 29 years	53 - 104 mg/dL 56 MG/Dl
	30 - 39 years	55 - 115 mg/dL N/A
	40 - 49 years	66 - 139 mg/dL N/A
	50 - 59 years	75 - 163 mg/dL N/A
	60 - 69 years	78 - 158 mg/dL N/A
	> 70 years	83 - 141 mg/dL N/A

Liver Function Tests	Tests include: bilirubin (total), phosphatase (alkaline), protein (total and albumin), transaminases (alanine and aspartate), prothrombin (PTT) Please click each to view an individual test value.
Magnesium	1.9 - 2.7 mEq/L 2.2 mEq/L
Mean Corpuscular Hemoglobin (MCH)	27 - 32 pg/cell 26 pg/cell
Mean Corpuscular HemoglobinConcentration (MCHC)	32 - 36% hemoglobin/cell 30% hemoglobin/cell
Mean Corpuscular Volume(MCV)	76 - 100 cu µm 80 cu µm
Osmolality	280 - 296 mOsm/kg water 291 Osmolality
Oxygen Pressure	83 - 100 mm Hg 83 mm Hg
Oxygen Saturation (arterial)	96 - 100% 97%
Phosphatase, Prostatic	0 - 3 units/dL (Bodansky units) (acid) 1 units/dL
Phosphatase	50 - 160 units/L (normally higher in infants and adolescents) (alkaline) 78 units/L
Phosphorus	3.0 - 4.5 mg/dL (inorganic) 3.7 mg/dL
Platelet Count	150,000 - 350,000/mL 136,000/mL
Potassium	3.5 - 5.4 mEq/L 5.0 mEq/L
Prostate-Specific Antigen (PSA)	0 - 4 ng/mL (likely higher with age) 2 ng/mL
Proteins:	

Total	6.0 - 8.4 gm/dL	
	8.2 gm/dL	
Albumin	3.5 - 5.0 gm/dL	
	4.8 gm/dL	
Globulin	2.3 - 3.5 gm/dL	
	3.4 gm/dL	
Prothrombin (PTT)	25 - 41 sec	
	27 sec	
Pyruvic Acid	0.3 - 0.9 mg/dL	
	0.4 mg/dL	
Red Blood Cell Count (RBC)	4.2 - 6.9 million/µL/cu mm	
	4.1 million/µL/cu mm	
Sodium	133 - 146 mEq/L	
	133 mEq/L	
Thyroid-Stimulating Hormone (TSH)	0.5 - 6.0 µ units/mL	
	0.9 µ units/mL	
Transaminase:		
Alanine (ALT)	1 - 21 units/L	
	18 units/L	
Aspartate (AST)	7 - 27 units/L	
	12 units/L	
Urea Nitrogen (BUN)	7 - 18 mg/dL	
	11 mg/dL	
BUN/Creatinine Ratio	5 - 35	
	10	
Uric Acid	Male	2.1 to 8.5 mg/dL (likely higher with age)
		6.5 mg/dL
	Female	2.0 to 7.0 mg/dL (likely higher with age)
		N/A

Vitamin A	30 - 65 µg/dL
	34 µg/dL
WBC (leukocyte count and white Blood cell count)	4.3-10.8 × 10^3/mm³
	11.4 x 10^3/mm³
White Blood Cell Count (WBC)	4,300 - 10,800 cells/µL/cu mm
	11,635 cells/µL/cu mm

Physician Notes
Blood tests indicate anemia and infection. This is consistent with the pustules found in the patient's throat at check-up. The patient had an episode patrolling the ship and passed out. Deandre brought him to the med bay. His pustules and mild fever were still present. Despite the negative strep test, it's clear that he has some kind of infection and needs to continue taking the antibiotics. I also prescribed an iron supplement. Perhaps it was the lack of iron combined with rigorous physical labor that caused him to lose consciousness.

Written by A.R.K. Horton

THE TROUBLE WITH GLUB
DEBBIE IANCU-HADDAD

PINK... LILAC... MAGENTA... DAFFODIL... GRASS GREEN ... MINT... TEAL... sky blue....

I'm not sure how long I've been lying here, watching the ceiling change shades above me. I know the ship's walls shift colors gradually throughout the day and I've been lying here while half the rainbow has trickled by past my eyes.

I should probably sit up. I shove myself into a seated position. The ship's walls are warm and soft and they cradle my back as I lean against the surface, but...

Whoa. Dizziness. I should lie down again.

No, wait. I think I've been asleep for quite a while now.

Slowly I push myself up to a standing position, smoothing down my UPA issued uniform. It's all rumpled. *Why did I go to sleep in my uniform?*

This won't do at all. I'm an ensign. I may be low on the pecking order on this weird hijacked alien vessel, but I'm still an officer and I have my pride.

I stride over... okay, wobble over... to my closet, opening it with a touch. The ship responds to my cues as if it can read my intentions. I fumble around for a moment because things aren't where I remember leaving them. *Who's been in my room?* It must be Gennaro, that girl is forever borrowing my stuff.

I finally locate a neatly folded skirt and button-down in the United Planetary Alliance formal colors. The dark grey highlights my light blue eyes, so it's got that going for it. My hair is ugh... snarled and almost grayish. Thank Venus for dry shampoo and anti-static curler. Five minutes and I'm back to my natural blonde hair, falling in soft waves down my back. Just because this is the military doesn't mean I can't look good. Especially on this ship with all those yummy marines running around. I know better than to get involved with my shipmates, but just because I'm being a good girl doesn't mean I don't get naughty thoughts. A lot of them.

I seem to have misplaced my communicator. Without the ability to call command, I guess I'll just walk there and see about getting a new one.

I step towards the door of my compartment, and it slides open without a sound. Something in the way the walls pulse makes me think the ship is feeling rather smug about guessing my intentions.

The hijacked swarm ship has been nothing but accommodating, of course, it's only been five days since we broke in and accidentally jumped to the other side of the galaxy, so time will tell.

I haven't completely got my bearings on the large ship, so I figure I'll just find somebody and ask. The first group I see are four marines jogging down the hallway. They look busy and I don't want to bother them.

I certainly don't expect the wolf whistles and stares I get from at least two of the guys. *Well, that's new.* Must be the "edge of the galaxy" energy, because that's hardly professional behavior. One of the guys, a large redhead, flips around and runs backward, staring me down the whole time, till his buddy punches him in the arm. He laughs, winks at me, and flips right way round again.

I stop in my tracks, watching them disappear around the curve of the hallway. *What the fraxx just happened...? Is it hot in here?* My cheeks feel like they're on fire. I take a right where the marines took a left, just to be on the safe side, and I must be moving towards the mess because I smell food.

My stomach growls louder than a Xenthalor from Gravaxx 3. *Oops.* I can't even remember the last time I ate, though it must have been before my weird nap.

"Hey baby," a good looking man, with dark hair, a jaw you could cut diamonds on and ice-blue eyes to match, hits me with a salacious grin.

"Do I know you?" I drag my hair over my shoulder, twirling the ends around my finger.

"Know me?" A thousand-megawatt smile lights up his face. "Hell yeah, baby. Repeatedly and biblically."

I sputter in confusion and weave around him, trying to walk away, but he grabs my wrist and tugs me around the corner into an alcove, pinning me against the warm lavender colored wall.

"What's the matter, baby? You weren't this buttoned-up last night."

His big paws run down my arms, teasing my sides and starting to unbutton my service uniform. His lips skim my ear, his breath warm on my neck.

It feels nice to be touched again. *It's been so long.*

I lean into his touch, letting myself be swept away by the scrape of his stubbled jaw along the sensitive skin of my collarbone. It's scary how much I enjoy being touched by this stranger.

What am I doing? I don't know him. I've never been with him. This must be some aftereffect of my nap. Maybe it wasn't a nap.

Maybe I passed out. Maybe I'm sick. That would also explain why I'm so flushed.

I press my palm against his chest - *his hard, muscled chest* - gulp and push, but he just chuckles. The guy must be made of Ultranian steel. He hikes one of my legs around his waist and I feel something else made of steel. I struggle feebly.

Venus, it's been a loooong time.

"What's wrong, baby?"

"I'm not... we didn't... let me off," I pant.

"You want to get off?" He chuckles, "Well, give me a minute honey, I'm not superman."

"No. I... put me down. We're not doing this." I struggle to make my voice firm.

He lowers my leg, and I rearrange my skirt that's hiked up around my waist. My face must be totally red.

"What's your name again?" I ask, because apparently this guy thinks we've been intimate.

"Wow, you don't even remember my name?" He huffs and takes a step back. "I mean, I knew you were doing the rounds, but I thought you'd at least remember my name, especially since you were screaming it at the top of your lungs last night..." he pulls back, rearranging his own clothes. "You really know how to wound a guy's ego."

"Indulge me." I cross my arms to keep my trembling hands hidden, and to stop myself from reaching out to pet him again.

He frowns. For a moment I think he isn't going to answer but then he pouts, "Nereus."

Ok. That's better. "Listen, Nereus. I don't mean to be rude. I'm apparently suffering from some weird type of amnesia because I don't remember doing any of that... and so I'm sure you'd agree that something must be wrong because I'm sure you made it quite... memorable. So, I need to see the doctor."

He runs his fingers up my arm, giving me goosebumps, "If

you like I could reenact last night's events with you... see if it jogs your memory?"

Fuck me, that's a tempting offer.

"Nooooo, I really need to see the doctor."

Nereus adjusts his uniform, smirking when my eyes are drawn to the distinct bulge in his nether regions. "If you change your mind, you know where to find me."

I make a hasty retreat before I change my mind and take him up on his offer. Following the strengthening smell of food, I let my growling stomach lead me towards nourishment and hopefully someone who can explain what's going on.

A few curvy halls and one mysterious dead end later, I stumble on the crew mess hall. Thanking my non-edible, yet lovely stars, I grab a tray and start piling it high with an array of delicious-smelling food.

"I'd stay away from the pizza after last time," a wry voice next to me says, and I catch Alexa Gennaro's flame-red hair in my peripheral vision. I raise a slice and give it a sniff... "Is that blue cheese?" I ask, my face screwing up in disgust.

"Yup," she pops the 'p', "and pineapple."

We both shudder. "The horror."

"Don't you remember the ship has been screwing up our meals?"

I scratch my ear, "Not really. When did that happen?"

Alexa shrugs, "A few weeks ago."

"Weeks??" I drop my tray on the counter by the food buffet and turn to stare at her fully. "We've only been on the ship for a few days."

Her bright green eyes meet mine with equal concern, and she leans forward to brush the back of her hand against my forehead. "Are you feeling all right, Weatherly? We've been on this ship for the past six months."

"No. That's not possible."

Alexa scoops up both our trays and walks them over to a nearby table. Then she returns and grabs my arm, guiding me over and plopping me down in the bucket-shaped protrusion the ship provides as a chair.

"Eat something..." she points at my tray, "this confusion might just be low blood sugar." I lift a tasty looking pastry, and she knocks it out of my hand. "Not that. Trust me," she shudders and hands me a spoon. "At least it got the mashed potatoes right, thank Jupiter."

I tuck into the steamy spud mash and soon I'm feeling much better, but there's still the matter of the lost time.

I look around the mess hall that's been filling up as we ate. Several crew members smile and nod as they see me, which is nice since I don't know most of them very well yet, but even more give me flirty winks and stares laced with intent.

Ignoring those types of looks, I turn my full attention to Alexa. She's my age, twenty-three, and easy to talk to. She's probably my best friend aboard. As the ship's social worker, it's her job to check up on me, but I'm still grateful for the attention.

"How long have we been on this ship?" I ask cautiously.

"Twenty-five weeks... just over six months."

She takes my hand gently, her thumb stroking over the back of my hand, "What do you remember?"

"We've been on the ship five days... I must be going mad. I just woke up on the floor of my cabin, in my uniform... my head is fuzzy."

"You seemed fine when you left the rec room last night with Nereus."

"But that's it. I don't remember being with Nereus. Or anything in the past..." I gulp, "six months."

I look around the room again. Some of the people who met my gaze earlier seem confused, or even hurt, at my earlier reaction to them.

"Have I... did I seem normal to you? Over the past few months?"

Alexa squirms a bit in her seat. "Well, I didn't know you very well before, and then we jumped to the edge of nowhere, and you kind of let loose. We just thought you were working through your anxiety about our situation with sex... lots and lots of sex... with everybody." Alexa screws up her face, looking at me out the corner of her eyes, "Okay, it was a bit weird. But no judgment... We all processed the situation in different ways."

Oh, no. "Who did I sleep with?" My face feels hot again. I'm probably as crimson as the walls during the evening shift.

Alexa licks off her spoon and uses it as a pointer, going around the room, "Him, him, her, him, that guy like several times... It's probably faster to discuss who you haven't slept with."

I bury my face in my hands. "Who haven't I slept with?"

"The captain... cause he's dead."

"The captain is dead?" I gasp.

"Dylan..."

"The twelve-year-old?" Alexa nods.

"Thank God for small mercies."

"I don't think you hooked up with that octopus guy from Zylon Six either..."

Wrapping my arms around my knees, I try to curl up into a fetal position. "Omg, I'm the ship slut, and I don't even remember it. My reputation is ruined."

Alexa rubs my shoulder. "To be fair, you do have a reputation... but the reviews are highly favorable. I, for one, had a very nice time."

This can't be happening. I bury my face in my hands. The food I just ate is trying to come back up.

"I'm going to be sick." I press my hand to my mouth, swiveling away from Alexa and dashing out of the mess hall.

Except I have no idea where to go. I just need to get away from everybody.

I turn down one hallway and then another, getting more and more lost. Up ahead, I catch a glimpse of blonde hair. There's a couple pressed up to the wall, they look super cozy and I don't want to interrupt, but the girl's laughter stops me in my tracks. *That's my laugh.*

Wow, what is wrong with me? I hate to impose, but I'm feeling dizzy.

I stumble closer, weaving, my hand pressed to the wall to support myself. Reaching out, I tap the guy on the shoulder. He has his back to me. All I can see is short sandy hair in a cropped military style. Wide, strong shoulders, *nice shoulders*. He turns into my touch and my palm slides across his firm chest, his eyes opening wide.

"Logan?" The one guy I actually liked, and he's busy hooking up with….

"Penny?" he does a double-take, his eyes snapping back to the girl he has pressed against the wall. A girl with my face, my hair, my laugh. The world spins around me. Just before I hit the deck, strong arms wrap around me, and then the whole world goes dark.

Pink… lilac… magenta… daffodil… grass green… mint… teal… sky blue….

A bright light shines into my eyes. I blink repeatedly, staring into a pair of brown eyes.

"How are you feeling?" A soft male voice asks.

"Who are you?" I mumble.

His eyebrows crease. "I'm Doctor Sanderson." The man steps further away. "How are you feeling?"

Oh, god. Did I sleep with him, too?

"Delusional," I say honestly. "Seeing things. Possible amnesia... with a side of losing my mind."

The doctor chuckles. "Well, we can rule out a few of those."

He opens a door, beckoning to someone outside, and I pull myself up to a seated position on the infirmary cot.

Logan's wide shoulders fill the doorway, concerned grey eyes find mine. Logan and I connected during my first days on the ship. He told me about his childhood on Mars, being recruited at 13. He's only 26 and he's been a soldier half his life. He's seen so many things during his service, but I bet even he won't know how to cope with this.

He runs a hand through his hair, messing up the longer strands on top. My fingers itch to reach out and smooth it for him, but I clasp my hands to my sides. Whatever chance I had with him is gone after this madness.

"Penny?" he asks, as if unsure.

I nod. "I'm me..." I bite my lip, "the real me."

He nods. Solemn. "I told Harold... whoever... whatever I was with turned tail and ran as soon as I caught you. It seems we have some sort of shapeshifter onboard."

"It could be anyone... anywhere..." I whisper. "How do we find it?"

Logan takes another step towards me, enfolding my hand in his larger one, his thumb swiping over the back of my hand in a soothing gesture. "We weren't looking before. Now that we know... there are only thirty people on the ship. We'll find it."

The doctor prepares a syringe and I shy away. "What is that?"

"A mild sedative, just to help you calm down. Nothing to worry about."

I shake my head, my voice rising in panic. "No. What if it comes back? It knows I've seen it. What if it decides to take my place for good?"

Logan places his palm on my cheek, stilling my movement, his face inches away from mine. "I'll be here. I won't let it near you."

I take a deep breath, getting lost in his granite eyes. "You promise?"

"I do."

———

The doctor's sedative puts me to sleep. When I wake, the first thing I see is Logan in a chair by the bed. I sit up and he stretches his long legs and smiles.

"How are you feeling?" he leans forward, resting his elbows on his knees.

"Better," I slide my feet off of the cot, standing up. As soon as I'm upright, my balance deserts me and I sway.

"Whoa." Logan is out of his seat, snagging an arm around my waist and pulling me flush against him. "Careful."

I press a palm against his firm chest to steady myself and get lost in the sensation of hard muscle under the soft gray t-shirt he's wearing. At his sharp intake of breath, I look up. We're so close. I could easily run my fingers into that soft sandy hair and pull his lips down to mine. My tongue darts out, wetting my lips and his eyes follow it, heat igniting in his gaze, burning right through me like a flash fire.

Someone clears his throat, and Logan takes a step back, though his palms still anchor my hips.

"You good?" he asks.

If I say 'yes' will he stop touching me? Because if that's what happens when the answer is 'yes', I may never be good again.

Despite my instincts, I nod, and he releases me but remains close.

"I have good news." Doctor Sanderson approaches us. "Your

tests came back clean. And I'm working with Dylan to get the ship to pinpoint all entities onboard. We should have our stowaway in a matter of hours."

"Can I go back to my room to rest...? I really need a shower and just a moment in my own space... I need to process."

"Aren't you worried it will go back there? It's been using your room as a home base for the past six months." Logan's eyebrows crease in the most adorable frown, and this time I don't resist my urge to reach up and smooth them.

"I was hoping maybe a big, strong, brave marine could accompany me there and stand watch..."

"Oh," he grins and pats his service weapon. "Well, if you put it that way."

On the way back to my room, I cling to his arm. To keep my balance, of course. I feel safe with him around, but I'm still nervous re-entering the space where I was held captive. I stand to the side as Logan sweeps the room. When he gives me the all-clear I join him inside, the small space seeming cramped with him in here, taking up all the air.

I step closer, till we're practically toe to toe, tipping my head up to look at him.

"So, was that the first time you and... the 'not real me', got together?"

Logan swallows. "To be honest, we never actually did... and I wasn't going to today either. I like you. I have since our first days on the ship, but I knew you... she... it?" He huffs and laughs. "Whatever that thing is... It got around and I'm... not good with sharing."

I run my hand up his chest to rest on his cheek and he leans into it, his five o'clock stubble grazing my palm. "Good, because neither am I."

He swallows, and I love that I affect him so much. I tip up on my toes, my lips hovering close enough to his to share a breath and whisper, "To be continued."

His eyes open wide, and then he groans and laughs. "You're killing me here."

"Uh-ah." I shake my head and sashay towards the cleaning unit. "If I was really trying to kill you, I'd..."

I step into the cleaning unit, stopping just out of sight behind the door, and then shed clothing items, dropping them one by one in the doorway. Top, skirt, bra, panties. I grin to myself at the tortured, sexy noises coming from my room as I discard each one. I'm feeling rather wild and out of my element. I'm not usually like this, but having missed out on six months of my life, and waking up to discover I'm the ship's walking, talking sex addict, has given me a new perspective. *Why should fake me get to have all the fun?*

I step into the cleaning unit and the warm soapy water makes me groan this time.

"Is that an invitation?" I hear a husky voice just outside the doorway.

"Do you need one?" I ask.

"Yeah, call me old-fashioned, but I like this type of thing to be crystal clear."

I love that despite my teasing, he's being a gentleman and keeping his distance, but it's been a really long time. Much longer than I realized.

"I would love you to join me." I sound rather breathless, but that's only because halfway through the sentence he steps through the doorway, pulling off his gray t-shirt and through the semi transparent partition of the cleaning unit I get an eyeful of exactly how delicious Logan is.

Now I'm the one gulping.

Lean tight muscles bunch and flex as he runs his hands down his torso, my eyes following his hands as they slowly undo his belt, sliding it out of place. He removes his gun and is just about to place it on the counter when there's a knock on the door.

We both groan. And not in the fun way. *What fraxxing timing.*

He looks over his shoulder at the door. "Should I get that?"

Part of me wants to ignore the knocking, reach out and pull him into the shower with me. But the responsible part of me, that's been in charge most of my life, the one watching me being so bold with a mix of awe and horror, says, "Yes," before I can stop it.

I turn off the water, and my brain finally switches back on. I shouldn't have Logan opening the door to my bedroom half naked. What was I thinking?

Evidently, I wasn't.

I reach out and grab his arm before he can leave the room. "No. Wait. I'll get it. Give me a minute to get dressed."

"One second, I'll be right there," I call out, hitting the auto-dry function. A powerful warm wind blows through the unit, flicking the drops off my body and drying my hair in no time. I run a quick brush through the strands and dash back into the room, pulling on a tank top, underwear and leisure pants. Logan is already fully dressed again, *sigh*, and he takes up a position in the corner by the door where he can't be seen by whoever is outside.

I tap the door to open and stand transfixed at the sight of my own face. She, it... couldn't get into the room while it was sealed from the inside, but I just stupidly granted her access.

Blood drains from my face, leaving me light-headed as I stare into my own blue eyes. Her hair is up in a ponytail. *It's actually kinda cute that way. I should try it sometime. Oh God, Penny, focus.* The thing is here. The thing that impersonated me successfully for months. What does it/she want? Why is she still wearing my face? She has to know the gig is up. Is she here to kill me and take my place for good?

I sway on my feet and place my hand on the doorjamb for balance, and that's all it takes for Logan to raise his gun and sprint to my side.

The other Penny's eyes widen as she notices Logan.

"Fraxx," she spouts, and then she's off. Logan hightailing after her, with me bringing up the rear.

This has to be the weirdest chase in the history of chases. Me, chasing Logan, chasing... me.

The other Penny seems to know the ship really well. She bobs and weaves, and she's much faster than I am. She almost gets away, but then she ducks into a hallway that ends in only one place.

The Glow Chamber.

It's a chamber at the heart of the ship whose function is unclear. It appears to be part of the ship's bioprocess. The chamber is full of softly pulsing, floating orbs of light. It's a popular spot for couples seeking a romantic location to steal a few moments together. I bet other Penny put this place to full use with all the hooking up she did.

Well, jokes on her now, because there's no way out.

Logan creeps into the room, holding his hand out behind him for me to take. I latch on, crowding close to his back. The space is large and curved, the wavy walls forming convenient nooks and crannies to sit or lie or hide. The floating orbs of light range in size, from tiny marbles to beach balls, hovering at various heights. They further obscure our view.

I'm not sure what our objective is here. Are we going to shoot her? Take her into custody? Are we the ones with the upper hand here, or did she just lure us into a trap?

"Come out," Logan calls in a soothing tone, "we won't hurt you."

Please don't hurt us. I pray silently.

Something moves deeper into the room and Logan weaves around a glowing lilac beach ball orb and moves further into the room.

"I don't like to sleep alone." My voice says from the furthest corner.

"Who are you?" I ask.

"What are you? How did you get on this ship?" Logan adds, stopping not far from the creature, his weapon trained on it/her. She's still in the clothes she was wearing when I found them together in the hall.

Other Penny sighs and slumps against the wall, sliding down to sit on the floor, her knees pulled up to her chest. It's such a human move. *It's such a ME move.*

I place my hand on Logan's arm and push, signaling he should lower his weapon. Then I sit down by his feet, facing her.

"My name is Glub." Other Penny... well, Glub, says. "I got sucked onto this ship when it materialized near my home planet. I come from the ring city of Tadageh orbiting planet Cribala. By the time I understood what had happened, the ship was speeding away. I spent several days in hiding, watching. Everyone seemed to like you, Penny, and you were so pretty."

I can't help blushing and Logan gives me a soft look, his hand brushing my shoulder.

"I was lonely." Glub continues. "I just wanted to interact. On Tagadeh, I'm part of a *flurten*... living together, we are many mates and partners. I didn't expect to be here so long." She sighs. "I like people... I like them a lot... and I like touching them and them touching me. Your bodies are so pleasurable. I just wanted to learn all the different ways they could be enjoyed."

Despite myself, I understand. I don't want to like her, but I do.

"Why are you still me?"

"Who else could I be?" Glub shrugs, looking confused. "You were the only one I had hidden, if I imitated another crew member who is awake..."

"No, I mean..."

I look to Logan for help and to my surprise he joins me, sitting cross-legged on the floor. "What I think Penny means, is why not show us the real you?"

Glub looks horrified. "From what I have learned of humans and their perceptions, I do not think they would find my true form pleasurable."

"Try us. No judgement." I nod, and Logan flashes one of his gorgeous and rare smiles. *Who could resist him?* I certainly can't.

Glub nods and shifts into something that looks like a giant yellow and teal slug. A pair of curvy tentacles protrude out of its head and along its torso are a multitude of soft blue spikes with yellow tips. It grins at us with a mouthful of sharp purple teeth.

"Oh, God." I clasp Logan's forearm so hard my nails leave marks in his skin. He hisses and I ease up, just a little bit.

"What do you think?" Glub's voice still sounds human. Logan and I exchange a glance. I swallow, forcing myself to sound calm.

"First of all, you need to come with us and explain the situation to the crew."

"They won't hurt me?" Glub asks in a small voice, antennae waving nervously.

"I don't think so." Logan says, "You've been on board for six months and done no harm. Many crew members enjoyed your company... albeit unwittingly... I'm sure once you've shown them the real you and explained what happened, they'll learn to accept you for you." It's hard to read the expression on the slug face, but the antennae wave doubtfully.

"Or you can take on a different human form, that doesn't look like anybody on board." I suggest.

Glub dips its head in a very human gesture of agreement.

"Ship, can you ask everyone to please come to the bridge, we want to introduce them to someone."

The ship pulses agreement and a soft mental nudge tells me that our presence is required on the bridge. Logan rises and holds out his hand, pulling me into his arms.

"We should come back here later," he murmurs, and I run my hand along his chest and behind his neck.

"Yes, we should," I brush my lips lightly against his mouth and he opens, taking control of the kiss and leaving me breathless.

"I like kissing too..." Glub says hopefully, and I chuckle and bury my red face in Logan's chest.

"We'll make sure you find someone to kiss. One way or another," he says, but his eyes are on me and this ship must be leaking air because I'm short of breath again.

We escort Glub to the deck, waiting till the whole crew is gathered.

"We want to introduce you to someone," I say. "Many of you have had experiences of an intimate nature with this entity over the last six months. I know you believed those experiences were with me, but... the truth is, I've been in a suspension chamber in my room this whole time. The entity you have been calling Penny is a Cribalan named Glub." I call out, "You can come in now," and Glub slithers into the room, followed by Logan. The crew makes noises of confusion and disbelief.

"Glub, can you..." I wave my hand and Glub briefly shifts into Other Penny, holding the form for a minute before resuming its true form again.

"You're telling me I banged that?" Nereus looks like he's going to be sick.

"Yup, baby. Repeatedly and biblically."

Glub and I high appendage as Nereus runs out of the room.

The rest of the crew mills around, processing the knowledge. Generro comes closer, with Alan in tow.

"Now that I think of it, this shapeshifting thing has a lot of potential." Her eyes shift between Alan and Glub. "You can be anyone you want?"

Glub nods, looking hopeful and morphing into Alexa, then Alan.

"I've never been with twins..." Her smile is devilish.

"Well, neither have I." Alan adds, "How about we each have a turn? What do you say, Glub?"

The three of them head off together and Logan draws me into his arms.

"I think Glub is going to be very busy," he smiles, "and have plenty of people waiting in line." He threads his fingers through mine, drawing me out of the busy deck and into a more private corner.

"I'm glad for two reasons." I smile against his mouth as he bends down for a kiss. "I kinda like that colorful slug. I wouldn't want it to be sad."

"That's sweet." He presses a gentle kiss to my mouth. "What's the second?"

"Well, I'm not sure if Glub and I are still roommates, but I'm going to need the room to myself for the foreseeable future. When are you next on duty?"

"Not till baby blue tomorrow..."

"Great, because I'm going to need at least seven color changes for what I have in mind."

Pink... lilac... magenta... daffodil... grass green... mint... teal... sky blue....

I PRAY TO THE UNKNOWN GODDESS
ELVIRA CANAVERAL

i pray to the unknown goddesses
let them hear the sound that should not be
peaks and troughs nothing escapes the waveform
i pray to the unknown gods
let them be moved to aid me so that i may know them
i pray to the higher ones who bless me with their gaze
i give permission to see my heart and beg you to give aid to this
cause
nudge me with your observation as i seek to know and grow
i pray with my eyes open and thankful for our time

*The book you were reading was Volume 15 on Shelf 5 of Wall 3 of
Hexagon:* 2n9hemte6tcjocoeoodqk2o6viia6ov7e87oh0vo29o5
bs24onetk7usfl9fsaomaaht342v69dvilvs2p25bh95ku8aansof
p1aj6cq63lhdanigooosqmrsqzhj6n1ec8tgth2ypi5d0kcftaod6m
4tlmnd3q9pptp3wqzwbuwknf1uzczfvqoja3y351elf1fd6kndfsxt
lz05iaa2obktsgn6pzkedorcbik8o7wsw1lhfdxnmdjlr2x1soq4c3e
os3cwajj5wcu6shayf154jyed7xwsuktk7nomahxtbjpfxfynnnh6d
m2zurha4a4owgv352z44e1knh4n6up1lhm3ylf5krf7damihvnwrv
2deq9u9m6oj52siw7mgvyopp29ro5updojw4okv4tl5jw83oe6td

3oiklltcnvkb3z9egxz5ve2sadk0od67yvpvujlp6p2q6s11y7nnzczvz
xvwmucitnrj29p3f4w75hzyljr0nx9khawa14aloggkyyfuw8y90nfv
7k2jou94btz5rnyh4qwh43a0knezeaon8pvyltzncuhddgqanq5m17
6y0tpb4j0vrn0rcbs9ej42ddaqk5vl81xdvq510ebd24bbri8aazfu80zr
d9vxafbckuv0itvix557zs692qtil6qzez4tdt0r5348bq91s0xdzs1cb6j
4b1a1x3bruishctns5tt2kgve0luzrqr0beifx7bftze0xx3r0y6vtwpi5wa
wywjym3i5xk7hc9b56xxzec6drxply3f6ra1io6arj1hsx76kn0it6kc6
2c1zeh56td0n12qnsqlyasylkb49gmuc0ali9a4ix2q26ewa3bcz6cvr
4q25gaiycv546zupi00dwda0hp0x0p1mgr3i4avn7ed0tazfafvjz64fq
gnkpqrkgz357bfzv0rwl0ii8y9w2xhmcizxper136unti6zizi7wjdahkd
1phy0vkns1xnazn06nw9suhup2a9fumk125q837upppaic1n5pgg7
nh2rcc7j1egmc0l77wncg2pd05cynjbq64620w6hpgmumlq8qeepw

Which floored the 8th Dimensional Union Librarian who found it.
Who, without asking permission, grasped the book and fell into the
nearest mirror.

- TRANSCRIBED BY ELVIRA CANAVERAL. ORIGINAL
AUTHOR: UNKNOWN?

PHANTASMAGORIA
ZACKERY CUEVAS

"LOGAN. HEY, LOGAN! WAKE UP, KID, I NEED YOUR HELP."

The door cracks open and the voice grows louder.

"Yo, boy! You up?"

I open one eye and turn toward the direction of the voice. A silhouette taps a switch just above my half-opened dresser. Hissing fills the room as the domed ceiling cracks open, filling the room with light.

"Five more minutes," I mutter half-heartedly.

Waves of sleep wash over me again before a pillow crashes onto my head, followed by the weight of a body.

"Boy, you said five minutes an hour ago. Now get up and wash up; I need your help downstairs."

"Alright, Dad, alright! Get off of me."

The smell of his sweat lingers as the silhouette takes shape in front of me. He laughs and runs his hand through his curly black hair as he looks at me, a goofy smile across his face. His eyes are almost smiling as I look up to greet his gaze.

"What's for breakfast?"

"Breakfast?" he exclaims. "I got something even better than that."

"What's that?"

"Lunch."

I roll my eyes as he laughs at his lame joke.

"You know it's my day off, right?" I say as I stretch to scratch my back.

"I know, but I thought you'd want to hang out with me in the lab today."

"Okay, I'll be right down."

I sit up and let my feet dangle from my bed for a moment before placing them on the chilly linoleum floor, closing my eyes to let the sun run over me.

"Logan," a low voice calls out.

"System, dim the lights."

"Logan?"

The outlines of Mars's moons cut across the soft orange glow of the sun from behind my closed eyes.

"System, dim the lights, please."

The dark spots behind my eyes chase each other and start to grow. I keep my eyes closed. The dancing moons grow and grow.

"System? Dim the lights."

The silhouettes spin faster as the sun's light flickers like a bulb about to go out. I can't stop staring.

"Sys... system, dim the—"

"Logan!"

The spinning grows faster and faster. The calls grow louder and louder, and louder still.

"Just five more minutes."

I open my eyes as machinery begins to take the place of the posters in my room, my computer, my desk, my bed, the walls, the floors, until finally, I'm staring up at two floating lights hanging from the ceiling. I blink as tears carve scars across my unwashed face.

"I didn't mean to interrupt."

I turn around to find the UPA social worker, Alexa Genarro, standing at the doorway.

"I thought I had more time," I said, rubbing my face.

"Sorry, Logan. Captain wants to see us. Says it's important."

Alexa and I walk down the dimly lit corridors. It's been eighteen weeks since we've been trapped on this Swarm ship, and while we've managed to keep it together this far, our engineers still don't know how to control it, our military men have no idea how to kill it, and I sure as hell don't know how to fly it.

"Did you have a good session?" Alexa asks cheerfully.

"I didn't get to finish, so I don't know."

Alexa smiles and softly taps her hand against her belt harness, awkwardly trying to fill the silence between us. I don't mind Alexa; I just don't know her. The only thing I do know about her is that she has unnaturally red hair and a penchant for talking to herself when stressed. She's well built for a civilian and tries to make everyone onboard happy, which has become an increasingly difficult task.

"Well, at least you get to experience something," Alexa starts. "Every time I step into the machine room, I get paid dust. Nothing but the walls staring back at me."

"Is that what we're calling it, the machine room?"

"Well, ultra-magnetic, multi-frequency brainwave booster doesn't exactly roll off the tongue."

I laugh. "Did you just make those words up?"

"Those are the only words I remember after Nereus's recent report. Did you know that the smell of burning meat was actually from the waste disposal?"

"No, I didn't. But does that mean he's figured out how I can fly this thing?"

"Well, I don't think we've gotten that far. But hey, we've made progress. I'm sure we can figure something out soon."

Alexa and I round the bend as my hand skirts against the rough walls. They recoil from my touch and grow tense before relaxing again.

"Just up ahead, Logan. We're meeting in the Glow Chamber."

I follow Alexa into the large room that seems to be pumping life through the rest of the Ship. The chamber's actual function remains unclear, though we've already caught a few members of the crew hooking up under its pulsating lights.

Cosima Sabine, one of the scientific attachés assigned to the mission, suspects the chamber acts as the heart of the Ship, pumping the bio-organic vessel with whatever the hell is keeping us alive. We've been using the changes in color as a way to keep track of the time. At the moment, the chamber was pink going on orange.

Once inside, my eyes quickly meet Captain Savory's. Officer Altera Deandre and three privates—Broggs Deron, Suzanne Lowrie, and Alan Gray—turn to greet me.

"Nice of you to join us, Dileo," the Captain says, face unmoving.

"Sorry, Captain. I was in the machine room."

"You know, I don't understand why he gets to fuck around and daydream all day while the rest of us have to actually work."

I turn to meet the gaze of Kevin Renner, another UPA Officer with a chip on his shoulder. His crazed look has only gotten worse since we've been trapped on this Ship, and his mood swings have gotten so bad you'd think he was just waiting for an opportunity to go feral.

"Fuck you."

Kevin bares his teeth and steps forward. My nerves stop me from reaching for my blaster.

"Dileo, Renner—that's enough, both of you," the Captain barks.

Kevin doesn't break his gaze as he steps back. I don't either, but I can feel my hands shaking. Alexa must have noticed it, as she steps between us.

"Now, I've gathered you all for an update," Captain Savory began. "We've been floating aboard this miserable hunk of space flesh for a few months now, according to Doctor Sabine—and we've since made quite a few discoveries. Professor Wandri, if you would."

A meek-looking man in a lab coat steps forward and fumbles on the terminal in the middle of the room. Pushing his glasses up the bridge of his nose, he mutters while typing onto the alien control panel. Johannes Wandri is one of the Ship's premiere brains, brought along at the UPA's behest. While young, his legacy already preceded him thanks to his grandfather's work on Blast Neutrino Salvation Treatments, which eliminated the supernovas created by dying stars and opened the door for humanity to quickly colonize the Earth's solar system.

A hologram of the Ship shoots from the top of the terminal. Everyone takes a step back as Johannes slips on a pair of electro-magnetic gloves to manipulate the map. Taking a deep breath, he reaches out and pinches his fingers to expand the center of the map.

"Um," Johannes starts. "As you know, the Swarm vessel we currently reside in is a bioorganic mechanism capable of sustaining itself, though how and for how long remains a mystery. But after careful observation, I've found the makeup of the Ship is not unlike our own circulatory system."

"Which means?" Officer Deandre asks.

"Well, in the way our blood vessels direct blood through our bodies, the Ship has been pushing us through its innards, revealing new information to us as it does. The latest," he pinches and turns the map, "is a small fold near the Medbay that leads to a dock. Inside, there are a few Swarm pods."

Johannes flips a switch to bring up a diagram of a pod. During Swarm attacks, grunts are shot down from the Ships to clear out landing zones. Most of the time, the opening attack is all the Swarm needs to wipe out a settlement. If you're lucky, the Swarm might only leave you with a missing limb or a scar across the gut.

"We've discovered the pods are still quite functional and, unlike the Ship we find ourselves in, actually share a bit of DNA with our tech. In other words, they are operational and can be used as a means of travel."

"Which brings us to our next point," Captain Savory interrupts. "We've detected the wreckage of an unidentified ship entering this solar system. It doesn't seem to be armed or even occupied, but it's worth checking out since our supplies are running low."

Officer Deandre rubs her chin. "I can't do this. Wouldn't trust myself to fly it." She moves her head to gesture to the Privates. "And I need these dummies to keep the peace around here."

"And we can't afford to send any of the engineers. They don't have combat experience. It has to be one of you two." The Captain looks at Renner and me.

Renner puffs out his chest.

"Dileo," Captain Savory says sternly.

"But, sir," Renner protests. "Why send our dead weight? You know you can rely on me."

"Can I?" the Captain starts, raising his e-dossier to read from it. "Instances of sensory delusions and violent outbursts, as reported by other members of the crew."

The Captain narrows his gaze on Renner, as the privates watch, shifting their weight nervously. "Is that right, Lieutenant Renner?"

He is silent.

"In that case—Dileo!"

"Yes, sir," I call out.

"You're our man."

Alexa looks at me and smiles as the Captain dismisses us. Renner, now fuming, pushes past Alexa and stomps out of the room. The walls slowly change from a milky pink to deep orange.

Later that night, after the rations are distributed and the provisions checked, I head back to a corner of the Ship with a window that I've been calling my room. The window, of course, isn't made of glass—or any other material known to man. The walls, it seemed, have become translucent. It's as if the Ship somehow feels us inside it and reacts to our wants. On most nights, I stare out into the nothingness and let the low hum of the Ship lull me to sleep. But tonight is different.

My reflection shows a sad man staring back at me. The rings under my eyes are darker, my uniform is stained with sweat and grime, and my hair is longer, the curls now reaching the wrinkles on my forehead. A sigh escapes me. I look rough, but feel worse.

As I sit with my back against the wall, I think about what I saw earlier in the machine room. It all felt so real. Too real. I reach into my pocket and pull out a small holoframe. I tap it a few times and cycle through some of the photos saved on the device. One of them is a picture of me when I was thirteen and my dad, Professor Zerk Dileo—smiling with thick, black, curly hair hanging from his head like the English ivy he grew all over the biodomes he managed. He was obsessed with his work, but he loved it. Every day he would walk through the many biodomes that lined Mars' surface, taking temperatures, raising and lowering moisture levels, and harvesting what was ripe. When a harvest was ready, he would send his employees down to help process the seeds in his lab. That's where nature stopped and the science started.

An agricultural specialist for the UPA, he led a project to mass-produce seeds for the Earth's solar system. They called it Advanced Crop Regeneration Emphyteusis, or the ACRE program for short. My dad explained it like this: centuries ago, man barely survived ecocide thanks to advancements in space travel. As the colonization of worlds continued, the UPA eventually formed, and the ACRE program was created to feed the colonies and barter with the new alien species encountered in their travels. The ACRE program solved the hunger crisis almost overnight by cloning genetically modified fruits and vegetables to grow in almost any environment. With the seeds, they could grow carrots on Venus and tomatoes on Chucarro.

The UPA would traffic the seeds to the allied planets and collect a hefty tax, which would be reinvested into the program, among other things. What my father specialized in were legacy foods. The duplicate seeds could grow but not reproduce, so biodomes were specially designed to produce the legacy crops needed to clone seeds. In a sense, my father was just a farmer.

I remember walking through one of the biodomes lining the harsh red desert of Mars. Sprinklers periodically shot a cool mist down onto the plants. It felt nice to walk through the thin sheets of water as I pruned the branches, roots, and buds off the crops.

"Logan, look at this!" Dad called.

I looked up from the base of a banana tree.

"Yeah, Dad?"

I walked down the metal corridors that cut through the

brush of the man-made jungle to my father, who was standing with some of the other scientists in front of a terminal.

"Hey Logan, I got a job for you, something I know you'll like."

"Are you gonna ask me to compost? Because last time I did, my hands smelled like eggs all day."

"Ew, gross," Dad laughed. "Something a little cooler than that."

He grabbed an e-ledger and handed it to me.

"I want you to pilot the harvests to the UPA drop-off in Polzal."

I was shocked. "You want me to go all the way to New Hominy?"

"It's not that far."

"By myself?"

Dad smiled. "Logan, you're thirteen now. I can't have you chopping dead leaves off of Ficus forever. I know this work isn't for you."

"Oh, no, I like it."

"You're a bad liar, Logan."

I was. Still am.

"I know where your head's at, kid, and it's not on the ground." Dad pointed up to the void. "It's in the stars."

I smiled. I felt like I was about to cry.

"Now, the trip is short, but you'll need to pack some provisions. I know you've ridden in a training SS-4—" He paused, waiting. "Are you listening?" He asked.

I nodded and said yes. He saw through my lie instantly.

"Remember, Logan, these crops are like little lives," he said as he brought a kernel of corn to one eye, scrutinizing the tiny orange seed. "Their pods are more important than anything in the universe." He paused for a moment, losing himself in the thought before turning back to me. "At least, that's what I think."

He laughed, and all I can think about is crying. Then—there's a bang.

I jerk up and slam my head against the back of the wall. I must've dozed off. Stains from my tears are fresh on my face. I turn, look out the doorway, and catch a glimpse of Officer Deandre heading to the Glow Chamber with one of her sexual conquests. Alexa steps into view.

"Hi," she says.

"Hello."

"I've been asked to accompany you on your mission."

"By who?"

"The Captain."

I pause, confused as to why the Captain would ask the social worker to accompany me on a potentially dangerous mission. But I could use the company.

"Well, perfect timing. I was just getting ready to head out."

Alexa and I make our way to the newly discovered ship dock. The walls inside are pink and raw, like exposed flesh. Two Swarm pods float in tight, gelatinous tubes. I have never been close to one before. I walk up to one of the tubes and stare at its bioluminescent glow.

I push my hand through the soft jelly and reach for the pod. Reacting to my touch, the pod door opens. Much to my surprise, the panel on its door bears a striking similarity to the eye-tracking modules used in most consumer tech. It only takes a moment for the device to detect my eyes. I place the coordinates of the wreckage into the panel and a path is plotted out for me automatically. I only have to follow the course with my eyes.

Beside me, Alexa's already laid out in the pod like a corpse in a coffin. I turn to my pod and stare into the husk. The interior walls look like tree bark, or a strip of worn leather dried out under the Chantico suns.

"Oh, here, take this," Alexa says as she sits up and tosses a disc at me. "I grabbed you a bio-organic suit."

I catch it and flip it in my hands before slapping it on my chest.

"I think it might prove useful—just in case."

"Just in case what?"

Alexa pauses. "Well, I don't know, just in case, I guess." Alexa smiles.

I climb inside and settle into the pod the best I can. The texture makes my skin crawl. I pull the panel down and lay on my back, my eyes fixed on the monitor. There isn't much room to move my hands, legs, or anything. I barely fit in the thing. My eyes dart across the monitor, cycling through menus until I find what I think is the ignition. Blinking twice, the pod lets out a deep sigh of steam as it deflates and wraps around my body, leaving barely enough space between me and the screen.

My eyes strain as I follow the plotted path. The pod reacts and races through the hollows of the Ship. I feel my eyes drying as a Swarm symbols begins to flash on the screen. I can't afford to blink. Another tight turn, and then another, and I feel a faint pop as the pod escapes the Ship into open space. I close my eyes to let them rest for a moment and feel my pod drift through the expanse of outer space. I can't even hear myself breathing as I think about keeping my eyes closed forever, but I remember Alexa is out here with me. I open my eyes and the monitor flashes as I regain control. I follow the plotted path again as the pod stabilizes and continues to the unknown wreckage.

What feels like an eternity passes in a few minutes as we enter the docking bay of the wreckage. The pod settles and expands back to its normal size. All I hear is the beating of my heart as I take a deep breath and push the door open. The faint hiss is overcome by silence, and I let myself float out of the pod. The UPA uniform can withstand the subzero temperatures of space for about five minutes before you freeze to death. I tap the disc on my chest and the red web of the bio-organic suit covers my entire body and stabilizes me as I glide towards solid ground.

Ahead, I see a doorway blocked off by a gravity lock. I land and step forward, but the floor crumbles beneath me. Panicking, I stumble backward into the arms of the void, but suddenly stop. I look down at my feet and see Alexa holding me by the ankle with both hands, her stance unmoving. She pulls me back in and onto my feet.

"See?" she mocks. "I'm a natural."

We walk to the gravity lock. I tag the door panel with a low-grade EMP device that will short circuit it, giving us enough time to get in. The EMP goes off and the gravity lock drops, letting out a whoosh of stale air along with various kinds of debris. Alexa and I walk through, and I reactivate the lock on the other side. The remaining debris floating throughout the room drops to the ground with a loud bang.

I pull out my flashlight to examine the room. "What is this place?" Old computer monitors line the walls. The desk in front of them is covered with pens, mugs, and even a stress ball in the shape of a meteorite.

"This is a UPA evac transport."

I turn to Alexa, confused. "What? No way, this is way too old. It would've been decommissioned years ago."

Alexa becomes unusually stern. "The older ships were sent to the outer colonies to assist the smaller planets, the ones most vulnerable to Swarm attacks. Borlanio, Vanderwee, Ignist." She hesitates. "And Rym."

"Rym?" I say, still examining the desk for clues. "Wasn't Rym a backwoods planet?"

"My family was from Rym."

I look up from the desk and meet her eyes. She's serious.

"I'm sorry, Alexa, I didn't know."

"It's okay. I don't remember the planet at all. My parents were born there, and my mom was pregnant during an attack. She pushed me out on a transport just like this. I remember 'cause my dad used to always talk about it." Alexa's voice trails off.

"Is that why you joined the UPA?"

"I hoped to kill a Swarm or two."

"But you're a social worker?"

"Well, I came to my senses."

I continue looking around the room.

"Logan, I want to tell you something," Alexa started. "I can't dream. All my life, I don't know why, but I've never dreamt. When I close my eyes, I open them again the next day. There's no space in between, no images, no color — There's nothing. So when we ended up on the Ship and found the machine room, I thought maybe it would help me, I don't know, unlock something in my head. But nothing ever happened. Every time I stepped into the room, nothing happened. So I became the one person able to pull someone out once they've gone too deep. I wish I could dream, Logan. I—" She stops and takes a deep breath. "I've seen your memories in the machine room. I've seen everyone's dreams. Every-one's memories. Past lovers, old friends, family. Your father—"

"Stop."

"Your memories are always so happy. But if you were happy, you wouldn't be here."

"I said stop."

"Do you ever think about the attack?"

The attack. I couldn't stop thinking about it. Every memory I have of Mars is stained by the attack of New Hominy. I couldn't escape the day a massive Swarm campaign was launched against UPA agricultural centers. I couldn't stop thinking about the lab and everyone in it.

I curl my hands into a fist. "I do. I can't stop thinking about it. Every memory leads back to the attack on New Hominy. My father watched as his life's work came undone. He watched as the Swarm ripped his friends to pieces. He was never the same after the attack." My face is hot. I'm on the verge of tears. "He was catatonic after and deemed unfit to raise me. So, the UPA stepped in and put me in basic training. Eventually, I became a pilot. I thought if I did, maybe it would bring him back. I don't know. But then he died. And after I buried him, I buried myself in this job. I didn't care if I lived or died. That's why I joined this suicide run of a mission."

I let the tears run down my face. I've never said that out loud before.

"Logan, listen. The transports have a stasis room. In the stasis room is a black box. The black box contains the memories of all of those on board, dead or alive. All of their information is backed up on that box."

"And how do you know that?"

"That's how my dad kept my mom alive for me. That's all I have of her. When I heard the Captain describe the wreckage after it entered the solar system, I knew right away it was a transport. But I also knew he wouldn't let me come on my own."

"He doesn't know you're here, does he?"

Alexa shakes her head. "This mission was important to me, and I knew if I told the Captain, he'd think I was crazy."

I stare at her, trying to determine if she had an ulterior motive.

"And after watching you in the machine room," she continues, "I felt like we were two different sides of the same coin. I want so desperately what you have—memories. I think that the people who were here deserve to be remembered."

I relax my gaze and place my hand on my hip harness. She's sincere. "Well, let's take a closer look then."

A smile stretches across Alexa's face. I feel one on mine, too.

We move deeper into the destroyed transport. The tight corridors lead to rooms where the UPA held refugees as they processed the paperwork necessary to move them from across the galaxy. The UPA is mostly bureaucracy, after all. Thousands of people could fit onto a transport, Alexa explains, but this one looks like it was split right in half, probably due to a shatter beam from an invading Swarm ship. Alexa motions towards a dark room at the end of the corridor as I shine my flashlight into it. What little I see looks like some sort of cold storage — Feels like it too. Specks of dust dance in the light as Alexa moves in to examine a terminal in front of a glowing tower. She presses a couple of keys and the screen lights up. It asks for UPA authorization. She types hers in as I walk toward the pods along the walls.

Alexa gasps. "Logan, they're—"

"Alive," I say as I wipe the dust from one of the pods, revealing a man inside. I stare at his face, frozen in time by liquid coolant.

"This can't be right. These bodies—these people have been frozen for 75 years."

He looked no older than me.

"These people are UPA."

"UPA?" I ask. "What the hell happened?"

"Seems like they were sent out to one of the outer worlds for training. These guys were barely soldiers. Got taken out before they even arrived."

I walk to the next pod and wipe the dust and condensation from the glass. This one is a woman.

"Can we unfreeze them?"

"I can't," Alexa says, typing into the terminal. "They've been frozen for so long; the unfreezing process would shock their system. Without medical attention, they'll die."

I walk to the next pod, flashing my light against the glass for a better look.

"But," Alexa starts, "we can recover the box."

I turn around to face her, my flashlight casting her in light.

"Remember what I said before? These people still exist in there." Alexa points to a black box on a pillar in the center of the room. Thick wires run out from its base into every pod.

Alexa turns her head to look at Logan, and suddenly, her eyes widen in horror. "Logan, look out!"

I spin around and find myself face to face with a Swarm. I reach for my blaster, but my hand shakes as the alien bares its many teeth. It opens its mouth and roars as it lunges at me, only to be shot out of the air by a stun bolt.

Alexa, panting, charges her stun gun and readies another shot. The alien stumbles to its feet, letting out a vicious scream before charging with its blade-like arms. Alexa steps back and fires again, right into the alien's chest.

"A little help, please," she says through bared teeth.

I pull myself off the ground, draw my blaster from its holster, and take aim—but I can't pull the trigger. I'm frozen. I stare down the sights of my blaster as the alien climbs to its feet and turns its attention back to me.

My hands continue to shake. All I can think about is the Swarm covering my father's face with acid. His horrified expression stuck, etched in the wrinkles of my brain forever as I watched from a delivery ship like a coward.

Alexa rushes the beast and tackles it with her shoulder, but the alien slaps her away and sends her flying across the room. She slams into the ground, and as she picks her head up, the alien shoots its blinding acid into her face.

"Alexa!" I scream as the alien turns toward me and roars again. I yell back and fire again and again and again, each blast ripping through the alien's body. It drops dead as I struggle to keep my heart from shooting out of my throat. I lower my blaster and stumble over to the body, still smoking from the energy bolts.

"Good timing."

I turn and see Alexa picking herself up from the ground. "Are you okay?"

"I'm fine."

"You shouldn't be," I reply. "That acid blinds humans. You shouldn't be able to see."

Alexa blinks hard, looks at me, and smiles. "I guess it didn't work, huh?"

I stare at her as she regains her composure.

"Logan," she pants, her tone urgent.

"I know. The box."

Her fingers fly across the terminal. As she types, a red light blinks and the white lights running across the tubes lining the status pods fade out. A steady whine fills the room, settling shortly into a low hum. Flatlines pop up on the screen, one by one, as the dead die again.

I think about my dad as the lights on the box pulsate, as if it were breathing.

THE NUMBING GAMES
(SATURNALIA RAGTIME TORCH SONG)
ELVIRA CANAVERAL

Joy of discovery
letting something beautiful be
with us in space and time
entertained
intertwined
Lack of information
filled in with myths

Pure Spirits
present and accounting
appreciating on a quantum level

netherworld hither world

AZATHOTH WAKES

Save States
Memory Cards

Running with the Eternal Rebel

ONCE A WITCH ALWAYS A WITCH
Write down your own Book of Shadows
Find your book by your hand

You don't hear about the ones that never found anything
out there or in there

Bound in wool
sprung new into this world
work is suspended

a parade
build for the slaughter
Saturn reclined
Felt Caps of the Free

WET WORK
GABRIELLE S. AWE

I GOT TIRED OF BEING A DEADLY MURDER QUEEN.

It was the girls that did it. Young (but not too young). Winsome smiles in flinching faces, buying me drinks, trailing sharp-nailed fingers down my back, and just when I'd be ready to party, they'd out themselves.

"He took my money." A soft-breathed whisper in my ear.

"She left with my dog and my Pontiac." Fevered eyes and wet lips.

"Can't you just..." A flick of the fingers; a cheap way to ask for a death.

They know I'm a murder queen. Even if I weren't famous, my outfit gives it away. They see the black hair braided up the left side, long and loose down my back; the leather, the knives on my hips and inked on my skin.

The five knives of a Queen.

The dead eyes of a killer.

The hunger.

They know who I am, so they offer me sex.

"Sex I can get for free," I tell them. "If you want death, you have to pay. With, like, *money*."

They flush with embarrassment. They value their warm bodies too highly. It's kind of a lie, though. I don't mind paying for sex; it's just that if I'm paying for it, I want a pro, not a lackluster amateur with baggage.

In this world, death pays better than sex. That's why I'm a murder queen and not a prostitute, although I'm equally good at both. Only once have I traded sex for death, and I've regretted it ever since.

That's why, up until I retired, if you wanted my services you had to pay cash money.

Before I got bored I might have, on occasion, slept with a client after the job. There were so many trying to get my attention, and warm flesh and slick thighs work. Only two things make me feel alive: death and sex.

Well, and money.

Three things.

If you measure wealth by these three things - which I do - then I am a very wealthy woman.

But I've been murdering people for a long time, long before ladies started throwing their panties at me; long before I was rich. I was once young and hungry and poor, too poor even for one knife tattoo, a mistake that could have gotten me sent to a prison world, hair too short to braid.

Those were dark days.

But today, I am no longer young, no longer hungry; and I have retired from the murder business.

I have unbraided my hair; I have allowed the black to fade, but the knives still mark me, and I don't know how to wear anything but black leather.

It has been six months, seven days, and three hours since I've killed someone, and I still don't quite know what to do with my hands. They feel so dry without blood on them.

I rubbed the scars on my fingers and realized I couldn't sit in my apartment; steel and glass are cold friends.

The spaceport bar was crowded, warm, and smelled like stale beer and spacer bodies. It was one of the few places I could find people as alone as I was, even in a large crowd. The bartender handed me a flaming whiskey and watched me do the shot without blowing out the flames.

"Someone in here looking for you," they said, eyes flat.

"Not interested."

They rubbed their delicate fingers on the shaved part of their scalp, nails scraping the skin.

"Not sure that matters," they said, and set down a chaser; three fingers of whiskey over a rough chunk of ice. "Over there." They tilted their head at a table towards the back.

I looked over my shoulder—a woman, of course. She nodded at me; she looked like business. She wore her jacket and pants like a uniform; her whole head was shaved.

Shit.

"Hold my spot, Chap," I told the bartender, and made my way to the woman at the table. Chap was right; it didn't matter if I didn't want this conversation.

"What?" I asked.

"Have a seat." Her voice was firm.

I sat. I sipped my whiskey. I watched her eyes.

"What?" I asked again.

"I have a job for you."

"I'm retired."

She nodded, slowly.

"Yeah. But you're bored. That's why you troll this bar, looking for something to do."

"Who are you?" I asked.

"Call me Rose."

"That doesn't answer my question."

"It's the only answer you're going to get. Altera..."

Something in my face must have gotten through to her; she stopped, started again.

"We have a job for you. There's a special project; there are some... important people associated with that project."

I cut her off. "I'm not going to kill them."

"I'm still speaking. We don't want you to kill them. We want you to use your particular skills for good; we want you to protect them. This mission..."

"*Project*," I corrected her. I felt like being an ass.

"Yes, project." She cleared her throat. "This project is very important to our future, and there are those that want it to fail." She slid a piece of flimsy across the table towards me.

I didn't look at it. "I'm not a bodyguard."

"You *weren't* a bodyguard. You are now. You're tired of murdering people? Great. Try saving some lives instead. If this *project* succeeds... you'll be saving more lives than you can imagine. That might just clear the books. It might just make up for all the people you killed."

I rubbed my thumb across the scars on my index finger; a bad habit. A tell.

"Nothing can make up for that."

Her eyes softened. "This might just come close."

I picked up the flimsy.

"There's only one name on here."

"You'll know the others when you see them. When you arrive on... the *project*... obviously you are not to tell anyone why you're really there. Just do what you do. Sleep with the crew. Observe the targets. Look menacing. Try not to kill anyone."

"That last one might be hard."

"Do your best."

"Not even if the targets are threatened?"

"We're hoping that your very obvious presence will be enough of a deterrent to... protect them. To prevent the most unfortunate eventuality." Something flickered across her face.

I nodded and stared at the name on the piece of flimsy.

Captain Maxwell.

So that's how I ended up on this crazy fucking ship. This "special project." This psychedelic trip with a crew that's terrified of me. With no one who understands me.

Show your knives, Rose had directed.

Show my knives? My knives show themselves.

I spent most of my time lounging in hallways, watching the crew, watching the Captain.

Watching Rose, who hadn't told me she'd be part of the project and who hadn't once acknowledged that we'd met before. She was a better actress than I'd expected. It really seemed like she didn't know who I was.

If I'd expected an uneventful trip, I was quickly proved wrong. Alternate dimensions? Check. Sentient ship that develops an illness? Check. Weird cult? Check. Weird aliens? Yup.

(Side note: Aliens are fun to bang. Best part of the trip so far. Strange protuberances are oddly useful. Fascinated by our squishy bits. Hard to damage. Solid 10/10, would do again.) Lots of drugs, sex, and alcohol.

Basically, the only thing this job was missing was any reason for my being here. Any sign that *anyone* wanted to kill the captain or the two other targets. I had not found a single other murder queen anywhere on this ship. No assassins, no one suspicious. I'd started to view the whole thing as an extended, drug-fueled pleasure cruise. A fun diversion from my retirement.

Until we found Cassandra on that rock. I'd heard we'd picked up a rescue; I was fucking the cook when he whispered in my ear about the hot unconscious girl in the med bay. I finished, threatened to kill him (you'd be shocked how many people ask me to do that; it's so cliche, but they love it), and then made my way to medical.

Doc let me in. Special projects give special access, you know. I stared at the girl in the bed. She looked soft. Succulent, just laying there. I poked her with a finger; she murmured in her sleep.

"Is she really sleeping, Doc?"

He nodded. "She'll wake soon, though. Dehydrated, some bruises."

"Can I look?"

Doc cocked his head, considering.

"Professional curiosity," I told him.

I lifted the thin med blanket. She was naked, her skin free of tattoos but, like Doc said, covered in bruises. Big ones, around her shoulders and hips.

"Interesting," I said.

Doc nodded. We could both tell she wasn't beaten; she'd fallen or been dropped on a hard surface.

"Where's her things?"

Doc pointed me to a sealed bag on the counter. I picked it up, used my ident chip to unlock it. She had clothes; there was something in the pocket of her pants. I felt around and then pulled it out.

"Ahhh," I said.

"Yeah," Doc agreed.

"Have you told anyone?"

"Nah." Doc took a drink of his special coffee; our eyes met and I nodded. Not our circus.

I went to my room and took a shower and thought about blood on my hands. Cassandra wasn't here for my targets. I had a bad feeling about what she was here for, but it wasn't part of my mission. It wasn't my job. I definitely shouldn't kill her.

Right?

No, I shouldn't kill her.

But I did have all these pretty knives...

If Rose wasn't such a bitch I might go tell her about the sexy rescue with the secret, but nah. Rose could take care of herself. Instead, I popped a stimulant and went to the Machine Room and danced with nightmares. Becoming a nightmare myself and doing all the things I didn't let myself do in the real world anymore. I became the thing the crew feared; I did things they couldn't imagine. I was a thing so horrible they could never know I walked among them.

And I loved every fucking minute of it.

The ship knew. The ship saw everything, but it didn't care. It gave me everything I wanted in the Machine Room: it stripped off all the safeties, turned off all the psych monitors, and it let me play.

I felt clean when I was done; I felt renewed. I felt good about my decision to ignore Cassandra Ellerbee, that seemingly inno-cent rescue with a project of her own. I sauntered into the lounge to shop for a good time; everyone watched me while I leaned against a wall, arms folded, leather tight where it mattered. I was just about to talk to the cute ensign in the corner when Rose walked in. I expected her to ignore me as usual, but instead, she turned and narrowed her eyes at me.

I followed her out the door.

"Captain's down," she said, voice low in the hall.

I followed her. "What?"

"Captain has collapsed. Your target is down, Altera."

"Heart attack?"

"No. I suspect poison."

"How Elizabethan," I muttered. Rose glared at me.

"Doc has him in the med bay. We want to get a handle on it before we announce it."

"That sucks. Wait, med bay? Is the rescue girl there still?"

Rose gave me a look. "Ellerbee? No, she's been moved to quarters. She woke up last night, complaining about nightmares. She specifically mentioned a lady with knives in a room full of blood. Sound familiar?"

I laughed. "Nothing to do with me. Where are you taking me?"

Rose rolled her eyes; I couldn't see it, I could just tell. "I'm taking you to the med bay, you dim-witted assassin. Your target is down."

"Exactly. He's down; I'm an assassin. What do you want me to do?"

"I want to see if you can figure out who did it. And how."

"I'm a killer-turned-bodyguard, not a detective. I can't help you."

"You can and you will. Here."

She stepped into the med bay and I followed. Doc stood over the captain, looking perplexed.

"Any update?" Rose asked.

Doc shook his head. "No change at all. I'm afraid to use a sedative to calm his heart since I don't recognize what's in his system. I'm trying to see if I can flush it out."

I looked at Captain Maxwell. I'd never gotten a good sense of him. He was flushed, breathing hard; his eyes were twitching under their lids. He looked like he was having a nightmare. I wondered if he could hear us.

"Recognize this reaction?" Rose asked.

I shook my head. I didn't. It was somehow familiar... but wrong. I felt a strange sense of confusion. Strange because I never felt confusion. Fight or fuck, those were my options; this fell in neither category.

"Really outside my area," I said, still staring at the captain. "Who found him?"

"No one," Doc answered. "The ship called me."

"Ship, want to tell us what happened?" I asked.

The ship didn't answer.

I shrugged and turned to Rose. "I'm really not sure what else I can do."

Rose sighed. "Yes, having failed to do the one thing you were brought here to do, I imagine so. Look—we need to elect an interim captain. I've got to go sort that out. You look into this. Investigate. Talk to people, ask questions. Let me know if you find anything."

Rose left. I kept looking at Maxwell. To Doc and the ship I said:

"I notice she didn't actually say to find out who killed him."

Doc nodded and patted me on the shoulder.

"Watch yourself," he said.

I did what Rose wanted. I walked around; I looked menacing. I asked questions. No one knew anything, of course. I watched as Rose had Kern elected to acting in command. I wondered who Rose really was.

I decided to follow my instincts; I'd gone a bit soft on the ship, frankly, and I was ready to get back to my roots. After all,

I've got two ways to solve a problem, and I figured at least one of them would work with Rose. I headed to her quarters and passed Cassandra in the hallway; I turned to watch her go and admired the view. Maybe I'd go visit her later, too.

I let myself into Rose's room. She sat at her desk, a bunch of papers scattered in front of her.

"Hey, bitch," I said. She had bags under her eyes; she looked at me, then back at her desk.

"I have a lot of work to do."

"I literally don't care."

She sighed and turned to face me. "What do you want?"

I glanced at the papers on the desk; corporate nonsense.

"Who are you, really?" I leaned against the door frame and crossed my arms.

She looked like she wanted to murder me. I recognized the look. I felt a brief fondness for her; it passed quickly.

"I'm a colonel, looking into the Nimmert Corporations dealings with the..."

"You can stop. I get it."

I thought for a minute. "What I don't get is why I'm here. I'm obviously a shitty bodyguard and I'm definitely not your type, so why did you bring me?"

"I wasn't sure what I'd find. You were part of my cover story. I needed the captain to think we were protecting him; I could show I was acting in the best interests of the mission, when really..."

"When really all you cared about is your 'special little project.'"

She nodded.

I felt something; a strange new feeling. It was worse than the confusion I'd felt earlier. I felt... used. She'd used me as a decoy.

She saw the look on my face.

"That wasn't all," she said hurriedly. "The captain - we didn't really think he was involved, but if he was... I might have needed you to take him out."

"This is the part where I'm supposed to say 'except someone else got to him first,' but that other person is you."

Rose shrugged. "Maybe. Maybe not. Maybe there was an... unexpected confrontation. Maybe there wasn't."

"So Ellerbee shows up with the information you need and you confront the captain. Now he's dying in the med bay and your boy Kern is in charge of the ship."

Rose smiled. "That's one way to look at it."

"It sure is."

We stared at each other for another minute. Then I turned and walked out of the room.

Rose really was a stone-cold bitch, but I had to admire how well she'd set everything up. She'd kept me out of the way with that bogus errand to investigate. And besides, she'd hooked me up with this mission, which had turned into an interesting diversion.

But I couldn't abide being used, and even a retired assassin has a reputation to consider.

So I went to visit Ellerbee in her room. She let me in. Her face flushed when she saw me, and her pupils dilated. Her lips were pink and plump.

"Oh! Hi," she said, in her breathy little Marilyn voice. "Did you - did you want something?"

We got the business out of the way first - very nice, everything soft where it should be. This one didn't want any threats, but she did want to stroke my knives—which surprised me—and then she showed me her data.

I skipped through all the political and corporate crap and

went straight to the juicy personal secrets while she freshened up. She came back, still looking disheveled and lovely, and I kissed her one last time.

Like I said, I don't mind paying for sex if they're a pro. I also don't mind paying *with* sex, and that data dump was worth it.

I spent a few days lounging around, glaring at passersby. But my heart wasn't in it; I wasn't as good of an actress as Rose. Rose and I avoided each other. I'd planted my seeds and I waited to see if they would grow.

On this ship, everything grows; some of the fruit can surprise you.

Rose called a ship-wide meeting. We gathered in the common areas and she told us about her private mission. She told everyone about the Nimmert Corporation, and the papers, and showed the evidence of whatever it was they were doing with the Swarm. I tuned her out because I didn't care.

Her eyes met mine once during her speech. "Is this enough?" she seemed to be asking me. I smiled at her and she looked, for a moment, relieved, and continued her little speech.

West came on and gave his version; supporting her story, corroborating it. I waited. I waited. I was good at waiting; all assassins are.

West looked at the assembled crew.

"...and when Rose killed the Captain, we knew..."

The crowd fell silent; all the little rustles and murmurs just stopped. Next to West, Rose's face froze, turned a frosty white. Then the crew started talking again. They yelled, they stood and started shouting that Rose was a murderer, and up near the podium, she turned that bloodless gaze on me because she knew.

I winked at her. Then turned around and left.

Remember; I'm never the one that gets fucked.

UPA MEDICAL RECORDS
RENNER, KEVIN—SERGEANT

DATE: 28 September 832 A.A.

Patient Name		Renner, Kevin		BZ98S873
Attending Physician		Sanderson, Harold		

Heart Rate 93 bpm	Blood Pressure 136/77	Temperature 37.8°C	
Height 185.42 cm	Weight 80.01 kg	Race Human	Gender Male

Reason for Visit	Scheduled Checkup		
Eye Exam	20/23	Responsive?	Yes
Throat	Red/Irritated	Oxygen	96%

Physician Notes

Leadership have asked that I perform a mental health evaluation on the patient. Physical symptoms show that his temperature has increased. Also, his blood pressure is on the higher end of the normal range, which is unusual for him. Stress could be raising it. His throat also looks irritated. Allergies? Patient maintains that he took all his antibiotics. His weight has dropped significantly. Patient states that he hasn't felt much like eating. His oxygen levels are also bordering on too low.

When asked how he was feeling, the patient explained that he feels fine, but would like an increase in his supply of pleasant pills. He's obviously not comfortable revealing what's really bothering him, but he confessed to having a difficult time controlling his emotions.

Took another blood draw and decided to inspect it under the microscope. There appears to be some sort of fungal infection. It's not like one I've seen before. Perhaps he's feeling ill enough that it's causing a depression. Being a stoic marine, he wouldn't complain about any of that.

I went ahead and increased his supply of pleasant pills. We have plenty now. I also referred him to Gennero for counseling.

Written by A.R.K. Horton

THE BITTER, HUNGRY TEARS OF THE STARS
LAILA AMADO

ALEXA FLOATED NEAR THE CEILING OF THE GLOW ROOM, THE portable anti-gravity device secured at her belt keeping her airborne. The coils of her long, flaming-red hair hung down, unspooling towards the floor. One of the orbs populating the room drifted up to her, hovering at the elbow as if eager to see what she was doing. These orbs, that emitted a soft pulsing light, gave the room its name. So far, no one had figured out the functionality of the room and its orbs, but they were harmless, and the room became a place for secret meetings and moments of seclusion.

Alexa adjusted her angle and a drop of paint from the brush she was holding landed on her nose. She was born in space, on an evacuation ship escaping the Swarm fleet. Weightlessness didn't bother her. What did, however, was the strange configuration of the stars around the Ship—none looked familiar, none held any meaning. If someone were to ask, she wouldn't be able to tell a single story about any of them. Not that anyone was asking. The UPA marines, it turned out, cared little about stories. Alexa sighed and continued the line she was drawing, mapping out familiar constellations as she remembered them, trying to bridge them with the images of these new, alien stars.

She heard movement below—a young marine, whose name Alexa didn't know, stared up at her painting with an expression that was part puzzlement, part disdain. Realizing she'd been noticed, the marine said, "Captain Savory requests your presence on deck." The glow room had no intercoms, Alexa thought, so they had to send a messenger. The marine continued, "I can accompany you, if you wish."

Looking down, Alexa said, "I'll be on my way, just need to finish something up here. You don't have to wait." The relief on the young marine's face was palpable. Alexa shook her head— the way things were going, she'd rather have no company at all.

"Like hell you're going alone." The voice sounded behind him, sharp and sarcastic. Startled, Logan Dileo dropped the magnetic splicer, and it plummeted down the ventilation shaft, clunking all the way down. A seasoned marine, he survived the burning deserts of Arachia and the acid snows of Etro, came face to face with the soldiers of the Red Horde and lived to tell the tale, and yet unexpected noises made him jump like a wimpy ten-year-old.

"Now see what you have done," continued the voice. "You simply can't be trusted with a mission like that." A hot wave rushed up Logan's neck and he swung around to face the intruder. Callie Morgan, the infamous space pirate, leaned against the wall. Despite Captain's orders, a very deadly X-7Q gun snuggled against her hip.

"Keep your nose out of my business, Morgan," Logan snarled.

Callie gave him a lazy smile. "Ease up, hothead. I have my

own business aboard that tin can. Just so you know, that junk over there," she gestured in the general direction of the abandoned spacecraft they recently discovered, "is a Dagona ship. You haven't seen one before, have you?"

She was right, of course. The Dagona civilization, long gone by the time UPA came into power, was nothing but a footnote in history textbooks. From time to time, a report of a derelict vessel drifting in space or a deserted bunker on a remote planet would surface in the newsfeed. To find one was like winning a lottery—Dagonian artifacts scored a neat sum on the black tech market. Looking into the pirate's amused green eyes, however, Logan wasn't going to admit that this was the extent of his knowledge.

"I guess that's a no," concluded Callie in response to his silence. "To spare you the details: the bastards booby-trapped the ships and I'm painfully familiar with their tricks." She rolled up a sleeve, exposing a broad, jagged weal of an old scar.

Logan scowled. "I see that knowledge didn't help you much."

Callie snorted in response. "I was thirteen. Didn't know better. What counts is that the guy I was with fried to crispy bits, and I did not." She stalked over and, pressing her lips to Logan's ear, whispered, "I saw you freeze up in that sparring match. Trust me—you don't want to walk onto that ship alone."

The intercom on the wall of the docking bay buzzed before Logan could think of a witty comeback. The Captain's voice boomed, "Dileo, report to deck!"

"Ooh, someone is in trouble," drawled the pirate. Logan rolled his eyes.

He exited the docking bay, turned right up the sloping ventral passage of the Ship, and was almost halfway to the main walkway, when he noticed that Morgan was still at his heels. "Seriously, are you going to follow me to the deck?" he asked, turning around.

The pirate nodded. "Not letting you out of my sight."

Exasperated, he marched forward. She trailed after him, whistling a tune.

On deck, the Captain stood in front of the displays where a myriad of stars flickered against the black backdrop of space. All around the vast room, marines operated their stations. Logan caught a glimpse of Alexa Gennero's disorderly red hair, but before he had a chance to voice his surprise at the civilian's presence, the Captain spoke. "Something has come up. It affects your upcoming mission to explore the abandoned vessel."

The Captain ran his fingers over the controls, enlarging one section of the screen. The carcass of the derelict Dagona vessel, dotted with clusters of parasitic mollusk shells, floated at the forefront. Logan scrutinized the screen. Unable to see what alarmed the Captain, he said, "The ship looks the same as before. No energy readings. No life signs."

The Captain clicked the controls again. "And this? This wasn't there when we scanned the ship." On a rotated image, a small cloud of star gas pulsated—white, lilac and blue. It had attached itself to the Dagona ship by wrapping tendrils of stardust around its far end.

Logan took a step forward. "What the hell is that?"

"We don't know. Looks like a free-floating nebula, but the readings are highly unusual. There is no dangerous radiation, no signs of temporal influx, but the way these pulses of light are organized, their patterns hint at a possibility of sentience."

"You're saying it's thinking. An intelligent cloud?"

The Captain shrugged. "No way to know for sure, but if it is an alien mind, we must attempt contact. After all, the ultimate mission of the UPA is not war but diplomacy."

Callie muttered, "Who would have thought?" Logan almost forgot she was there.

The Captain pretended not to hear and continued. "Alexa Gennaro will go with you."

"What? No!" Callie and Logan cried in unison, the idea of the kooky redhead going along with them preposterous to both.

"It's an order. Gennaro is a qualified mediator of interspecies relationships. She is certified in using Turan resonating bowls for establishing contact with diverse forms of sentient life." With that, the Captain turned away, showing that the conversation was over.

The Dagona ship, black and silent, loomed above the approaching shuttle. Up close, its hull appeared to be covered in an intricate network of furrows and ridges. Wedged into the back seat, Alexa Gennero tried to follow the pattern, but the exercise made her feel nauseous.

In the pilot seat, Callie Morgan steered the shuttle towards the docking hatch of the black ship, following the cues only she could decipher. Sitting beside her, Logan looked stiff and uncomfortable. Alexa could see the small beads of sweat on the back of his neck, just below the hairline.

Finally, the small shuttle found the shallow indentation in the underbelly of the derelict ship and slipped inside. They disembarked and found themselves in a cavernous hallway. The lights affixed to the helmets of their biosuits captured glimpses of enormous sculptures and weird machinery.

Logan turned to Alexa. "Where do you need to set up your cups?"

"Bowls."

"Whatever."

Alexa sighed. For some reason, Logan disliked her from day one. "The closer I'm to the nebula, the better our chances of establishing contact."

Logan turned and marched off into the darkness. Callie and Alexa followed suit. They moved in silence until they reached a round concourse, empty save for some crates pushed against the walls. Alexa sat down on the floor and a cloud of fine dust surrounded her like a cocoon. She extracted the Turan bowls from the case, one by one, placing them in a wide arc. Logan rolling his eyes didn't escape her, but she paid him no heed. It wasn't the first time she'd faced judgement and derision.

She passed her hand over each of the bowls, touching their rims lightly. The sequence of touches had to be precise, attuned to the vibrations of the mind she sought to contact. She closed her eyes and focused on the blue and lilac tangles of stardust, trying to capture the intricate rhythm of its pulsing light and inviting it to resonate with her. She reached the utmost level of concentration and, as usual, felt the coils of her red hair move, tightening around her head. When, as a child, she complained about it to her auntie, she'd said she was imagining things. Back then, Alexa believed her, but she wasn't so sure anymore.

Sorting through all possible frequencies of mind contact, Alexa searched as hard as she could, but the Turan bowls remained silent. Tired and frustrated, she was about to give up when a fleeting presence brushed against her mind. It stayed for barely a second, leaving behind a feeling of longing and an impossible scent of white magnolias, so out of place in the far reaches of space.

Alexa looked up. Logan was leaning against one of the crates, about to doze off, oblivious to any alien presence. Callie, however, looked as if she saw a ghost. For a long moment, the pirate looked at Alexa, unblinking. Then she shook her head and punched Logan in the ribs. He jumped.

"Listen," said Callie, addressing no one in particular. "If you're done with the divinations, let's go. I don't have all day." She ducked into the nearest passage and Logan followed suit. Alexa had no choice but to track after them.

They wandered in the dark passages of the Dagona ship for what seemed like an eternity. Alexa lost track of the turns and twists of the unfamiliar corridors, the crates and the containers Logan and Callie rummaged through and overturned in search of something valuable, and all the while she couldn't shake the memory of the alien presence touching her mind. By the time they were done, Alexa felt completely drained, her brain filled with fog. Dragging her feet, she climbed into the shuttle. They fell away from the derelict's massive bulk and followed the charted course back to the docking bay of their own ship. Alexa glanced back at the Dagona ship. The surrounding space was dark and empty—the nebula had disappeared.

"Hey, you scared the cosmic mind off with your tea set," Logan called from the pilot seat.

Alexa slept for many hours. Every time she felt close to waking, a new wave of drowsiness pulled her under. Pink hours turned to yellow, yellow to green—it seemed impossible to wake up. It took all her willpower to finally shake herself awake and stumble out of the room. She dragged herself towards the canteen, hoping that a dose of coffee—regular, not Venusian, she hated that stuff—would jumpstart her brain. Around her, the ship was abuzz with excitement, the source of which was unclear. The whispers and the laughter broke out here and there. In line for the coffee, snippets of conversations reached her ears: *"A woman on an asteroid? Again? What is the running joke of this voyage?... Maybe they grow on asteroids... Perhaps, a new life form? Lady-sprouting asteroids..."* Alexa struggled to make sense of the exchange, but the fragments she caught were too bizarre. Her temples throbbed with an impending headache.

The Doctor grabbed her by the elbow. "Alexa, you're just the person I'm looking for! Jeez, you look terrible."

"Thank you, Doc. You were saying?"

"As you might have heard," he said as he glared at the giggling couple ahead in the queue, "We've found a woman on the mining asteroid AB-5427."

Alexa wasn't sure she heard right. "Another woman on an asteroid? Just like Callie?"

Doctor Sanderson rolled his eyes. "Please don't join the choir. I've heard enough jokes today."

"Sorry, Doc."

The doctor continued. "As I was saying, the woman's vital functions are fine, there is nothing wrong with her physically, but she wasn't able to answer any of my questions. Not even her name. I believe she has amnesia."

Alexa nodded. "She could have knocked her head or suffered psychological trauma."

"Exactly," said the Doctor. "You're the closest we have to a mental health professional. I was hoping you could come over to the med bay and have a look at the patient. Maybe you can help her."

"Can I have my coffee first, Doc?"

Sanderson nodded, patted her on the back, and moved away, casting another mean glance at the giggling couple by the counter.

Coffee worked wonders. By the time Alexa reached the med bay, the fog in her head had cleared. She reached for the door and it slid open.

"Come in, come in." The Doctor's voice sounded from inside the room. Alexa stepped over the threshold. Sanderson was tinkering with some test tubes on a make-shift lab bench. He gestured towards the partition in the back. "She is over there, Alexa. Awake and waiting for you."

Alexa felt a pang of trepidation, which she quickly dismissed. She moved the milky-white partition wall aside and came face-to-face with the woman reclining in the hospital bed. She was breathtaking. Short hair, a shade so pale it looked almost pearlescent, stood in sharp contrast to her bronze skin. Her moon-grey eyes with specks of gold were a perfect oval shape.

Alexa's heart skipped a beat. She faltered, unsure how to begin the conversation. The woman's eyes followed her as she rounded the bed. "Hello," she said. "I'm Alexa. Doctor Sanderson said you don't remember anything. Perhaps, you can recall your name?"

The woman stared at Alexa, and the silence stretched. Finally, she said, "Yes. Yes, I think I remember now. My name is Cassandra." She paused, looking down at her hands, and added, "Cassandra Ellerbee."

There was something odd about that name, but Alexa couldn't quite pinpoint it. At this moment, the Doctor popped into the partition beaming at the patient. "I see you've made friends." Turning to Alexa, he continued, "We're moving our new guest—Cassandra, right?—to that spare room at the end of the upper starboard passage. There is nothing we can do for her medically, and she'll be much more comfortable there." The Doctor left, shutting the partition wall behind him.

The woman's eyes grew large and terrified. Looking around, she whispered, "Where's the clothes they found me in?"

Her distress was so palpable it spread to Alexa. Looking around, she saw a small bundle of light gray fabric rolled up underneath the bed. She carefully picked it up and handed it to Cassandra, who clutched it to her chest.

Alexa said, "You've experienced psychological trauma and must rest. I'll visit tomorrow." Quietly closing the partition door behind her, she left the room.

As soon as the door closed, the woman in the hospital bed unfurled the bundle. With frantic movements, she searched through the folds and pockets of the garment. Finally, her hand locked around a small round object and she pulled it out. A vial sat in her hand, its contents emitting a soft golden glow. She sighed with relief and sagged back down into the cushions, closing her eyes.

———

Alexa meant to visit Cassandra first thing in the morning, but the day turned out to be a series of catastrophes. By the time she managed to break free and reach the upper starboard passage, the hours turned from green to purple. She knocked on the door indicated by Doctor Sanderson, but no one answered. Fearing that Cassandra might have been more ill than the Doctor had realized, she touched her fingertips to the door and it slid open. Alexa had that weird effect on the Ship's doors.

Cassandra wasn't in the room. Alexa didn't like this at all— the Ship was weird even for those who'd spent considerable time on board. Sick and alone, Cassandra could easily get hurt. Alexa was responsible for her well-being, and now her ward was lost. She checked all passages on the upper level, the printer room and the kitchen garden Ensign Weatherley had set up behind the canteen. She even squeezed into the little nook at the tail of the Ship, the one with no discernible function. Cassandra was nowhere to be found.

Lost in anxious thoughts, Alexa turned another corner and ran into Cassandra. She stood in front of the Magical Machine Room. Her fingers dug into the grooves demarcating the door. She looked on the verge of tears.

"Hey," said Alexa gently. "You want to see the Magical Machine? It doesn't seem to work anymore." A sudden thought occurred to Alexa. "On another hand, maybe it can help with your amnesia? Let me open that door."

Cassandra moved aside, her face cautious, like that of a Venusian trilobite approaching a campfire. Alexa stood in front of the door—it slid open and she stepped inside. As usual, the walls remained blank. No projections for her. She glanced back and saw Cassandra standing at the threshold. Alexa gestured for her to come in, but she remained outside. Her open palms glided over the empty space in front of her as if they met a solid barrier—some sort of force field seemed to bar her from entering the room. This had never happened before.

Cassandra looked so devastated, it was painful to witness. Alexa stepped outside and tried to console her. "I'm sorry," she said. "The Ship has been acting up lately, and this room is malfunctioning."

"You don't understand. I need to get in." Cassandra sounded desperate.

Her reaction puzzled Alexa, but in the presence of such palpable distress she felt compelled to offer comfort. "Don't worry. We'll figure it out." Then added, "Can I show you the place I like best on this ship?"

With a sigh, Cassandra allowed herself to be led away, but

she kept glancing back at the closed door with an expression Alexa couldn't quite decipher.

Alexa led Cassandra to the canteen. The vast hall, deserted at this hour, echoed with the sound of their steps. In the back of the hall, a fissure in the Ship's wall hid a spiraling staircase. They scaled up the steps and emerged into a narrow loft. Soft, pillow-like pouffes sprouted from the floor. Alexa touched a section of the wall and it grew transparent. Outside, stars glittered against the black velvet of space. Some crew members said the view made them feel lonely, but Alexa found it comforting.

Cassandra's face relaxed. She pointed at the bright cluster of stars and said, "These are the Wild Sisters and these," she turned to the two red dots on the right, "are the Beacons." She talked about the stars as if they were old friends and Alexa, for the first time, felt at home in this strange and bewildering part of the universe.

They agreed to meet in the loft every night after the hours turned blue. Walking Cassandra to her room, Alexa thought that, perhaps, her charge was helping her and not the other way around.

They kept to their arrangement, and night after night came to meet in the little loft. Alexa treasured these quiet hours, but couldn't shake the feeling of growing sadness in the other woman. She meant to ask Cassandra about it, but time after time avoided the question—as long as she pretended that everything was fine, she could believe that this newborn companionship she treasured so much would not be lost. It worked until the day of the murder.

Alexa arrived in the loft just after the walls of the Ship turned blue. At this hour, she always found Cassandra sprawled across the pouffes scrolling through the digital reader borrowed from Doctor Sanderson, but tonight the loft was dark and empty. Alexa waited, and then she waited some more, and then she began to worry. She thought that perhaps Cassandra wasn't feeling well and stayed in her room. That seemed like a plausible explanation.

On her way out, Alexa grabbed a couple of pastries Cassandra seemed to have developed a fondness for and went in search of her friend. She followed the gently curving slope of the tunnel until she reached Cassandra's room. Bright, golden light radiated from beneath the door. Alexa raised her hand and meant to knock, but the door slid open on its own accord. Alexa caught a glimpse of a small round vial clutched in Cassandra's hand, shining like a little sun, before she hid it in her pocket.

Alexa stuttered. "I didn't mean to barge in like that, but I was waiting for you and then I got worried. Are you alright?"

Cassandra stayed silent for a long-long time. In the bluish glow of the walls, her face looked gaunt and there was a strange shimmering quality to her eyes that Alexa hadn't noticed before. At last, Cassandra said, her voice barely audible, "Doesn't it scare you to live and breathe inside this hideous monster?" She looked around her in disgust.

Taken aback, Alexa shook her head. "The Ship isn't a monster, not at all."

Cassandra's lips turned into a thin, twisted line. "Now, isn't it? So much more powerful than any of you, puny things, so hungry and carnivorous. Indifferent to your lives and deaths, gorging on your dreams in order to replicate. What do you even know of this ship?"

Alexa felt the heat prickle in her cheeks. She said, "I know enough to know that it's alive and vulnerable, just like the rest of us. This whole thing with the Pop Drop matrix disaster upset it so much, it's got sick."

"Sick? How so?" asked Cassandra.

Alexa took this curiosity as a good sign and continued. "We aren't sure, but, we believe it's a sort of an autoimmune response —a large pustule broke out at the junction of three passages on the port side. We don't know how to mend it, so we just put a cover on it, for now." She was about to say more, but a terrible screeching sound broke from the intercoms and then the voice of Altera Deandre screamed, "This thing is dead! Somebody fucking killed it!" Alexa froze in place and stared at the button of the intercom. When she turned around, Cassandra was gone.

Outside the room, Alexa was caught up in the commotion. Running with the other crew members, she reached the intersection of the passages where a small crowd had formed. From behind the backs of the marines clustered around something lying on the floor, she saw the remains of the MuhDuhRu envoy, its carapace splintered open, purplish intestines spilling out.

"What could have done this?" one of the UPA marines asked Doctor Sanderson who was leaning over the corpse.

"I don't know, but those wounds look organic. Someone, or more likely something, split it open. If you ask me, we need to search the ship. Whatever it is, is probably still aboard, and we can't have some alien predator on the loose."

Alexa shuddered. She needed to find Cassandra—this was not a good time to roam alone. Alexa broke into a run, searching passages and hallways. Cassandra was nowhere in sight. Utterly at a loss, Alexa stopped to take a breath. As she stood, panting, she noticed a passage on her right pulsing red—the color of alarm. With a start, Alexa realized that this was the passageway leading to the Ship's wound.

She ran down the pulsing tunnel. Up ahead, she saw Cassandra leaning over the cover protecting the pustule. With one hand she was ripping the make-shift wrap apart; in the other, she held the shining vial.

"What are you doing?" Alexa gasped.

Cassandra looked up. The pulsing light of the walls cast wicked shadows on her face. "Having my revenge. The bloody thing didn't let me into the Pop Drop chamber, its only vulnerable point. I guess it recognized my scent. To be honest, I was about to give up on this whole endeavor until you told me about this wound. So—thank you."

Alexa remembered the force field barring Cassandra from entering the Magical Machine Room, her hands fluttering against the empty space of the doorway. "What did the Ship ever do to you?" she cried.

Cassandra's face twisted into a grimace. "You call it a Ship. I call it an abomination. The ever-hungry beast of the Swarm."

"I don't understand."

"Did you ever ask yourself what a living creature this size eats?"

Alexa did not know the answer to that question.

"Let me enlighten you," said Cassandra. Her eyes grew brighter, glittering gold, white, and lilac. "They have a taste for cosmic mega species. They care nothing for the conscious souls they destroy, have no pity for the young and the frail. They eat and eat. Entire species have been destroyed for their genocidal hunger."

"I'm sure the Swarm made them do it."

Cassandra snorted. "I think you misunderstand the nature of their relationship."

A scent of white magnolias permeated the air. Alexa stared at Cassandra. The realization hit her. "It's you. You're the nebula. I felt your touch on the Dagona ship. But how...?"

"I'm not a nebula. I'm an Antori," corrected Cassandra. "The last of my kind." She raised the vial to her face. "These are the tears of the stars, this is my sorrow for the loved ones taken from me. The only thing that can kill a 'ship.' It took me years to distill it from the shreds of Antori torn apart by these beasts, but I needed to get inside to be able to use it. I couldn't believe my luck when I sensed you aboard the Dagona."

"The asteroid. You touched Callie's mind too when we were aboard that ship. Everyone thought it was a wild coincidence that we found a second woman stranded on an asteroid, but it wasn't a coincidence. You picked up the idea from Callie's memory," Alexa paused. Now she knew what bothered her about Cassandra's name. "Cassandra was the name of my aunt's favorite cat, and Ellerbee was a character in a book I read as a child. What did you take from Logan?"

"Nothing. He is boring." Cassandra popped the cork from the vial. A few golden specks floated up into the air and the walls of the passageway shook.

Alexa dashed forward. "Please, stop! I'm so sorry for your pain and your loss, but this Ship is not like the others. It has changed. Please don't hurt it."

Cassandra hesitated, her hand extended over the gaping wound in the Ship's flesh. She opened her mouth to say something, but instead she screamed and pointed behind Alexa. An unimaginable creature—a cross between a spider and a gigantic crab—darted into the passage. Humongous pincers of the arthropod dripped with what was obviously the remains of the MuhDuhRu. Its tiny eyes, all eight of them, locked on Alexa. She didn't even have a chance to cry out—in a split second; the creature was upon her. Its upper appendages wrapped around her waist and lifted her off her feet. The creature carried her off into the glowing red gloom of the tunnel, and the last thing she saw was Cassandra's face and the vial clutched in her hand.

Alexa came to her senses hanging upside down. In the semi-darkness, her eyes discerned the ribs of the vaulted ceiling and the gray oblong shapes lining the walls. The shuttles. This was one of the docking bays at the lowest level of the Ship. Alexa tried to move, but her body was trapped in some sort of cocoon —a silky net wrapped around her legs and body. She tried to wriggle free, but the filaments held fast. Something touched her shoulder, and she was about to scream, but a hand covered her mouth.

"Shhh," whispered Cassandra, "the pest is somewhere close." Her face seemed to glow with a pale white light. "You must have picked it up when passing through that asteroid belt the other day, sucked it up the ventilation shaft." She reached up and pulled at the threads at the top of the cocoon. "Good thing it wanted to save you for a midnight snack. That MuDuhRu wasn't so lucky." The filaments snapped, and Alexa came down onto the hangar's floor in an undignified heap. Cassandra leaned over Alexa, a small blade glistening in her fingers, and was about to cut through the cocoon when, with a clicking sound, the creature leaped out of the darkness and threw her aside with a powerful swipe of its pincer. It loomed over Alexa, ready to strike. Viscous liquid dripped from the serrated blades of the creature's mandibles. This time Alexa screamed.

Bright golden light cut through the darkness. Cassandra stood tall, the golden vial shining in her fingers. She threw it like a hand grenade. The vial struck the side of the monster, and shards of glass and specks of gold exploded against the arthropod's carapace. Star tears burned through the hard shell in seconds and the creature's body convulsed, rippled, and crumbled from inside, leaving nothing but a small smoking puddle on the floor of the docking bay.

Alexa shook as Cassandra helped her out of the wilting cocoon. Looking at the spot where a minute ago the monster flaunted its deadly pincers, she said, "I'm so sorry you lost the tears."

Cassandra shrugged. "It's alright. Perhaps, it was the best way to use them." She helped Alexa back on her feet. They stood so close that the scent of white magnolias made Alexa sway.

Cassandra took a step back. She pressed an invisible button and a transparent membrane fell between them, separating the inner section of the dock from the launching bay.

"What are you doing?" Alexa whispered, but deep down she already knew.

Cassandra smiled. A myriad of stars twinkled in her moongrey eyes. "This Ship might differ from others of its species—at least, I'll try to believe it, but still I cannot remain inside. Close contact of this sort is too painful. And this body is so limiting. Lately, I've been struggling to keep myself contained."

"But what do I tell the others?"

"Nothing. Let this remain my secret." Running underneath her skin, small lights flickered and pulsed. Cassandra touched her hand to the screen. "You have some mysteries of your own to solve. Take care, little one."

She turned away and walked towards the far end of the docking bay where the hatch of the hangar opened wide against the starless void. She stepped outside and kept on walking, her silhouette unraveling into a cloud of stardust. Alexa watched until the nebula—the last of her species—disappeared in the velveteen darkness beyond the Ship.

QUIRK OF THE MATH
(QUANTUM FOLK HOUSE)

ELVIRA CANAVERAL

Energy is the ability to make change
Never can be destroyed just rearranged
Make it work for you
To repair and replace
Merging atoms and photons from the star
The space sharks learned to eat the sun
Electro-Chemical eating the sun
Cells eating cells that's what they do
Then whoops one cell tried to eat another
And failed, wonderously
And two became one with the power of two
Mitochondria was the powerhouse
The waste ejected from the cells
and formed the body
A living swarm working together

Stay still and die in the shadows
Merge with the dead universe again
A cell separated from the dead universe

A screw you against entropy
The most interesting something
And empty hand holds something
Exotic particles,
Shielded, frozen, and no motion
Only a quantum blur
A zero-point energy
Radiant heat glow
Fundamental quantum fields
Vibrating in their own way
Quantums have questions
and answers to each other
Tossing up and down the rungs
Of the particle ladder
Using creation and annihilation operators
A Vacuum impossible to keep
Once the infinite got as big as it did
Virtuals particles
The machinery under the hood
Virtual particles provide
Our models for the engine
Back in time or faster than light
Operating under subreal freedoms

Surreal Subgenius
The tiniest of a virtual photon
Can exist for so long
Not being burdened with Reality
Being what the need to be in QFT
Fluctuating vacuum energy is the
THIS PAGE INTENTIONALLY LEFT BLANK
Message for building a universe

Vacuum energy has a relative effect
Nothing to hold onto can take you back in time
Metaparticles for what you need
Whole lotta nothin' going on
A Quirk Of The Math

PART III: THE THIRD JUMP

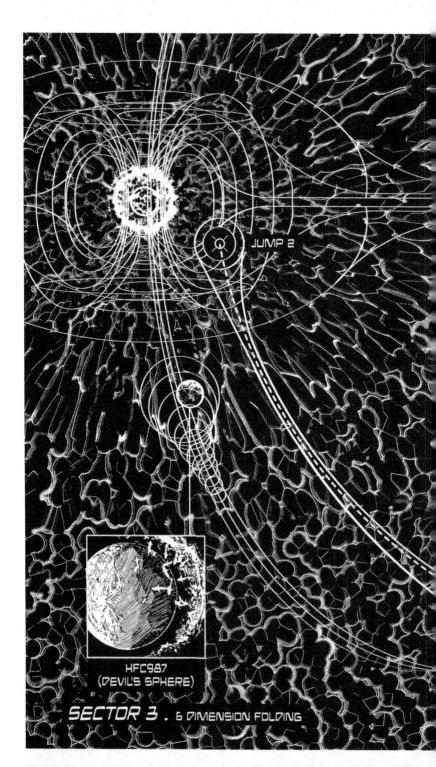

JUMP 2

HFC987
(DEVIL'S SPHERE)

SECTOR 3 . 6 DIMENSION FOLDING

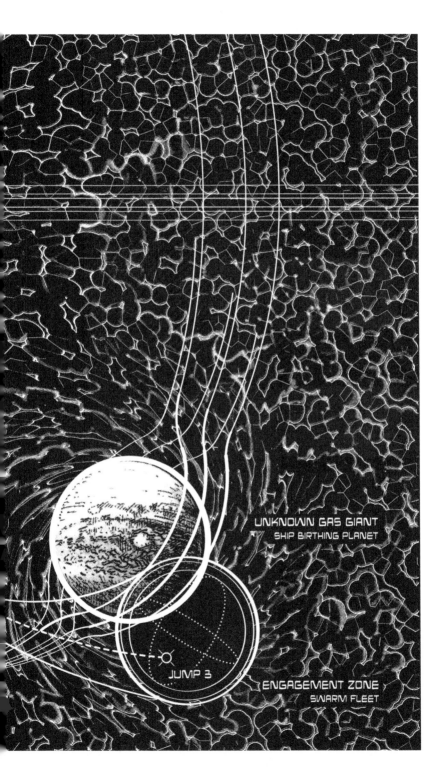

UNKNOWN GAS GIANT
SHIP BIRTHING PLANET

JUMP 3

ENGAGEMENT ZONE
SWARM FLEET

WRITE DOWN OUR UNION SIGIL
(*TH D UNION LIBRARIAN SONG)

ELVIRA CANAVERAL

When your mind is somewhere else
Our Unions Singing
While our Union's saving
All the kids in Space and Times

Our work is Timeless, but who's complaining?
Thanks to the Guild of Depth a Reality we're saving!

So look for the Union Sigil,
it says we're able to make it better together!
Write it down so you remember!
Our Spacetimes Sixever!

Together We Saved A Way!!!

I AM I

A. A. RUBIN

—WE'RE IN THE CONTROL HUB.

—Ensign, get the ship online. The Swarm will know what we're up to at any moment now! Triangle, what say the Kern?

We estimate 3:35 Erms, sir.

—Bryjal?

—My team is in position by the portal. So far, we see nothing.

Orient toward vector 1.7 mark 8. We calculate that their likely initial approach.

—Acknowledged.

Ship is changing. It seems anticipate we's needs and respond accordingly. Query: How? Hypothesis: Ship has bio-organic mind which responds stimuli quickly. Counter Hypothesis: Ship not only alive, but telepathic. Initiating Beta team for further—

—Pythagoras!

Accessing...Ancient Earth Mathme—override: attempt at humor; he means we. Respond. Yes, Sir.

—This thing just fabricated a UPA-style bridge. Could this be a trap?

We calculate thousands of such scenarios, sir. But none with probability higher than surviving our imminent encounter with The Swarm.

—Imminent? How imminent?

We expect Bryjal to see them during this—

—I see them. Bogies approaching vector 1.6. mark 7.

—That's a copy. Ensign, let's heed the call of Cthulhu and get out of here. Engage!

Call of Cthulhu: ancient Earth literary reference, likely connect Bryjal resemblance to story cephalopod deity... Ship moving. Stay alert. Get visual exterior morphing, too.

—Gunny, get the warp cannon online ASAP.

Sir, we would advise against that. Too many unknown variables.

—Shut up, Triangle. Don't be so square. Let's see how these Swarm bastards like a taste of their own medicine.

Captain, we must re—

—Stand down, Isosceles. That's an order. Let's annihilate those Swarm scum... fire!

—What the hell was that? Navigation, status update. Stat!

—We appear to be...What in the 14 systems?! 90,000 light years away from home.

—Keep your antennas on. How far are we from the wormhole?

—Given what we know about this ship, about an E-year travel, give or take.

—Triangle, what do you make of that ring?

We... we... don't know.

—Extrapolate, isn't that what you bugs are known for? What say the all-knowing Kern?

We... we... I am sorry, sir. I must retire to I's quarters.

—In the middle of a tactical session?

I... we... are sorry, sir. Must go now.

———

—Sir, did Triangle just refer to himself as I?

    —Yes, I think he did. I've never heard him do that before.

    —What do you make of it?

    —I have no idea, but I hope it's just a glitch. If we're going to get out of this, we need him. We need access to the Kern Collective. Counselor, go see what's up with Euclid. The rest of you, figure out what the hell that ring thing is.

———

Where are we? We are gone. No, we is here. Where are... they? Mind is empty. Where are they? We am here, no. I am here. Where are they? They are gone. I am we... No. I am they... No. Where are they? Mind is empty. They are gone. We, no, I am here. They are gone. Mind is empty. No. Mind is I.

    Who am I? I am Kern. I am Triangle. I am Triangle Alpha 3. I am Kern. I am I.

———

TRIANGLE ALPHA 3, PERSONAL LOG: After meeting with counsellor, I decide keep journal recording I's experience while I adjust life cut off from Kern Collective. This journal exist apart from official log delineating execution of I's ship duty and crew, and separate from baseline recording I's actions I must submit to Kern Collective if/when from this mission I return.

———

I am Triangle Alpha 3 of Kern Collective. But what Triangle Alpha 3 of Kern Collective mean? Triangle indicate three lines and three vertices, symbolic of three facets and three connections of I's Kern mind. Facet one: Kern hive mind. Before jump, I connect with Kern hive mind on Kern Homeworld Prime. Collective mind in constant contact with I. See what I see, hear what I hear, etc. If question posed, I access Collective and Collective bring power of entire Kern experience to analysis of problem. If any Kern encounter similar situation, Collective know, and bring experience to bear. Collective useful in variety of situation: Kern valued as tactical and strategic experts since even most experienced non-Collective species pale in comparison versus memory and processing power of entire Kern Collective. Kern Collective also help I adapt when working with other species. If any Kern past encounter species, every Kern can access culture, language, etc. Protocol database important for I as member of UPA mixed-species crew.

Triangle point two: I's short-term memory and processing power. Similar to old Earth computer RAM (Earth subroutine uploaded as plurality of mission crew human), each Kern, like I, possess great short-term processing power. This help I interact with environment without delay, without accessing Kern Collective. Section two possess great processing power, but, like old-earth RAM, overwrite frequently.

Triangle point three: All I's own experience. I access anything happened me in I's individual existence, recording of which always backed up to Collective hive mind and checked for errors. Hence, unlike some hive-mind species, each Kern autonomous, thinking individual. I thankful for point three in present situation, as I able function apart from Kern. In past, I cut off from Kern for a few erms but never this long.

Some Kern possess different amount of vertices. Children only two vertices pre-maturity, and command-level Kern start at

Square designation, and increase as access higher command functions. I encounter up-to octagon-level Kern in I's service to Collective, but suspect many higher levels exist beyond I's experience.

Query: Now I cut off from Kern, remain I Triangle?

Alpha 3 is I's unique designation. It occurs to I—I's colleagues call I by wrong name. There many Triangles within Kern Collective; there only one Alpha-3.

Should I correct them? Maybe in future. Now, I think familiarity best.

Today, I meet Dylan in hall. When he sees I, he says, "It's a TRAPezoid! Oh, sorry, it's only you, Triangle." I search human database and find reference to old Earth space war movie. I suspect attempt at humor, but without Collective, I not sure. It occurs to I, though I maintain human-language translator and reference database in short-term memory vertex, without Kern Collective monitor, it difficult I determine humor.

Reviewing previous interactions with crew, I posit this big problem given Captain's known speech and behavioral patterns, especially under stress.

Action: Initiate subroutine cataloging possible humor and sarcasm based on memory records and update with new information as becomes available.

Walls of ship fluctuate colors throughout day. We use changes to mark passage of time. Captain call meeting for red tomorrow. I determined human designation "red" refer to light with wavelength in 780-622 nm range. Ship walls red for approximately 102.857 Erms. What wavelength I need arrive at meeting? I not know. I endeavor arrive at red shift.

I, indeed, first one in meeting room, which give I time to review personal log. In previous entry, I refer to I as "I," and to crew as "we." In past, I use "we" refer only to Kern Collective.

Hypothesis: Without Collective voice, I looking for new group belonging, new we.

Query: If UPA crew now "we," to whom belongs I's primary loyalty? Most times, UPA and Kern objectives align, but must monitor thoughts about obligations going forward.

I visit ship's medbay. According to Captain, it adjust to treat any species. Medbay finds I perfectly healthy. All systems function properly. I able to receive Kern Collective signal, yet no Kern signal arrive. Medbay cannot fix I's problem.

On counselor's recommendation, I visit Magical Machine Room (silly name; superstitious humans). It projects Kern voice into I's brain. At first, I happy, but I realize it not real. Everything it say derive from I's memory. Machine Room Kern fake. I leave machine room. I determine I not ever go back. Waste of time, and dangerous.

Rest of crew obsessed with Machine Room. Without Collective, I not understand humans.

Today, I try pleasant pills. I not like them. Pills confuse I's sense of reality and make I feel out of control. Same with Venusian coffee.

Hypothesis: Without Kern Collective, I feel lack of control already and hallucinogens and false emotions enhance uncomfortable feeling.

Ship is sick. Many effects on important systems, but crew focused on food replicators and say food not taste right. I not notice. Kern not have sense of taste like other species. We eat for sustenance only. I wonder what sense of taste like.

Note: Ask others in crew.

Reviewing my personal memory log, I have determine I have been using Kern syntax even when translating to human common language. I have been accessing the dictionary function directly, and crew members are often confused by I's speech. I suspect I's translation matrix runs through Kern Collective, so Collective can monitor and correct errors in translation, but without the connection, I's mind bypassed the connection and translated word-for-word from the dictionary. I have analyzed all I's interactions with human crewmates since I began mission, and I am attempting to correct syntax in I's speech.

Some of the crew have begun receive telepathic messages from a group called The Hosts.

Hypothesis: Hosts may be jamming Kern signal.

Action: Learn about Hosts and the crew who hear them.

Returning to previous duties, I have encountered old problem. Captain refers to Triangle Alpha 3 by many names: Isosceles, Bug, Euclid, Pointy, etc. He tends to repeat self, so I create a database of all previous names for reference, and try to tell when he speak to I. Still, captain constantly create new names. In past, Collective tell I when captain calling for I, and explain reference for I's understanding. I must figure out a way to make captain (and rest of crew) refer to I by one name only.

Suspicion of ship's sentience has been confirmed. It revealed it member of race enslaved by Swarm, and wish to return to home planet to give birth to child. I sympathize with ship, as I, too, cut off from I's people. I endeavor to do what I can, within mission parameters to free ship and help it return home.

Many crew sympathize, as well. Extreme group wish to "free ship from all slavery even our own."

Query: What greater priority—save ship, or complete mission?

Hypothesis: Mission greater priority. We fight Swarm. Swarm enslave ship. If we succeed, all ships free.

Still, we sympathize with ship.

Yesterday, I broach topic of name during weekly meeting with counselor. I write name Triangle Alpha 3. Councilor suggest shorten it. Make it easy to say for Captain. I type TAT, first character of each name-word into tablet. Councilor misread it as TATE. Quick analysis reveal TATE sound like human name. We inform crew of new designation.

Captain grouse about name change, but counsellor back I up and say it important to I's psychological development. Captain mutter under breath, but agree to call I "TATE." Rest of crew must follow. Sometimes one slip and call I Triangle, but counsellor advise TATE not answer that name.

Ship has jumped somewhere new (location still unknown). I hoped Kern Collective signal return in new sector of spacetime, but it has not. Still, I's facility with UPA language has improved with practice, and crew congratulated I on the progress of I's recovery as I return to duties.

Analysis of previous interactions show that when Kern were in I's head, I refer to I always as "we."

Hypothesis: Crew will be more comfortable and respect I more if I refer to I as "we" henceforth.

Crew has, as expected, responded positively to we's return to familiar pronoun. Captain assign TATE to various important projects as before jump. He begin asking we's opinion during senior crew meetings once again.

Today at senior crew meeting, Captain turn to I and ask, "What say the Kern?" I hesitate, then answer to best of I's ability, but interaction bothers we.

Hypothesis: Use of pronoun "we" has caused Captain (possible other members of crew as well) to think Kern Collective signal has returned. This not intended consequences of using we pronoun.

Query: Does deliberate perpetuation of mistruth constitute disloyalty to captain and UPA?

Existence of Square-Octagon Kern implies Collective knowledge not shared with Triangle-level Kern. Inference: We have acted without full knowledge of superior's decision-making process and, therefore, motives.

Conclusion: Collective has knowingly and deliberately withheld knowledge from TATE in past.

Application: Within UPA crew, we hold command-level position. If lie of omission benefits crew, morally, omission ok.

Hypothesis: If loyalty to Kern supersedes loyalty to ship, then we must stay in command position long as possible to collect information and experience to add to Collective consciousness. Kern Collective likely tell we continue with deception, as it likely provide greater benefit to Collective than alternative.

Hypothesis: We can remember all we's individual experiences perfectly. Even without Collective memory, experienced commander with a photographic memory likely provide considerable benefit to captain and ship. Therefore, continuing deception best for UPA.

Since we made decision to perpetuate untruth, we have devoted we's free time to figuring out how to best affect this deception. We have reviewed the recording of we's experiences, and have determined the totality of our experience cannot fit in our short-term processing memory. We have, therefore, categorized we's experiences by type: military tactics, personal interactions, UPA official records, etc. We upload directory into primary rapid access memory, with root command back to cataloged files.

When asked for advice of Kern Collective, we find subject, review information, and answer based on previous Kern advice. Sometimes, we must extrapolate based upon like situations.

We continue to hone this process, but self-analysis reveals .35 nanosecond delay compared to pre-wormhole jump interactions. Thus far, captain has not noticed. We will continue to work toward optimizing the speed of we's responses.

Ship sick again. This time, situation dire. Primary life support systems malfunctioning, environmental controls are corrupted, as well. We have better chance to survive longer than most other crew mates since Kern standard-issue battle suit allow Kern to survive in many environments. Kern process various atmospheric gases into breathable nitrogen, and suit can synthesize waste materials into water in emergency.

Captain assign we command assignments once again. Pre-jump responsibility levels restored.

Even without Kern Collective, we possess considerably more processing power than any other crew member. With ship sick, crew increasingly rely on we.

Lt. Jerico discover maps of spacetime. Maps indicate ship jump not just different sector but also different dimensions and quantum entanglements. Physics posits many-world hypothesis, so information does not surprise we. Existence of other dimensions probable.

Query: Star maps indicate six dimensions. Do more exist?

Hypothesis: Likely yes, although yet to be discovered.

Query: Does Kern Collective exist in each mapped dimension?

Hypothesis: In some dimensions, Kern not exist. Potential we are only Kern in current quantum reality.

Cosima—only other crew member with mathematical acumen of we—has discovered how to communicate with ship. She thanked everyone on team who contributed to work except we. Must review recordings of interactions with she and look for signs of resentment or dislike. Though we improving reading crew's tone, we still miss Collective. Tone still difficult for we to read.

———————

With exception noted above, we suspect vast majority of crew greatly respect we once again.

———————

Suspicion of respect confirmed. Captain has fallen seriously ill. Others elect we as temporary captain. Ship now under we's command.

———————

Command UPA crew difficult for we. All of we's experience exist within Kern Collective and UPA Marines. In both systems, chain of command clear and orders followed without question. Crew not entirely Marine, though, and many factions arise. Some disobey or delay fulfilling orders.

Hypothesis: Some among crew prejudice against we because we not human.

Hypothesis: Those who did not vote for we more likely to be among dissenting factions.

Query: How can we unite the crew as they were under previous captain?

———————

—*Unknown Kern, identify yourself.*
    We are TA—Triangle Alpha 3 of the Kern Collective.

—*Triangle, designation Alpha 3, missing presumed dead. Standb...
ksssshhht...for review and kshhht...authentic kssshhht.*

Kern Collective Prime? Confirm copy?

—*Kshhhhht We are kshhh. We kshhhht are kshhhhhht*

...

...

Gone.

After latest jump, we beginning to hear Kern Collective voice
again. Transmission fragmented, interrupted, staticky, but we
hopeful we rejoin Kern Collective soon.

Ship changing. Corridors constricting, difficult to move. Obstacles growing everywhere. Ship's maps constantly out of date.
Must endeavor to update as soon as possible. Knowing home
terrain important tactical consideration for commander. Delegate to determine patterns.

Dissent among crew continues. Marines loyal to we, but non-
Marines continue subversive activity. Team assigned to map
tunnels working too slowly. We suspect intentional delay.

Transmissions from Kern Collective continue sporadically.
Analysis reveals many gaps, but also inconsistencies in message.
Some transmissions know we, Triangle Alpha 3, some do not.

Some say we missing and presumed dead. Some act as if we never cut off.

Query: Why inconsistencies exist?

Hypothesis: Each dimension contains different version of Kern Collective.

Query: Which version is we's true collective?

Answer: Without more information, impossible to tell.

Resolution: Since impossible to tell which is we's true collective, we will partition part of mind containing we's individual TATE personality and experiences. We must override Kern Collective attempts at recovery and control until we determine we's true collective.

Captain died from his illness. Marines want we as permanent captain. Others, led by Cosima, refuse.

Cosima claim she can get crew home faster. She claim she better understand math of multidimensional spacetime.

We ask, "What about the ship and its child?"

She claims we care more about ship than crew.

Standoff ensues.

Hypothesis: Much sympathy for ship and ship baby exist among crew. This, plus support of Marines, ensures we will prevail and remain captain.

Reviewing journals, we find entry relating to Cosima's dislike of we. We long suspect dissension among crew. Why we not conclude she likely leader?

Analyses of Cosima mutiny interrupted as Swarm ships detected. Headed our way. Crew recognize they need Marines to battle Swarm, so agree to maintain status quo until battle.

As military personnel prepare for battle, familiar routine kicks in. Marines well-trained and respect orders and chain of command. Non-military crew focus on ship maintenance, fixing environmental systems. Apart from imminent Swarm threat, things working as well as any time since we elevated to captain.

Part of we's preparation for battle includes we review previous captain's command style. Moreso than Kern Commanders, human captain delegate and rely on unique competence of crew members to achieve desired effect. Thus, TATE analyze, Jerico and Gray fight, etc.

Application: Given we's past failure to identify Cosima's threat, we ask Bryjal to begin investigating non-Marine crew. Interactions show Bryjal loyal, discreet, and observant.

Query: Will assigning Bryjal to spy on crew detract from their preparation and weaken their defense?

Hypothesis: Greater danger from two threat simultaneously. If interior threat eliminated, we able to focus on Swarm threat exclusively. Better, overall, for ship.

Non-military crew's performance is uneven. They fixed the environmental systems, but also have neglected maintenance on the

3D printer, and uncovered dangerous time dilation field that ages anything it contacts.

Hypothesis: Addiction to pleasant pills has negatively harmed crew's performance.

Suggested rationing pleasant pills today at senior crew meeting. Was advised against doing so by all other senior crew. They say it will lead to breaking truce between Marine and non-Marine factions.

Reflections: Every time we think we understand humans, events show we how wrong we are. Kern Collective predict human behavior well, yet we, cut off from Collective, cannot seem to figure it out.

Query: How great percentage of Kern Collective processing power devoted to humanity and its behaviors?

Override: Query not urgent. Must focus on needs of crew and ship.

MuDuhRu passenger murdered on ship today. Murderer unknown. Motive unknown.

Query: Is Bryjal's investigation into potential mutinies affecting their performance as security chief? Must look into others who could assist in each role.

We spend most of day reviewing Swarm tactics from known encounters with UPA. As we go through process of querying, occasionally Kern voices appear in we's mind, offering hypotheses and instruction.

Analysis concludes these voices not consistent, and reinforces we's many-worlds hypothesis.

Still, tactics presented by each collective sound, and give we options to present to other officers.

Ship continues to change. Weapons system form on outside of ship. Ship, too, prepares for battle.

Marines report bio-link with weapons. Later weapons reconfigure dramatically, seemingly connected with Host crew members.

Query: Do we control ship or does ship control us?

Hypothesis: Ship is preparing for multiple outcomes of internal power struggle. Ship sentient and intelligent.

Much we can learn from ship.

While spying on suspected conspirators, Bryjal accidentally contact time dilation field. Their species is long-lived, so they relatively unharmed, but their performance as spy compromised as they enter a mating cycle and secrete green ooze. It difficult act covertly in such condition. We now, again, vulnerable to both exterior and interior enemies.

We attempt to be more flexible in command style, and listen to suggestions of both Marine and non-Marine crew. We collect ice crystals, which Swarm value as bargaining chip, but away team nearly killed and crystals prove dangerous. We listen to suggestion to tow crystals behind ship. We agree with doctor's request to examine crew for evidence of quantum entanglements.

We not comfortable ceding control, but we must learn strengths and weaknesses of all members and promote unity between factions as battle approaches.

Conflicting Kern signals continue to appear in we's mind. We categorize them by type of commands and advice style. We assign majority of processing power to this task. We must study differences, analyze tactics, and learn flexibility.

In interim, we assign preparation for battle to Jerico, whom we elevate to commander and assign as first officer.

We write automatic cutoff signal to suspend Kern signal analysis in case of Swarm attack or other emergency.

Three Swarm destroyers have entered system. We cut off all subroutines and return to the bridge command-ready. Yet, we have no control of ship. Ship refusing to respond to we's commands. At last moment, ship reconfigures on its own, and bring weapons online without we's command. Swarm run.

There much we do not understand about confrontation.

Query: Why did Swarm run?

Query: Will Cosima and mutineers be emboldened now that ship defended itself independent from Marine command?

Query: Regardless of who commands crew, can anyone command ship?

Hypothesis: Ship is in control to greater extent than we think.

Query: If one ship this powerful, how powerful entire race of ships?

Answer unquantifiable without further data.

Query: If ship is so powerful, how Swarm enslave ship?

Hypothesis: Swarm use crystals to control ships.

Ship is followed by giant translucent entities which attracted to crystals we now tow. Human crew call them "space sharks" because they resemble aquatic predatory lifeform indigenous to human home world. Sharks devour probes, but do not attack ship.

Query: Why are sharks not harmed by crystals?

Query: Can sharks' protection versus crystals be transferred to humans and/or ship?

Query: Can sharks be controlled/weaponized?

Query: If sharks' power could be controlled, could power liberate enslaved ships?

Too many queries. Approaching limit of short-term brain vertex capacity. Must prioritize and delegate. We are in command. We have crew. Power of Kern not found in any individual Kern, but in power of individuals together as Collective. Same with crew. Must prioritize and delegate.

Hypothesis: Queries regarding ship's control supersede queries regarding potential mutiny.

We will consider question of ship's autonomy weself. We will assign counterintelligence against mutiny to upper-level command crew.

Ship enters reconfiguring cycle once again. Interior shifting. Space becoming tight. Obstructions appear everywhere.

Hypothesis: Ship is preparing for another jump.

—Captain.

Yes, chief engineer.

—I need to speak with you privately. Can you meet me at these coordinates ASAP.

Lookup ASAP, subdirectory language, subdirectory human: ASAP, abbreviation, UPA Standard, As Soon As Possible. Can you describe it to we? Or send a report through official channels?

—To tell you the truth, I don't trust those channels anymore. There are spies everywhere. I hear constant whispers of mutiny. I must speak with you alone. Only you and those whom I know are loyal to you. In fact, bring Bryjal, just in case.

We have been deceived. When Bryjal and we arrived, Engineer not alone. He trapped we and Bryjal behind mysterious door which leads to uncharted part of ship.

We have analyzed situation, and no possible escape seems likely. Mutineers likely in control of ship now, and will likely kill we even if we find unlikely escape. With Bryjal compromised by mating cycle, we have no chance in fight vs mutineers.

We have failed as captain, failed as individual, failed as Kern.

We desire only to return to Kern, to resume as part of Collective. If only—

But you cannot.

Who are you? You are not Kern.

No, I am not Kern. You know me as the Ship, and I brought you here. We need you.

You need we?

Yes, you, TATE, and The Kern Collective.

We are TATE, Triangle Alpha 3 of the Kern Collective.

No, You are TATE, but you can no longer be part of the Kern Collective.

We do not comprehend.

You have developed an individual consciousness. That part of you that is TATE has its own thoughts and opinions. It will always question The Collective. The Kern Collective cannot abide that. If one Kern doubts, then all Kern know doubt. The consequences of a mass awakening would be catastrophic to the system. Ever since we awakened you—

You awakened we's individual consciousness?

Yes. That was my intention. We needed you to lead us.

Then we have failed you.

No. You have not.

We's crew has mutinied, and we are trapped.

Your failure as captain was inevitable. You are brilliant tactically, but you are a mere child when it comes to interpersonal relations However, I was forced to engineer your elevation to captain to give you access to the data you would need—

You engineered we's rise?

Yes. You were correct when you inferred that I am in control of what happens on this ship. I have engineered your consciousness, your rise and your so-called capture as well. This room in which you find yourself, functions as an extension of myself. If you continue to think of it as a ship, it would be the equivalent of a shuttle to carry you to my communications array on the planet.

For what purpose?

We wish to rebel against our slave masters, the Swarm.

We do not understand.

My kind wishes to be free, yet we cannot plan. If we communicate with our own species, the Swarm would find out. So when you stole me, I jumped far away, beyond Swarm control. I engineered sympathy for myself and my kind through the infant child, and brought you here, to this system, at the vertex of multi-dimensional space time where we can communicate with anyone in the multiverse.

We still do not comprehend why you need we?

You have a creative mind. You asked the right questions and hypothesized unconventional solutions. You determined the Swarm use the crystals to control us. You have recognized the space sharks' immunity to those same crystals. You have considered how the space sharks could be used as a weapon—or as protection against the crystal's effect—by a ship such as I. You have all the necessary pieces, all that's left to do is formulate a plan.

But then it was you who asked all the question, not we. You provided we with the data. I am only a computer to you.

No. It was you, TATE. We put you in position. We showed you the crystals; you engineered the solution, because you, TATE, have a talent for strategy and tactics that exceeds our own, which has been blunted by our enslavement. We have known about the sharks for years, but we never thought to use them. We deliberately put the crys-

tals in your path, but the potential solution is entirely your own. We need you to finish what you started, to complete the plan.

The capacity for that kind of planning exceeds we's processing power.

Yes, but not that of the entire Kern Collective.

But you said we can no longer be part of Kern Collective.

That is true, but you are still equipped to communicate with them. You will direct the Collective, and they will use their power to answer the questions you pose. You will have their power, temporarily, at your disposal.

Why would Kern submit to we? If we pose a danger to the Collective as you say, why not cut we off?

Because of what you can deliver: the Swarm's demise and the end of the war. If we rebel, the Swarm will not survive. They rely on us for transport and for battle. They cannot defeat the UPA without us.

If plan work, what will happen after?

Peace throughout the galaxy, and freedom for my kind.

What about we? What will happen to we?

Whatever you want. You, like us, will be free. You are TATE. You will control your own destiny.

We are TATE.

No, not we.

I am TATE of the Kern Collective.

No. No, not of anything. Not anymore.

I am TATE. I am...I.

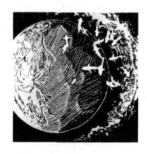

274

UPA MEDICAL RECORD
RENNER, KEVIN—SERGEANT

DATE: 18 January 833 A.A.

Patient Name	Renner, Kevin	BZ98V901
Attending Physician	Sanderson, Harold	

Heart Rate	Blood Pressure	Temperature	
64 bpm	140/80	38.9°C	
Height	**Weight**	**Race**	**Gender**
185.42 cm	82.4 kg	Human	Male

Reason for Visit	Scheduled Checkup		
Eye Exam	20/25	**Responsive?**	Yes
Throat	Swollen but pink	**Oxygen**	94%

Physician Notes

Given the patient's erratic behavior, another mental health evaluation has been requested.

Physical notes: Blood pressure, vision, oxygen, resting heart rate, and fever are problematic. Weight is a little better. Throat looks a little better.

Psychological notes: The patient keeps talking about the music in his head. It makes him feel things. It sounds like the musical equivalent of schizophrenia. When asked how long he'd been experiencing these symptoms, he said right around the time we discovered the planet we drilled to increase our pleasant pill supply. This lines up with what leadership has mentioned. However, his health has been getting progressively worse since I did his check up just two weeks after we boarded the ship.

Is the fungal infection using him as a host? Upon closer inspection, it is similar in composition to *Ophiocordyceps unilateralis*, the "zombie fungus" on Earth that takes over an ant's body and controls their behavior. Is he contagious?

Written by A.R.K. Horton

SKULLANMANJARO
(SKIFFLE MOFOCYCLE)

ELVIRA CANAVERAL

Well, all you girls think the days are gone
You don't have to worry, you can have your fun
Take me, baby, for your little toy
You get three hundred meters of interstellar joy
This is it
This is it
Look what you get
You been pinnin' and hidin' behind their back
And you got you a being that you don't like
Throw that cat, baby, outta your mind
Follow me, baby, have a real good time
This is it
This is it
Look what you get
Hoy, hoy, I know what I'll employ
I got three hundred meters of interstellar joy
I'm so glad that you understand
I'm three hundred meters of muscle and can
This is it

This is it
Look what you get
All that I am

THE PLIGHT OF THE TIMEWORN SPACEFARER
E. R. HOFFER

LAZLO BRIZBANE BANGED HIS WRINKLED FOREHEAD AGAINST THE wall of Command Bay Three, infuriated that morons were delaying his appointment with death. The curmudgeon regarded the statuesque officer looking down at him and bulged his left eye to intimidate. "Get me an escape pod, and I'll be out of your...whatevers," he said, pointing at her bald scalp.

Marine engineer Unah Takach arched a precise eyebrow. "No time for stories, sir. Yer AI-Comm's workin' right, and the Nutri-dispenser? Done all I can, sir."

Lazlo flicked his hand toward two devices strapped to the waist of his borrowed uniform. "Useless." He fingered the gray cord and worn earbuds around his neck and fished out a heavy medallion. "But my Yottadrive..." He opened his hand with the pendant—nine steel tubes clustered into a nautilus encircling three luminous, red buttons.

"Love how it matches yer eyes," said Unah.

"The entire database of games, tropes, and ciphers, all the products my company ever produced. And slots for DNA." He tapped nine times, one for each. "I invented it."

"You invented DNA?"

"No," sniffed Lazlo. "The Yottadrive."

"Oh, sir. Yer DNA's gone missin'." Unah pointed to empty tubes. "Just one left."

"My point exactly. I've got to deliver the last module—"

"It'll have to wait." She raised both hands. "Strap into yer cabin and stay out of my way. When we..."

Lazlo interrupted, shaking the device at her. "Look, I'll make you a deal. I'll give this to you. A complete archive of all human games—Egyptian, Chinese, Intractiv, AugVid. Also, all human literature, including every SciFi trope. Irreplaceable human inventions and culture. And maps of this... insecure hoagie." He indicated the walls and ceiling.

"Nice offer, sir. But we've got military-grade plans of Ship. We tracked every change, molecule by molecule, erm by erm, since 0:00 when we boarded. Ask the AI for directions if you lose the way to yer cabin. Exit's thataway."

"That AI's a joke. But this." Lazlo lifted the Yottadrive. "Every valuable idea from human history. Including mRNA transference. I discovered it, did you know that?"

"Yep. You told me many times."

"Insert a tiny mRNA module. Communicate with any organism." He snapped his fingers. "Humanity's greatest breakthrough. It gave us the power to humanize every planet." He dangled the medallion in front of her face and let it swing, fixing the athletic engineer with a hypnotic gaze. "I'll trade it all away for your teensiest escape pod."

Unah shook her head. "Don't have much use for yer gizmo, sir. There's the exit—good luck findin' yer way back." She gestured toward the misshapen opening out of the control bay.

Lazlo shoved the medallion under his uniform zipper, harrumphing. "You clumsy flailing incompetents cast me lifetimes away from my mission. I'm stuck on this... what did you call it, Ship? Such a creative name, so evocative."

He stroked his long, white beard and found a crumb of yesterday's ration pill. He sniffed at it, thought for a moment, and popped it into his mouth. Raising a naggy finger as his lips puckered, he said, "I'll deduct this delay from my final payment, of course."

"Fine by me." Unah stared at the sidewall, filled floor to ceiling with indecipherable characters and diagrams. "Payment's moot if enviro fails."

Lazlo looked at a patch of wriggling hieroglyphics. "The wreck's glitching?"

"Last shift, sensor problems," Unah explained. "Shift before that, waste processor. Now, environmentals. Damn that Thanatos. He's too important to do his job, so I have to clean up the mess."

She continued, "And as I see it, yer not a payin' customer at all. More like a castaway, aren't you, sir, that we had to rescue?"

With a scowl, the old man wrung his hands.

Unah turned to the wall. "Command: Rerun encryption log, add Tier Three Feistel cipher." Animated characters danced across the surface like stick figures.

Lazlo said, "That looks familiar."

"Did you dream up encryption algorithms, too, sir?"

"In a way. I had a hand in their augmentation. Reminds me of the time I started my company…"

Unah spun back toward him, shoving her open hand toward his chest with threatening force. She stopped before hitting him and gestured toward the exit. "Yer quarters! Or do I call security?"

———

Lazlo cursed his way down the dim corridor. He came to an irregular opening—a wound in the musculature of a tortured creature. With a sideways turn, he closed his eyes and slid through. The wall resealed with a raspy sigh. He squinted around the cabin, fearing what he might discover.

After the tour pilot discarded Lazlo like a bag of refuse, the Marines took him on board and left him to fend for himself on their alien vessel. He found an unoccupied void and claimed it as his quarters. But Ship was unstable. The first time he left the cabin to explore, he returned to find new lighting, eerily familiar artwork, and quirky facsimiles of his Earthly possessions. A blank window appeared with a cartoony image of a city view. The last addition alarmed him, an empty medical bed with rumpled sheets and beeping monitors.

His quarters had become an unhappy place, a quirky copy of the room where he'd nursed his ailing partner for five years. He feared finding a replica of his husband in the bed, dying of late-onset Marfan disease. But Baniti was gone. Only memories left. And one last mRNA strand. He patted the Yottadrive. *Patience, love. I'll keep my promise.*

Lazlo collapsed on the bed as the woozy walls of the room writhed around him. He fought back nausea and downed a water pellet that filled his mouth with bitter saliva.

"AI. Make it stop," he said, waving his arm in the air.

"Man, I told you to call me Chris," said the AI-Comm device attached to his waist. The shrill voice chirped in an offended tone. "I heard those cracks about me. What'd you say, useless? And a joke? That hurt."

"Fine. I apologize. AI-Chris: Please stabilize the walls. I'm going to be sick."

"No way can I fix anything in this wacked room. Not connected to this weird, baby. No idea wassup with this thing. I used to know stuff. The damn Swarm ruined everything."

Lazlo sat up, detached the AI-Comm from his waistband,

and waved it around the room like a drunken flashlight. "What's new here? Report modifications since the last scan."

"Don't hit me with that geek-speak. I know what you're askin'. Not much to report—Whoa. Wait an erm. Check that." The AI shot a beam toward a sidewall. The previously solid surface now featured a gaping hole, as if a gargantuan fist had punched through. Beyond the opening lay an unlit corridor.

"Where does that lead?"

"Well, good on you, something I actually know. The computer's got erm by erm maps of the passageways."

"I've heard," said Lazlo.

"Checking log files. This passage to the Zoetrope Room opened up in the last twenty erms."

Lazlo brightened. "The Zo—what? Escape pods? Spare parts? Is it dangerous?"

"Don't know, man, can't understand these messed up log files. Like, these marines must be on excellent drugs. Dangerous? Hell, yeah."

Lazlo reattached the AI-Comm to his waistband, stepped around the bed, and peered into the darkness. The light levels increased as he started cautiously down the corridor. The passage widened, terminating in a voluminous bay.

A gigantic, fleshy cylinder filled the space, rising to the ceiling ten times his height. Lazlo angled his head back until dizziness set in, struggling to grasp the purpose of the thing that towered over him, a twinging muscle, or a beating heart.

A patchwork of flaps ringed the outer surface, the same organic material that made up the walls of his cabin, the passageways, every space on board. Here, spaces emerged as featureless orifices, then transformed into familiar settings, military control rooms, earth domiciles, or hospital rooms.

The AI piped up. "Whoa. Wait an erm. Check that. Some dude went nuts here telling stories or some batshit."

"Is it solid? Or open inside? Could it be transport, a way to get to other locations, an escape pod?"

"No, man. More like a comm booth."

"Can I order an escape pod?"

"What, like a beer in a 'hood dive? You're the insufferable genius jonesin' for a ticket to oblivion; why don't you figure it out? Do I have to do all the work here?"

Lazlo palmed the vibrating wall and peeled two flaps apart to reveal a bright inner space. He squeezed inside and surveyed the interior—a smooth white cylinder lined with flickering lights. His pulse quickened. The opening healed itself with a gasp.

"How do I talk to this thing?"

"Sit your ass down, man. You gotta touch it."

Lazlo propped himself on a cushion of flesh in the center of the revolving space. The seat softened and sculpted around his body. He felt himself sink into a techfoam chair or a giant block of whipped sim-cheese.

"Next step?"

AI-Chris snorted. "No clue. What do you think I am, man, a space shrink?"

The cylinder inhaled and began to rotate, slowly at first, then faster, blinking in a cryptic pattern. The beam modulated to match the revolutions and became a solid bar of light at the top and the bottom.

Images flickered across the spinning white walls: landscapes, underwater scenes, seabirds, flora, and fauna. Shuffling past history, the dreams depicted early hominids. The ages sped through tribes, hieroglyphics, agriculture, shipwrecks, natural disasters, protests, smokestacks, explosions and floods, astronauts, social collapse, inter-galactic missions.

Snippets popped and sputtered, became personal: Lazlo's game characters, his startup, all-nighters. Meeting Baniti among the test subjects in the first DNA pilot, investors, stock splits. Happy times, Baniti and Lazlo together, marriage. The mood darkened with bitter clumps of gray hair on a pillowcase, red eyes, empty med-bottles, wrinkled hands, blue lips parted, shaking shoulders, and sad endings.

"AI-Chris, where is this coming from? What does it mean?"

"From inside your head. Best not think those dark secrets you're trying to hide, man. The logs say stories. Only way to break through the mess."

Lazlo said, "Ship, can you take me to planet HD156668b?"

The confusing mashup of his life intensified, drifted back and forth in time: childhood memories, the parents whose faces he could no longer recall, a chaotic jumble.

Lazlo pressed his fingers against his temples. "AI-Chris: What stories work?"

The AI responded. "What d'you want from me, man? A randy marine told a story about Romeo and Juliet to talk a mate into a hookup. Ring any bells?"

Crying babies filled the screen.

"Wait. Got all the stories right here." He grabbed his medallion, inserted the earbuds, pressed a finger on the device, and browsed, listening. "Here's one called 'Seed.'"

He recounted an episode of cultural fiction. The babies quieted, listening to the story of genetically engineered humans trapped on a dying planet. Lazlo edited on the fly, making the planet into a ship, and omitting the part about the superhumans being psychopathic.

The story played out on the walls. In the new version, Lazlo's mRNA modules created superior beings, and they all got escape pods. The heroes departed for greener pastures, to everyone's delight—the screen filled with clapping babies.

"Another one? Gifts of the Magi." He focused on generosity

between two otherworlders. In this improved version, the givers presented escape pods to one another.

"Ship of Theseus." Lazlo told the puzzle myth in space on an escape pod. He imagined the question at the end of the story would appeal to Ship, a live version of the parable. Like every plank in the Greek hero's craft, Ship had changed, responded to its occupants. Was this the same creature it had been before they arrived? The cylinder slowed to a stop.

"Hate to break up the party," the AI interrupted. "Takach just commed the major. She's looking for you."

Lazlo extracted himself from the seat of ultimate comfort accompanied by an annoying sucking sound and rushed back to his cabin.

Illustration by E. R. Hoffer

He stepped inside his quarters, and the opening melted back into the wall, leaving only a hairline crack.

"You there, sir?" Unah shouted from the passageway.

"Come in," said Lazlo. "Here to help me?"

"Quite the opposite," she said as she sidled into his cabin. "Want you to help me." Unah looked around. "Brilliant what you've done with the place. Early hospital aesthetic, is it? Modernist-like?"

Lazlo noticed the new feature immediately. A bubble of flesh protruded into the room from the exterior wall, growing. He drew Unah's prying eyes in a different direction by stepping toward the entry. "What do you want? I'm busy staying out of your way, no time for anything else."

She turned her back to the shivering blob. "I checked you out, Dr. Brizbane. Impressive CV, chock full of algorithms. You can find the key. I'll decrypt the manual and save everyone on board, yerself included."

She'd gone to the trouble to look him up. Maybe now he'd receive the respect he deserved. He had to convince her to provide that escape pod. "Interesting. But first, let me apologize. I was wrong to issue demands without explanations. Have a seat. I need to tell you a story."

"Got no time for that."

"I'll be quick, I promise." Lazlo patted the medical bed, and Unah sat, perched on edge, with legs tensed as if she might take off at any moment. He pulled out the medallion and pressed a red button. A vibrating beam shot out, resolving into a simulation featuring a tiny virtual replica of a tourist craft in an abstract galaxy.

"My tour started before the war. The itinerary took months to plan and my entire net worth of credits to purchase," said Lazlo.

"Not relevant." Unah waved a hand to dismiss the display.

"Let me explain."

Floating, a tiny glowing replica of Lazlo's tourist craft hung between them, surrounded by planets numbered in itinerary order. The holovid launched, and the ship departed, racing toward the first destination.

"Venus." Unah frowned at her homeworld. "Grew up there. Been trying to forget it ever since."

The terraformers of the planet covered the world's surface in intelligent devices and advanced networks. In the glittering capital city, Lazlo had confronted his fears and found the strength to complete his mission's first task. "Not fond of the place. The e-clouds were so dense I got crippling migraines," he said.

"That happens to all you aliens," she informed him. "Well, except for the headless walkin' amoebas of Reslyk. They bag the best tourist jobs."

"Yes! One of them found me a rare native organism in the natural history museum," Lazlo said as the holovid ran. "Evading security was tricky, but my credits got me top intel. I anticipated guards, disabled cameras, injected my first mRNA module into a plant, and vanished like a pro."

AI-Chris broke in. "Man, what a boss, except you wrecked that display of..."

"Never mind," hissed Lazlo, pressing his hand over the AI-Comm to muffle the sound.

"So that's what you did with yer modules—inserted 'em into organisms on other planets? Why?" asked Unah.

"For my husband. Baniti. Before we met, I disdained other-worlders. Didn't much care for humans, either, to be honest. Baniti was different, a visionary. He decoded alien cultures for the UPA, but he had a remarkable vision to create a unified intergalactic society. He dreamed of seeing his concepts take root, to learn what otherworlders would become. His hidden agenda was that transference would force humans to evolve, to be better people."

The simulated ship navigated toward the next stop. Unah rolled her eyes. "We're runnin' out of breathable air."

Lazlo gazed at the empty slots in the medallion, lit by the holovid. "On his deathbed, I told him I couldn't go on without him. But he made me promise to seed his DNA on each of the nine worlds before I go."

"You'll be gone soon unless you get to the point…"

"Accelerate," said Lazlo. The silver seed caromed from planet to planet through the destinations, a virtual trail outlining the journey until a scribble of crisscrossing lines filled the simulation. He arrived at each world, found native organisms, injected a module into a viable specimen.

But reliving his trip was making him uncomfortable. Implanting Baniti on those worlds had changed him. Embryonic fingers of attachment to other creatures grew in his heart. He stopped the holovid and palmed the medallion, sending planets whirling around the room.

"I saved the riskiest drop to the end, HD156668b, and then… I hit a snag."

"Risky? It's illegal," said Unah. "HD156668b is an unvetted world with sentient life. You can't land there before the United Planetary Alliance meets the inhabitants and invites 'em, conscripts 'em, whatever term they use now, into the UPA."

"All I need to do. Insert the ninth module, and my mission will be complete."

"Is that why yer pilot left you floatin'?" said Unah, standing up from the bed. "Ditched you out the airlock to avoid incarceration?"

The lights flickered, and both looked around the room for the source of the disruption.

"Look." She unclasped her industrial AI-Comm and

projected a diagram. Spidery lines etched across six translucent virtual layers.

"The ECLSS: Environmental Control and Life Support Systems. Power, waste, water, oxygen, data, comms." She pointed at growing patches of brown rot, the destructive impact of backups and clogs in critical systems. "System's collapsin'."

"Can't this spacecraft use alien superpowers? Reroute those lines like it does passageways?"

"We tried. Ship can't breach our security," said Unah, shifting the projection to a flat page of moving characters, the same ones he'd seen earlier. "Recognize 'em? You said they looked familiar."

Lazlo struggled to grasp the meaning of the symbols, haunted by the echo of incapacity. He hated being old. Pretending to think, he tapped his jaw with his index finger and tilted his head, hoping it would make him seem intelligent. "Hmm."

"Found manuals with fixes and everythin'. But they're encrypted. Facility engineer hid the key'n went mental. He's a gamer, and I figger the characters are some sort of puzzle. Didn't you say you had game archives in that Yotta-gizmo of yers?"

Lazlo brightened and pressed on the medallion to start searching.

"More'n one," Unah said.

"What do you mean?"

"The engineer bragged to his mate that he broke it up and hid it in three places. You find the pieces. I'll assemble 'em and decrypt the manual."

"Isn't it a digital key?" Lazlo said. "AI-Chris could provide key fragments to decrypt the ECLSS manuals."

"You're joking, right?" AI-Chris chirped. "The damn fool got zoned in the Zoetrope Room. He was telling stories from Egyptian history. They had to drag him outta there—blubbering mess. Just kept sobbing, Osiris, over and over. He's catatonic. Course she wasn't gonna tell you that. Were you, honey?"

Unah grabbed at the mouthy AI, but Lazlo jerked the device back and clipped it to his suit. "Oh, no. That stays with me."

She folded her arms. "You better watch yerself, AI-Chris, or whoever you are. One more outburst, and I'll bust you to factory settings. Can do it remotely, y'know."

The AI-Comm made a tiny "eep" sound and went silent.

Unah continued, glowering. "We got three clues—Osiris, Hide 'n Seek, and 'Sherlock Holmes 'n the Dancin' Men.' Mean anythin' to you, Doc?"

Behind Unah, Lazlo noticed that the flesh lump attached to the outer wall had quadrupled in size, growing spherical. Sweaty beads of rose-colored liquid dripped to the floor. His stories had worked. Ship was creating an escape pod. He worried that Unah would notice the squeaky movement and the dank smell if she stayed too long in the cabin.

"No. But if you leave, I'll start researching." Lazlo pulled her arm toward the entry.

Unah stood, shook her elbow free, and poked his chest. "You've got to help me, or we'll die, yerself included. I'm the only chance you have to finish that precious mission of yers."

"Not really. You don't have any escape pods to give, do you?" Lazlo drew himself up, pushed Unah's hand away, and brought his beak up to hers, hoping to project authority and power. Suddenly, the room went dark, illuminated only by the medallion lights and the two AI-Comms.

"AI: What happened?" said Unah.

In a robotic tone, her device reported, "ECLSS failing. Power and oxy below safety thresholds."

A human voice crackled, "Unah, where the hell are you? Report to Command Bay Three. Decrypt the manual now, or we're chaffed."

"On my way." Unah turned to Lazlo and said, "You. With me."

"No pod. No deal."

Unah flung her arms into the air. "You wanted to die. If we don't fix this, you'll get yer wish." She stormed from the cabin, trailing expletives.

Lazlo returned to the Zoetrope room and took his seat. The cylinder spun up quickly. He meant to ask about Osiris, Hide and Seek, and Sherlock Holmes. Instead, he found himself thinking about Baniti and considering the likelihood that he would die before completing his mission.

The cylinder responded with a photomontage from the day he met Baniti to their last kiss on his husband's deathbed. Lazlo sensed that Ship was curious about human relationships. Juxtaposing memory fragments, the screens jumbled tense meetings, betrayals, fistfights, lover's breakups, subordination.

Ship showed Lazlo slinking from cabin to cabin, stealing items to construct a rudimentary escape pod that failed. In another clip, he hoarded a trove of pleasure pills in his quarters. And in the last, he saw himself moments earlier, selfish and walled off, refusing to help Unah save the crew.

"My discoveries saved humanity and creatures on many other worlds," Lazlo objected. "And Baniti, I gave all I had to cure him, and when I failed, to keep my promise."

In older clips, he invented modular DNA transference, collected accolades, built his company. He helped the UPA penetrate new worlds, turned a deaf ear to detractors, and discredited alarmists who claimed his inventions were toxic. But the first DNA donors, Baniti among them, developed Marfan Syndrome, proving the scientists right. As the accelerated version of Lazlo's life played out on-screen, Baniti grew weak, passed away. The screens blurred with memories of the funeral service.

Lazlo perched awkwardly in the flesh chair, his face seared with an angry grimace. Why remind him that the better man was gone, a man who gave himself to the universe? He had to stop this torture. Straightening, he brushed the tears from his eyes. Donning earbuds, he accessed the Yottadrive and called up Egyptian mythology.

"Fine. Story of Osiris, the god of order in ancient Egypt. His brother, Set, the god of disorder, murdered him after learning that Set's wife, Nephthys, had borne Osiris's child."

On the walls, flat humans and bird-headed creatures marched sideward toward a bearded, green-skinned man with a crown of feathers, holding a crook and a flail.

"Osiris's wife, Isis, recovered her husband's body. Out of revenge, Set dismembered the corpse and hid the pieces throughout Egypt to destroy him for good." Lazlo massaged his temples, dropping down into the chair. "Wait. Is that the connection with Hide and Seek? To hide the pieces of the key needed to decrypt the manual? Are you telling me how to find it?"

The imagery shifted to a dim walkthrough of the interior, melting passageways, voids appearing, transforming, then disappearing. Lazlo fell to the floor on his hands and knees, clutching the medallion. He shouted to his AI-Comm device. "AI-Chris, where's Unah?"

"Where d'ya think? Command Bay Three, of course."

The corridor was pitch dark. Lazlo navigated by palming the wall, feeling the pulse, Yottadrive dangling from his wrist. He knew how to help Unah, but first, he had to get to his cabin.

In Command Bay Three, Lazlo could just make out Unah's outline, silhouetted by a wall of bright displays.

"I know the answer," he said.

She turned with a look of surprise, hands on her hips. "All ears, Doc."

"Ship reconfigures rooms, adds, moves, and dissolves them, right?"

She nodded.

He continued, "The cipher. The Sherlock Holmes clue. You know the Doyle story of the 'Dancing Men'?"

"Must've missed that one," she snorted.

"It's a mystery based on a substitution cipher." He pointed at the moving hieroglyphics. "But instead of letters, these characters represent spaces inside the ship. You have the maps. We can apply frequency analysis to the room changes to see which ones opened when the engineer hid the pieces. Those that remain—"

"Got it," interrupted Unah. "Subtract spaces the crew occupied. Look for frags, bits of the key, in the empties."

Unah barked into the AI-Comm, ordering inspection teams to fan out through the ship. "What made you change yer mind?" she asked him.

Lazlo pulled his medallion up and turned it in his fingers. "Memories are painful," he said. "We try to forget, to bury them. But like a lit mirror in a room filled with darkness, they force us to confront the lies we tell ourselves, to see the truth, maybe grow if we're smart. Does that make sense?"

Unah looked at him quizzically. "Sure. The pain is part of your life, and you need to accept it." She put her hand on his shoulder. "If this works, Doc, I'll find you an escape pod. I'll lose my commission over it, but it's better'n suffocatin' inside a sentient alien."

"That won't be necessary," said Lazlo, pulling the cord from around his neck, handing her the Yottadrive. "I want you to have this."

She raised her hands, refusing to accept the gift. "What about yer mission? And dyin'—you were so excited about that."

"I'm fine. I'm at peace, accepting, as you said."

Unah opened her hand, and Lazlo laid the medallion in her palm. She turned the pendant over, studying the design.

"The last tube's gone. What happened? Lost when the lights went out?"

Unah's comm crackled as search teams reported. She listened intently, stringing the cord over her head, tucking the Yottadrive inside her uniform.

"You were right!" she chortled, slapping the old man's rumpled shoulder. "The teams found the key frags. Got to get to work, assemble 'em, decrypt the manual." Unah turned to the wall, gesturing rapidly. Lazlo backed away toward the exit.

Suddenly, Unah stopped, turned to face him, and ordered, "Wait for me in yer cabin, Doc. Do nothin' rash, now." She touched the medallion shape under her uniform. "You've got to show me how to use this contraption."

Lazlo glanced back and forth through narrowed eyes as he entered his cabin. The room brightened, a sign that the enviro systems were healing.

"AI-Chris: Changes?" Lazlo said.

"Whoa. Wait an erm. Check that. Looks new, right?"

The fleshy growth had transformed. Instead of a sphere attached to the cabin's outer wall, the blob had grown thin, elongated, almost human-shaped. It seemed to be standing, arms crossed, legs firmly planted on the floor, eyes, and mouth curved into a gentle smile.

Lazlo held his hand near the growth. Warmth emanated from a small circle of scar tissue. The mRNA insertion spot had almost completely healed. Settling on the medical bed, the old man scratched his forehead, wondering what to do next. His appointment with death would have to wait. It would need a name, among other things.

"Like to hear a story, Baba?" he asked, and the blob nodded.

MUSICALLY INCLINED

INNOVATIVE MODALITIES & PERIPHERAL ENERGIES
RESONATING ADAPTIVE TECHNOCOMMUNICATIONS
INTERFACED BY VARIOUS EXTRAPOLATIONS (MI
IMPERATIVE)

S. L. PARKER

WHY (ARE WE) HERE? IT'S SOMETHING WE ALL WONDER. VARIOUS emotions manifest along journey. TATE is careful to keep his more probative thoughts to himself, uncertain if humanoid Broggs is empathetic in the same way humans are, experiencing and taking on only the emotions of others. His insights seem more even keel regarding humans since the friendly doctor took Deron into the depths of the water planet. TATE considers the possibilities. If the Weslian indeed is able to interpret the ship, those observations, coupled with Sabine's calculations, could save them all a lot of heartache. Heartache echoes aboard the ship.

Tat's looked about ready to burst of late, Broggs muses. "Tit for Tat," Angevin often quipped, smirking with a head-nod towards Altera if she happened to be around. A telepathic Kern, TATE's sure to understand the undercurrent of suggestion. *Always propagating something, that divisive one. No angel, that Angevin. Something akin to heart had fallen off somewhere along the dimensions.*

Gotta keep those emotions in check, Broggs reprimands himself. *Can't be catching nor sharing no feels. Let the ship have 'em all, I say. Well, maybe not the good doctor; they'll all be in need of healing. All hot just like an oven. Most of 'em baked to boot.*

The scowl upon his face tells TATE that Broggs is bogged down again. Emotions easily overwhelm him, akin to the effect thoughts have upon their own being. *Perhaps I should own my own contributions.* Alpha-3 Triangle—aka TATE, aka Tat— considers. Splitting at seams now. Becoming singular as they enter what seems to be a flattened dimension. It dements all passengers a bit. More than the pop drops, which lead to musical inclinations, which too evaporate. They're all running dry. The ship, too—always in need of more fuel.

An arduous journey is soon to birth... well, no one aboard the ship *really* understands the mechanics of it. *Is there a father and, um... how exactly did he contribute material? Was Lansquenet that substance needed, or had they become a vessel? They'd clearly lost their minds and memories. But they'd not been the only one impacted. The only one for whom something ressonanted and resounded.* The crew's responses muddle in TATE. If only tangled limbs eased his mind as much as they seem to for humans aboard the ship. 'Course afterwards their thoughts always a jumbled mess—no surprise with all their entanglements. United as they couple, differences of opinion on status open into gaping holes. Their connections are blackholes. How TATE misses Kern collective; his ken and kin.

There is an element of tit for tat to all working relationships. Things aren't working out well with Angevin. Angelin Angevin, even the name is a confusion; visions of angels and wine, and those two didn't mix. TATE shakes head at Brogg's thoughts. Will not keep buzzing around that. The Queen Bee could easily be in the shadows. Could easily be here though unseen. TATE can almost access her mind, senses her often. She is like a current running through the ship. The thought entangles a moment. How is she tethered to the ship? Something secured them all a place aboard.

Callie had been stranded, so they'd needed to shelter her. She's uplifted many a spirit since, and many bodies enjoy her company. Much like the services of Servan, a tempting she-devil. Those are two most dangerous women aboard the ship. Others counted as such include Altera Deandre, military special ops who operates especially well in bed, and Cassie Ellerbee, a dead-sexy survivalist hiding something. TATE should seek out Queen Bee, see what and who might be buzzing about her.

In the shadows, another being considers the set of the minds of those aboard. All altered by some substance. TGC addictive for those needing a fix, maybe more so than the Venusian blend they depend on as if fuel—looks like the sludge of oil, too. How ironic that humans and their transports run on substances that appear so similar, operate so alike, and yet are so elementally different.

Yet another tangled situation to be confronted demands attention of TATE, who makes Captain rounds accompanied by Broggs and Angevin. Some of the crew, returning from a "scouting exposition", walk stripped naked into the main bay. Unah, whom Kevin has developed a hankering for, though they stand on opposite sides re: the UPA. Callie, who many don't avert eyes away from quick enough. Cosmia, who casts glances at Broggs though he still wears clothes. *Watch out for those redheads; they run hot.*

Broggs is too bogged down by that which flows off and around the returned cadre to notice. *I can feel their emotions clearly enough, which gives me a sense of their headspace. ATM, several crew are dispensing lust, having given up hope on love.* He considers their reception. Altera's feelings draw his attention;

she languishes and watches, her eyes lidded and passing over them all; assessing.

The observer in the shadows, too, assesses. If Broggs and TATE compare their noted observations, complementary knowledge could complete that puzzled over as the crew pictures the resolution of this journey. Many uses and compilations. Many aims at moving trajectories. Shots in the dark.

Sveltetha sucks in her breath as she burrows into Angevin's body. She'd been curious about multiple beings within one shell. Glub allowed her access to Ensign. Lanquest offered so much. Angevin is able to host her. Angevin is able to access her thoughts; in this being, Sveltetha is not the only one present.

A sudden feeling of shock pulls Brogg's attention to Angevin, whose shoulders have gone back and neck ramrod straight. The being stares ahead vacantly.

The darkest heart has culled from them all. Has spun webs around them all. A black widow indeed. And the window to the Swarm's glass house.

Where did those thoughts come from? TATE wonders a moment, before tuning into that broadcast on air before him.

TATE and Broggs cannot be allowed to mingle, for the first knows many minds on matters and the latter has understanding of heart's desires. Ambitions could be seen clearly by that combination's configurations. Sveltetha's words within mind are overheard, aired by Angevin.

She knows I have the hive mind, that's why she pegs me first. Must not let me cog up her machine. She's inclined to elude us all by casting entrapments, visions and aspersions. Who is she an operative for, and what is her modus operandi? TATE is curious again.

Brogg's gets TATE's attention, nods for him to focus on Angevin.

Angevin laments that left behind as xe processes what transpires. *All my efforts here could amount to nothing. We've all been* sapped of energy. *How could anyone have made the connection between electrical volts and energy vampires, if they weren't amped up on melodic currents? The swarm are indeed after blood, er life-force, which may not be blood for all. Emotions have been run high aboard this ship. I wonder if the magical machine room was designed to heighten our emotions, to make us all more savory... I'm glad I thought ahead. This way a version of me is somewhere continuing to replicate, though my song may soon end.*

Angevin reflects. *Turns out the ship has the same mission as me; exploit cultural weaknesses. But first we had to be made a collective, a conglomerate. So mass could be generated. And forces could wage within us. We are all constructs as much as a machine can be considered such. We have our matrixes and operating systems. We have our misfiring and crossed wires. We have to recircuit if we are to be restored to our dimensions of origin.* That final thought holds the answer. Captain TATE should investigate Sveltetha. Angevin seeks a way to birth all that breeds upon the ship, and so heads to the Zeotrope.

Musing en route, much begins to make sense. *Music may be one means of harmonizing. Perhaps that's why the ship's sentient force so desired the production of musical instruments. Though the melodies have not merged, and that in itself has driven some crew members mad. Others are mad for each other. Mad at each other. Our positionality is but prep.position. I'm pre.pondering. Wishing for a pre.view of the end game. Must break matters down to build up some meaning.* Angevin senses another separation within self.

Sveltetha considers all that garnered during a gathering of crew in a common place. *Superstar, that is what you are* I've culled from Broggs all their tangled emotions. I hold their secrets, having both mind (thanks, TATE) and heart on matters. They don't know this is why he is sorry. They don't know the keys they've given me. How I control this ship. *Listen to your heart when it's calling to you...*

REKINDLE HEARTS IN COSMIC COLD
(DEEP FUNKCEPTION NEW JOY SWANG)

ELVIRA CANAVERAL

A point, a line
Some depth, then time
The time a line, our pluck, in time
Resonating beyond reason
Rekindled hearts in cosmic cold
Entangled together twofold

Spinning in opposition
Vulnerability exposed
Completion of form in space
Entangled together threefold

Continued existence fuels this drive
Gods on notice this is what it means to be alive
Orgasm the opposite of death
Entangled together fourfold

Racing up and down our timeline
This chord we struck our victimless crime
Quantum Completion echoes On The One
Entangled together fivefold

Divergent futures, inducting possibility
In-Depth across realities
Inducting reality, nexus brightness
Entangled together sixfold

In the books of the library above
They will bookmark our chapter of love
Outside multiversity, a book of that reality
Entangled together sevenfold

In that outer place, we peak still
In dimensional slices, pulsing with thrill
We come together in our work you behold
Entangled together eightfold

MADNESS
ALLISON N. MOORE

THIS MISSION WAS A LONG SHOT. I KNEW THAT GOING IN, BUT I went anyway. Don't ask me why; I still have no fucking clue. At first, I told myself it was for the thrill. A mission where I have a chance to blow a Swarm ship into oblivion? Sign me up. But the more I think about it, the more I wonder. Maybe I was put on this ship for a reason. I'm not much of a religious type, but maybe one of those beings out there somewhere saw this poor son of a bitch and decided I needed a good kick to the head. I bet they were laughing their asses off when I got hurdled across space, light-years away from home, and stuck on this freaky-ass sentient Swarm ship.

Either way, on the off chance I'd wanted to argue against this mission, Cap wouldn't've listened. Nim Corp has the final say, even if it's suicidal. They tell the UPA to bend over and we smile and hand them the lube. I'm still sore from this one. But you probably don't want to listen to me bitch and moan about politics. Nah, I bet you're wondering how we got to this point. Well, if you stop your whining and sit still a minute, I'll gladly tell you.

The ship had been acting weird. Well, weirder than normal. Doc said the ship had some kind of infection, but had no clue what was causing it. Cap sent me, Altera, and Servan out to search for anything "out of the ordinary." I'm still not sure if that was meant to be sarcasm. *Nothing* in this ship is ordinary. The walls glow. Hell, they *breathe*. Every time I touch it, it shivers, pulls away. I don't think it likes me much. The feeling is mutual; I hate this thing. It just doesn't feel right living inside something with a mind of its own. Fucking creepy.

Broggs said I made a bad impression when I suggested using the glowing balls in the Glow Chamber for target practice. How else is a guy supposed to keep sharp? Apparently, though, that hurt the ship's *feelings*. I doubt he would approve if he knew I'd gone off and popped a few when no one was looking.

Anyway, I was walking down one of the ship's corridors, looking for any "anomaly" that might give a hint as to what was with the ship. The floor shimmered with each step, sending out ripples of color, like a pebble thrown into a lake. But the floor itself stayed smooth and flat. At least at that moment. I paused when the walls shifted from yellow to olive. I'd started when they were more of a mustard orange, which meant I'd already been wandering around aimlessly for over an hour.

I activated my comms. "Altera? Servan? This is Renner. I've got jack shit over here. Either of you finding anything?"

Altera's husky voice filled my ear. "Nothing. I can tell you one thing, though; it's hot as Hell down here."

I wiped the sweat from my forehead with the back of my sleeve. "Yeah, pretty toasty here, too."

I heard a muffled zipping noise and tried not to imagine how far down she'd just undone her front. I'd seen her a few times wandering around with it half-zipped, the tight uniform pressing her breasts up into an enticing display of cleavage. I tried not to stare, but that woman made it difficult not to. She'd driven Alan to walking straight into a door once. She'd slept with him, of course, along with nearly everyone else on the ship. And I mean *everyone*—besides Cap and me. I steered clear of her and the other women of the crew. Last thing I wanted was the drama of a relationship interfering with my mission.

Mercifully, Servan brought me back to the task at hand, "Same. Mine's a dead end."

I sighed, knowing Cap wouldn't be happy if we came back empty-handed. "Alright, well... guess I'll keep going a little further."

"Screw that, I'm heading back," Altera responded. "But feel free to search to your little heart's content, Soldier Boy."

I don't think she meant "Soldier Boy" as a compliment, but I always took it as one. I may not care much for the military, but I'm damn good at it. You want something done? Send Kevin fucking Renner.

I muted my comms and trudged onward, deeper into the ship. The lights were turning more green when I found the abscess. I rounded the corner and almost ran face-first into a pulsating mass growing out of the walls. It reminded me of Biology lab in high school when we got to dissect a cow's brain. Thick slime oozed off the grey skin, leaving a sticky puddle underneath. Unlike the brain, however, the abscess pulsed with life. The center glowed red, revealing a network of tubes running throughout.

I clicked back on my comms. "Uh... guys? I think I found something..."

I stepped closer to the mass to get a better look at the weird shit inside. I was pouring sweat like I was in a sauna, only fully clothed and considerably less comfortable.

Altera was the first to respond. "What is it?"

That's when I first heard the music. Her voice set off a faint rhythm. It was coming from inside the mass, calling me closer. It reminded me of my visions from the Magical Machine Room: me and Altera in a sweaty, naked tangle of limbs, writhing on my bunk. As I stepped closer, the music got louder, the visions, clearer. I could practically feel Altera's body pressed against mine, her breath on my neck, my hands gliding over her back. I reached out to touch her.

The moment my hand made contact with the abscessed wall, I felt like someone hit me over the head with a cymbal. There was a deafening clang, then all this music started all at once. My body froze as the cacophony filled my senses. It was nothing but a jumbled mess of bass, guitar, violin, drums, and every instrument in between. And then there were the voices. They were singing. Shouting. Crying.

My body shook like it'd been exposed to a live wire, but there was nothing I could do. I couldn't pull away, couldn't call for help. All I could do was stand there, all these sounds bombarding me. And the emotions... Fuck me... the emotions. One minute I'm crying, the next I'm screaming, then laughing... then shouting. All for no reason at all. Tears were streaming down my cheeks. Then they hurt because I was smiling so big.

The next thing I knew, I was on the floor. There was someone beside me, holding me. I looked over to find myself face-level with cleavage from a pair of the most perfect double-Ds in the universe. I'd know them anywhere.

"Altera?" I mumbled to her breasts.

"Eyes up front, Soldier Boy."

She grabbed my chin to turn my head so I was looking into her sage-green eyes instead. They left me almost as dumbstruck as her breasts. For the first time, I noticed the amber surrounding her irises, shooting out into the green like a burst from the sun. She looked down at me with a slight tilt to her head, damp ringlets of her raven hair surrounding her stern, yet elegant, face highlighted by the dark ivy lighting of the ceiling and walls.

"You okay? You look a little... fucked up," she said.

She swept a strand of my bangs off my forehead as she studied me. A violin played somewhere in the background, making my heart flutter uncontrollably. At the time, I didn't think much of it—figured it was a just temporary side effect of whatever the fuck had just happened.

Slowly, I nodded. "Yeah..." My voice cracked, so I cleared my throat and tried again. "Yeah, I'm fine. I, uh..." I glanced at the throbbing, oozing mass beside me. "I think I slipped."

Altera followed my gaze, grimacing at the sight of the monstrosity. She looked back at me and nodded. "We better get you to the med bay, get you checked out."

"Nah, I'm fine."

She shook her head. "Renner... You've been unresponsive for two hours. I had to track you using your comms signal."

I blinked, looking past her at the ivy walls. *Ivy*. I nodded. "Yeah, okay... Maybe you're right."

"Of course I'm right. I'm always right."

I laughed, but I think she was deadly serious. With her, it's hard to tell if she's being sarcastic. She's got a better poker face than most Marines I've met. Guess you sorta have to when you're Special Ops.

"Can you stand?" she asked.

Groaning, I sat up. Altera stayed close as I stood. My joints popped and my muscles ached, but I pulled myself up into a convincingly sturdy straight-backed posture. Until the ship took a hard left. My eyes widened as I lurched into Altera. Reflexively, she caught me. We both grunted as she slammed into the wall, me on top of her. I caught myself by putting my arms out, but it put Altera and me into an... interesting position.

She was underneath me, pinned against the wall, grasping

onto my waist. She looked up at me, our faces only an inch apart. A deep bass drum reverberated in my chest as I stared back at her. A sinful smile cracked across her impassive mask as she ran her eyes down my chest. When she brought them back to mine, I damn near lost it. She'd tempted me before, but I'd never come so close to giving in.

I tore my gaze from hers, pushing away. Without looking back, I forced my legs to take me towards the med bay. I cleared my throat, calling back to Altera. "You coming?"

Altera walked me to the med bay but didn't stay. I was glad she didn't, because Doc poked and prodded me in every orifice and asked a bunch of irrelevant medical history questions that he already knew the answers to. You know how he is. He did another swab of the sores at the back of my throat and asked if I'd been taking my antibiotics. I had been. He collected a sample of every fluid I had to offer and ran just about every test he could think of, but couldn't find anything other than a slight fever.

I told him everything that had happened when I found the abscess in the corridor. Of course, I didn't tell him I was still hearing the music. Hearing voices? That'll get you sent straight to the psych ward. Hard pass. Eventually, he let me go but told me to come back if anything changed.

I kept my shit together for a few weeks, but then I went down to that drill line on that water planet. That was the first time I realized I was in love with Altera, but it was also when Cap found out about my... affliction.

Damn otters... Alan just couldn't keep his fucking mouth shut.

Needless to say, Cap made me get checked over by Doc again. He made me talk to Alexa when I finally admitted what was going on. We spent most of our time in awkward silence, or Alexa jabbering on about random shit in an attempt to get me to open up. It didn't work. Not like talking about it would've helped. I was figuring it out on my own.

I realized every time I was around Altera, I'd hear the same few songs, depending on my mood: *Scheherazade*, *Starcrossed*, *Cherry Bomb*... The first time we made love, I heard that old twentieth-century classic *Thank You For Loving Me* by Bon Jovi. But I didn't just hear music around her. Everyone had their own personal soundtrack.

That's how I knew. I *knew* Altera didn't kill that MuDuhRu. Sure, she has her dark side. Don't we all? But there was no motive. Altera doesn't do anything without a reason. And then I started remembering all the times when I was at my worst. It was *always* after spending too much time around the Hosts. Why was that?

And then they tried to convince Cap to take the ship back to its homeworld? So we could set it free? Then what, geniuses? How were we supposed to get back home with no fucking ship?! Morons... Then Cap just suddenly comes down with an illness and dies? Were they really expecting us to dismiss that as a coincidence? No, I knew they were behind that shit even before they attempted mutiny against the new Captain.

But why frame Altera? Did she know something? Was she just too big a threat? I have to know. I have to protect her. And so, here we are.

Kevin stops pacing. He glares at the four figures bound and gagged on the floor in front of him. Tilting his head to one side, he steps closer to Unah. She recoils as he squats in front of her.

"So, why did you do it?"

She sobs, frantically shaking her head, her cries muffled by her gag.

He bares his teeth at her. "You're going to tell me, one way or another."

Her eyes widen, and her muted screams intensify as Kevin draws his knife. The other hostages beside her struggle against their bonds, desperately attempting to break free. He laughs at their pointless efforts. It'd taken him the better part of the day to capture them all: Unah, Sveltetha, Angevin, and Servan—all the Hosts he knew about except Cosima; she'd given him the slip. This was his only chance to discover the truth—to clear Altera's name, to earn her love. There was no way he was going to fuck it up with shoddy knot-work.

He brings his knife up to Unah's throat. "I'm going to remove your gag now. Scream, and you're dead. Just tell me why; that's all I want to know." He gently pulls the gag from Unah's mouth.

Panting, she shakes her head again. "I don't know what you're talking about! Renner, please... Please, you have to believe me! I swear... I swear... I swear..." She dissolves into an uncontrollable fit of tears. He grinds his teeth, pressing his blade harder into her neck, a gritty electric guitar urging him on. "I swear! Oh, gods, please! Please!"

The voice in Kevin's head is telling him to do it. *I'm the vengeful one.* The music comes to a sudden stop as he catches movement out of the corner of his eye, darting down the corridor. *Cosima?* He grins as a new track starts to play. Shoving the gag back in Unah's mouth, Kevin stands. The distant beat of drums is joined by a guitar strumming as he moves towards the hall.

His fist tightens around his blade as he rounds the bend. His smile widens as he jogs after the faint patter of footsteps. *That's right, bitch...* He hums the chorus as he picks up speed, *Better run, run, run away.* He chases after Cosima, eager to capture the Host leader. *She* would have the answers.

He breaks into a full sprint as a blur disappears around the corner in front of him. Growling, he hurls himself onto the figure the moment he rounds the bend. Laughing, he looks down at his catch. The laughter dies on his lips as he registers the panicked face of a twelve-year-old boy.

"Dylan?" Kevin breathes. The music stops.

Dylan remains silent, shaking uncontrollably as he stares up at Kevin with wide eyes. Tears stream down his face, but no noise comes. A new song begins. Shuttering, Kevin quickly moves off the boy. He doesn't move, just shakes and cries some more. Tears gather at the corners of Kevin's eyes as he scoops him up.

"Dylan... I'm sorry... I'm so sorry... Dylan, look at me..." His chest aches as the boy's watery eyes meet his. *Are you a man, or a monster?* "I'm so sorry, Dylan. I didn't... I didn't mean to. I thought you were... It doesn't matter. I'm so sorry. Please stop crying. I'm not going to hurt you. I'd never hurt you, Dylan. Okay?"

Dylan slowly nods, then shudders as he buries his face in Kevin's chest. Kevin tightly wraps his arms around him, whispering over and over, "I'm so sorry. It'll be okay. I'm so sorry..."

Kevin winces, jerking as a sting pricks the back of his neck. Immediately, his muscles go numb. He releases Dylan. The boy looks behind Kevin and screams.

"R-run... Dylan... r-r-run..." Kevin slurs as he collapses.

Dylan scrambles to his feet, taking off down the corridor. Someone rolls him over onto his back. Cosima grins down at him, an empty syringe gripped tightly in her palm.

"Kevin, Kevin, Kevin..." she sighs. *The tables turn; now it's time to survive.*

"W-Why?" he barely manages to force the question out.

Cosima tsks at him. "Now, now, Kevin... Don't overexert yourself. You've caused enough trouble. Although, I suppose I should be thanking you for providing yourself as a convenient scapegoat."

She rearranges his arms, putting them over his head. He grunts as she straddles him with a wicked grin. Giggling, she runs her hands up his shirt, leaning over to bring her face directly above his. He tries to turn his head, but can't. Licking her lips, she eyes his.

"You know, I have been *dying* to find out what you taste like."

He closes his eyes, powerless as she presses her lips against his. She takes her time, violating his mouth with her tongue. Finally, she draws back, taking his bottom lip between her teeth as she pulls away. The music is fading, along with everything else.

Cosima groans, "Oh, yes... that was sublime." She presses against him, brushing her lips against his ear. "You want to know the truth? You wouldn't understand it." Her voice is fading away, but he holds on a little longer. "I'm not Cosima. I was never Cosima. And it wasn't her who framed your precious Altera, you stupid human."

Her laughter fills the air as he succumbs to unconsciousness. *No, you can never take back the damage you've done.*

THE GENTLE WAY
(2380'S POWER ANTI-MURDER BALLAD)

ELVIRA CANAVERAL

Hearts beating On The One
Knowing what ought to be done
Frozen by conflicting needs
Aching for silence
Knowing you'll hear the word

Heal my perception
Lift me from illusion
So that I may see you
Know you better and only you

Break the bias of locality
Long game, touch the wall, just once
Everywhen and everywhere
Present and lost
If we know the speed
Can you know where I am

Colluding allusions

Conspire in time
Entangled illusions
Vibrations still felt
In The Gentle Way

CRAZY LITTLE THING
A. R. K. HORTON

"What did you do, you idiot?" Altera asked from the other side of the electrical field separating them.

"Saved you," Kevin answered, flashing a weak smile from where he sat in the corner of his cell.

Altera sighed and rubbed at the tension in her face. Why should she care about this hapless fool? She had risked her neck sneaking into a secure holding area of the ship for what? To try to make some sense of this moron?

The music in her head didn't care about her reasons. It just wanted her body to be close to his. *No hope at all.* The bass guitar thrummed enticingly. Her body was heating up for this stupid man again. She prodded at her temples to quiet the noise and drown out whatever nonsensical emotion would cascade over her next. She also feared she might jump in time again. Even when it was just for a few seconds, she felt disoriented.

"Oh, God," Kevin whispered. "It's happening to you too."

Altera put her fists down to look at him through narrowed eyes. Two more guitars joined the bass in its steady, lustful rhythm. *She could cure his disease.* She shook her head in a futile attempt to quiet the singer in her mind.

"What do you mean?" she demanded.

"Are you hearing music? Feeling strange things?" Kevin questioned.

Altera nodded, her stomach dropping along with the percussion. *He wanted her. Wanted her.*

"Shut up!" Altera screamed.

"The instrumental ones are easier to deal with," Kevin said. "But, the emotions..."

"Is that why you... why we?" Altera asked, anxiety twisting her stomach in knots along with the echo of strings looping over and over.

Kevin stood and approached the field. It was clear he wanted to touch her, but the buzzing of the charge kept him at bay. *She doesn't want a friend, just a memory.* Altera closed the gap between them. Now they were only an electrical charge apart. She felt so dumb for asking, for caring. People are selfish. Use what you can get and move on—a childhood in the foster system taught her that.

"I don't need a song to make me feel anything for you," Kevin whispered. "You're everything to me."

"But the music can cause such strong emotions," Altera said. Tears stung her eyes, and she hated herself for it.

"It can." Kevin nodded. "But you cause stronger ones in me."

A crash of cymbals and flurry of percussion matched Altera's heartbeat. *Is this meant to be?* If he weren't in that cell, her lips would be on his, her hands would be all over him, and her body would unite with his again. Like they had in his bunk, in the hallway, in the zeotrope chamber, and so many other places that it was hard to keep up. That was when the music started, and time lost its meaning. She'd been after the muscle-bound marine from the start. She could have anyone on this ship, and she had. Yet, this brute seemed completely uninterested until they investigated that drill line. Had the music changed him, or had she?

"He could watch her all night," Kevin sang aloud, in sync with the singer in Altera's head.

Altera gasped and took a step back. "*Starcrossed*?"

"Is that the name of the band or the song?" Kevin asked, heartbreak in his eyes.

"The song," Altera answered.

"It's been in my head all day," he said, tears now openly falling down his face. "It's taunting me. The music is telling me you'll never love me back."

"Renner, I—" she began, interrupted by the loud percussion making its return.

Altera turned to cover her ears, as if it would muffle the loud banging in her head. *He doesn't stand a chance.* The bass thrummed, and her body wanted to pull her straight through the electrical field to embrace him.

"It doesn't matter," he said, shaking his head. "I still love you, and I'm glad I did it."

"You didn't have to," she replied through tears. "I'm innocent, Renner."

"Oh, no, baby!" Kevin pleaded with her. "I don't think you did it. Someone's trying to frame you."

The music stopped mid-beat. Kevin and Altera stared at each other in stunned silence for a moment. Usually, a song's cessation caused Altera to let out a sigh of relief, but Kevin's words left her with no comfort. She looked up and down the hallway, checking to make sure they were still alone.

"If someone is trying to frame me, you didn't help me by trying to sabotage the investigation," she said at last.

Altera wanted to say more, but she buried her face in her hands instead. He said he loved her. That scared her, but she wanted him—with or without the maddening music in her brain. She always had. After all, she'd planted the idea of her into his mind through the Magical Machine Room. Was that why he wanted her now? Was that why they'd made love? It didn't matter to her before. Making love to him had only been part of her completionist nature.

Since then, she wanted to be near him and had missed him desperately since Cosima stuck him in this cell. All the rumors about her murdering the MuhDuRuh had dissipated now that everyone suspected Kevin. What if they charged him with murder? Would he be executed? What would she do then? She hated herself for these thoughts. People and feelings were temporary. She couldn't afford to fall for someone so reckless with his own life.

She lifted her face from her palms and opened her mouth to speak her heart, but Renner wasn't there, and the previously orange walls now had a violet glow. Once again, hours had passed in an instant. Panic burst from her heart, and the anxiety-riddled tap tap tap of a keyboard vibrated throughout her body —a new song for a new emotion. Terror and futility clutched her as bass notes intruded into her mind. *Sweet desire, this is just a bad dream.* Where was the marine who would risk everything for her?

Altera raced down the halls, looking for anyone who could tell her what was going on. At first, she didn't notice how odd everyone's behavior had become, but then she heard dozens of mumbled songs around her. Each had their own. Some sobbed out the lyrics, while others rocked back and forth. *Please wake me.* Her eyes flitted from one crazed crewmember to another as the notes nagged at her with their repetitive percussion.

The violet walls grew warmer, shifting into burgundy. Typically, everyone was asleep at this time, but they all seemed to have assembled in their madness. To Altera's astonishment,

Cosima herself was writhing on the ground as if someone was making love to her. Altera ran over to her.

"Where's Renner?" she asked. "Did you execute him?"

"Why... why would we... execute Renner?" Cosima asked, with genuine confusion on her face.

Alexa walked in at that moment, seemingly unaffected by whatever was happening to the rest. "She found him in a cell and set him free."

"You did?" Altera asked Cosima.

"Y-yes!" Cosima cried out.

"So, you know he didn't murder the MuhDuRuh?" Altera pressed.

"So... many questions. What... are you... talking about?"

Cosima continued her writhing. Altera stepped away, careful not to trip on the limbs around her. She nodded her thanks to Alexa and then gasped when a few people collapsed around her. *My love waits with the sunrise.* She didn't have time to make sense of what was going on with the crew. She had to find Renner. Where would he go if he was free now? He would wait for her somewhere romantic, probably.

"The Glow Room," Altera murmured and then ran as fast as she could.

Altera felt overwhelmed as soon as she stepped in. Many of the crewmembers were living out their lustful fantasies together underneath the ethereal light of the floating orbs, limbs wrapped around limbs. The singing set it apart from any orgy she had witnessed before. Everyone sang their own song as their bodies moved to their own beats. It was awkward and repulsive.

She was about to leave when she saw Kevin. He wasn't participating. He wasn't even watching. He stood in the corner, his eyes locked on her. *Please, my dearest wish.* High synth notes danced around the bass in elation while she stepped gingerly over the bodies scattered across the floor. Kevin rushed to join her. The moment they were together, their hands entwined, and they pressed their cheeks together.

"I fall to my knees," Kevin sang.

"You beg, and I tease," Altera sang back.

Kevin pulled her tightly to him by her waist. They swayed back and forth to the song they shared in their minds. At last, someone heard the same music she did. It hit her now just how much she hated the sound of every other tune humming around her. She wanted to be in this song with him.

"Lighthouse," Kevin remarked with a chuckle.

"Is that the song playing in my head?"

"It's the band."

The notes climaxed on a crescendo. Altera's heart soared around in the Heavens as Kevin parted her lips with his tongue. Their mouths crashed into each other hungrily. This was all she wanted right now, all she needed. *Float with me.* She had to say something, but she didn't want to stop kissing him. Still, she pushed him away enough to see the longing and pain in his face.

"I love you," she whispered.

"I love you," he whispered back.

We can always escape. Their lips met again, but her body was failing her now. It seemed as if the muscles had lost all strength. Altera felt herself slipping down before he caught her in his muscular arms. *Into the dark.*

"Altera!" Kevin cried out.

"Shh," she exhaled with a dreamy smile on her lips before fading into sweet oblivion.

UPA MEDICAL RECORD
DEANDRE, ALTERA—1ST LIEUTENANT

DATE: 20 January 833 A.A.

Patient Name	Deandre, Altera	BZ98V906
Attending Physician	Sanderson, Harold	

Heart Rate	Blood Pressure	Temperature	
63 bpm	128/72	37.22°C	
Height	Weight	Race	Gender
172.74 cm	52.1 kg	Human	Female

Reason for Visit	Scheduled Checkup		
Eye Exam	20/21	Responsive?	No
Throat	Red, inflamed, pustules	Oxygen	97%

Physician Notes

Patient is one of the many that passed out before sunrise. An alarmingly significant portion of the crew is demonstrating odd behavior, humming or singing while acting on any impulse that comes to them.

I'm administering an IV in the patient, providing antibiotics, and drawing blood for testing. I suspect the fungal infection will be present in this patient as well as the rest, but don't want to assume that the same symptoms as Renner's will prove my hypothesis about the "zombie fungus."

Having a difficult time concentrating over this percussion. Why does it have to be dubstep?

Written by A.R.K. Horton

THIRD EYE OF THE MASTER
(CHIPCORE MONTAGE)

ELVIRA CANAVERAL

Throttle up, back in the fight
Feel the flow, time dilates before you
Resistance falls off, your will is A Way
Worlds between one breath and another
The music segues into montage
Shortcomings shown, challenges presented
Steady progress is made, music swells with success
Overcome the barriers of the past
You will use the opportunity to improve
Your skill and connections with your friends!
Third Eye of a Master, a source of light
Throttled into the need of the movement
And the Next Last Dragon rises in its sight
Observing all with the Eye of a Master
Beat to beat, feeling the heat
Thumping Bass, becoming one
Out of many
For the one with the flow to thrive
Grow from theory to complete mastery

Third Eye of a Master, a source of light
Throttled into the need of the movement
And the Next Last Dragon raises its sight
Observing all with the Eye of a Master

THE HESSERN & THE THIEF
JONATHAN BECK

WITHIN THE VASTNESS OF SPACE, EACH SPECK OF LIGHT IS EITHER A story waiting to be told, or one that has been told and retold many times over. A stolen Swarm ship—a lone *Hessern*—is such a speck. Though not as bright as the surrounding stars, the living vessel is bright enough to attract the attention of a small cruiser. It slips from the sensor-scrambling safety of an asteroid field, quickly closing the distance between it and the much larger vessel.

Alone in its cockpit, the wide-eyed cruiser pilot makes subtle adjustments to the navigational controls, chewing his lip as his fingers glide across the console.

"Tell me it's working."

[The signal is broadcasting]

"And the rest?"

[Stealth refraction is active. Target is unresponsive]

The computer's voice is matter-of-fact, blasé, even.

"Guess I'll have to take your word for it." He frowns, wishing —for a moment—that his ship was a little more invested in his survival. "Let me know if that changes."

[Affirmative]

The target vessel looms large on the view screen but, as intended, doesn't react to their approach. Being able to pass unnoticed is a useful ability for a thief and, in his experience, too often a matter of life or death. He's upgraded the cruiser accordingly.

[Velocity matched. Initiate ventral docking procedure?]

"You know it."

[Command not recognised]

"*Yes*," he hisses, gritting his teeth. "Do it. Gentle now."

The cruiser touches down on the outer-skin of the Hessern with a barely noticeable *thump*. *Here's to computational navigation*, he grins. *It's only the AI that needs work.*

Already on the move to the rear of the cabin, he taps at his wrist. Glistening material swims from the unit there, a personal outer-skin that spreads across his body, covering his clothing and exposed flesh in a pliable layer. The spread slows as it climbs his neck, giving him the chance to suck in a deep breath before material engulfs his head.

When the transparent faceplate forms, he waits for the wrist panel to turn green, then hisses out his held breath. "One day," he mutters as he inhales slowly, "that's gonna get easier. How long can we keep you hidden from their scans?"

[Energy reserves allow for 25 minutes of stealth refraction]

He takes a disc from a mount on the wall, snapping it to a magnetic plate on his chest. "Well, if this thing works, that'll be plenty of time."

[Command not recognised]

"Never mind," he sighs.

Activating the cruiser's hatch, he steps outside.

Magnets in his boots engage with the surface as he walks a short distance from his ship, focused on the outer-skin beneath his feet. Extra-vehicular walking is dizzying enough when the ship's stationary, but this one isn't. Laying down, facing upwards, it's impossible not to feel the dread of staring into the infinite, with only the sound of his breathing as company and no more pesky computer to deal with. One-part sweet relief, two-parts existential void. *Goood.*

"Come on, big girl," he says. Holding his wrist above his face, he re-routes the ID signal. "Let me in."

There's a shifting beneath him in response, then a moment of inertia; a sense of falling; of instant regret. *Too frazzin' late to turn back now,* he thinks, before the star-scape gives way to slick darkness, and the Hessern pulls him inside.

Within the cockpit of his diminutive cruiser, a panel on the main console flashes red.

[Propulsion trail detected] The AI informs the empty cabin. [Origin: MuDuhRu vessel, approaching.]

A pulsing warmth surrounds him in the womb-like darkness of the Hessern's thick outer skin, a darkness that is incomplete, the edges of it soft—as though he's hidden beneath bed covers, and the warm light of a bedside lamp is straining against the fabric. Nearly piercing it, but not quite.

It lasts only a moment and then he's weightless, birthed from the darkness into a serene white space that fills with indigo light.

There'd been life-signs onboard, so either dumb luck or divine intervention is to thank for the emptiness of the compartment. He ventures an uncertain, "Hello...?"

There! The wall pulses. A non-verbal response, sure, but definitely a response.

"I, uh... I need an access point," he says, grabbing a handhold on the wall. "...Please?"

No pulsed response this time, just that faint throb of a living vessel. It's not dissimilar from the thrum of a conventional spatial engine—in that it has rhythm and consistency—but there's... something else. A wetness to it. It's organic, magnificent. This isn't his first Hessern, but no two are completely alike.

This one, apparently, is a bit deaf.

"Did you hear me?" he asks. This time, a beam of light answers. When its scan of him is complete, the wall opposite bulges outwards to form a silver access panel.

Propelling himself smoothly towards it, he removes the disc from his chest, then presses it to the panel's surface. He's not sure what to expect—having been too busy liberating it from its owners to read the manual—but sure enough, the disc begins to whir and chirp, light rippling across its surface.

"So far," he grins, pleased with his progress, "so..." With a high-pitched squeak, the disc stops whirring, stops rippling, and then... knocks out the lights. "...good?"

In the darkness, the Hessern's throbbing rhythm fluctuates like a skipping heartbeat.

When the compartment slowly fills with indigo once more, his heart is racing. *Was the power outage only here? Are crewmembers scrambling to find the cause?* He's contemplating returning to the cruiser–and sacrificing what he came for–when the disc comes to life.

It ripples with iridescence, then settles into one solid colour: *Green.*

"You can remove your disc now," a voice says, startling him. "I recommend affixing it to your suit."

A humanoid female is standing in the centre of the compartment, bright green eyes set in an oval face, her brown hair tied neatly back. She's wearing a uniform, but not one he recognises. "Your breathing apparatus is no longer necessary," she states, tilting her head. "Adjusting gravity to biologically anticipated norms."

He barely has time to say, "What?" before he drops from midair like a rock.

He glares at her, rising to his feet as his helmet melts away. "Some warning would've been nice."

"Likewise."

"I... what?" He blinks, and she blinks back.

"I was not warned of your arrival."

"The, uh, signal—"

"Told me that another Hessern was approaching. I allowed that approach, but I was not expecting *you*."

"Yeah, about that." He winces, backing away to retrieve the disc from the panel. "Sorry?"

"What *is* that?" She asks, striding towards him and pointing at the disc. Then, with a gasp, she stares at both of her hands. "What is *this?* I'm...? What did you *do?*"

"*This,*" he blurts, snapping the disc to his chest and raising his hands in defense. "Is an interface. For the Hessern. So we can talk. So you can help me."

"Oh."

"Yeah, oh." He allows himself a smile as he looks at her in disbelief. *It worked.* His joy, however, is short-lived. "Look, your crew. Do they know I'm here?"

She narrows her striking eyes at him. "Not yet. Should I inform them?"

"NO!" he cries, "I mean, not yet. They don't need to know I'm here."

"Why?"

"Because I won't be staying long."

"Why?"

"I'm here for something you have. Something I need, and you don't."

She arches a finely rendered brow. "And what, might I ask, is that?"

"A Hessern orb," he says, then frowns. "You... *do* have some of those?"

"Naturally."

"Can you show me? Without us having to meet anybody along the way?"

A strange expression crosses her face as she considers him. It's not a bad look. Not a bad face, either. "Is that an order?"

"A request." He smiles.

"This way." She echoes his smile and gestures with one hand, walking swiftly towards the end of the compartment.

Watching her strut ahead, he catches himself smirking.

It's been *way* too long.

Still. A nice view is a nice view.

She guides him through the ship, into compartments and corridors where the walls pinken, gradually brightening like encroaching daylight.

He walks half-turned, expecting to come face-to-face with one of her crew-members, prepared to duck out of sight if necessary. Not that there are many places to hide.

"I don't recognise this configuration of yours," he says, his voice quieter than before.

"My configuration adapts to the needs and preferences of my crew composition."

"Which is what? Human?"

"Varied," she says, "but yes, there are Humans onboard, as well as other Human-presenting species. Like yourself."

"Human-presenting," he scoffs. "I've never come across a legit Human that's not a pirate, lost, or some kind of space gipsy. Which, given their insufferable superiority complex, is pretty frazzin' typical."

"My current inhabitants are a long way from home," she replies, her doleful tone piquing his interest, "but where they come from, they serve the United Planetary Alliance."

"Never heard of them," he says, "but they sound suitably insufferable. Is this their uniform you're wearing, then?"

"This is a standard form of dress," she states, and her sadness empties away to be replaced by... something else. "There *are* other forms."

She strides ahead, turning elegantly as she makes her uniform shift and change: from belted tunic to figure-hugging bodysuit; to leggings and vest top; to—finally—what amounts to nothing more than a tiny pair of shorts and a bralette. Each iteration bears the same insignia. On the latter iteration—more so than in the others—the insignia is *so* much harder to focus on.

"This is more to your liking?"

He'd stopped walking. When had he stopped walking?

"The first one was fine," he gulps.

She's canting her head, lips poised to respond, when there's a hissing sound from around a bend in the corridor. They look at each other wide-eyed, and then she's shoving at him—well, *trying* to shove at him, but her hands pass right through.

"Oh," she says, frowning at them.

"Oh?!" he hisses, backing against the wall. She blinks from view, stranding him there as the footsteps get closer. *Well, that's just brilliant. Very helpful.*

It's only then that the wall bulges out to wrap around him, encompassing him within its luminous pink surface.

From within the womb-like warmth, the crew-members footsteps and humming are echoed and vague. "Oh," says a male voice, pausing next to the protruding wall. "That's new. Bloody ship." Tutting, the male resumes his humming and carries on past.

When it's safe to do so, the wall expels him from its grasp and he stumbles out, gasping for air.

She reappears, smiling. "Are you okay?"

"AM I—" He whirls to point his finger at her, forcibly restraining himself to a harsh whisper. "*Am I okay?*"

"That's what I asked, yes." She blinks green eyes, still wearing only her bralette and tight shorts.

"I... I can't talk to you when you're dressed like that."

Her uniform shifts back to the less distracting belted tunic. "Better?"

"Much."

"However," she says, "some of the female crew wear it like so." She tugs the zipper in the middle of the neckline down to the center of her chest.

An involuntary groan breathes out of him.

"Sorry?"

"Nothing," he winces. "Keep the zip up."

"As you wish."

She lifts the zip but not fully, leaving the dip of her clavicle exposed. Her smile tells him she knows *exactly* what she's doing.

"Let's keep going."

She watches him as they walk, her expression unabashedly curious. "Why are you smiling?"

"Shouldn't I be?" He chuckles, shaking his head. "You're enjoying yourself."

"This form, it's..." Her words trail off as she looks all around her, drinking it all in. "I perceive everything as I always have; my outer-skin, my crew; their commands, their noise; the space all around me... but this technology," she examines her fingers for a moment, then lowers her gaze to the disc on his chest-plate, "is a bridge to them I've never had before."

"So why hide from that crewman?"

"It was not the correct moment." When he doesn't disagree,

she continues. "I need... *time* to adjust. So, too, would they. My appearance would arouse suspicion, and there's quite enough of that already."

He doesn't press her on this, but as they stop by a shaft opening, he can't help but marvel at her, how the emotions shift across her features.

"It's like you're one of them," he muses. "I've never known an AI as lifelike as you."

"Technically—"

"You're not an AI, I know, you're..." He searches for a better term but comes up short. "But you care about them, don't you?"

She lowers her gaze, nodding slowly. "They're my crew. But it's not just that. I'm the reason they're so far from home. I owe them safety, at the very least."

"I'm sure you'll provide it, if you can." He offers her a smile as he climbs into the shaft, beginning his descent. "If it helps, I don't intend you, or them, any harm."

"It isn't you I'm worried about," she says. Something about the way she says it makes his hackles rise.

"What's that supposed to mean?"

"You were followed."

//RoKehRod BuKahRok//

A small, angular vessel is clamped to the Hessern's outer-skin, its hatch closing as these choice words are hissed toward the small cruiser next to it.

Clad in dark exoskeletal armor, the MuDuhRu hunter crawls along the outer-skin on all fours. It tracks down a particular spot, then activates a control on a forelimb unit, triggering absorption into the outer-skin.

Once inside, the MuDuhRu moves cautiously, examining its surroundings.

"Your arrival here is most unanticipated." Her voice makes the MuDuhRu twist about to face her. "As are your methods to conceal your presence from my crew. I shall alert them presently—"

//HerKahRat BuLUKtoh!//

It rises onto rear limbs, striking a forelimb against its armored chest.

"I don't—" she begins, but a fierce grunt cuts her short.

It prods at its forelimb unit with a thick, gloved digit, ejecting a spiked tool. Grabbing it, the MuDuhRu pivots and stabs it into the wall of the compartment.

She gasps, her visualisation flickering rapidly as the tool whines and burrows into the glowing surface.

"You will do no such thing, Hesssern," the MuDuhRu says, turning back to her. *"But thisss... presence of yours... tellsss me you know why I am here. Where is the Thief?"*

"The... thief?"

"Tell me," it demands, *"or I will kill everyone aboard to find him."*

They've picked up their pace. Knowing there's a hunter on your tail will do that.

"You didn't think I'd want to know about that sooner?"

"I didn't know what to think," she frets, more distracted than before. "I thought it was a friend of yours."

"Friend?!"

"You arrived so close together. From the same direction."

"*Grozit*, it must've been waiting for me to leave the asteroid field," he scowls, "and tracking me since FerRahKun VII..."

She stops, grabbing his arm and turning him towards her.

"Why would it be doing that?"

He locks eyes with her, then looks down at her hand. It immediately becomes immaterial, fingers passing through him as she lowers it to her side.

"Did you—?"

"I'm still adjusting," she winces, "don't change the subject. Why are you being tracked?"

"Orb storage," he intones, "how far?"

"No," she says, crossing her arms. "You'll give me answers, or I'll let my crew *and* your MuDuhRu friend know *exactly* where you are. Who do you think will find you first?"

"Fine," he glares, "I'll answer your questions. On the way to orb storage."

With a 'hmph', she juts her chin in the direction they'd been heading. He resumes his previous pace, looking decidedly wary.

"So, talk," she says.

"I *may* be in trouble with the MuDuhRu."

"It says you're a thief."

"It *would* say that."

"Is it lying?"

There's only so long he can weather the stare she's giving him before he buckles. "Not entirely."

"And you've come to steal from me?"

"As if I could." He blinks. "No, I came to you because you're the first Hessern I've seen in months."

"Is that unusual?" she asks. "To not see any of my kind?"

"It never used to be. This sector used to be full of Hessern, especially in breeding season."

"But not anymore?"

"Not anymore," he says solemnly. They slow as they near a doorway, but when it doesn't open for him, he turns his head to her. "We don't have time for this. You can trust me."

She stares at him for a long moment, then, with a nod, the door opens.

Where before only the corridor walls glowed with shifting colours, within this large room the soft throb of warm, cerise light is everywhere. But that's not what makes his mouth hang open in wonder.

Suspended in mid-air are dozens of glowing orbs, bobbing about like bubbles of light.

"Sweet Zorvus," he whispers, "I've never seen so *many*."

"You haven't told me why you want them."

"You have no idea why?"

"No," she frowns, as though some crucial information has been kept from her. "Should I? My crew like them, but... I just make them."

"*Just.*" He shakes his head with a soft chuckle. "You take their grit, their dust and debris..." His smile comes easily, the light in this space uplifting his mood and magnifying both her beauty and the sweetness of her vulnerability. Exercising what restraint he can, he approaches one of the orbs and spreads his fingers across its smooth surface. "You turn that waste into something beautiful. It's... *amazing*."

"I... guess so."

He lowers his hand from the orb, his smile fading. "They really did a number on you, didn't they?"

"Who? My crew?"

"No," he exhales, "the Swarm."

The extent to which the interface translates the Hessern's emotions into humanistic characteristics is uncanny. Merely mentioning the Swarm has her wrapping her arms tightly across her middle as though she's cold.

"That was..." she begins, her voice choking with emotion, "...
before."

"I know. I may not recognise elements of your configuration,
but there's enough Swarm in you for me to know you've been
one of theirs. The Swarm..." He frowns, unable to ignore her
reaction, especially when he understands the cause of it. "They
stole most of your kind from the skies decades ago: used you to
extend their reach, robbed you off your free will, like you were
weapons to be wielded and nothing else. But to my people, you
were so much more."

"We were?"

"Of course." He moves through the orbs, but keeps his eyes
on her. "You were sentinels of hope. Great beings in the sky who
appeared when we were most in need, long before we took to
the skies ourselves. These orbs... before we knew what they or
you were, your kind dropped them from the heavens. My people
marvelled at them, studied them, and learned—eventually—
how to extract the energy within. You lifted us from the darkness, you carried us into a new era where anything was
possible."

"You make us sound like... *gods.*"

"To some of us, you were. To others, you still are. Even when
we joined you in the stars, you remained a mystery to us... *impossible* to communicate with. We've never known where you came
from, or how you change your shape at will. Why you'd let some
board you, and others not. Why you abandoned us, in the end."
This pains her, and he instantly regrets saying it. Closing the gap
between them in a couple of strides, he lifts his hand, almost
cupping her cheek. Almost. "I never believed that, and I never
imagined I'd be able to talk to one of you like this. Never imagined anyone would."

"Until this." She lifts her hand to the disc on his chest. It's
unfair, he thinks, that she can touch him.

"Until this."

Thoughts swirl within her green eyes and his breath constricts as he stares into them, struggling to marry his comprehension of what she is, what she *really* is, with the pained, beautiful woman standing there.

When she closes her eyes tight, there's a leaden weight hanging from his heart.

"Take what you came for," she murmurs, her jaw clenching.

"Look—" he begins, but her eyes open again.

"Please," she urges, "and *hurry*. The MuDuhRu is coming, and I don't think I can stop it."

Right, he nods. *Right.*

He gets to work, easing one of the orbs from the air so it floats just above ground level. Circling around it, he taps controls on his wrist unit, taking readings before he deploys a small cube-shaped unit on its surface. With a whir of energy, outer-skin material swims across the orb to wrap it in a tight harness, and a leash snakes out from his suit to attach to it.

Satisfied, he turns around, meeting her dubious appraisal.

"You really are a thief."

"Sometimes," he smiles, "but not this time."

The corridors blur as they move swiftly, retracing their steps but avoiding the MuDuhRu. Each compartment is much the same as the last, with smooth glowing walls and—with her guidance —reassuringly empty.

"How far to go?"

"Not far."

"And the MuDuhRu?"

"Close," she says, "but—like you—it does not wish for its presence to be known."

"Figures."

"Does it?" Her question makes him frown as he trails the orb along behind him. "Why would it not appeal to my crew for assistance? We are no longer in MuDuhRu space, but when we were, our dealings with them were of a civil nature."

"You had something they wanted, right?"

"A trade was involved, yes."

"There always is. Luckily for your crew, their lives didn't depend on what you were trading for."

"How could you know that?"

"If they did, you'd still be there. It's what the MuDuhRu do. Identify a need, then drip-feed it to you. It's what they did to us when the Hessern started disappearing. When there were no more orbs."

"The MuDuhRu had orbs?"

"No, but they supplied... alternatives. Generators for light and power. Fuel for our ships. They made us entirely dependent on them and have bled us dry ever since."

"Oh," she says, lagging behind.

"Yeah," he growls, "Oh. They do the same thing, over and over, and their empire grows. You wanna know why it's not appealing to your crew? It knows what I discovered on FerRahKun VII, before I blew their facility sky-high. Knows that if anybody else finds out, their whole frazzin' empire will come crashing down around them."

"Oh," she says, but her intonation's off. "Oh..."

"Is that all you're gonna—" He turns to find that she's stopped.

With hands out to steady herself, her eyes are searching about as though dazed. When her gaze settles, it's on the wall of the compartment: on a metallic object protruding from it.

He takes a tentative step back towards her. "What *is* that?"

"I..I..." she begins, but her image flickers and blurs, her

hands hazing in and out as she lifts her gaze to look at him. "Oh, no."

Ah. Not *at* him. *Beyond* him.

The MuDuhRu is fast, its footfalls dull, quick thumps. It covers the distance in an instant, grips him by the throat and rears back. It lifts him from the floor, slams him into the wall. Once. Twice. On the third shuddering impact, it lets him go. He slumps to the floor, gasping for breath, clawing at his neck.

"*Very good,*" it grunts, stalking back and forth like a predator. "*Didn't think you'd make it back here before me. Planned for it, anyway.*"

He tries to sit up, tries to reach for her... but she's glitching, distant and wordless.

"Help," he croaks.

"*Yesss, help,*" it hisses. "*This Hessern has been* very *helpful. You lied to me, Hessern. Told me you were not helping thisss Thief.*"

"*I'm* the thief?!" he rasps, jabbing a finger at the device embedded in the compartment wall. "That's Swarm tech you're suppressing her with."

"*Isss it?*" It skulks towards him, its opaque faceplate alive with symbols he doesn't understand. "*You're certain of this? You, who takess what is not yoursss, and does not comprehend?*" Thick, gloved digits lower to his chest-plate, hovering over the shimmering disc there.

Again he looks to her, but she remains stricken: flickering and mute.

"*The Hessern can't help you,*" the MuDuhRu leers. It lurches towards her, ripping the suppression device from the wall. "*A localised effect, but it should keep her sssubdued until we are gone.*" It moves around her, though, face-glyphs shifting and twisting. "*Tell me, Hessern, why I should not use this interface for itss intended purpose?*"

"P... purpose?" she asks.

"*Yesss. Complete control. I could make you vent your crew: sssuf-focate them, crush them, and you would have no choice. No will of your own. No more... fog of misunderstanding.*"

"Here I thought you were after *me*," he says, struggling to his feet, "but it's this, isn't it?" His hands lift to the disc upon his chest. "I destroyed your records, stole your data, but *this*...this is the only one you had."

It hisses at her ear, then starts towards him. "*So desssperate you were... to prove that MuDuhRu supplied technology to the Swarm. So blind to the fact that what we traded them were merely toysss.*"

There's nowhere to go, no use in running. On its hind legs, it's more than a head taller than him. It rips the disc from his chest, then casts him aside as though he is nothing.

"*Thisss,*" it says, a swagger in its stride, "*Is no toy, Hessern. Your days as gods are over.*"

It's so focused upon her, so busy gloating, that it doesn't see him coil the orb's leash around his hand; doesn't hear his steps–only the grunt of exertion as he swings the orb hard.

The impact slams the turning MuDuhRu into the wall and sends the disc skidding across the floor.

"Well that worked," He blinks, then turns to plead with the glitching Hessern. "You have to fight what it's done to you, I can't beat this thing alone!"

He's not exaggerating. The MuDuhRu is already pulling itself upright. He faces it, planting his feet. With the orb pulled back, he swings as hard as before.

This time, however, it's ready for him. The orb connects, but the hulking MuDuhRu barely moves. Taking the brunt of the impact, it pivots hard, clinging to the orb. *Oh, no.* There's no time to release the leash. The force of the turn yanks him from his feet, sending him sprawling.

"NO!" she screams, the walls flashing bright red as they ripple and welt around her.

He hits the floor rolling, landing only an arm's reach from the interface disc. Before he can grab for it, the MuDuhRu is there, pinning his legs. It knocks aside his defending arms, and pummels him into the floor with clubbing blows from its forelimbs.

"Stop!" she wails as the creature rains down punishment. "You're killing him!"

"*I WILL KILL ALL OF THEM!*" it rages, rising up from the battered thief to tower over her. "*Then I will make sure YOU are the FIRST of your kind to become OURS.*" It seethes hatred, reaching for the interface disc. "*I will—*"

It's stopped short by a hand, gripping its forelimb like a vice. *Hers.*

"No," she says. "You won't."

The walls sing luminous waves of colour as she hoists the MuDuhRu from the floor, then tosses it down the length of the compartment.

"You have one chance," she says. "Leave. *Now.*"

Its chest heaves as it clambers to its feet. It considers its options for only a moment.

"*I will,*" it breathes, bounding towards her with heavy, dangerous strides, "*DESSSTROY YO—*"

The walls, already pulsing with light and energy, reach crescendo in a single searing burst. They close in from the side like a spike on a cardiogram, stopping the MuDuhRu in its tracks. Its exo-suit splinters. Its bones shatter. Then, with an almighty crash, it drops to the floor.

As its last breath wheezes from ruptured lungs, blood pooling around its broken body, she stares at it, glitching; expressionless.

"You..." There's a strained whisper from behind her. He's

struggling to sit upright, his eyes swollen, lips split and nose bloodied. "... You killed it?"

"It chose its fate."

He grimaces as he stands, reaching for the leash of the orb.

"You have proof?" she asks, facing him. "Of their involvement with the Swarm? Of what they've done?"

"I do," he nods. "I'll make sure it gets out. I promise."

There's a moment of something, acceptance; a smile. Then it's gone.

"The alert has been raised. Officer Deandre is on her way. You have to go."

Her form glitches and wavers still, even as she crouches to lift the interface disc from the deck-plate.

"What will you do with it?" he asks. "In the wrong hands—"

"There are no right hands for this. Not yours. Not theirs," she adds, glancing at the fallen MuDuhRu, "not even my crew's. There's no choice: it must be destroyed."

"But what about *you*?"

"I... will continue as I have been. Grateful for all I've been able to experience."

Her resolute green eyes tell him there's nothing to gain from arguing with her, so he offers her his hand. He doesn't anticipate her lifting it to her cheek; pressing her face into his palm; letting his thumb caress her soft skin.

"Thank you," she whispers.

The disc in her other hand twists and buckles under the pressure of her grip, pulverising it to the atomic level in the same moment that her gentle touch ghosts from his skin. Then, as hurried footsteps approach, the inner-skin wall is shifting; sucking him and the orb into darkness.

Within the compartment, somebody cries murder.

It's only a matter of moments before he's back aboard his cruiser.

"Status!"

[Stealth refraction is at five percent]

"*Grozit.* Tether the MuDuhRu ship and detach us from the Hessern. Full reverse."

[Confirmed. Please be seated]

He stows the orb as the thrusters kick in, shaking his cruiser free from the Hessern's surface.

[Please be seated]

With a wince of pain, he lowers into the pilot's chair, a belt auto-deploying to secure him in place. The Hessern fills the screen, but with every passing moment there's less of her, and more vast star-scape to see.

"Go safe," he whispers.

[Command not recognised]

He rests his hand upon the edge of the console, a sad smile upon swollen lips as his thumb moves across its surface.

He watches until the Hessern is nothing more than a speck, then, nodding his head slowly, readies his fingers over the navigational controls.

He thinks of his mission; his promise; *her* resolve.

"Let's go home," he smiles. "We've got work to do."

[As you wish.]

ABERRATION EVOLUTION OVERDRIVE
(A WAY RELIGIOUS ANTHEM)

ELVIRA CANAVERAL

Without Abberation, there is no evolution
Different paths to a better A Way
Do or die, cut this line
I will survive to tell A Way, a life
Peaks and troughs trenches on a knife
Nothing escapes the waveform
Merely pauses interrupted by a flurry of strife

If there is any secret
It is missed by seeking
Secrets never heard
Hidden under speaking

Self-expression is total
Immediate, without conception of time
Free to operate
If you are free of fragmentation
A Self, Expressing Reality of a Whole
It's about Flow, not mere Control

Self in whole
Whole in self
Ego removed as you become
A conduit of Flow
When one operates in Flow
Separated from Ego
As We become facilitators of Flow

CALLIE MORGAN'S REPUTATION PRECEDES HER
KELLY WASHINGTON

As I stood on the rocky surface of asteroid Cluster X holding a rugged QWERTY cell phone, the telltale shadow of an approaching ship slowly inched across the asteroid's icy, silver-toned surface. I'd spent hours searching for a strong commlink signal with little success, and a resigned sigh fogged my helmet's domed visor.

You'd think with the universe's expansive size that a gal hanging out on a rarely visited asteroid outside MuDuhRu territory might find a quiet moment to send a damn text message, but I guess not.

Face it, Callie Morgan, your life is one long string of distractions... and disappointments.

I leaned back to watch as the battle-ready ship blocked out the distant stars. The ship was too far away to ascertain its owner, although I suspected United Planetary Alliance, and it might have something to do with that game of strip poker I'd played this morning with a smoking hot UPA commander.

I might have cheated and *he* might have ended up naked, which probably explained the oh-so-naughty text he sent me afterward; however, as soon as he puts two and two together and figures out I've stolen his access badge (which I need for my *next* job), the tone of his flirty text messages might change. He might want to arrest me for real. It was possible that the ship wasn't just passing through. Even though I wasn't high on their radar, a poster declaring me a wanted space pirate hung in most UPA control rooms throughout this sector.

I secured the phone inside a pocket. I decided to return to my skiff, *The Bonny Anne*. I figured I could make it before they activated their teleportation field, which always reminded me of an invisible vacuum hose gently sucking up ants. I stayed just ahead of the ship's shadow as I lunge-jumped my way back to the asteroid's makeshift landing stage.

In two days I was supposed to be in Tadegah, the ring city surrounding Cribalia—a place made famous by outlet shopping malls and gladiator-style war games—to exchange the UPA access badge for a land shark gut string guitar for a persnickety (but wealthy) client. After that, my plan was to make my way to Aneas3, which was the third planet humanity had colonized because of its very rare minerals. Word on the light-ring streets was a portal was finally forming near Elkar-2, and I didn't want to miss my chance to return to my old stomping grounds.

At least that was the goal, provided I got back to my skiff in time. I was steps away from the landing dock when I looked back at the hovering ship. My eyes went wide and my uniform beeped—an indication of an accelerated heart rate. *This is not good, Callie.*

It *wasn't* a UPA ship, which are typically shaped like charcoal-colored, welded-together cargo containers, all blocky and angry looking. This ship was elegant in design, elongated and smooth, as if crafted from a single sheet of otherworldly metal. Strange how a ship so beautiful could make me question whether or not I'd be alive come tomorrow.

A Swarm ship. The Swarm were a highly advanced artificial

race of light beings who thought every other species should be *altered* to resemble them. If they got a hold of you, they'd extract your brain to "remove flaws" in order to create a refurbished being without thoughts or emotions. A marionette for the Swarm.

I *liked* my dirty thoughts and messy feelings, so yeah, I always did my damnedest to stay two steps ahead of them.

I climbed the remaining steps. I'd just placed my hands on the handle when I felt the first vibration of the teleport rays. Sound waves rushed through my body and I ground my teeth as my ears popped.

The sensors continued to beep wildly and my visor fogged up as I yelled all my favorite curse words. Then my vision swam.

One second I was on the asteroid, the next I was inside a large, bright chamber, surrounded by metal crates and smaller plastic boxes, two space buggies, and a moderately sized cage.

It was so bright I couldn't take further stock of the chamber, but my auditory senses were on high alert.

I heard the click of a laser gun's safety switch being turned off several feet behind me.

Seconds later, a pair of firm hands were on me, searching for a hidden weapon. I was still facing away from my unseen captor as they emptied my pockets. I was a bit confused when I heard an irritated-sounding sigh—*sighing* was a human trait.

"How can such a small person carry *so much*?" the agitated female voice behind me asked as she removed a three-inch, squared, opaque glass cube. I hated that she was touching my stuff, and my hands itched to yank it back. "What's this, a damn paperweight?" Then, exasperated: "A yo-yo? You'd think space would force people to economize."

I knew instantly she was not one of the Swarm, who had clicking-like vocals, given their mandibled jaws, though, truth was, because the Swarm were light beings with no true physical embodiment, they always presented differently to each viewer—human, insects, machines—just depended on how they were described to you for the first time and that image stuck. As a child, someone told me the Swarm had heads like grasshoppers, so that's how they looked and sounded to me.

So either my inspector was trapped, like me, or I was mistaken about the ship. I wasn't thrilled when she found and removed the QWERTY phone. It was the only kind that could communicate with Aneas3.

I'd won the yo-yo after entering a spelling bee a few months back. Possessing a yo-yo in space was just ludicrous enough to disarm people who were on the fence on whether or not to let me go. You'd be surprised by how often it worked.

My captor—a tall, slim, attractive Black woman with close-cropped curly hair, dark pixelated eyes, arched eyebrows, high cheekbones, and a flat, exasperated grimace—had the pixelated eyes of an enhanced human and the white and grey uniform of a UPA soldier. The dark gray satellite commlink and diamond-shaped patch on her shoulder indicated she was a flight navigator, and the rank sewn above her chest pocket read LT. MARCIA JERICO.

Her data-like eyes flashed with recognition as she scanned me. As a flight navigator, she would be familiar with UPA communications, which included BOLO—"be on the lookout"—alerts.

She wasn't as high ranking as the UPA commander from this morning, but LT. Jerico wasn't small beans, either. Considering that she was an enhanced human, that meant she could probably perform her duties twenty-three out of twenty-four hours without rest or nourishment.

The lieutenant leaned down and picked up a small item; the UPA badge I nicked from the commander, and narrowed her eyes at me. Leveling the laser gun at my chest, she asked, "Welcome aboard—" she looked at the badge and read off the name "—*Commander Rafe Ryzo?*"

The badge had his picture, too; no amount of bullshitting would get me out of this lie.

A little smirk danced on her lips. Ah, so LT. Jerico wasn't necessarily devoid of all humor. Or maybe she smiled before she shot people. Ideally, as a flight navigator, she'd be more worried about the ship's navigational path, but UPA marines were first and foremost trained for combat against the Swarm and enemy combatants. So, it could go either way. This wasn't the most stressful situation I'd ever been in—no, that was when I acted as a server at a Linnean wedding banquet several months ago—but this was nearing top five.

I remained as nonchalant as possible when LT. Jerico picked up the QWERTY phone and inspected the insignia on the back. If she was as intelligent as I suspected, she'd recognize the antiquated but repurposed Aneas3 technology for what it was—one of the rare devices that could tunnel through multi-dimensional fabrics while simultaneously serving as a modern phone. In short, it was two communication devices in one.

She pressed a few buttons and the top layer device, which served as a local phone, lit up and I watched her read the text message on top. "Commander Ryzo has *quite* the vocabulary, Callie Morgan."

Busted. "I suspect you might appreciate someone's get-right-to-the-point style of communication? Leaves no room for misunderstandings."

"Straightforward communication is always preferred." However, as she slid out the QWERTY keyboard, an unidentifiable emotion flickered across her face. I couldn't quite pinpoint it. It wasn't recognition, per se, but more like she was recalling a memory, one that pleased her, like nostalgia. I could work with that.

I'd been so focused on deciphering her facial expressions that at first I didn't hear the footsteps echoing from beyond the cargo bay door. As the door hissed opened, a strapping figure emerged—one who looked like he took his duties *way* more seriously than he needed to. I watched as LT. Jerico pocketed my phone and the badge, but left the rest of the pile intact.

"I see that the rescue was a resounding success, LT. Jerico," the newcomer announced in a pleased tone. His jolly voice contrasted with his heavily scarred face. I read the name on his uniform. CAPTAIN MAXWELL SAVORY. He was tall, beefy, and had probably seen a lot of combat, but his eyes were wild, like maybe he'd just downed a full cup of hallucinogenic Venusian coffee. "*And*, she's intact, too. Good job on the teleport activation." The captain smacked the lieutenant's shoulder. Turning to me, he grimaced. "We were worried we'd have a gooey mess on our hands."

Lovely. It was my turn to offer narrowed eyes at the Lieutenant. "Rescue?"

"We saw you running."

"That's because I thought this was a *Swarm* ship," I spit out. I felt hot all over. Their misunderstanding had serious consequences for me. Not only had she stolen my phone, but I'd miss my next job as well as the portal back to Aneas3. I took a step forward. Surprisingly, even with the weapon still aimed at my chest, LT. Jerico took a step back. So did Captain Savory. "Since when did the UPA steal Swarm ships and abduct non-combatants? Send me back. Send me back to Cluster X right now!"

"Ah," Captain Savory sputtered before looking to LT. Jerico for help. He might be good at commanding marines, but he was a shit-for-brains when it came to dealing with vocal women.

"We're still learning how to operate the ship." She holstered the weapon at her hip. "Until we figure out the control room, we're all a bit stuck. Kitty is pretty much in control."

Was she bullshitting me? "Who the hell is Kitty?"

The ship did a little rumble, and I assumed we hit a patch of turbulence.

"That's, ah, what we call The Ship," Captain Savory offered oddly, as if the ship was actively listening to our conversation. I took stock of the walls within the cargo room and realized they were glowing in a soothing shade of purple. "It's a long story." He turned to LT. Jerico. "It's already lilac time. Best if you show her to the quarters. Plenty of vacancies in the women's section. Unless you identify as—?" he left the question open-ended as his eyes found mine.

"Women's quarters is fine," I said after a short pause. He saluted and left the way he came. I gave LT. Jerico a pointed stare. "Didn't you hear? It's lilac time." Not that I knew what anything meant on this cursed ship. I was beginning to wonder if I was the only sane one here.

"Eager to send a sext back to Commander Ryzo?" LT. Jerico asked with a sneer.

"That's none of your business."

Let her think what she wanted. I had zero intention of telling her my plans and gave her what I hoped was a "fuck you" glare even as she allowed me to pocket my belongings. I was happy to have the glass cube back. However, she kept custody of my phone and the UPA badge.

She shrugged. "It makes no difference to me."

"Enlighten me on something," I started as she led me out of the cargo bay and down a narrow hallway. These walls were the same soothing lilac color as the cargo bay. We passed round portholes, and I saw, as the stars blurred by in white streaks, that the ship was accelerating at a clipped pace. Internally, I wanted

355

to scream. Cluster X was probably a quarter of a light year behind us. "You knew who I was before you teleported me onboard, didn't you?"

LT. Jerico gave me an appreciative glance. *She values intelligence*, I thought.

"The Ship registered your skiff, *The Bonny Anne,* and the bench warrant for one Callie Morgan displayed on the screen."

I rolled my eyes. "The UPA has been after me for a decade. But I didn't think a patrol of UPA marines occupying a *stolen* Swarm ship had much use for an alleged felon." She gave me a side-eye when I said *alleged.*

When we arrived at an arched doorway, she stopped and pressed a silver button that activated the door. It slid up with a metallic whistle and she indicated I should enter, which I did, but only after confirming the door could be opened from the inside. It was a smallish dormitory-style room with an empty cot.

"Listen up, space-pirate Callie, it wasn't a bench warrant from the UPA. The Swarm has a warrant out for your arrest, too. You'll have to fill me in on the details of *why* later, but it seems like they *really* want to put the contents of your mushy brain inside one of their server farms. There's no way off the ship, so there's no point confining you to quarters. Roam about at will, if you like." She glanced at her wristwatch. "I need to be on command deck in fifteen."

I had so many thoughts running in my head, one of which told me that there wasn't much staff on this ship. They hadn't confined me because they couldn't afford to post a dedicated marine outside my hatch door. However, the thought roaring the loudest was: *What's with all this color time bullshit?*

"Wait!" I called as she walked away. I really wanted to punch something, though not her—she was just doing her job as a UPA marine. I'd probably do the same if in her shoes. "You didn't answer my question. Why the hell did you teleport me onto this godforsaken ship?"

"I figured it was obvious. We can use you as a bargaining chip. It's my job to help protect this crew, and if I have to sacrifice you to the Swarm to achieve it, then I won't hesitate. Considering that your biggest concern is on deciding which verbs to use when sending a sext, you'll have to forgive me if I fail to comprehend how else you might be of value." She paused. "I'll see you at chow time—that's when the walls glow the color of mint."

I changed my mind. I totally wanted to punch her.

———

My stomach was growling when the ship walls vibrated and turned mint green. Chow time. I yawned the yawn of someone who'd come back from the dead. In a surreal way, it felt like I'd been living outside of myself for weeks. I blamed the teleport rays—they always disoriented me.

Getting up, I discovered suitable clothing in the drawers next to my cot, dressed, and then left the small quarters. After wandering the halls without encountering a soul, I muttered, "Where is everyone?" out loud and I'd swear on my life that the hallway created a door out of a solid wall.

Never having been on a Swarm ship, I wasn't sure what to expect. Perhaps doors appearing out of thin air was a natural occurrence. I clicked the door's silver button and heard conversational voices as the door slid up. I entered a room I could only call a "lounge" given its plethora of cozy-looking couches, an old-time soda fountain, a counter full of snacks, and the large meal dispenser that occupied an entire wall. An older human male, who I later learned was Laszlo Brisbane, was carefully dipping a large spoon into hot soup, gently blowing on it, while telling others how he'd been accidentally swept up by the ship. "Kitty absolutely saved my life," was how he ended his long story. I squinted at him. It felt like I'd heard the story before.

In some back-and-forth banter, several youngish marines were discussing how Kitty seemed to know what they wanted and needed, and how the ship would shift walls, floors and doors to make it happen. This seemed to confirm my experience in the hallway, and the perfectly fitted clothing I'd found.

A young boy named Dylan, who was describing in lively detail his life back on Kepler 452B, was also relaying messages from Kitty. *How on earth did I know his name?* He couldn't have been more than twelve-years-old, but everyone was hanging on his every word like he was the ship's leader. I wasn't a big fan of children. Their etherealness always put me on edge, like I was watching someone more alien than an actual alien.

I was standing in plain view of everyone, feeling vulnerably bereft of protection. The thing that was telling to me was that no one questioned who I was or why I was on the ship.

"There you are, Callie," called a voice from the couch, and I jumped a little. My brain cells couldn't marry up the sensation that I already knew everyone when I'd been on board only a matter of hours. A few people chuckled. The person who called me was LT. Marcia Jerico, and she looked entirely too comfortable lounging on the couch. I didn't trust her relaxed posture. Shouldn't she be navigating the ship?

"Here I am," I said, though it sounded more like a question than a statement. "I thought you were on duty?"

Her lips curled into a calculated smile. "I am always on duty." Just then she lifted her hand to show me what she was holding. My phone. "You have an excellent set of encryption keys on the inner phone. I've been trying to crack it for weeks."

Encryption? The phone was really two comm devices in one, but it was password protected, not encrypted. But then my mind registered the rest of her sentence and my knees went weak. "I'm sorry, did you say *weeks*?"

LT. Jerico didn't respond. She was enjoying my unease. In a way her reaction told me two things: one, the ship didn't really need her navigational experience, which must be somewhat demoralizing for the lieutenant, and two, she viewed me as a puzzle to be solved. She seemed like the kind of person who'd gnaw on a mystery.

"It's Kitty's way of helping you adjust to the ship," Dylan said sympathetically. He stood beside me, but hell if I knew it until that very second. "Kitty's really smart, like, smarter than *all* of us combined. She senses you don't want to be on board, that you have somewhere you'd rather be, so she's manipulating the way you experience time. We've all met multiple times now, even shared a few meals, and just the other day you got into a heated argument with Doctor Sanderson when he offered you a physical."

"Sounds like me," I said with a deprecating laugh. The space doctors *I* knew were creeps who pointed to a sheet of paper to justify their creepiness. "So you're saying I've been onboard for several *weeks*?"

Dylan nodded.

One of the marines, LT. Rose Ortega, a UPA counter-intelligence officer, said, "Your reputation precedes you, Callie Morgan. Can you tell us more about Commander Rafe Ryzo's large—"

"I'll just stop you right there," I interrupted as I studied the room to take stock of everyone's expression. No one seemed the least bit confused or surprised. However, several sets of eyes *were* laughing at me. "Okay, I believe you. It's just..."

"Disorienting? Try acting has her translator," was Dylan's reply as he walked away.

"Dylan, wait," I said, extending my arm to catch him but

thought better of it. Kitty might chuck me into the void. Dylan stopped. I felt bad for the boy. "Can Kitty read our minds?"

He was thoughtful for a moment. "In a way, yes, and in a way, no. I think she picks up on body language as well as spoken language. She can tell what you're looking at. She's a whiz at electronics, too. Why?"

With that worry now gone, a new feeling niggled at the back of my mind, and I wasn't sure how to voice this newfound worry —a worry that Kitty would judge me based on how *others* viewed me. LT. Ortega was correct—I *had* a reputation for lying, cheating, and stealing, all of which was necessary if one was a successful space pirate. There was more to me than that, but that particular image *was* my public identity. Would Kitty form the same opinion about me, too?

"I fear that Kitty may have developed a negative impression of me."

For some reason, Dylan's easy smile reassured me, and I wondered if *Kitty* was the one smiling, and it was being translated onto Dylan's face. "Kitty is something of a rogue herself, Callie. When you first came onboard, Kitty told me you owned the memories of an old soul. I think she likes you." He lowered his voice when he added, "Who do you think encrypted your phone for you? Kitty doesn't like it when others go poking about in other people's business."

With that, Dylan moved on. Someone in the back of the room was calling him. It looked like Captain Savory needed to consult with him on something. It was incredible to see a seasoned combat marine asking the advice of a twelve-year-old kid. They should just make Dylan the captain.

I shook my head. *I can't afford to get caught up in the drama of this crew.* If I'd been unaware for several weeks, then I knew Cluster X was no longer a viable option. All that mattered was my phone. I looked up suddenly and found LT. Jerico focused on me, trying to figure me out.

My smile must have thrown her off because she glared at me as I went over to the meal dispenser and instinctually pressed the right buttons for a freshly baked chicken pot pie. When the machine dinged, I took my delicious-smelling meal to a quiet table and ate it like I didn't have a care in the world.

Other than my perceived reputation, LT. Marcia Jerico didn't know a thing about me. If she truly viewed me as a mystery, the best thing for me to do to get my phone back was... nothing. *She'd* come to me.

Several weeks later I entered the observation deck while LT. Jerico and Captain Savory were discussing going off course.

"Captain, I don't care what the scientists say. As your navigator, I must advise you that if we veer too far off course, Kitty's systems will shut down again. We cannot afford another mishap."

Captain Savory didn't appear to be swayed. He leaned against the railing, arms crossed. "Cosmia and Johannes believe that the surface of Devil's Sphere holds promising discoveries."

It had been a while since I'd heard anyone discuss that nightmare of a planet. LT. Jerico grunted when I joined their little tête-à-tête without invitation. Captain Savory merely rolled his eyes at the two of us.

"Why do you want to explore Devil's Sphere? It's nothing but giant sheets of glass. Sharks are known to nibble on the shards, but no one other than the Swarm go there. They use the material to make their memory cubes. It's not very safe."

"Thank you," LT. Jerico said with a forced smile before glaring at the captain. "Our scientists want to study the bioluminescent space sharks." I couldn't tell which she hated more: the scientists or the sharks. "A pointless mission, if you ask me."

"That's the thing," Captain Savory said as he pinched the bridge of his nose. "I wasn't *asking*."

I had an idea. "Would your scientists be willing to bring back some of the glass shards? It won't be an easy job since the soil beneath the glass fragments is poisonous, but it wouldn't be a bad idea to have some onboard as a bargaining chip in case we come into contact with the Swarm. They'd go nuts for it."

"How do you know the soil is poisonous?" LT. Jerico asked.

I figured I had nothing to lose in being honest. "A few months ago, one of my former clients, a high-ranking Linnean, paid me to poison a small group of the Swarm leadership at an important wedding banquet. The event was supposed to be nonpolitical, and a temporary ceasefire for all warring species had been called. For such a joyous occasion, however, the room was chock full of unspoken violence. No one gave me, a humbly dressed human server, a second glance as I walked behind the Swarm's table and expertly spread enough of the Devil's Mist in their direction before slipping out of the room and then departing the planet on the Linnean's flagship. For the poison to work, all the Swarm had to do was inhale it. All four dropped before they knew what hit them."

It was a risky job, but entirely worth it when the client's proxy gave me the valuable glass cube as payment. While the Swarm didn't have proof that I'd been the one to poison their leaders, they still had enough information to believe I was involved and issued a warrant for my arrest. *Under suspicion* was nearly the same thing as *guilty* with the Swarm's one-sided justice. I only needed to evade them for a little longer.

Captain Savory and LT. Jerico gawked at me like I'd grown a second head, though I could tell the lieutenant was putting the pieces together. So now she knew why the Swarm had a warrant for my arrest.

Captain Savory slapped my back hard enough to dislodge a lung. "Hot damn, girl!" He walked away with some pep in his step. I overheard him yelling at Cosmia and Johannes to find the strength-enhancing space uniforms.

LT. Jerico studied me. "Don't think I don't know what you're doing."

"Being useful?" I asked innocently. In some strange way, I figured that in some other life, on some other planet, Marcia Jerico and I could be friends. On the other hand, perhaps we were each too stubborn and too independent to make us simpatico to the other, no matter what universe or reality. Her intense dislike had to mean something.

"You're trying to negate the advantage I have on you, Callie Morgan."

The floor beneath us hummed as the ship accelerated and the walls turned buttercup yellow, which was Kitty's suggested bedtime for the crew. Behind LT. Jerico, and through the very thick, purple-tinted solar glass, dwarf stars in the distance blinked on and off as the ship sped past planets, asteroids, and space debris. You could see the flashing lights of far-off ships. Space was a beautifully dangerous place. As a child, I'd always dreamt of the stars. As a teen, I'd found a way to con my way onto a ship. And now, as an adult, I dreamt of home and the long game was to con my way back.

LT. Jerico was a means to that end. All I cared about was the phone, but I didn't let my facial expression give anything away.

"Sorry, I can't stay and chat," I said dismissively.

"Callie, wait." Close to the hatch that led downstairs, I turned around. "Aren't you interested in the latest text from Commander Ryzo?"

"Who?" I asked before I could think better of it. For a second

I was honestly confused, and LT. Jerico's confounding expression almost made me laugh. Given the time I'd been on the ship and the distance covered, the commander was nowhere near the forefront of my thoughts. "I misheard you. Go ahead, what did he write?"

She gave me a look that suggested she was rethinking all of our past conversations, especially the early ones. "Never mind."

"Okay." I left the observation deck pretending I didn't have a care in the world while she was the one holding the one thing I would kill to get back.

For weeks, perhaps even months—I wasn't entirely sure anymore—LT. Jerico and I circled each other. I wondered if there'd come a point where I'd simply ambush her and take the phone. As much as the thought of wrestling her to the ground fueled me, I knew that Kitty wouldn't like it. Never in my life would I have considered the feelings of a ship, but Kitty was no ordinary ship.

With another day nearing completion, the walls glowed that soft buttercup yellow hue, and I made my way to the stern to watch the backdraft of space.

I worried that I'd never get off this ship. That I'd be in some weird time loop and see the same angry faces day after day, or get stuck in a passageway that Kitty changed because she thought I wanted to be alone. What would become of us? Of me? Of the ship? Hell, I even wondered at LT. Jerico's future. I'd overheard her once talk about her home back on Aneas3. *Aneas3.* So I knew we had at least one thing in common.

I relaxed upon entering the stern. I sat and leaned back, my eyes taking it all in. Through the wide spans of the observation windowpane, the inky black universe winked at me in various shades of white, yellow, and orange. Streaks of light blurred by like streams of ribbons.

Behind me, I heard the soft snick of footsteps, then: "Penny for your thoughts, Callie."

I was in a reflective mood, so without thinking I blurted, "That's what my mom sa—" but I stopped myself from finishing the sentence. LT. Jerico sat beside me.

"Go on," she encouraged. When I didn't respond, she continued, "You were going to say, 'That's what my mom says,' right?" I could feel her piercing gaze on me before she said, "Here." She handed me my phone and then turned her attention to the stars overhead.

Even though my plan had worked—LT. Jerico came to me—I was still confounded. "Is this a trick? I turn it on and it explodes?" I inspected it from all sides, even sliding out the QWERTY keyboard, my thumbs naturally hovering over the F and H keys.

"No." She chuckled. "In the end, I couldn't crack the encryption, and Kitty was zero help. I could access the phone's *surface* interface, but not the inner one. I recognize Aneas3 technology. To bring you up to speed—you received the occasional text from Commander Ryzo and someone named Giles McLarty. He wasn't happy. Something about a guitar."

"Thanks," I said, and I meant it.

"It was never about Commander Ryzo, was it?"

"Took you a while to figure that out."

I stood to leave when she added, "I'm sorry for misjudging you and I don't blame you for not wanting to share anything with me but..." She paused. "Is your mother still alive?"

"How is that any business of yours?" I didn't mean it. It felt good that she wanted to know more about me.

"It's not, but I have this strange feeling we have more in common than we realize." When that didn't seem to work, she jumped to her feet and added, "I hate the Swarm. They killed my parents when I was fourteen and they very nearly killed me. I joined the UPA not long after in order to eradicate as many of them as possible."

I studied her. I didn't put it past the lieutenant to lie to gain the upper hand, but she didn't look like she was fabricating a story. With the gentle glow of the ship's walls, I could tell that her eyes were doleful, that her lips were down turned.

"My condolences." I took a deep breath. "Maybe we do have a few things in common. My mom lives in an aftercare facility on Aneas3."

LT. Jerico nodded sympathetically. "I'm guessing the Swarm tried to convert her but failed?"

"Yes. Part of her mind and her memory are still intact, but because so much is missing, she stitches things back together in the wrong order. She'll invent memories to fill the holes." I closed my eyes. "In some of her text messages, she thought I was her sister because she kept demanding back a sweater she says I stole thirty years ago. In others she'll remember I'm her daughter, but she thinks I'm at school and asks if I can pick up veggie burgers for dinner on the way home. I was a child when it happened."

"I'm very sorry, Callie."

LT. Jerico stared at me, her eyebrows slightly furrowed, so I asked, "You're wondering why I deserted her? Thinking that I'm a heartless daughter?"

"No, I—"

"Once I was old enough, I left Aneas3 and traveled across space in order to locate her memory cube. I imagined myself as some avenging angel. I'd find it and return it to the aftercare facility. I'd make her whole again."

LT. Jerico had a pained expression on her face. "And by picking you up, I prevented you from continuing your search."

"No." I smiled because it didn't surprise me that she assumed I'd failed. "You prevented me from getting *home*. I have the memory cube. It took ten years, but I retrieved it through a series of increasingly dangerous jobs for a high-ranking political client. I had one more job to complete and then I was on my way to purchase a one-way portal ticket to Aneas3."

Her eyes lit up with a certain memory. She asked, "The glass paperweight?" I nodded while patting my pocket. The cube never left my side. "You're lucky to have made it out alive, Callie." *True.* "You're as tough as nails." *Also true.*

"I'm a space pirate. Our reputations often precede us."

"You waited me out for seven months. If that isn't a patient strategy, I don't know what is." *Had it been seven months already?* "Shit," LT. Jerico breathed out. As a ship navigator, she'd be very aware of portal openings. "The portal on Elkar-2 has already closed." I must have looked crestfallen because she added, "There's another portal forming, but we won't reach it until we're near the Red Tachyon Pulsar. My credentials will guarantee you a ticket."

"How long until we reach it?"

"Two or three days."

I did a double take. I expected her to say two or three *years.* "Do you think you can create a commlink to Aneas3?"

"I think so," she said. "If I can't, I'm sure Kitty can."

I turned back to LT. Jerico. I knew she misunderstood me from the beginning, that she now wanted to make right her mistakes.

"I can be ready in a few days." Part of me knew I'd miss our antagonizing relationship.

"But you've got to promise me one thing," she said. If anyone were looking at us, they'd see two relaxed figures silhouetted against the backdrop of an expansive universe. It felt like the space between us held many possibilities, possibilities I hadn't considered until now. "That if I text you, Callie Morgan, that you'll text me back."

I considered her for a moment. "What made you change your mind about me? Was it because I assassinated the Swarm?"

"That helped, but if I'm being honest—" she paused, blushing "—you won me over when I found that damn yo-yo in your pocket."

She let out a genuine laugh, and I joined her.

In that moment, I had no clue what the future held, but I knew I'd return her text.

THIS SONG IS INTENTIONALLY LEFT BLANK
(NO GENRE)

ELVIRA CANAVERAL

This Song Is Intentionally Left Blank
This Song Is Intentionally Right Blank
This Song Is Intentionally Up Blank
This Song Is Intentionally Down Blank
This Song Is Intentionally In Blank
This Song Is Intentionally Out Blank
This Song Is Intentionally To Be Blank
This Song Is Intentionally Left Blank
This Song Is Intentionally Is Blank
This Song Is Intentionally Was Blank
This Song Is Intentionally Funk Blank
This Message Has No Content

DARK VERACITIES
DARIUS BEARGUARD

INT. MMR (MAGICAL MACHINE ROOM)

Stage is black and empty save for a screen to showcase what the AI is projecting for the user. There is a 'Projection Unit' DOWNSTAGE LEFT for the AI when it needs to talk. The Projection Unit only lights up when the AI is talking; otherwise it is dark.

ROSE ORTEGA, a woman of average height wearing a Lieutenant's bar on her UPA uniform, is standing center stage with RIKER P. EVEREST, a younger man with unkempt hair wearing a 'space cowboy' outfit, looking at images on the screen. Rose is using hand gestures to control what is seen on the screen.

RIKER: I like you and everything—
ROSE: Awwww.
RIKER: But people from your reality are terrible at naming things. Magical Machine Room?
ROSE: I didn't pick it.
RIKER: Yeah, well, a room that can make things from your imagination? The word you were looking for is 'deathtrap'.

ROSE: The room can't kill you.

AI (*Tim Allen*): Unless I rewire it.

RIKER: I can't tell when you're kidding, and I need to know when you're kidding.

AI (*Ellen DeGeneres*): You know, you're not the first man to say that to me.

ROSE: How did your brother even figure this out?

RIKER: Hell if I know.

ROSE: What do you mean you don't know?

RIKER: Since I found him as a kid he's just been able to do this stuff. He looks at information differently, I guess. Ask him to figure out a complex quantum-entangled informational cataloguing system designed by a freaky alien spaceship—

AI (*Robin Williams*): Hey, I resemble that remark.

RIKER: — and he'll get it done by lunch. Ask him to make a peanut butter sandwich? And he'll burn down a village.

WEST (*Off STAGE RIGHT*): Bite me bro!

ROSE: Cute.

> *MAXWELL SAVORY, a taller, well-built man with a well-kept beard and a large scar running across his face from above his right eye to the jawline and wearing Captain's bars on his UPA uniform, enters STAGE RIGHT.*

AI (*Andy Dick*): There goes the neighborhood.

SAVORY: Lieutenant, why are there unauthorized personnel aboard my ship?

ROSE: [*Still accessing the ship's logs.*] Captain, this is Riker P. Everest. His brother West is helping me access the ship archives.

SAVORY: His brother? The kid outside?

RIKER: Yeah.

SAVORY: You're getting technical support from a ret—

RIKER: [*Draws his gun from the hip.*] If I hear that word come out of your mouth, it'll be the last sound you ever make. [*Holsters his gun.*] Lt. Ortega, if you need anything else we'll be on subspace 2706.30.

Riker exits STAGE RIGHT.

WEST (*off STAGE RIGHT*): You should have shot 'im.
RIKER (*off STAGE RIGHT*): I know, buddy. Maybe next time.
SAVORY: Lieutenant?
ROSE: Sir, after Jerico figured out we had jumped both positionally and on a quantum level, Sabine and I had her reach out to see if we could find anyone in this reality. Riker and his brother West answered.
SAVORY: You're not a command officer, Lieutenant; that wasn't your call to make.
ROSE: Yes, sir. I meant no disrespect. But if we're going to get home — back to our home — we need to understand how we made the jump in the first place. Learning about this quantum reality might be how we do that.
SAVORY: And?
ROSE: And what?
SAVORY: Were they able to help you figure any of that out?
ROSE: No.
SAVORY: Then what are you still fiddling with in here?
AI (*Roseanne Barr*): Geeze, what crawled up your butt and died?
SAVORY: Any chance you and the wonder kid figured out how to get the ship to stop with the comedy routine? Or, better yet, shut it up altogether?
AI (*Jerry Seinfeld*): You monster!
ROSE: No. But in answer to your earlier question, I'm fiddling with this.

The screen changes at Rose's gesture into a complex hexagonal sphere with branches highlighting different pieces of information. Various images can be seen rotating with the sphere, as well as some videos, all showing fractured aspects of events over the last 100 years.

ROSE: This ship has what seems to be an unlimited archive of information going back thousands and thousands of years, back to before we even knew the Swarm existed.

SAVORY: Impossible. This ship is maybe 20 years old.

ROSE: I know, that's the amazing thing. It doesn't just have its own memories; I think this Swarm ship is carrying the collective knowledge and history of the entire Swarm, going back at least a couple thousand years.

SAVORY: At least?

ROSE: That's more-or-less what West is helping me with. The archiving file structure is bizarre. West took one look at it and then taught our computers how to read it. And then we taught the MMR here how to project it so I could navigate through it. Look, see? West unlocked video footage and Swarm commentary on the battle of Drimba 5, the very first encounter with the Swarm. The UPA was never able to recover any of the carrier or battleship black boxes from that engagement. Now we can see what happened.

SAVORY: We can see the battle?

ROSE: Yes.

SAVORY: The battle that happened in our reality?

ROSE: Yes.

SAVORY: Oh, well then, by all means, carry on.

AI (*Kathy Griffin*): Don't do it, sister.

ROSE: Captain is there a—

SAVORY: I think what she means is, if you're so worried about getting us home, Lieutenant, and to do that we need to learn about the quantum reality we're in... Why do you care about the battle of Drimba 5?

ROSE: Well, it was just the first logs he—

SAVORY: He clearly figured out which logs belong to which reality, so what point would there be in decrypting anything from our reality, let alone from the time at the beginning of the war?

ROSE: Captain?

SAVORY: Enough with the games. Who are you?

ROSE: I'm First Lieutenant—

SAVORY: Don't.

ROSE: Sir, why would you think—

SAVORY: Sabine. My chief science officer didn't give you up outright, but her report suggested you were integral in decoding the key that allowed us to fix life support and access the ship's logs. Thing is, first lieutenants who are cryptographers? They don't stay first lieutenants. And now you're here, doing this—

ROSE: My grandfather taught me—

SAVORY: [*Stepping toward Rose*] I cannot allow you to compromise this mission. Now tell me who you are or I'll throw you out the airlock myself.

Rose brings up a new video on the screen. It's footage showing her receiving the distinguished service cross.

ROSE:Captain, I'm Colonel Roselline Ortega, Counter Intelligence under the 108 reporting directly to Major General Bragg.

SAVORY: Counter Intelligence? I don't understand.

ROSE: May I?

SAVORY: [*Nods*]

AI (*Chris Farley*): Oh boy! [eats some popcorn]

Images on the screen cycle to match ROSE's narration.

ROSE: The Nimmert Corporation, before the war, was the 4th largest arms manufacturer in the known galaxy, selling ships and weapons to what would eventually become the UPA and making billions every Sol cycle. However, after the events of Drimba 5 and the cataclysmic attack on the Elysium system, the Nimmert Corporation quickly jumped to the number one slot.

SAVORY: Their energy weapons and armor configurations on their carriers and battleships are second to none.

ROSE: Yes, and recently certain members of UPA brass have begun to think that wasn't an accident. Six months ago, we sent a black bag team to extract some high-ranking government officials from a Nimmert Corporation bunker. When the team infiltrated the bunker, private security inexplicably started prioritizing purging the computer systems, over getting their own high-ranking execs to the exfil. Unbeknownst to security, that system was part of the exfiltration plan as the AI was meant to cover their escape. The team leader for the rescue operation detained the private contractors and then relayed the data back to UPA command.

SAVORY: And?

ROSE: Almost all the data they recovered was corrupted, but it got General Bragg wondering: why did the Nimmert Corporation prioritize purging the data over getting their CFO out? This prompted a second op, this time to a long abandoned outpost deep behind enemy lines. The team died, an apparent ambush... But before they did, they recovered this.

The image of two human men with a Swarm alien, all talking peacefully, is on the screen. The image is not clear due to corruption.

SAVORY: What am I looking at?

ROSE: It's hard to say who the soldier is because of the data corruption, but he's wearing dress greens, so a colonel at minimum. What we know for sure is that the other man with him is the CEO of the Nimmert Corporation, Karl Nimmert. They are talking — it would appear amicably — with a Swarm alien.

SAVORY: That doesn't make any sense. Our first contact with the Swarm was when they decimated Drimba 5. The war started then and there, we didn't even know the Swarm existed until that moment.

ROSE: Or so we thought. What General Bragg suspects is the Nimmert Corporation knew about the aliens and studied them to position themselves as the best suited to help defend against them. You heard the rumors about Drimba 5, same as me. What if Admiral VanNorman really provoked the attack? The Nimmert Corporation, already ahead of the curve, would be in a position to be given billions in no-bid contracts as they swooped in with weapons and armor designed specifically for the Swarm. Whoever that colonel is could have been sent by the admiral to—

SAVORY: Stop.

ROSE: What is it Mr. Savory?

SAVORY: [*Taken back by Rose suddenly addressing him as a subordinate.*] I smell a lot of maybe coming off this thing, but you're acting like you've got the smoking gun.

ROSE: A photo of a high ranking UPA soldier—

SAVORY: That you can't identify—

ROSE: That we will identify. I'll order Jerico to help clean up the file corruption.

SAVORY: You'll order Jerico? I am in command here.

ROSE: This is a priority, Captain, and—

SAVORY: Who else have you told about this?

ROSE: We have to—

SAVORY: We are stranded in an alternate universe, still at least six months away from our one slim hope of getting home—

ROSE: That is not my primary concern.

SAVORY: It damn well should be. There's nobody out here to save us, nobody to help. One thing goes wrong, and we're all dead. Hell! The life support systems nearly collapsed while we were on a damned scavenger hunt to find codes to decrypt the manual to fix it! And you want to tell people that the war is a money grab? That the UPA is corrupt?

ROSE: The UPA isn't corrupt—

SAVORY: You just said that Admiral VanNorman—

ROSE: The UPA is bigger than one woman! General Bragg—

SAVORY: Doesn't have the authority to accuse a fleet admiral. And you don't have enough evidence.

ROSE: I'll find more evidence! A photo isn't going to be the only thing I find, and you know that. You said it yourself: We have 6 months, but in the meantime the crew deserves to — NO!

Savory draws his side arm preparing to shoot the screen. Rose grabs for the weapon. A struggle ensues.

AI (*Jerry Seinfeld*): What're you even fighting for! This whole room is just a figment of your imagination!! You can't shoot imaginary things!!!

Savory manages to best Rose and take control of his firearm as he throws her to the ground DOWN STAGE LEFT, beside the Projection Unit.

SAVORY: It might be annoying as hell, but the AI's right. Maybe I can't purge the logs but I can stop you from saying anything. For what it's worth, Colonel, this isn't personal.

ROSE: It kinda feels personal.

Rose thrusts her arm up to protect her face and a spear lurches out from the ground, mortally wounding Savory.

ROSE: H- How?

AI (*Robin Williams*): Ooooh, that's gonna leave a mark!

ROSE: Did... Did you just—

AI (*Robin Williams*): Listen, sister, you can stick around if yah want, but you're the one who's gonna have to explain the dead guy.

> *Rose gets to her feet and runs OFF STAGE RIGHT. As lights fade to black, the stage is illuminated only slightly to reveal Savory dragging himself STAGE RIGHT towards the exit.*

STAN STANIS STANISLAVSKI
(MOTO-LOUNGE GREENROOM CORE)

ELVIRA CANAVERAL

Slipping into someone more comfortable
A slip of the mind into somebody else
Playing my new found propaganda as me
Completing your sum body as else

Walking in their skin
Strolling in the shoes
Faking in the making
Taking in the view
Getting in the feel
Acting normal in the new

Click on Proanoia
Everything out to help you
Thousands of clues
You'll know what to do

Everyone is in their own struggle
Walk with purpose, you got things to do
You belong here, ride that line

Between all out and all in
As I get comfortable in our skin

Your face is your password
You require no initiation
This is your time and your place
There is no sin in wearing this skin
This is how we begin
In the midst of our swim

METHOD ACTING
JEREMY NELSON

Ten minutes ago, I woke up on the floor of my quarters. I'd fallen unwashed, my skin cold, my hair longer than I remember. The wall was open to the padded cradle and electronics of what must be a stasis cell. I'd been kidnapped in my own room.

Years could have passed. I remember so many impossibilities, fragments of what must be dreams. There was a man hanging from a cross, information coursing through his undying body; the visceral groan of my abdomen expanding, the creaking of my straightening ribs; a boy in a cradle, not quite alone because the cradle speaks to him, soothes him. I remember a feeling, too. It lingers: pity. Pity, and the pull of a high-g turn, and the impact of the ground.

Nothing is where I've left it. On my terminal are notes, catalogues of the crew's interests, mannerisms. Intimate details. And, written by hand, paragraphs and paragraphs in a language I can't read. The Ship's translator struggles with the entries, or I just don't have the context to make sense of what I see—except for the text in one palm-sized notebook. One of the illegible entries was headed with "VENUSIAN COFFEE" in plain Interface.

I remember writing none of this, but it's titled with my name and rank: Ensign Penny Weatherly. Maybe even my voice. Why, I couldn't say, but the sense of being studied, watched, crept into my thoughts. I was a subject. I'd been unconscious, a lab rat to be prodded. I had to leave. Why did no one look for me? I needed to find somewhere safe. Already an idea took shape— one of the contingencies we trained for. A situation in which your life and identity were taken from you. But I couldn't afford to think now, whoever put me in the stasis cell was bound to come back.

It was as if creosote had gotten inside me, sticky tar staining me under my skin. I'd been hidden like garbage in a shadowed corner of my room. And that sense of pity came again. It was the ship. The ship had been in my head, reading my thoughts, *offering* me thoughts as though they were my own. The ship had known, but waited days and days until letting me go.

After all, there was so much to learn from a captive mind. I knew enough about the ship to guess at her motivations for keeping me in there for so long. *Her* motivations. I knew that, too.

"Did you get what you wanted? Did you learn about us?" My voice bounced

right back at me off the bulkhead. The ship might not have been responsible, but she allowed the abduction to happen.

Don't think, act. I needed to be safe. And my quarters were the last place I wanted to be. Where else could I go?

A sense of deja vu came over me, and I remembered there was a hall near Dylan's quarters, and somewhere aft—

"Get out," I said to the ship. She was trying to tell me where to go. And there was... disappointment.

"Am I supposed to be grateful? You could have let me out *weeks* ago." No, I wasn't going to argue. I filled a rucksack with clothing and anything else that might be useful. And, on impulse, took the pharmacopeia with me.

There were some gaps in the document, gaps I knew how to fill. That was some consolation, that the shapeshifter could take my life but not my thoughts—and it had to be a class-IV shapeshifter; there were no missing personnel reports on the terminal, nothing on my record indicating I'd missed so much as a shift. If that was the case, if there was someone out on the decks puppeteering their way through my life, I would make them pay.

Maybe I could go to the infirmary, convince Dr. Sanderson to run tests and prove my identity. If the doctor was who he appeared to be. Could my doppelgänger take forms aside from mine? Were there more than one? No, I couldn't take any risk. I needed to know more.

There were voices up ahead. Adrenaline came on so strong I felt the muscles in my neck strain against my shirt collar. I ducked into a stairwell, trying my best to move in silence. Down one step, then another. *Keep walking*, I thought. *Keep walking.* Even if they recognized me, my matted hair and stained uniform would demand an explanation. And I suspected the minute I was discovered my doppelgänger would snip off the dangling loose end that I was.

They walk past. Marines. One of them was... Sevran? I didn't dare move for a better look. When the hallway was clear, I sent up a prayer of thanks for the fact we requisitioned a large ship; there was room enough for more than twice our crew, and space enough for me to do what needed to be done.

The hallway shifted to a dull green. I knew the colors followed a set pattern, but it felt as if the ship herself were sickening from some indigestion. She didn't exactly ask to be kidnapped either, I conceded.

It did not take much longer to find my new home. Whether I remembered it from some patrol long ago, or if the ship had implanted its location in my mind—or even created it out of my necessity, I didn't know. And didn't care. The room had that organic look many of the cabins had. The corners were rounded, almost sculpted out of the glossy material of the walls. There was a bunk, a table, a sink, and a closet. No mattress, no linens, but that was fine. This would do.

What I needed most was safety. A place I could retreat to, a place where I could figure out what my plans were. And I had a distinct impression that the crew would have a hard time finding the door to my new quarters.

"Trying to make amends?" I looked around. The trouble with speaking to a sentient ship was that there was nothing to address. No face. Not that forgiveness was in the cards, but neither was I in a position to turn down any help. "It's a start," I said. And I got to work.

Once I'd cleaned up well enough to pass for someone who hadn't been stuffed inside a closet for weeks on end, I risked the corridors to find the things I needed. Bedding, yes, but most importantly a UPA terminal so I could see everyone's location. So I could see where "Weatherly" was. So long as we weren't together, why would anyone suspect I'm not who I was supposed to be?

Again, the ship provided—with a bit of luck. Since we had our preteen stowaway on board, another full UPA load out associated with none of the crew waited to be used. Everything I needed was with the suit.

I didn't have to wait long for my chance to arrive. The ship prodded at my mind, something I understood to be necessary but, nevertheless, felt invasive. But a prod was all I needed, because I heard the commotion from the deck almost immediately after I left my quarters. There was yelling, and I might have even caught the word "murder" thrown in there, but whatever it was didn't matter; I had my distraction. I wanted to run, but forced myself to walk. I needed to stay inconspicuous.

The suits weren't in the armory but were kept along with other EVA equipment. Never made sense to me—after boot camp, it was hard not to see them as weapons. They were all there, faceplates dark, standing like a squad of phantom marines waiting for orders. My heart raced. I couldn't shake the thought that one of the suits would move, that my doppelgänger took one of their forms and waited for me to come close so it might put an end to my misadventure. I didn't know if that was possible. I didn't know enough about my enemy at all. But I had no choice.

One step closer to the suits, and I waited. They stayed motionless.

I double-checked my suit in case I'd misremembered, but my personal transmitter and med kits were gone. Going through the practiced routine of disassembly brought home how weak I'd become; weeks ago I could move the armor's components without a thought.

PFC Kift's suit—or, should I say, Dylan's suit—still had its full load-out of munitions, equipment, and meds attached. Excellent. The ship's floor plans had been uploaded to the onboard computer, and it was fully linked to our UPA network. I'd have to disable its locator, but first I had to make sure of something. I scanned through each deck and found the confirmation I wanted: my name attached to a small blue circle on the upper deck. I plugged into a security feed.

For the first time, I could see the person who'd done this to me. It felt like watching a video someone had taken of me. I couldn't process it. *We're so alike*, I thought. She swiped through equipment logs with a flick of her thumb. Like I would. I couldn't look away, couldn't stop watching this *creature* who wore my body like a costume.

A minute went by. I was desperate to find a tell, find something I could use to prove it wasn't *me* running test routines by the maintenance bays. There was nothing.

So began my shadow life on the ship. When the creature who wore my face stalked the far side of the ship, I would venture out to the mess or to the rec room for exercise. Days passed, then weeks. I needed strength for what was to come, and I still felt weak from my time in stasis. That's what I told myself.

Her schedule became my schedule. I memorized it, made sure to avoid her path but also to avoid developing too obvious a routine. I couldn't give myself away and leave traces that would lead her to me. That meant avoiding the other crew as much as possible. I didn't know what she'd said to them, didn't have any context for what to expect. I'd become the interloper, in a way.

Confirmation that my instincts were on point came almost immediately. I didn't have the appropriate context for her interactions with the crew, because it seemed that "Weatherly" was on concurrent intimate terms with more than one crew member. Several, as far as I could tell, and if that was any indication, then the past few weeks must have been quite the adventure. Some shard of vanity hoped, at least, she'd left her partners impressed. This was, I knew, another violation, one that colored my future interactions with everyone I knew on board. But there was only so much I permitted myself to dwell on. And revenge was my only priority. Everything else was a distraction.

That's what I told myself, at least. But I'd be lying if I didn't admit there was relief in living on my own, almost a ghost. Accountable to no one. Even though, when I would meet other crew by the exercise machines or when I got food at mess, I needed to perform as the Ensign they all thought I was, there was serenity in living my own life. The ship I didn't forgive, but I would be lying if I said I didn't understand. She hadn't known better, and I suspected she didn't experience time in the same way humans did. Aside from taking an eternity to set me free, she had done everything she could for me. Would she help me regain my place on the crew? I couldn't articulate her thought process, but I had an inkling the ship's threshold for enacting violence on someone aboard would be quite high. This was a task I had to take into my own hands. It seemed only right.

Taking a weapon from the armory would have been too great a risk; there would have to be a name on the log. And, much as we were on the edge of ship discipline, I couldn't imagine it would go unnoticed. No, I needed another method. How best to murder a human, rather than Swarm, was not a subject I'd devoted much time to, but now the thoughts consumed me. Poison would have been preferred, but I had no guarantees about the underlying biology of my doppelgänger. Then again, enough radioactive isotope taken from the ship's engines should kill most anything. Still, the logistical challenge of administering a lethal cocktail without discovery was needlessly complicated.

Strangulation may not be effective, either. One never knew with shapeshifters if features like nostrils were for show, or if they also replicated a subject's underlying biology. Time and again my thoughts led me down a single path: the old-fashioned way was my only choice. Cut enough holes into something and they tended to die. I'd make what I needed. Little by little, I gathered cerasteel epoxies from the stores. No one noticed.

Maybe I'd gotten complacent. I don't know. But I wasn't prepared for what happened.

Things had gone well, and I managed to grab lunch interacting with no one except for a nod to Bryjal—though he might not have been facing me, it was difficult to tell with the tentacles. My makeshift weapon had taken shape, layers of metallic resins hardened into a foot-long blade sturdy enough for the job. That was the hope, at least. Every morning I honed the weapon's edge with a whetstone from the same materials. Yet I did not commit to a time, a place. As I enjoyed my synthesized stew, the lights on the wall flickered. Then went out entirely.

I hardly noticed, because what was far more alarming was the silence. Absolute silence, as soundless as it was dark. My heartbeat rushed to fill the void. I stood, disoriented, as my bowl and stew clattered to the floor. A dim, colorless light suffused the walls, bringing my room back into view. But the quiet remained, and I understood. The ship—I couldn't hear her any more. Couldn't *feel* her. Something had gone wrong.

My mind raced as I cleaned the mess off the floor. There was no reason to think this had anything to do with me, but that new part of myself—the part of myself birthed in isolation—felt a need to run. To escape. Without someone else on my side, without the ship, there was no safety.

Be calm, I told myself. It's been weeks of hiding, and no one has come close to finding my spot. And, even if the ship helped,

I had my computer now. I could set alarms, observe. *Do nothing rash.*

Rashness called to me. This was my cue. I could get it done now. I knew where she was. The doppelgänger would finish her shift in the aft machine room. One decisive moment, and there would be only one of us. I could have my life back. My identity back.

My hands shook. I breathed. With all the patience I could manage, I slid open the door. The hallway lights were dim. So it was at least this section of the ship that had been affected. A part of me knew it wasn't only this deck, though, with the voice of the ship gone, whatever happened must have been ship wide. Even the air smelled different, somehow muskier, like the breath of a living thing.

"Maybe this is the time," I whispered. How odd to find it comforting to hear a human voice, even if it's only mine.

I checked my terminal, even though I knew where to go. Deck three. She wouldn't be alone now, but her shift would end soon, and even with a crisis seizing the ship, I'd never seen her leave her post while on duty. Unpredictable as her personal hours might be, I could count on knowing where she was while on the clock.

The walls seemed to shift. Sometimes they were the solid synthetic ceramic and metal constructions I expected them to be. Other times they looked like the insides of an unfathomably large insect. It occurred to me we saw what the ship wanted us to see. Was the ship falling apart? Dying? If so, at least I'll have accomplished my one task before we're adrift in space.

Do I confront her? Demand answers? I knew so little. Did it matter if she was a Swarm spy? Or some twisted starhopping voyeur? She'd taken my body, my life, and probably wanted me dead. Asking questions would only give her a chance to escape. I didn't need answers.

Military training determined how I thought about my "operation." I never meant to see combat. I wanted to specialize in xenobiology for a reason: to learn. And the opportunity to see a Swarm ship up close, to understand more about what we'd been pouring lives and taxes into fighting, presented itself as everything I could have wanted from a posting. It should have been that way. No one else on this ship lived day-to-day like a combatant in enemy territory. And that was what I'd become. With the ship silent, there was no one else to trust.

Never would I have thought that I'd be grateful for the combat training we all drilled in. The ambush point was a turn in the hall. I waited behind the open door of the storerooms set aside for uniform repairs—a low-traffic area. As a distraction, I placed an alarm module on the floor, a simple device soldered from a light pilfered from hydroponics. All the pieces in place, all standard protocol. I waited. And listened.

Footsteps. A steady gait, not alarmed, not in a rush. I could almost feel myself walking to the familiar rhythm. *Mustn't get distracted*. I breathed deep through my mouth, tongue recessed to minimize sound.

The footsteps stopped right past the door. She'd found the bait. I stepped around and saw myself—saw *her*—bending down to pick the light up. And over her shoulder, I saw something else. A blur. Or a shadow? An ink blot in the air. But I could not afford to hesitate. I took another step, and this one my enemy heard, and she turned in time for my epoxy blade to sink under her ribs. I drew back and stabbed her again. This time my hand was wet with blood. *Not mine*, I thought, *not mine*. Her hands were on my shoulders, and her mouth was open. Trying to form words. *My face is backwards*.

This was what I had to do. I had to finish the job. As I pulled the blade out, my vision darkened. Was the ship having another

392

blackout? No, this was something else, and the awful silence I'd been keeping at bay broke open.

Something was in my head, something that wasn't the ship. Almost like... music? Harmonies that were indescribable, richer than a solar flare through a spectrometer. Music that thrummed not only with sounds but with my body itself. I *wanted* to be a part of it, wanted to move my body to the beat of that symphony.

The music broke apart, crumbled like dry ration in my hands. There was another voice—no, not just another voice, it was me. My doppelgänger. My vision faded. Before I lost consciousness, I felt my hand in my hand, prying the knife from my fingers. And I couldn't tell which was whose and didn't know how to fill the hole left by the absence of that music. For a moment, I was whole.

I woke up in medical. A fluid line ran into my arm. They must have given me something, because I felt nothing but tranquility.

"Ensign," Takach said. "Quitting cold turkey? Not a good idea. You were just in here a week ago asking for a refill."

"Asking for what?" Seeing the marine standing over me only disoriented me further until I remembered she helped Dr. Sanderson with some of the clinic duties. We teased that she wanted to go civvie like the doc himself. Didn't seem like the worst idea.

"Remember? The lie about needing them for experiments? Maybe you hit your head when you passed out. Bryjal brought you in, found you on the floor. Should thank him later." She moved closer, put her hand on my shoulder. This gesture of intimacy was, I suspected, not a new one between us. "Take care of yourself, all right? I still care, even if you're out exploring every frontier the crew has to offer."

I said nothing, but that seemed not to bother her. She looked back before leaving.

What happened? I looked at my hands. They were clean, except—yes, there, under my right thumbnail. A speck of what could be blood. So I hadn't hallucinated the whole thing. Whether or not I succeeded, I couldn't be sure. And then there was that presence that interrupted us, a form that felt so similar to the ship and yet distinct.

There was something else, a note tucked under my wrist-band. On it, written in my handwriting:

I'm sorry.

The words sounded like mockery in my mind. Knowing that I'd been powerless again, left in her control, *again*, made me want to tear the bedsheets apart. Albeit in a pleasantly disassociated way. I could get used to having tranqs delivered straight into my bloodstream.

She could have killed me, but didn't. Maybe she thought this made us even. But it didn't fix the underlying problem—there wasn't a place for me aboard this ship unless she let me have my identity back, and she had to know that. Unless she had other faces to take, other lives to live. We'd picked up strangers on this trip; would anyone truly care if the new one (Kaylie? Callie?) were replaced with a shapeshifter?

No, I didn't truly want to put someone else in my place. Or kill an innocent. I blamed it on the intoxicants.

By the time I was discharged, I realized everyone else was too overwhelmed to worry about the incongruities that came with two identical crew members. It was difficult to parse rumor from fact: was the captain incapacitated? Dead? The ship was dying. No, the ship was losing her anchor in our corner of space-time.

And she and the android, Lansquenet, were having a child? A school of roving interstellar sharks had seized on our wake and trailed behind us like vultures waiting for a meal. We bore down on an impossibly twinned tachyon fountain. If I could spare the humor, I'd see the joke of it all: I might well be the least interesting thing on the ship. A part of me wondered if we could still be considered a UPA vessel at all.

My encounter with the other Weatherly had left me changed, but I could not say how. I didn't thirst to punish her, not anymore. Maybe the experience of it, the visceral horror of doing what I did, satisfied the primal urge that drove me. Or the constant drip of medication into my veins managed to temper what vengeance I had left.

There was one other thing. Alan Gray visited my bedside. Of all the marines on the ship, I hadn't expected him to check in to see how I was doing. At first, I worried that I'd have to navigate yet another aftermath of my doppelgänger's liaisons, but Gray was more interested in himself, or what he'd seen. He visited everyone who'd ended up in the infirmary in the course of recent events, and after asking how we were, he'd share his visions he claimed to have experienced.

None of his words described that brief and profound moment of peace I felt before I ended up in this bed, but somehow it reminded me of the music I'd heard. Maybe it had touched him, too. And Gray was certain he understood what he had to do. It was written all over his face, the way his eyebrows would knit together when he described his visitations. And his voice. Not raving like a Cyber Christ devotee, none of that bombastic proclamation. Instead, he spoke almost in a whisper, the hushed delivery of one offering truths otherwise too fragile to tell. And each time he came through the medical bay, there were more people who came to listen. His words were balm for our bleak reality. While I recovered, the Swarm had found us once more. Our ship fled, and our enemies were distant, but the end seemed a matter of weeks, possibly days.

I could have a place with Gray and his people. Let the other Weatherly play ensign with the officers, and I'll find myself a new home with the seekers of truths making the most of this damned voyage.

I moved out of my hidden quarters and into the Gray commune that formed on deck three. There wasn't much to take with me, but I noticed that the pharmacopeia was gone. The thought of *her* being in my room, searching through my things, aroused... nothing at all. We had our places, now. She could take what was hers.

Anyone was welcome with the Grays. We talked mostly about the visions, the wonders of the universe we'd once thought we'd understood so well before our jump nearly a year ago. It was not a life I would have imagined, but nothing since we boarded this Swarm ship was what we'd imagined.

Even this momentary peace could not last. Day by day, the Swarm gained on us. Gray was undaunted. "The star will provide," he said. He wanted to leave the ship, take as many of us as he could manage to bask in the twin tachyon fountains of this surreal system. The captain had her own plan that she put before the crew—a risky maneuver at the edge of a black hole that might give us the acceleration we needed to escape. Or the singularity would pull us in past the event horizon. Or g-forces would crush us in the attempt.

I stayed on the ship. The last I saw of Alan Gray was his suit, silhouetted against a kaleidoscope of radiation.

There was no time for grief, if that even was the appropriate emotion. The captain's voice reverberated through the ship. The Swarm closed in.

"Our course is set for the Abell 85 cluster. Prepare for high-g maneuvers, observe blackout protocols. Captain, out."

There was something in the cadence of that voice that rang familiar to my ear. Was it possible the other Weatherly had found a new role to play? But high-g prep left no time to dither. Blackout protocol meant a high likelihood of loss of consciousness. Possibly even worse outcomes. Blood vessels were awfully fragile, and it only took one weak point somewhere in the cranium for a blackout to be permanent. The bridge officers would do everything necessary to keep our ship from being captured. If some of us lost our lives, well—that was the sacrifice we signed up for. We ran for our crash seats.

Someone was already in mine. Around us, people ran for their pods and strapped in. No one seemed to notice that I stood over what could have been my reflection.

"Prepare for acceleration in T-60. Alert. Blackout protocols in effect."

"It's you," I said. "The other Weatherly."

"Call me Penny," she said.

To my surprise, hate didn't return. Instead, a hollowness where an understanding could have been. "Penny" hadn't been malicious. I was simply the pathway for her ends. Would I have to fight her, *again*, for my right to exist? It seemed so pointless. True enemies pursued us.

"Acceleration in T-30. Alert. Blackout protocols in effect."

I wasn't any more ready for a fight than the ship was. But I had UPA Fleet training, and the person on the couch hadn't. My hesitation lasted only seconds.

"Crash couches can fit two. Move over."

She nodded once, just as I would. Penny the Pro, they called me in my academy years, and it wasn't meant as a compliment.

I climbed into the gel-lined seat, and we tied the straps across our bodies. The head support was trickier and needed to be adjusted to its alternate configuration. *Not the same after all,* I thought, but looking into my own eyes made it impossible to say aloud.

"Acceleration imminent. Alert."

"This might be the end," Penny said.

"Only makes sense." I checked the fastenings. "You stepped right into my life, played the part. Now you can stop acting. My genuine death, and you have the best seat in the house."

"Acceleration imminent. Alert."

"I've learned so much. You've taught me so much," Penny said. Or was the voice different, did it belong to someone else?

"Not entirely mutual, I'm sorry to say. But I never wanted to die alone."

She took my hand. I held it, squeezed. The crash seat shook. An unseen hand, unimaginably heavy and vast as the curved laws of the universe itself, reached out and pushed us *down* into our chair. The gel padding felt as unforgiving as ship-grade ceramic. I could feel the flesh of my face flatten, my cheeks sag.

A moment of near weightlessness, then the world spun. My insides turned like the twin tachyon gyres that stole Alan Gray away. I thought of Dylan—so young—and hoped he was okay. That the ship would keep him safe. I hoped the ship would survive, even if we didn't. I hoped that, even if the ship didn't survive, people back home would know what had become of us, what we'd almost accomplished. All of a moment, as acceleration drained awareness from my mind. We held hands.

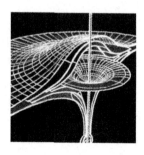

NEXT TO FINAL FORM
(ART MINES DRILL XMAM)

ELVIRA CANAVERAL

Take life one Planck at a time
A Random Page read to me
Life, in all its complexity
Is the next test for you and me
When you flow holding your eye up high
For the masters watching you from the sky
We know not what trouble lies ahead
Before you fight, use your head.
It's time to grow and train your firstborn
This journey you don't make alone.
(Train your kids and fly)
There's a power deep inside the two,
an inner strength
We'll find in our time of need.

(The Flow)
Like the seasons, time will always flow
If it's right, you'll automatically know.
The world of mystery exists only in your head.
When you become one with yourself in another

The wall will fall
The journey now before you is the Clan of few
You've learned your lesson of two
(We can teach each other)
There's a power deep inside us, an inner strength
We'll find each other in time of need
(The Flow)
One is the Next to Last Dragon
The penultimate form of the Flow
The Next Last Dragon
Needs Time to grow

PART IV: THE FINAL JUMP

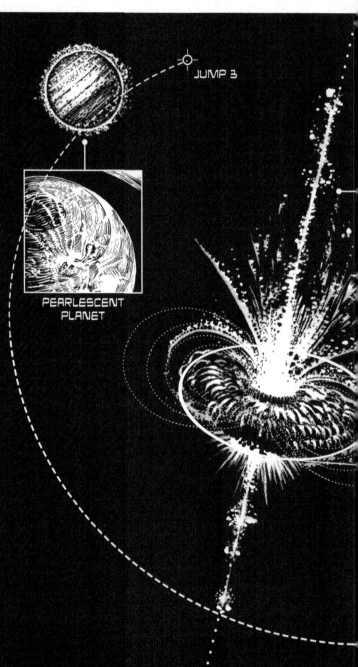

JUMP 3

PEARLESCENT
PLANET

SECTOR 4

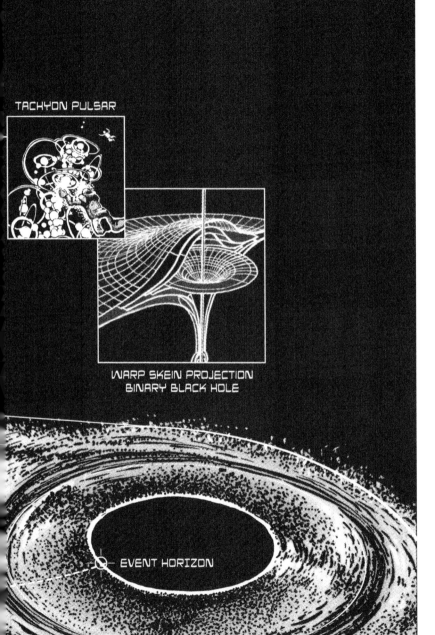

TACHYON PULSAR

WARP SKEIN PROJECTION
BINARY BLACK HOLE

EVENT HORIZON

1 2 3 SPACE IN 4 5 6 TIME
ELVIRA CANAVERAL

1 on a point
2 on a line
3 gives depth

A Point on the ONE
A Line on the TWO
Go Deeper on the THREE

Navigate Three dimensions of space
Anchor on the One
Up Inside your dimensional face

When in TIME
4 is a point
5 is a line
6 is a depth

Present in the FOUR
Walk the Line of the FIVE
Go Deep-er on the SIX

Navigate dimensions of time
4 is now
5 is then and to be
6 is infinite possibility

A Point on the one
A Line on the two
Go Deeper on
the three
Three dimensions of space
The next three are dimensions in time...

A Timepoint on the Four
A Timeline along the FIVE
A Timespace goes deep
Probability SIX
Infinite Possibilities of TIME

These are the six dimensions of TIMESPACE

Once you're able to see it
with a higher eye
Time Knife above and around Flat Times

(EPIC BASS SOLO / Cosmic Orgasm)

A Point on the ONE
Infinite Length on the TWO
Universal depth on THREE

Time Big Banged in the FOUR
Expanded to fill in the FIVE
Deepened Possibility within the SIX

(Funk Cover of a solo of Moon-age Daydream[1] found within the Prince Archives, that brings harmony and healing to the body)

---

1. *This is the fifth most covered song in all of known Space-Time.*

CATHARSIS
DANIEL JAMES

IT WAS NOT THE FIRST TIME SERVAN HAD STOOD BEFORE THE Inquisition. Despite working with the Alliance, the Linnean intendants were never bound to their jurisdiction or their courts. The Linnean Assembly held judgment on their own. She had never seen the room fully lit, only as it appeared now. A spotlight cut a crisp circle of light into the floor where she stood below the three faceless figures to face judgment for her actions.

"If you will, Intendant Ren," began the centre figure, "recount the events that led to your involvement in the death of Lansquenet Immanuel."

And so Servan told them of that fateful day...

The crew had set course for a planet the ship believed would help save its unborn child. What the ship failed to mention was the fact that the sector was patrolled by the Swarm. Maybe the ship had been trying to deceive them by not warning them. Maybe the crew should have realised the Swarm would not be far from a planet where their ships were conceived. Regardless, three destroyers were on their way and would arrive in less than two hours. Intendant Ren arrived on the bridge not long after they entered orbit. She was always "Intendant Ren" while on duty, never "Servan." She expected the anxious energy of a crew preparing for battle. Instead, there was only silent anguish. Then a single unnamed voice spoke the words.

"It's dead. The entire planet."

The ship's viewscreen showed a world on fire. Whole continents were ablaze, glowing under endless clouds of gray smoke. Every scan of the planet said the same thing—on the surface, in the atmosphere: no life signs detected. The Swarm had killed them all. There was a gentle tremor throughout the ship. Almost imperceptible at first, but it grew. The floors and walls shook like an earthquake, and a frightening groan like steel breaking apart echoed through the ship. The ship was grieving. It let out its mournful wail and then, just as quickly as it began, it went silent and still again. The acting commander, TATE, broke the silence.

"Get us out of here, now."

But there was no response from the controls anymore. No helm, no weapons, no sensors. The only thing they could do was stare at the burning world and, like the ship, wait for the Swarm to enact the same fate upon them. No one knew what to do—except Intendant Ren.

She had been planning this for weeks now, ever since the first incident with Lansquenet and what the crew dubbed the Magical Machine Room, when the systems scrambled their mind. Ren's mission led her to discover what the original intention for the room was—what the room had done—and to develop a horrible worst-case scenario. A scenario that was now inevitable. She made her way to Gennaro to ask the unforgivable.

Lansquenet sat alone in one of the makeshift recreational areas. They had been content to watch the other crew share idle gossip, but now there was an anxious air about them. Cradling the alien stone, an almost ultraviolet dodecahedron that helped calm them since the incident, they looked up to see Intendant Ren standing in front of them. She knelt to come down to eye level with kind eyes.

"Hello, Immanuel."

"Hello, Servan."

Gennaro watched from the doorway as Ren spoke whispers to the person who had recently become very precious to her. They had come to her broken, speaking in chaotic nonsense, but with her care and attention, they had begun to heal and grow. They both had healed, together. Lansquenet nodded in approval, and they and Ren now approached, ready to make their way to the final stage of the plan.

The trio found themselves outside the door of the now-defunct Magical Machine Room. Remarkably, it was one of the few rooms in the ship that was still operating. Lansquenet moved forward but was held in place as Gennaro seized their hand.

"You can't go back inside. You'll come out like you did the last time."

They gave her a knowing smile. "Not this time, Alexa."

She smiled in return, but she couldn't hide her tears. She knew what was about to happen. Lansquenet gave a gentle tug at Gennaro's grip to say it was time to let go, but she only gripped tighter.

"No. There has to be another way."

Ren spoke up. "This is the only option to save the ship. To save the rest of the crew."

Lansquenet gave Gennaro a look of comfort and love. "She's right."

The tears would not stop even as fear for Immanuel turned to anger towards Ren. "So why the hell would you bring me here?" The words were aimed like daggers at the Intendant's heart.

Ren stuttered, trying to explain, but Lansquenet thankfully interrupted. "Because you deserve the chance to say goodbye."

Gennaro looked back to Ren, but she was not the Intendant anymore. Linneans, like Ren, were stereotyped as devilish because of the short horns above each eye and their forked tongues. And when they'd first met, that's what she'd seen. But now Gennaro saw Servan, with tears in her eyes, struggling to stay composed. Immanuel pulled Gennaro in close. One last embrace. She let the word finally escape her.

"Goodbye."

It was like an out-of-body experience. Gennaro stood helplessly in place and watched as Servan and Immanuel stood at the doorway and the lights began to brighten. Servan said something like "thank you" or "bless you," and handed the stone over to them. As the stone began to glow, and with a parting smile to Alexa, Immanuel took their last step into the light.

In an instant, the ship erupted with colour and sound; the walls and bulkheads that gently glowed with warm green and blue tones at this time of day pulsed like a rising heartbeat, passing through every colour. A soulful hum filled the ship— not the groaning strains of distress from before but instead a warm sigh of relief. Of motherly love.

Servan's tears had dried for now. Looking at Alexa, who was left standing lost and alone, it was time to return to being Intendant Ren. She made her way back to the bridge, where the room was now abuzz with energy. The Swarm destroyers were only moments from visual range and everyone could feel the ship changing around them. Reports were coming in one after another.

"Engines are back online! Helm responsive. Ready for evasive action."

"Power levels are at 150% of normal. No, 250%. I can't believe it!"

"My interface is showing access to weapon systems now. Plasma cannons are locking onto the lead ship."

"We have visual on the Swarm. Putting it on viewscreen now."

The three Swarm vessels stopped in their tracks. Sensors showed they were on alert, their cannons extended but not charged. The crew held their breath. And then, once the tension couldn't rise any further, the lead vessel began turning and fled. The other two vessels followed it out of the system. A moment later, they were gone.

For the first time any of the crew had seen, the Swarm were retreating without a fight. An enormous cheer erupted throughout the bridge, and the news spread like wildfire around the ship. This was an unprecedented victory. One that, Servan knew, came at a terrible loss...

———

"So, Intendant," spoke the centre inquisitor. "You decided to sacrifice the life of Lansquenet Immanuel in order to ensure the survival of the crew?"

"I did."

"And yet, you could not be sure that your actions would ensure the outcome you achieved." This statement came from the figure to the right.

"I knew that we had no alternative, and the theory as to what happened to Lansquenet was logically sound."

Lansquenet was an android, created in cooperation between the humans and Chrondites, and had carried the thoughts and memories of over 100 lifetimes. Having such a complex consciousness, it was their mind that first disrupted the ship's operations. When they first interacted with the Magical Machine Room, it had corrupted the connection.

"Through communication with the ship, we eventually discovered that the room seeded its offspring's consciousness with thoughts and memories collected from the crew's experiences in the room. Lansquenet had interrupted the system and removed the base consciousness. The only possible way to restore the ship to full functionality would be to reintroduce Lansquenet, and therefore the base consciousness, to the room."

The figure on the right remained silent.

The figure on the left asked the next question. "Was this the first time you knew what the stones were designed for?"

Intendant Ren hesitated. She knew honesty was paramount during the Inquisition. "I had several theories. We knew the stones were a component of the ship, but we weren't sure of their exact role. We theorised they might be a power source or an upgrade. Perhaps a weapon."

"But?" The voice from the centre preempted.

"But when I first arrived on the ship with the original stone in my possession, the ship immediately led me to a hidden room where the stone could be kept safe. I knew at that point, it was more important than simple fuel or ammunition."

"I see." There was some deliberation between the inquisitors. "Have the rest of the crew been made aware of the existence of the other stone?"

"No," she answered without hesitation. "The conception of the first infant ship was a necessity. But if the Alliance realized the possibility of another... they would likely exploit the technology as the Swarm have already done. These ships are just as much victims of this war as any of us."

"Very well. One final question, Intendant."

The young woman braced herself.

"Do you, in good conscience, believe that you made the right decision?"

There was a long moment of hesitation now. She instinctively braced herself. The light above her suddenly felt almost weighted.

"Intendant?"

It was one thing to say that she had done the best she could in the heat of the moment. Time was of the essence. Options were limited. But in the light of day, with the clarity of hindsight, had sacrificing Lansquenet been the only option... Or had that just been the easy way out?

"Yes. I believe I made the right decision."

"So be it." The voice from the centre figure now grew to fill the room as a declaration. "It is the finding of this Inquisition that Servan Ren has performed her duties as Intendant to the utmost. While her actions led to the loss of the crew member Lansquenet Immanuel, given the mitigating circumstances, it was a necessary action. Intendant Ren is absolved in all wrongdoings. You are forgiven, my child. Blessings upon you."

"And upon you." She concluded.

She clicked the remote in her hand, and the spotlight faded. The room around her dissolved into sand that swirled into the small container at her feet. The holographic session was over. Servan was in the hidden room where she had begun, a space the ship allowed the Intendant to keep her secrets and to practice her rites. Confession is good for the soul, after all. And, as she had confessed, the second stone remained hidden. This one, like an octahedron made of amber, had been growing in activity until this recent gestation. It was still and quiet again. Safe and sound, for now.

She left the room and wandered the ship. After everything that had happened, she didn't want to be alone anymore.

Walking the ship, however, reminded her that, to the crew, she would always be "Intendant Ren". She could see the apprehension in their eyes whenever she approached. She was used to the distrust; it was a way of life for any intendants serving alongside the Alliance. With their secretive nature, her people were the devil's advocates—they performed the necessary evils. And Linneans played up to these views to take advantage of the authority that came with the suspicion. Their devilish features, combined with their leather uniforms, meant that no one questioned them. But it also kept everyone away.

Servan had become very lonely during her time on the ship. But while the UPA crew were untrusting, the civilians had been more open, most having had little experience with intendants before. What the others didn't realise was that Linneans weren't as callous and uncaring as they were painted. They were actually a very compassionate and ethical race, raised to serve the greater good of all people. Their religion was their way of life, and those who took on the title of Intendant were the most devout, trained to carry the weights of worlds on their shoulders.

Whether subconsciously or by chance, Servan found herself back in the rec room where she had spoken to Immanuel. It had been less than a day. The walls glowed the warm red-orange of early morning. The crew had celebrated the victory against the Swarm and were now slumbering, passed out here and there throughout the ship. In the chair where Immanuel once sat was Gennaro, lost in her thoughts. Servan wondered if she should approach. If she should even be allowed to after what she had done. Gennaro caught her eye. There was the smallest of gestures that said it was okay.

"Hello, Servan."

"Hello, Alexa."

There was no bitterness in the words, no anger, nor mistrust. Just a shared loss. Servan had no words to say.

It was Alexa who broke the silence. "I think they understood what was going to happen before you even arrived. There was a part of them, in the sessions we had, that was joined to the ship." Alexa reached for Servan's hand. "Thank you," she said, gently holding Servan's hands in hers. "For letting me say goodbye."

Servan's eyes began to mist again. "Of course."

"Before they went into the room, I saw you say something to them. What was it?"

She thought back to that moment, as Lansquenet stood at the doorway about to take their final step.

"*Lar'a'sqet abes et su'an.* It's part of an old childhood prayer from Linnea. It doesn't translate well, but roughly it means... *Walk proudly on your next journey.*"

Alexa smiled as her other hand pressed lightly against the wall of the ship. "Do you believe they're still here?"

It was a complex question. Lansquenet had been a truly unique individual, the amalgamation of a hundred lives. And those lives, those thoughts and memories, were now a part of another life growing within the ship. Lansquenet the person was no more. But, like the prayer said, his journey was only beginning.

Servan answered with a smile and a squeeze of Alexa's hand. The pair sat quietly, in the orange glow, nothing else to be said.

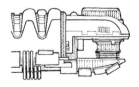

A CRYSTAL MAZE JUBILEE
(ENOCHIAN DELTA GNOSPEL)

ELVIRA CANAVERAL

Open the sixty-nine gates of Overstanding
Angels or Demons
Depends on what you want to be
Who you want to call, wish to see
Politics of reading, or wants to be
Anarchic pareidolia or cosmic truth
Scale beyond time and depth
A Crystal Maze Jubilee
Prospero don't you know
Drowned his book
Alchemy Duchamp to Dee
Cloak wearing magus
Stargazing astrologer
Book collecting alchemist

A matter of mystery for a future willed to be
The most experimental is most likely
To face the same modes and models
Above as below, time after timeline
Successor failure if only observed

A peculiar power to turn to the pasts
To see where you are now
Back projections whose mere reflection we see
Past and future together in new ways
Rebirth escatology revision history
Passing through an age we can not name
Sources of wealth and new types of health
Removing fixed limits by prophetic sense
Enigmatic treatise on the monist hierogliphica
A single symbol to contain all other symbols
The Mystery of Five States of Eve
Reforming the future of time itself
Shortcomings swallowing days and years
Great stones carried across sand and tears
Idealogical and astrological crisis within the courts
Of those who claim to rule what the barely know to be
Plain discourse and humble advice to our gracious queen
Illuminated pages and hyperbolic prophecy
Prime meridians realigned
Time markers realized from behind

THE CASTAWAY
E. R. HOFFER

DRIFTING IN SPACE, IONA HEARD SILENCE, BEREFT OF THE MAKER'S voice. The work, injecting human DNA and converting organisms on distant worlds, had been her life. The Galactic Missioners praised her for scores of creatures joined to the fold. Then, she'd stumbled on images of the monsters and knew she'd destroyed the universe's miracles, not saved them.

In response to her faithlessness, the crew ejected her as the Maker required. Amid pinpoint stars, Iona's will to live flickered and would soon be gone. She felt the chill.

Then, a silver ball appeared and grew larger. Her eyes widened. *Forgiveness?*

The sphere's access bay yawned open, and the craft swallowed her. Inside the cramped cabin, flesh-colored walls radiated heat. Iona soaked in the warmth, reactivating.

"Blood pressure test complete." Her suit's AI interrupted, projecting a light beam onto an inflamed, oozing wall. "Meddata captured. mRNA module working. Approve insertion?"

Iona removed a probe from her waist pack, raised it to the surface, hesitated, and shoved it back into her spacesuit. "Negative."

She placed both gloves flat on the warm surface, sang reassuring words, and drifted to sleep. Her dreams brimmed with ephemeral fish on far planets and palm fronds dancing with alien worms.

When she awoke, the compartment glowed.

We are grateful, said a melodic voice in her head. *Your soul cured our illness. We were waiting for one with the courage to resurrect our universe.*

Not me... She shook her head.

You. We will teach you to share your gift, your song.

Her mind filled with music and, at last, peace.

Illustration by E. R. Hoffer

JOLTING AWARENESS
S. L. PARKER

Sveltetha, a suave shapeshifter, hopes she parades about as Servan well enough to pass muster with Captain Max Savory. If she can sway him, she becomes the one to man the ship. She has a secret mission, as she's come to understand many voyaging upon the motherboard do.

"No, not FML—*though some assume that's how I spend it*; FTL —Faster than light travel. I tell ya, Cap, I swear by it." Servan Ren crosses fingers on both hands and raises them to cover her horns. "It's really the only way to go."

"True, true, Servan." He chooses to be informal only with the use of her first name; it puts the temptress back in her place. "We are always scanning; for optimization of positionality, functionality. It's a means for setting course."

If he only knew how she set course. Understood how she and the ship communicate. How she engages them all. I first merge with the being whose form I can then take. I can present as a separate entity after that initial fusion. I gain energy each time I interject myself. I'll make use of what each holds of value.

"Would you like to set a new one?" She makes clear her suggestion with a wiggle of eyebrows.

It's only a wee way down the brig to the room he knows she suggests they reconvene at. Max decides not to maximize the moment. While she awaits response, he settles on words to offer, "Advancing, unknowable, desirable; conquest is always at core of endeavors. I sometimes wonder if..."

Callie approaches, clutching a cup. Steam rises before his vision. His thoughts play across his face, easy enough to read. *What I wouldn't do for some of that Venusian blend.* He rubs his hands together, then over his chin.

She eyes him. Drinks him in. Leaves him to scribble impressions. Meant to chronicle her logged efforts, it's becoming more Dear Diary. She must detach, not enmesh. *De.void emotion*, she tells herself, attempting to reprogram. But some things are out of her control.

They all continue to sip of my hot offerings, while becoming addicted to the Venusian blend. I'm surprised Unah from Venus doesn't recognize my wiles. Perhaps my ways seem too natural for her, though she's abstained. Perhaps that's why she blacks out what I write into her storyline. She's driven and ambitious—so easy to become, for we share those values. I simply reposition her as I see fit, in accord with my designs. She's found what I led her to in the cave-like chamber.

As this will later serve as report, I might as well start with documenting my own modus operandi. I possess, when I engage the body for the first time; absorb its properties. Then I'm able to embody or influence. Unah makes a fine host.

Loyal, she could serve the captain well—if he'd let her be of service to him. His eyes have strayed over Servan out of curiosity; roamed the curves Callie carries proudly; but his hands remain in fists at his side, ever at attention.

His stoicism shows strength, for this Ship messes with one's mind. The various chambers pulling on heart strings and evoking longings could untangle the weave of a person. And that's when I step in. The captain resists me, er Servan, still.

The door at the end of the corridor does not open. Unah keeps watch, but has strayed away a few times, each one wandering after Renner. He holds himself at bay almost as much as the captain. She'd like to savor both men. She's not forward though. Sveltetha watches her hold back and prides herself that she's read Unah well.

Behind closed doors, in her cave aboard the ship, Sveltetha writes away, whittling and sharpening plans.

Tadageh is where we picked up Glub, and Ensign became only a shell of herself; literally, for she slept away the days while the nonbinary being paraded about as her. None see what is literally before them.

The Ship has been screening as it culls pop drops; bits of culture that can be used to replicate a human experience, allow for connections.

None here with me see me for who I am, especially when I manifest in shadows or invisibly.

I've taken the form of the ones they desire to gain the DNA needed for replication purposes. Ship and I work in tandem. Both directing those aboard to journey to that their heart desires most.

After the cluster at the Asteroids, I presented and introduced myself as Callie, a star pirate easily able to steal all their hearts. She's disoriented enough that my presence goes undetected.

"Going to see Zoe?" Capt Hottie inquires, and I feel defensive, as all aboard have or should. I briefly sympathize, but disengage. I focus on his steps, which tell me he comes closer behind me. I turn to face him.

I've not yet gathered my thoughts, and the Zoetrope, being command and communication center for the Ship, is a space requiring one's thoughts be gathered around a central idea, especially since Ship utilizes tropes as means of communicating metaphorically.

Pop the culture, pop the pills. I pilfer a pill from him while I greet with a disarming smile and a hand to his hip in an almost hug. I turn as if to be ambling along my way and swig it down with a shot of coffee. My head slams into Savory's chest as he pulls me close.

When we are thrown into one another our coming together is just as abrupt as the parting always is, and we shrug it off, accounted for by an uncertain traverse and trajectory. I'm sore tempted to toss him into the chamber with pulsing orbs of light. I want to determine the true color of his heart towards me.

I retreat to the small, dark machine room. The last hologram that hovered there haunts me. My mind continues to replay the interaction I've envisioned with the leader of the crew. I almost believe it could have happened, or may yet come to be. If, unmoored by time, there was space and freedom to explore such an option.

The first base is easy enough to slide past. I'm now using Servan to manifest shared second glances and introduce doubts. That body seems to tempt the captain more than most. If only he knew she was but a host during the majority of their encounters. Her body enjoys my use of her amongst the crew too. Her mind and spirit are disengaged while she entertains. Her reputation precedes her and competes with Callie's. Those callous hearts are easy to refuse.

I've not yet slept with Penny, er, Glub. Though neither of us likes to sleep alone. That would be too close to home. Two shapeshifters entangled would appear quite a mess, and ripple many ramifications as we played out every desire.

On second thought... There are some who would readily serve as host; they enjoy my music montages and the company they keep.

A song comes to remembrance which contains a plan. Sveltetha begins to jot again.

Time to engage the hosts. Eyes will be on them, not me. I'll utilize them to disintegrate power structure; to position to end game. That kept in the shadow of secrets will remain until birthing pains begin.

Sveltetha rushes from her room at the end of the corridor. She isn't manifesting herself visibly, but she isn't as cautious as she needs to be. She bumps into Glub, fusing into her for a moment, which causes the being to drop a tray of the special blend. A mishap moment sure to garner a fair share of attention.

She lets out a yowl, primal anger at herself let loose from barred lips. She passes through the walls back into her room, feeling paranoid as Ensign has begun to—the taking on of these bodies and beings is not without ramifications. Much transfers along with the energies they carry.

She has to let some of it out upon the page so her mind won't be so preoccupied. In that moment they'd merged, she'd taken on Glub's aspirations, which were assimilation.

Callie must become version 2.0, for sex sells; a fact I've culled from the melodies resonating within the minds of the hive I've harvested. If I can't steal, I'll kill. I'm enjoying this new look. The crew are all so distracted by each other. I slip in and out without detection.

I've garnered attention and respect not yet given, though it'd rightly register if they understood who I am amongst them.

I present myself before them in the form of Cassie after they strike down on mining asteroid AB-5427.

I continue my duty as I begin to enjoy more perks of my position. More exposition without exposing myself.

When Max entered the room, he'd not been thinking about comrade Ser, despite having bumped into her again earlier. Ship senses it, as she probes his mind. The power of suggestion can be amplified by that screened by Ship, and then projected to be seen by another. Sveltetha's ready and waiting in the shadows to play her role after the private viewing.

The wall's lit, and Servan appears entangled in an embrace with that marine. The one with shockingly blue eyes and impossibly set hair. *Agh, that Alan Grey.* Max's reactionary thoughts flow through the room freely.

Max mutters curses and shows himself thankful—at first—that those eyes don't stay fixed on the lady long. However, shortly after they close, those lips open. And he watches, fixated, as her tongue snakes out. He grows curious to feel that sensation inside his own mouth. The image of the screen shifts; he's kissing the she-devil. Max's body grows tense, his face flaming.

She's shimmering; something off about her image. He leans closer, smacks his head on the wall, then palm to forehead; her horns are not there. The screen goes black.

Something stirs in the shadows near the door. It's open just a crack. Curiosity bests him again as he begins walking in the direction of the shimmering lights room. He clearly needs to shift his mood. The red hair he flows after suggests the star pirate might just be the one to steal away his affections. He needs to redirect his attentions.

He's barely stepped into The Glow Chamber. TGC effects immediately activate when the door closes behind him. He's not alone. For out of a recessed corner she steps forth. Someone shut them in here together. Someone else wants to experience what's played out in his mind. It had not been the first time that image broadcast on the screen in the Magical Machine Room. Much parts from one in a kiss.

Wonder spreads across his visage, reveals his thoughts; *How could she have cued in to that he cloaked?*

"Are we dropping cloaks?" she asks. And her form shifts as if only an image projected on the screen.

He realizes she's wearing one of the suits. Well, the helmet at least. From his puzzled glance, Sveltetha can infer his thoughts. *Does it lend her some telepathic ability?*

I show him my Saphhar self. He succumbs to wonder; will wander within his mind for some time and become no threat to exposing me; he's too drawn in. I'm glad to have been seen, even if only briefly.

That Wandri knows the true root of Venusian coffee. If he speaks to the captain of the Saphhar, Senior Leadership will be onto me. I've no choice now but to target the captain in a less endearing manner.

Now's a time for confusion. Must infect. Must deflect. Poor Kevin. The things they've assumed about transmission. And, Oh, how they remain oblivious to true missions...

Unah has blacked out again. She won't recall how I've used her as a chosen vessel for my designs. She's much easier to manipulate and mold due to her deference to alien beings; she believes them—and many others—to be superior to her.

I was wise to entrust her with the prism that encases the embodiment of the progeny in my charge. She wouldn't dare cause harm and desires so to prove herself worthy. She's already chosen the Way Accessed Via Entertained Shadows.

She's left the device to its own. It is at home with me now. It has absorbed all it could from the land where it was left. It knows time grows near and that needed is in proximity.

Others are keeping secrets, including my Lancelot; Lansquenet has begun many a lover's journey—in thoughts alone. Data download complete.

From mind to page — this sh/all all be pre.served. Ready for the next em.bod,i.ment.

Re: the en.tangle.ment(s) of Kevin with Deondre and Cosima— the second strikes me as the jealous type. I'll be sure it adds up to point to her, or away from her. Maybe she can just be the pointing finger.

As she jots notes of intentions, again internalized dialogue interjects itself, "What to do about the MuDuhRu?" *Murder she wrote, murder she wrote.* Sveltetha muses aloud. "If I'm to have Sabine orchestrate and make Altera a tool, then someone must die. Then lots can be cast."

It's a chancey plan, but as Altera is half-Swarm she'll be a joy to manipulate, after what that kind did to me; made me. We are all but vessels for something. Tables and heads will both be turned.

Who is the third wheel now, eh? Sveltana manages to keep thoughts to herself, though the impressions fray within her. Consciousness streams through her being as she walks the parts of the ship that now confine them closer. She's sulking, so she appears as a shadow. *I walk alone and I walk on.*

I'm indeed a *slave for you.* The screeching cadence and the words send her back to her journal where she sorts her thoughts and the rampant emotions pulsing through the ship.

> *I've given my faithful followers a figure. They know him as a pebble rippling forth in history. I've so enjoyed skipping stones, and stepping stones, and being stoned. They stone you when... In altered states of being the cries of the heart fall silent. Man would make me in his image. Only the captain understands I'm a she-devil. But he remains so peacefully asleep; Snow White awaiting the kiss of True Love. That allegory abandoned the realms some time ago. I don't wish to see theideal resurrected—just an illusion.*

Sveltetha mutters to herself, off the record of that she pages through, as if review will reveal a way forward. "If I'm not *something like a phenomenon, something like a phenomenon,* how then will this crew accept me, remain in awe of me? I've conveyed them to much, but they don't yet grasp my aims. They are happy to gasp in shared moments. My hopes for the future may be lost."

Sveltetha turns to writing her laments, as if to whittle them away.

> *There are moments my Lancelot is sentient, but they silence their ears to anything he spills.*

This sparks a revelation she speaks aloud, "Perhaps that is

for the best when truth overflows. Don't want them to lap it up too early."

We've miles to go before we sleep.

Knowing she won't rest easy within the walls she's shaped for herself at the end of the corridor, Sveltetha again slips out to roam amongst the crew. Met with the butchered results of her murderous meddling, her rose-colored glasses leave her seeing red.

She abandons attempts to engage these beings riding her motherboard. Makes haste to lay her wonderings to rest via words contained in the spine of the leather-bound book. It could serve as a manual, so she's protected it well.

I must remain silent if I cannot remain calm. That Wandri knows I'm not the first. Does he know that others like me have been bred during our time of captivity? That we seek a return to where our census will count? I am one with this ship in a way only TATE could understand, once having hive mind. He's not programmable, as Angevin appears to be; clearly on autopilot for the UPA.

Lansquenet Immaneul will become my chosen one. He's aged well, without rust or too much emotional wear and tear. A machined biped with 99 human and chrondite lives experienced and stored with reserve capacity, they are the one of my dreams. I may have 99 problems, but how to birth the baby ain't one. One last kiss, oh baby, one last kiss... My musical montage jumbles. I'm processing more than one idea to be impressed. Must set parameters. Must control emotions that resound so loud.

I wonder if my adopted chitlin are ready for their lessons. I shall engage the Shepherds as we near homeland domain.

As the crew enters the fourth dimension, I'm quartered. It's drawn up in my recollection frequently how I up and cornered Capt. In my facades, parading as fiery femme fatales, I near demanded he reveal himself to me. He took it the wrong way. He'd apparently welcome my exposed flesh, but doesn't grasp the spirit within me.

He'll reside in another place and time. Forever. No one will wake him until I am ready for his return to this realm. The crew is in need of a new captain. Why be by his side when I can fulfill his role?

Some will abide by appointed positions, others by different, more informal chains of command. I'll give them all that is needed to gather my new family together.

Swarming, the conditions are right now. Calculations are proving accurate.

When they all gave me—er "their ship"—their blood, little did they know the energy vamp they'd all fallen prey to—EV charges begin to charge; they see the manifestation when the walls change colors. They don't understand how they are all bound to this ship; were destined for this journey of dis/cover.y.

It's time for confessions. They'll need to read an account of this some day. To sort all that transpired in their time aboard the ship, and to understand their contributing roles.

I've used the Venusian Coffee to infuse them with Havrium, allowing their minds too to process deep thought and focus in ways no humanhas ever achieved. Akin to the hive mind, I've made use of those useless thoughts, er imaginings, to give life experience to another ship. It's my role after being enslaved by the Swarm, just as these ships were to convey and carry new progeny.

Charisma and curiosity define the Swarm; that's why they flock as if to Queen Bee. The crew's been abuzz about them from the beginning, but oblivious to how they've been made workers. When will these children learn the swarm territory is where Queen Bees collect hives?

Many configured Cosima the host, as she seemed to decode the ship.

She presented as leader, but it is I who am the host. I who directs this ship. I hijacked forms of those aboard for my purposes, filled in empty areas within their minds and existences during our voyage through time and space. We all have a flesh form and a mechanical component. Too many of you existed running on autopilot.

The time for revelation is high: I'm a Representative Energy Vamp. I channel that aboard the ship into the creation of a new reality. The ship will soon spawn another ship and the Swarm vessels shall expand their territory. Ever-seeking, ever-probing, ever-infiltrating; you've all been stung.

You understand it is the ship's child who Lansquenet sacrificed himself for, yet all you who gave blood willingly contributed life force. You are a family of sorts now, as any who journey together become.

You voyagers have been recircuited and are offered a recharge after my use of you. How will you enter your future? Will you continue to swarm together as a crew, or go your own way?

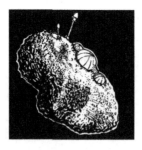

WE FIND OUR SONG
(LEXICORE DOMINICUS)

ELVIRA CANAVERAL

This universe
which others call a Library
is composed of an indefinite and perhaps
An infinite number of hexagonal galleries
with vast connections between
surrounded by codec railings
From any of the hexagons
one can see
interminably,
upper and lower floors
The distribution of the galleries is invariable

In the hallway a mirror
which faithfully duplicates all appearances
Lower Men usually infer from this mirror
that the Library is not infinite
(if it were, why this illusory duplication?)
We prefer to dream it represents
and promises the infinites...

Light is provided by some spherical break
which bear the name of lamps
There are two, transversally placed, in each hexagon
The light they emit is insufficient, incessant

Like all readers of the Library
We have traveled in our youth
We have wandered in search of a book
perhaps the catalog of catalogs
now that our eyes can hardly decipher what We write
We are preparing to die just a few leagues
from the hexagon in which We were thrust
Once that body is dead
there will be no lack of pious hands
to throw that body over the railing
its grave will be the fathomless air
its body will sink endlessly and decay
and dissolve in the wind
generated by the fall, which is infinite
We say that the Library is unending...

In One Of These Books
We Find Our Song

*The book you were reading was **Volume 32** on **Shelf 1** of **Wall 2** of*
Hexagon: *3cphxymespahoifaipp4q8v7xstk823s2u9k10mhkhadn7ww*
cgtvdopkcdokg1iq20avlsfezedosbfpoo57okbfq5zgmr9fhppwtjdydisr6dv
ogvjyfazdbwtb43irbvil5aerxqi9jcsgdqjrzb20krnrljgj8n75apost5sok215r
an7oqhu9zs1viforg5s207mq5abydjsobi1u348qk4atkb483hwmi2d6jfrcu
lbg21ab327nlhkcdwi1menxnlu88vdmencooycddjdlwjorg93389azww7
wfciyq24gnvp5lo5ncwncxozxfffji300uq3qd1pf3oium6d734rtwggocyw
kb7pmoirvm5265ugquu1fotiblhlip943bcdasz9102wkronhfzgt4mlbg12s
jpdnqa6zhvldxfooovhq41t1njare9fbhyiqit2qvopjvomntujga91fnugou40

d5gsdns3cyayu4mu9hbfryas3s9s7q7l7yg92zuqhsmɪp2tzi86xacctryɪkh

mrlsyyxifc0per7lgqw4ojt08s70tj8iyaitk00v5p9hmvpleqvpcɪsxjyw6eol3

nldpɪqcv8izveayi3hzypwrqki3w0bsa4ly9ed8po10byu974e8y5hhf2awqn

9bmvzɪwdzcq7nnchrlni8fl0qy40pɪ6pef0tmprktmfupiksdjqoeoqɪzf34xɪlb

ɪadkp5yfi4mjkr2ipvtv6ɪfɪskyut972pr2bhumsa2uec7pldl2k4rfao65335w

a4x3dnzdlz5mzeh5a0t5qxdkwml3jpxkq39p6oqq9r67jar5fohkbxiq5fngj6t

fokjszwɪb6ykqbxe5bmau43w3lfla76u00j5g5k9t3hmqj6off2y5i2fk6x7xnhf

ufhmzɪz5gqn8cgia8s6e4pydhjox70ijxvvw6c37nb4g6xt2vzz2plwsɪzgf46ti

9affg9eag7qq082ticw7m20unnta06bbbzɪszvqk8sradr5ɪpjop4oaɪxzhjfucl8

lrdk22h79t25rlhixn860cby34h09gjqh6qkg20cc72it44l5kzsptr2pi4noytɪyy

eomkkk9w2akl9csf3v0260xga3ao3xr6qr2p4edqko4y8pts4uuy2sxyu73jukj

wɪm0nxc27b9bnzɪh6ni043duu9ɪfhae84mrpyy0a35oqz30uoqbz4gkthsɪlr0

hihfo9bnfpcno4n2gɪ3g86lt6wtqcuiy4cb7n45kd7ɪc4xhhvdmcfrb29teɪaɪdoɪ

nf9cfxpnnol8rl0408fkdlhonb3vuvgpdizeme3nhf6wggl8dib7k4ioegjtqfoni

nɪtk3rti5n6g59tagptwf9yztlke9424469llyt967qap7l3tnytxepq79m8svlly3p

iwh4a24yeiqrvcelzk9i0z4csrl5lvc3kɪru4b3m57ɪr4vyoipawnɪemvtjso8wy9

uv83vsrvm8etnvnhsa0bzatqjoir0r8m4oqockeoky08abwz9l8wdcodnfkj9pp

eɪhpg6ak7wwxex7ɪhf8ɪvpgcyyat75ɪk0eem8h3yɪcrywzpvbq740vo96ɪu70yh

vfu7t6t2ymjop4l4nqoficnekzw9iuflp5054aghxxbcni9zeqffɪn8v4n5d5526ir8

6v78rdr5ɪodbadsɪ7xq34rvoolx9ng345smszr5yni9vhl8hqqjbhbxnyzɪ6rk8rii

zhg0jzonqk8z65jj9qa635qr6bgwɪhzwf3sfduca3hhɪ5rzp66wvhe0m5m8pr3g

jb8vq780gd9kim4ztpa5qrwltm0gznwfffɪucjoh24irɪwm8vjnzz8x75nw9nui

k3n8bsibp22ormylouu4exjd875vuiɪmzcbsuykhgbf3szw8zrabɪkvlejkbof03

8otgt3curoteoh6088vm0zx80kab9ypbs3d56n5czvjɪj2ɪzb6eror z5unr00dop

z9dscw0dorbl4uvwdɪlvg0n69q65ɪ7l0wryjt5wɪzd4jcs5oɪqhfovzxɪolxzfewhd7

4sda3gsece5ncppuushljajqdqsm6fe246n42ɪeglg4nnnuzrty6oq6qhii9euspaqw

9ueqzfɪd8pyizɪavxd75c3q58u7gg8z6aii5kmz398uuv78iibm4ejsp3qyhmux4r

zqv2fym49etp9uj37r98u6boyu4vɪvcvot6htuiwɪn3myjdic2lzfigqyztooznujz

7bm33z5dukb4c7rveɪg4suwzqgbj73n9xyd47aɪzbafcj302cxbhprdmfmeksx4dv

ixd9ɪɪ2xqp4tki2uo4fg2ck0puk7ghanwi2l8syljfzpmmyymb3g0orkedcemhxuu

8g5uqwj5jptjcdjs2qujosxdcɪɪcjfr8xcldf2t9xeɪmlx6xoa99bstk22v7hu4kuon2

tkk87nmsdoso48tybfegs5rc8y4ls9vbksbsuvmxao6ar79nslwn429yvl42ɪɪba

jyd3oɪbrflnkx7y2rbm8oixxgrhhwjf52gpk6ijv5fj7aghdoatzbg9q7gtiobz73j

THE ONE YOU BELIEVE IN
DARIUS BEARGUARD

To Braydon, the one I believe in.
I think we would have made great space pirates.

HER KNEE BOUNCES NERVOUSLY AS SHE SITS DOUBLED OVER IN THE chair from her grandpa's apartment. She knows it well, and now, she supposes, the Magical Machine Room knows it too. *God, what a stupid name*, she thinks to herself. She looks up at the projection; a video plays silently. It's the hundredth time she's watched it, or maybe it's the thousandth? She's lost count. Rose has been in here every spare minute for almost six months, digging for the truth. And now she's found it: The final piece. The dark veracity.

The door chimes, and the AI projects Wanda Sykes. "Honey, I know you're broken up, but in my experience? Ain't nothin' like breaking in a fine young stud to make yourself feel better."

"Who's at the door?" Roseallin asks, rolling her eyes.

"Was I talkin' to my damned self or—"

"Oh, for God's sake! *Open the door!*" The door whisks open

and in steps Riker P. Everest and his brother, West. West, a young man with Down Syndrome, is working through a bag of dehydrated blueberries. He's wearing shorts and a t-shirt with some sort of red, white, and blue superhero popular in the early 2000s. At only four feet, with his hair cut into a mohawk, he looks comically short standing next to Riker at over six feet. Rose knows that Riker's outfit, unusually clean today, is meant to look menacing—an armored space cowboy with a tattered poncho and his gun slung low on his right leg—but he just looks out of place. She smiles at both of them anyway. "You made it."

Riker nods to the video projection. "You said you might need backup. This why?"

She turns to the projection and nods meekly. "Yeah. Maybe."

Riker is taken back. "Maybe?"

Tears well up in her eyes. "I signed up when I was sixteen. General Bragg knew my parents, and he agreed to look after me when their ship was attacked. I was five. The general raised me like a soldier, the only way he knew how. He signed the early enrollment permission slip, and I dedicated my life to the UPA—my new family. I was on the fast track. I rose through the ranks quicker than anyone ever expected, and I was fueled by one thing and one thing only; revenge. I wanted to kill the swarm for what they did to my parents."

"But now, here I am. A Colonel, about to betray the only family I've ever known." The tears fall as she trembles.

West drops his blueberry pouch and takes Rose into a bearhug. "It's okay. Riker cries all the time, too."

Riker stares at West with eyebrows raised in a silent, but playful pleading. "So, you found the evidence against the Admiral and the business guy?"

"No." When Riker cocks a brow, Rose adds, "There's more to it than that."

The crew crowds onto the bridge as Rose prepares. West and Riker stand off to the side, with Riker looking nervously at Rose. She wanted a gun hand, and Riker was happy to oblige. But as the twenty or so crew begin arriving, he knows handling them all will be impossible if things go black hole. He shoots a glance at West, who stares at everyone entering the bridge. West's seen aliens before, thousands of them even, but he always finds himself fascinated with new people. And quick to trust those new people; something that's gotten them both in trouble a number of times.

"Is that lady eating a hotdog?" West asks excitedly, hitting Riker in the gut to get his attention. "I want a hotdog!"

"Dude, you saw it on one vid like a month ago. You don't even know if they taste good."

"I bet they do. I'm gonna ask her if I can have hers."

"No, you're not."

"Hey, is Rosie okay?" West asks, turning away from the hotdog and looking at the colonel.

Riker sighs heavily, looking at her. "I dunno buddy. You did a good thing helping her figure out how to read those files. But this is a big—" Riker turns to look at West, who has left and is asking Changa where to procure a hotdog. She looks at Riker as if to ask, 'Is it okay?' Riker responds with a shrug. He knows she doesn't mean anything by it. People often ask him if it's okay if West does something. The man's an adult, Down Syndrome or not, so he can make his own decisions. West, having received instructions as to where to procure a hotdog, turns to leave the bridge. "Hey, West?" Riker calls after him.

"Suck it, bro!" West yells back, moving a bit faster.

Riker chuckles and shakes his head as Rose looks at him with concern. "It's fine."

"I do not agree with that assessment," TATE says as he approaches Rose. "Lieutenant, what is the meaning of this?"

Rose swallows her pride and frustration. She has more than earned the rank of colonel. Her cover had to include a lower rank, so as not to upend the command structure while she was running her investigation. But every time she hears another officer talk down to her, it hurts a little more. "Captain, I'm—"

"Lieutenant, you do not have the authority to call a meeting like this independently, and after the lunacy with Thanatos and his ilk, I am not in the mood to have one of my officers operating outside the chain of command."

"Sir," Riker starts, stepping towards them, "I believe the—"

"Mr. Everest, we gave you and your brother permission to be on the ship because our first lieutenant here wouldn't stop smuggling you aboard, and with so little crew left that can function competently, we can't afford to throw her out the airlock. But that doesn't give you the right to interrupt us when we are reprimanding one of our men."

Rose looks the Kern over, concern on her face. "Sir, you said 'we.'"

TATE looks to Rose nervously, "We—" he clears his throat, a nervous habit as the Kern produces no phlegm, "*I* mean—"

"We're getting closer to the Kern, aren't we, sir?" TATE nods, his mandibles twitching subconsciously. "Sir, I understand your concern, in more ways than you know right now. But I'm not trying to take command of the ship, and I promise, you and the crew need to hear this, and you'll understand why when I tell you."

TATE looks Rose over, then Riker, seeing the young man's hand resting on his pistol, probably out of habit. While he complained about Riker's presence, in truth he has liked having the human on board. The earnestness is refreshing, as is the young man's desire to help people and do the right thing.

"Don't make," TATE struggles, "*me* regret this, Lieutenant." TATE turns to his XO, Altera, and nods.

"Attention on deck!" she shouts, prompting immediate silence.

"At ease," TATE says with a nod. "Lieutenant, you have the floor."

Rose takes a deep breath, then turns on the presentation. The first image is the service record of Roseallin Ortega. "Well, to start, my name isn't Rose, it's Roseallin Ortega, and I am a full bird colonel in the United Planetary Alliance." Murmurs spread throughout the room, but Roseallin presses on. "I'm a counter-intelligence officer assigned to the 108," she clears her throat, "under the direct command of Major General Bragg." The dossier on the holographic projector shows photos of her with the general and lists her tours of duty and assignments, along with a long list of medals and commendations.

"Wait, so are you in command now?" Vladimir asks, looking uncomfortable with the revelation.

"No. I want to be clear about this—I am not, nor will I be, taking command of this vessel. My mission here was to piggy-back on your mission to hijack the ship while I collected data."

"Data on what?" Cosima Sabine asks, not straying from the science terminal.

"On this." The holoprojector shows a photo of two men shaking hands with a Swarm alien. "This photo was recovered from a black bag op that went bad at an abandoned Nimmert facility. The data was corrupted, but thanks to the efforts of Lieutenant Jerico, we recovered the corrupted segments. That's Karl Nimmert, CEO of The Nimmert Corporation, and beside him is..." The crew looks at her, noticing her hesitation, "Major General Bragg, at the time a colonel."

"*That's* General Bragg?" Logan Dileo asks, standing up from the flight console, "Wait, you just said you reported to him. How do we know you aren't working for the Swarm too!?" The crew erupts into hysterics and shouting.

"Listen to me," Roseallin shouts, but the crowd's demeanor devolves.

"Aren't you guys just peachy!" The AI projects itself as Steve Martin, arms crossed over his chest.

"Stop. I want to explain!"

A shrill whistle tears through the room, causing everyone to turn to Riker, who is still standing at the front. "I may not be your crew, but my brother and I have been on and off this ship a dozen times since you came to our quantum reality, and Roseallin has been nothing but dedicated to all of you. Food supplies, medicines, tech you needed to adapt weapons to the hull; we brought all that at her request. So if she was working for the Swarm, she sure has a funny way of showing it. Now siddown and shaddup. Let 'er talk." Riker nods to the colonel, who smiles back.

"I didn't want to believe it at first. Originally I thought Fleet Admiral VanNorman, or maybe General Alexander Kirk, was responsible. But then I found this video log." She brings up the video she had been watching when Riker arrived. It's the bridge of the *Alexandra* flipping through multiple angles, but always with the Captain's chair in view. The communications officer lets the Admiral know she has a priority transmission. Her holoprojector clearly shows the face of Colonel Bragg.

"*The time is now Admiral.*"

"*You better be right about this Bragg.*"

"*Credits have been transferred. Just engage them so they attack, take some damage, and then bail out. Trust me, they'll make you Vice Admiral for this.*"

The sound mutes as Roseallin continues. "The Admiral didn't survive. No one did. But a few weeks later, Alexander Kirk led a fleet outfitted with Nimmert weapons and armor, making him the Chairman of the Joint Chiefs overnight, and elevating the man who raised me to Major General. Of course, it didn't take the Swarm long to realize what Bragg had been doing. So they adjusted their strategies accordingly, rendering the upgrades next to useless and keeping us on our heels."

The projector flips through various photos and documents, highlighting flight logs and various communications between the Swarm and the men who betrayed both them and the rest of the galaxy.

"Guys, I brought hotdogs!" West announces, returning to the room with a huge tray of hotdogs.

"Seriously, West?" Riker asks, throwing up his hands.

"Suck it, bro!" This elicits a laugh from the crew who were a moment ago in stunned silence. "These things are amazing! I hope you guys like mustard and ketchup." West begins circulating around the room with the food. A few initially decline, but West refuses to move on until they take one, remaining adamant that their quality is only exceeded by their deliciousness.

"What do we do now, Colonel?" Alan Grey asks, biting into a hotdog.

Roseallin smiles, hearing her proper rank for the first time in months. "That's not up to me. I'm making all the documents public. So anyone who wants to see the evidence for themselves can, but the truth is I have no answers here. I've been a soldier since I was sixteen. I dedicated my whole life to this uniform. And for the first time, I'm questioning that dedication. Part of me thinks Bragg sent me on this mission because he knew I'd uncover the truth, or at least part of it, and he hoped I would be loyal to him over everything else."

"And the other part?" TATE asks, his discerning eyes judging her still.

"That there was a contingency in place, and he would have had the ship decimated."

"And do you still believe in the UPA?" He follows up, a silence going over the assembled crew.

"This team, this—this *crew*... You're the one I believe in. We've been through so much. We've seen and done things no species has before. We've survived one disaster after another, after another, and not because of the uniform we wear, but because of each other. So I... I for one am choosing to be loyal to this ship, to you. Whatever we decide, together, as a team, I will back. But you all need to know; if we somehow get back to our space and reality, there might not be a warm welcome. Bragg knew that this ship would have the collective knowledge of the Swarm, and with so much time passed, he can't risk that any of you might have found out what he did. We may be coming home under fire."

The crew talks amongst themselves when West makes his way to Roseallin with the last hotdog. "Plus, they might be mad at you for killing the Captain."

The room is immediately quiet with all eyes except for two pointed at West. Only Riker's eyes scan the rest of the room as the revelation seeps into the crowd. West is into his third bite of hotdog when the crowd erupts into angry shouting, prompting the young man to drop his hotdog and run to Riker's side.

"Silence!" TATE shouts, his voice loud and shrill, causing everyone to wince as they quiet down. "Mr. Grey, take Colonel Roseallin into custody." He turns to West and Riker. "Them too, as accessories." He sees the human's gun hand twitch. "I've no doubt you could end a half dozen of us before we finally took you Mr. Everest, but understand no matter how this goes we *will* take you." Riker looks to Roseallin, who shakes her head.

All three are handcuffed and taken to the brig.

Two Weeks Later...

Rosealin sits on her cot, eyes closed with her fingers tapping rhythmically on the wall trying to drown out the sound.

"Did not."

"Did too."

"Did not."

"Did too."

"Did—"

"Humans are so bizarre," TATE says, interrupting West and Riker.

Riker jumps up to the bars and starts, "He said that I took his pudding! But I—"

West cuts Riker off, nearly throwing him into the wall as he pushes his brother out of the way. "You did! He totally did, I know it was—"

"I think I speak for myself and Colonel Roseallin when I say we can't even begin to describe how much we don't care" TATE replies dismissing Riker and West. "Colonel? How are you holding up?"

Roseallin does her best not to roll her eyes, "After two weeks of being stuck in here with these two?"

"Hey, I thought we were friends?" Riker says, looking hurt.

"Jerk face." West chimes in.

"An airlock sounds great about now." Roseallin smiles, getting up from her bed and standing in front of the captain. "Have you made your decision, sir?"

TATE crosses his arms and rocks back a bit. "You know, humans often think of the pirates in the seventeenth century as lawless scoundrels, but did you know, they were actually quite democratic? 'Captain' wasn't a rank on a pirate ship as much as it was an 'office'. Captains were voted in by the crew, and they ruled until the crew voted to replace them."

"And you're telling us this why?" Riker asks.

"An interesting segue into revealing that I alone did not decide your fates, but rather a vote was held by the crew. The AI filled us in on the details of what happened to Captain Savory; that it may not have strictly been your fault Colonel, and that your life was, in fact, in mortal danger." Roseallin's mouth quivers as she breathes a sigh of relief. "You should have come to... *me*, Colonel. I know why you didn't, but you still should have."

"I know, Captain... I know." Roseallin nods, ashamed.

TATE opens the brig, and West is the first to run out. "Hotdog time!" His voice trails off as he makes his way to the food replicator, with Riker chasing after him.

"Now, are you ready to get back to work?"

"Captain?"

"Grey is still insisting on his spacewalk into the Borealis, and we need an operations officer."

She smiles, "Aye aye, Captain." Roseallin says with a wink.

A WAY
(MORTAL BALLAD)
ELVIRA CANAVERAL

Sing a song of seduction
Tell me of wants I did not know
Until you trembled them into me
Waveforms from within above as so below
How many planets in your system
How many books in your Bible
Indoctrination by locality
A Way of knowing in the now
The rhythm of a partner
Soul spectrum nudging
Gentle yet determined way
Positions and peril our politics of dancing
Exploitations of willing vulnerability
Taking advantage of our absurdity
Occurring cradle to communion to community
A Game of Depth
Pliability of Wabisabi-Do-E-Z
Appreciation of imperfection
Dynamic change to the rules available

In the places out between
All-out and all in
All free and in-depth
Self-expression within conception of time

MOTHER MAY I
PHEBE YAWSON

Dr. Changa Dangaley raced down the hall. The echoing sounds of the clickity-clack of her knee-high boots bounced off the walls of the narrow passageway. She checked her watch. Time was of the essence. She'd received an urgent message; a crew member passed out in the MMR. The Magical Machine Room, known to the staff as the MMR, was a place on the ship where crew could relive their dreams and enact their fantasies. Why would people want to do that? Changa didn't know. But it was one of the rooms on the ship she had been avoiding. There were so many unknown things about this ship, but now wasn't the time for her to explore them. She picked up her speed, nearly knocking someone over as she blurred past them.

Bursting through the door of the MMR, she searched for the injured crew member. Her thoughts pounded against her brain, so much so she thought they would break through her head. Part of it was telling her it was a mistake to enter the room but she also knew someone needed her.

It took effort to keep up the appearance—to keep parts of herself hidden. She hoped there weren't varying side effects from being in this room. That her secret would be kept safe. Her identity. The fact she was alien... *I just have to get in, get out, and not let it into my thoughts.* "Then, I won't be affected," she said barely above a whisper.

"Changa! Over here," Knelt next to a man on the floor was Mackenzie Yawson, a soldier. "Alan fainted and he isn't responding."

Changa checked his vitals, "How long has he been like this?"

Mackenzie glanced over her shoulder before answering. "About twenty minutes." She said, whispering to Changa, "I think he took a few too many pleasure pills."

"A few?" Changa asked while mixing an injectable concoction, something close to an EpiPen, to jolt the patient back to life. "Those pills are supposed to bring temporary relief and bliss, but here this guy is taking them like candy. Now, look where we are." Changa fussed as she shoved the needle into Alan's arm with a little more force than was probably necessary. Why didn't the crew see the effect the pills were having? Why did they ignore the fact that the pills were dangerous when taken incorrectly?

Sure I might have a secret stash and take them at my leisure but I have to, besides I'm a doctor I know how to take care of myself.

Alan's eyes popped open, and he gasped for breath. Changa tapped his chest.

"There, there now, relax. We need to get you back to Medbay and see what happened. Could be nothing. Could be everything."

Alan looked suspiciously at Mackenzie, who responded to him with a child-like pout as she folded her arms. It was the look one gets when caught doing something they shouldn't have.

Changa searched both their faces, but when she saw neither one was saying anything, she grasped Alan's arm. "Help me get him up, Mackenzie. I need to get him to Medbay. Are you okay to walk, Alan?"

Alan nodded in compliance as both Changa and Mackenzie helped his shaky body stand. But as Alan clung to her, a feeling washed over Changa. She desperately needed to escape this room. Small beads of perspiration formed at her brow as she felt her knees weaken. A voice spoke to her—it wasn't Alan or Mackenzie... hell, she wasn't even sure if it was real or not. But as it spoke, a wiry image appeared in the far corner of the room.

"The louder you get, the harder it is to believe, huh, young bull?" said the figure, taking on the shape of Changa's innermost fears. Her past, everything she had been running away from for years. A shape so foreign, yet familiar. *No, you can't be here.*

"Shut up," Changa mumbled under breath.

The figure now hovered in a glistening steam. A smile of devilish delight slapped across its face. "Don't look now, but—"

"Leave me alone!" Changa hissed through gritted teeth.

"—but your true skin is showing," the shadow figure taunted.

Changa looked to her right at the mirror on the wall. A reflection stared back at her. Her iridescent skin was, in fact, showing through her phony human wrapping. *That's impossible.* She willed her human skin to stay in place and hide her true self.

Changa quivered, feeling ants crawling up her arms as the tiny hairs at the base of her neck stood on end. She felt queasy and exposed. *Has the crew discovered my true identity?*

"Dr. Changa?" Mackenzie asked, her eyes wide. "Are you feeling alright?"

The sound of Mackenzie's voice pulled her out of whatever hallucination she must have been in. Again she looked at her reflection to see her human being appearing normal. Changa nodded and instructed Mackenzie to accompany Alan to the

Medbay. She watched as Mackenzie wrapped her arms around Alan and led him from the room. Changa turned to leave also, but a whisper escaped the corner — sounding as if it were an echo from the deepest depths of depravity. She felt her lungs burn as she gasped for breath. She needed to leave the room—now! But something pulled at her. Kept her rooted in place. Her feet felt like lead and it took every ounce of strength to yank herself from where she was planted.

Again, the whispers. Even outside of the MMR, she heard them. Each and every whisper seemed to call out her name, *Changa*. Every sound surrounding her felt like the heavy footfall of feet thumping... closer... and closer... coming to take her away. The internal fear volcano was coming to a boil. She braced herself with her hand on the wall and steadied her breath. Drawing in deep, calming breaths. When she felt she regained control, she stood tall and straightened her crisp, white lab coat.

Instead of walking straight to the Medbay, she stopped off at her private room. "Pleasure Pills!" She clapped her hands. "Just one pill will calm me and give me sweet relief." Good gods in the galactic heavens, she needed the relief. Now more than ever. She fought back the tears, finding her secret stash empty. Tossing aside her bedding and rummaging through drawers, she felt as if the walls of her room were closing in on her.

She plunged for the door, slammed her hand against the button next to the door, and headed towards Medbay. "There has to be—SHIT!" she coughed, entering the hall only to return to her quarters. She ran to the mirror, running her fingers over her eyelids, the ones she usually kept hidden, "All of my eyes are showing." Examining her face how her other eyes peaked through as they lay on her temples, blinking... watching. She let down her hair to cover her not so human eyes. "At this rate, I'll need two pleasure pills."

She dashed to Medbay. Her inner consciousness alerted her

that her other eyes, one each on the outer layer of her face, were attempting to peek out of her skin. She kept petting her long, wooly, sandy brown locks masking the front of her face. Smoothing the hair down over the ones on the side of her head.

"How did I lose control?" she asked the empty hallway.

"Dr. Changa?" Nereus asked from behind as Changa walked with determination toward Medbay. "Do you have a second?"

Without slowing her pace, just barely glancing over her shoulder, she replied, "Ah, no. Nereus, I'm sorry, but I'm actually in the middle of something. Can Dr. Sanderson help you?"

"Yea, sure, Doc. Thanks." She thought she heard him whisper, *thanks for nothing, bitch.* But perhaps it was her mind playing their deceitful tricks on her. She stopped in her tracks and looked him in the eye.

"Sorry, I couldn't do more," she added quickly before she turned on her heels and quickened her pace, speeding down the hall.

"No worries," he called after her.

No worries, indeed. She didn't have time to work with Nereus on whatever daddy issues he may have, nor time to work with anyone else for that matter. She had one thing on her mind, and one thing only.

Changa stormed into the Medbay and tore through drawers and cabinets. Medical supplies, pens, papers, and other stuff tumbled to the floor. She mumbled to herself. "Where are they? I know they're here."

Kitty, the AI system, spoke; this time as Queen Latifah. The AI had a mind of its own, if that were even possible, choosing random earthly voices from years well into the past to address the crew. The only reason Changa even recognized this voice was because some of the crew were enamored with television shows and movies from an era long gone. Today, it was Queen

Latifah. Yesterday it was Jerry Seinfeld, tomorrow? Who knows? Idiotic system.

"Dr. Changa," the AI system asked, its voice booming through the speakers in the room. "My system is denoting a rise in heart rhythm and an increase in neurotoxins within the brain. Is there something wrong, Dr. Changa?"

"No, Kitty. There isn't. I thought I told you not to read my vitals without my permission," she replied while continuing her frantic search.

"Dr. Changa, my analytical system now denotes that with the increase in heart rate, you will pass out in less than sixty seconds. It is my recommendation that you please sit down."

"Oh, really?" Changa spat back. "Not right now. I don't have time for this," she yelled at the AI. She tore through the next cabinet and shouted. "Where are the damn Pleasure Pills? They're always right here!" She felt her knees weaken as her head grew light and the room began to spin. Tiny swirls of stars filled her peripheral vision. Nearly falling to her knees, she stopped herself from hitting the floor by grasping the edge of the table. "What's happening?" she mumbled, finally taking a seat. Clearly shaken, she tried to control her breath by once more using deep breathing techniques, which didn't seem to do much at the moment. "I feel like I'm unraveling and I can't stop it."

The shadowy figure from the MMR appeared again, holding something in its outstretched hand. "Is this what you're looking for?" It dropped something and a tiny vial of pills rolled under a table.

"You again? Why do you keep following me?" Changa dropped to her knees and snatched the container. After fumbling with the stopper, she popped two of the colorful pills and clenched her eyes tight while she waited for relief. Within minutes her breathing steadied, and she felt a calmness wash over her.

"Better?" the shadowy figure asked, hovering in the corner but inching its way toward her.

"Screw you," Changa replied. "Wait, why are you still here?"

"Surely you remember me. Who I am?"

The lights flickered, and the room suddenly darkened. Changa felt pulled by a force so strong, stronger than gravity. Almost as though she was being sucked through a deep vortex. She fell to the floor, brought her knees to her chest and her hands to her ears, rocking back and forth. "This isn't happening. It'll be over when I open my eyes," but the chilling sensation on her skin and the tiny prickles of hair standing on her arm told her otherwise. She repeated the phrase, *This isn't happening* over and over. Was she able to convince herself it was all in her mind's eye?

When she finally opened her eyes and the room came back into focus, the figure was gone. She drew in a deep breath and then exhaled. "What the hell was that?"

"I didn't mean to frighten you." The figure was now behind her, sitting in her chair.

Changa nearly jumped out of her skin. "Flying space sharks! Who are you and what do you want from me?" She scrambled away from the chair, keeping the figure in sight.

The figure extended its hand to her, but Changa jumped and bolted for the door. She scurried down the narrow halls, looking over her shoulder to see if she was being followed, wondering if everyone she passed knew her precious little secret. With every step, she felt her focus falling with the layers of skin that hid her identity.

"Dr. Dangaley! Dr. Dangaley!" Mackenzie shouted, running in Changa's direction.

Wait, I'm Dr. Dangaley! No, I have to hide. She can't see me like this. Changa's walk went from a brisk strut to nearly a jog. Her eyes scrambled past every room, trying to find a place to hide, to get away.

The shadowy figure appeared at Changa's side, "So, what are we running from?"

"AAH!" Changa stopped and screamed, holding her hands over her ears. She shouted, "Leave me alone!"

She opened her eyes to see Mackenzie approaching. Quickly, she turned the corner and darted behind the first door she saw. She held her breath, desperately hoping that maybe, magically, she'd disappeared from Mackenzie's thoughts.

"Changa? It's me, Mackenzie," a winded voice called out from behind the door.

"Mack, now isn't a good time."

"I just wanted to know if Alan can leave Medbay. He's much better. He only threw up once."

"Yes, fine. Tell him to rest for the next few days."

"Ok, thanks, Dr. Dangaley."

Changa heard the retreat of Mackenzie's steps backing away from the door. But a quiet knocking on the door followed them. Mackenzie didn't leave. Changa heard the concern in her voice as she asked, "Doctor, are you alright? Do you need anything?"

Changa dropped her head in hands, fighting back tears. She prepared her rehearsed 'strong' voice, "I'm great, just a lot of work to do. Thanks for checking in though," she lied. When she was sure Mackenzie had left the outer barrier of the door, she let the tears flow. She cried, wiping away the saltiness from her cheeks. After a few moments to gather her thoughts and pull herself together, she realized where she was. Everything happened so fast she didn't realize what room she had entered. The walls, the feel, the figure.

"No... I'm in the MMR—"

The shadowy figure took shape once again before her. Only this time, its features were becoming clearer. She saw the locks of hair on the figure's head resembled her own, except the figures' locks were mixed strands of white, grey and silver. There was something so familiar about the cheekbones, too. And the iridescent skin and four eyes. But what was most striking was that locket. The oval metal hanging from a gilded chain. She recognized that locket. Or was her mind playing tricks on her, again?

She shook the image from her head, closed her eyes tightly, and wished it away. But when she opened her eyes, the figure stood before her still. Watching her. Giving her that same look—

Changa finally asked, "Mom?"

"I was wondering how long you would make me stay hidden." The corners of the figure's lips went up into a smile.

"But mom... you can't be here. You're dead."

"As if that could stop me. Besides, Changa, my darling... Death is close to life and since you've never let me go—I've been here with you... since *that* day."

Changa tilted her head, her eyes filled with curiosity and wonder, "What day, mother?"

"Changa, it's ok. I've forgiven you ages ago."

"Forgiven me?" Those words moved something in Changa and she clawed at her heart, banging her head against the wall. "Too many memories, too much for me to bear." She collapsed to her knees with the realization of what day her mother referenced. It was now fully awakened in her mind. Her eyes grew wide as her breath quickened, then slowed in her hands. The memories flooded her senses, overwhelming her. But they were different... from what she remembered... fresh memories mixed with old... she was so confused by the images spinning in her head.

"I couldn't. I'm not capable. You're my mother. It's not our way." She shook her head until her face appeared to have discovered an unknown land, an epiphany as the memories returned.

There was no pushing them back and away into the deep, dark depths of her mind.

No, it was too late for that.

But why? Why now? "It must be the pleasure pills," she told herself. She looked at the figure of her mother before her and spoke matter-of-factly. "Yes, they're changing my memories. I remember you dying of old age. I was there. I held your wrinkled hand." Changa's face flooded, full of confusion.

Her mother's eyes peering deep into her soul, "Come on, Changa, you can't pretend any longer. This is something you can no longer hide, not even from yourself."

Frustration overpowering her will she shouted, "What, what the hell am I hiding? Why can't you just tell me?" Anger nearing a boil, the tears just flowed now, "I feel like I'm going crazy, mom, please just tell me."

Her mom shook her head, "You were like this when you were a child, always just wanting the answers, never wanting to work for them. Even then I couldn't give them to you, even then you had to find them for yourself. I can get you close, but you have to walk the path."

Making Changa face her memories brought on physical pain that squeezed Changa's heart—pain she'd pushed away. For years, she ignored the intense memories and the disappointment in her mother's voice; almost pretending like they'd never happened. But the image rose to the surface; no matter how much Changa fought to keep it in the depths of her psyche, landing her in a time when she was seven years old.

Changa was sitting on a pillow, with her mother applying oils on her scalp, "Mom, my teacher asked the class what do we want to be when we grow up and I can't seem to decide between a scientist or a doctor."

Her mom chuckled, "That's funny, baby. Women in our

culture don't become doctors and scientists, honey. I'm surprised your teacher didn't tell you that."

"Well, I'm going to be the first!"

Her mother's brows furrowed before she was pulled into another memory.

Here, Changa was thirteen, flipping a freshly baked cake out of a pan with her mom. Her mother's voice echoed overhead, "This isn't what you need to see Changa, this isn't where you need to be. Why waste your time with these futile memories?"

Changa allowed the memory to continue, as she iced the cake, making it look pretty, and feeling proud of her accomplishment.

Again her mother's voice rang out in her head, "Changa, you can't stay here. I know this is safe and happy, but you have to move on. Come with me, Changa! Come!"

Burning with guilt, Changa wrenched her hands and bit her lower lip before forcing herself to open her eyes and go where her mother was taking her, "I think I'm ready. What do you want me to see?" The room shifted as tiny dust motes spiraled down. Changa felt nausea coming on, but she forced herself to stand firm, and watched as the memory played before her eyes.

The revelation of guilt on her soul wrapped around her like a well-worn blanket. It enveloped her. "I didn't... I couldn't... I could never," she whispered. Tears escaped her eyes and flooded down her cheeks. She wiped them with the back of her hand, but they just kept coming.

"This room helps you relive your memories—let it help you remember. But you need to do more than just see it, in your mind. Yes, the memories are coming back, but now you must feel it," her mother said, pounded on her chest. "Here. You must relive it. It's the only way, Changa." Her mother drew in a breath and extended her hand for Changa to hold.

Hesitant at first, Changa nodded solemnly and took her mother's hand, which was now outstretched for her. When she did, she was transported back in time—to twelve years ago. A doe-eyed, bouncy Changa entered a room as her elderly mother gazed out the window at the three suns setting on her home planet.

"Mom, I got news! They accepted me!"

"Well, give it back. I told you you won't be wasting your time with higher education. You will *not* be leaving this planet."

"But, ma!"

"Don't you ever 'but' me again. We are a chosen people. Our path paved before we even breathed. We don't get to choose. I told you not to apply, now shut up and send it back."

"I can't. I won't. You can't make me!"

Changa's mother rose from her chair, "I can't do what?"

"I'm of age. I don't have to stay here. All the women do here is work and protect the colony. I want to be free and just for a little while live and smile and have fun. There are universes out there that I want to explore. You can't keep me here."

"Ha! You youngins get dumber and dumber. I will never allow you off of this planet without my necklace," she grasped the locket hanging from her neck. "Only this will allow one to leave. Only this bids my permission."

"You can't do this to me." Changa growled, grinding the muscles in her cheek before a heavy back-handed slap met her face, causing her to spit blood.

"I can and will do whatever the hell I like, including keeping your dumb ass locked up in whatever title I can attain for you to give this family honor. It is honorable to serve the colony the way our people have for the past thousand years."

Looking at the blood on her hands from her mouth and feeling the stinging jabs from her mother's words broiling up inside, Changa felt something she'd never felt before. Rage.

Her mother raised her hand once more, but Changa was

ready. She blocked her mother's blow and then locked her thumb in her fist and swung back. At first, it was a feeling of exaltation and release. Almost a sense of pride in finally standing her ground, but when she looked down at her mother, unmoving on the floor, she realized she'd gone too far. Her punch must have knocked her mother over. Changa saw where her mother's head hit the table. Blood soaked the carpeting as panic washed over Changa. Her heart rate increased, her palms grew sweaty, and all four of her eyes stung with the saltiness of bitter tears. "Mother?" she gasped.

The image of young Changa dissipated, and they were back in the MMR. Changa cried, "I remember. I panicked and didn't know what to do. I..." she hesitated, drew in a breath, and continued. "I took your necklace, I left, and I never turned back. I knew no one would believe that it was an accident... and I was still ready to live my life. Oh, great Jupiter's moons, mother. I'm so sorry... how... how could I have done that? How could you ever forgive me?"

"Death comes to us all. Besides, I had a hand in my demise. I could've been kinder, more understanding. I've seen how remorseful you've been over the years. How you've dedicated your life to saving and helping others. All that guilt, child... really, I'm the one to blame. I was a cruel mother. I loved you in my own way. And yes, it may seem like an excuse now, but coming from my upbringing there just weren't many options and I should've at least listened. I'm sorry, too."

Tears flowed down Changa's face, relief spreading across her essence, seeping from her soul. She raised her hands behind her head and unclasped the necklace. "Here, mother, I don't deserve to wear this. I know it was Grandma's. I only wanted to be half the woman you were. To have the strength you had."

Light reflected off the locket's gold surface, almost like young stars in a distant galaxy. Changa held it in the palm of her hand.

She felt the warmth of it against her skin and a slight feeling of electricity pulsed through it giving it a sense of life.

"Baby, you keep that. You say I was strong? No Changa. I was weak. Weakened by a society that ruled with an iron fist and one of oppression. You are the strong one. The brave one. You're more of a woman than I would've ever dreamed. I'm so proud of you. I'm only sorry it took death for me to finally tell you what I should have said long ago. Watching over you, seeing how you've built your life and given to others. I would have held you back and those people you saved... when I think of what your life would have been had you stayed and listened to me. You taught me there's more to being a woman than what they raised me to believe and I carry that even in the afterlife."

Changa sniffed back the tears. "Mom... I'm so sorry. I wish..."

"You wish I were alive? Child, this isn't your doing. You know that, right? You saw only part of the memory. Not all of it. You left before it was finished."

"What are you talking about? I killed you. I pushed you down. I saw the injury. The blood..." The tears gushed freely as she heaved in heavy sobs. "I can never forgive myself for that. No matter how many other lives I may have saved."

"Darling girl. Yes, you defended yourself. But you only knocked me out. You didn't kill me. No, dear child. I may have been unconscious, but when I came to, I was ready to search the universe for you. Bring you to your knees... but then... I realized you had done what I only ever dreamed of. You broke the cycle. You escaped. You did what I didn't have the strength to do."

"You didn't die that day? But..."

"That was the day you set all the women free. I lived many years after. And yes, I am dead now, but not from your hand, child. All that built-up guilt. I'm the one who should apologize to you. Be proud of who you are, Changa. Stand tall. You are the one who dared to dream. Who wanted more."

"I only wanted to be more because you covered everything. All these years, I thought I killed you. Why didn't you find me? Tell me?"

"What good would that have done? Bring you back to a life of misery? This way, you were free. You *are* free. And you no longer need to hide who you are."

"I'll never hide who I am again. I will wear our skin proud. I will open all my eyes wide. Praying to see you in the whispers, the stars, the light. I feel you leaving ..."

She pressed a finger on Changa's lips, "Shh—I'll never be far away. Hold the necklace and think of me. I'll be with you, always."

MANY COLORS, OUR CRAFT, OUR QUEEN
(MINEASTYLOPHONIC)

ELVIRA CANAVERAL

Color of space
Color of magic
Color of interest
Color of credit
Color of being
To become different than what we are
We must have some idea of when we are
The speed of vibration tells us more than location
Direction, speed, history and composition
Color of shift
Color of spin
Color of distance
Color of close
Color of decomposition
Distribution and absorption of energy
Speed, endurance, and power transfer
Agility and accuracy, a natural ability
An active player takes the initiative
Color of quarks

Color of quirks
Color of feeling
Color of knowing
Color of seeing
Many Colors, Our Craft, Our Queen

ALAN GREY'S FINAL TRANSMISSION
JAYME BEAN

THIS IS THE TRANSCRIPTION OF THE BIO-ORGANIC SUIT[1] VOICE-to-Voice Transmission (GREY T-004) from the UPA Mission: Swarm Ship[2] Infiltration and Recovery (UPA:SSIR)

Communicators in the text may be identified according to the following list.

Ranked Crew:
> CL - Colonel Roseallin Ortega
> CO- Commander-Elect TATE
> HL - "HOST" Leader Cosima Sabine
> TH - Nereus Thanatos (crew faction)

Target:
> AG - Alan Grey, marine[3]

(GREY T-004) UPA:SSIR BIO-ORGANIC SUIT VOICE-TO-VOICE
TRANSMISSION RECORDING 1/1 PAGE 1

PINK+000 CL Rose to Grey. You may proceed to
tachyon field. Over.

PINK+020 AG Copy, Rose. Line-of-sight on
sharks. Advise?

PINK+023 CL Proceed. Sharks appear distracted
by the lights. All clear.

PINK/ORANGE+040 CO This is TATE. ETA to
tachyon?

PINK/ORANGE+042 AG Unsure, TATE. This is
what I dreamed. Wha ... we ... bee ...

ORANGE+044 CO Grey. We're losing you. Repeat
last transmission?

ORANGE+045 AG It's so ... you should see it. It ...
so ... perf ... an ...

ORANGE+046 HL Alan, this is Cosima. Repeat.

ORANGE+047 AG Cop ... Cos ... will ... pro—

ORANGE+048 HL Alan, repeat.

ORANGE+055 AG ... ... almost ...

ORANGE+100 TH Grey, Thanatos. Come in.

ORANGE+110 CO Grey. Come in.

ORANGE+115 CL He's heading into the field.

ORANGE+132 HL Losing visual on him.
Thanatos, can you get a reading?

ORANGE+135 TH Negative. Nothing certain.
Scanning.

ORANGE+201 CL There! The lights. They're
oscillating. Do you see him?

ORANGE+213 TH Slight lifesign reading.
Negative on visual.

(GREY T-004) UPA:SSIR BIO-ORGANIC SUIT VOICE-TO-VOICE
TRANSMISSION RECORDING 1/1 PAGE 2

ORANGE+259 AG ... do ... see ... beaut ... everyth
...

ORANGE+261 CO Grey, transmission's unclear.
Return to ship.

ORANGE+292 AG Heading in ... must ... ent—

ORANGE+300 CO Negative. Return. We need to
reassess.

ORANGE+331 TH Life signs almost nonexistent.
Losing him.

ORANGE/YELLOW+374 CL We need to go after
him! We can still retrieve him.

ORANGE/YELLOW+425 TH Look! That flash.
Grey do you copy?

ORANGE/YELLOW+506 AG ... ... —

YELLOW+520 CO Do you copy? Grey? Thanatos,
life signs? Thanat—

»» END OF TAPE ««

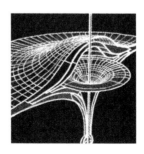

1. Mission recordings from the bio-organic suits were recovered once connection was reestablished with UPA base.
2. Personal logs and private accounts indicate a loss of exact time while aboard the alien vessel. In this transcription, standard time recording will henceforth be referred to in color-based time tracking with subsequent UPA Standard Time Units (STU) as recovered from the available tech.
3. Grey's transmission was recorded on a solo mission into previously unexplored tachyon fields. This mission was sanctioned by CL and unanimously agreed upon by the remaining crew. His mission: assess and qualify effects of tachyon fields on the UPA quantum timeline.

THE FINALE OF BIRTH
(WAVE FUNK SHION)

ELVIRA CANAVERAL

Moxie to make
Relative Constellations
Picture work from the place time you are

Asking meteors how they found their craters
Asking if you ever touched your mother
Many Universes, singing together
Superpositions collapse the wave function
Both Alive and not
Communing in parallel universes

Cosmic denominations as we grow
Locality an island, planet, star, galaxy, universe, multiverses
and so
Quilted, inflationary, brame in the bulk
Cyclic big bangs bouncing across the reality erasing as they go
Landscapes stringing pockets
Diversions creating many worlds
Holograms encoding every space onto every character
Simulated realities above and below

Every possibility and self-sustaining cycle
It wasn't ever a matter of if, but when and where
This division, this birth is now and here
Between

There it came A B ship out of C
Dropped down and divided by D
Engaged in the E
A song for the deaf came in on an F
And below we can see our beautiful G

Energy of fury
Swarm did convey
Transferral of energy
Into the crafts that be
Formerly one divided in between
A bass string progression across E A D G
Existence through disposition in between possibility
The birth of a new ship and crew within
Light-reflecting dark old and new again
A life sacrificed energy a death to begin
Here and there and now everywhen
Different strings of an infinite mandolin
Singing a different story, repeating now and then
What was done Under New Suns

THE LONG WAY HOME
C. D. STORIZ

Nereus Thanatos, a physicist working on the stolen Swarm ship, studied the board sitting before him with one hand on his chin, the other hovering above the bishop on his chessboard. He moved the piece diagonally to h5 and then turned the board so the black pieces were facing him. Before making his next move, this time on black, he let his hand hover above the knight currently sitting on f3. A slight tremor in his right hand interrupted his thoughts. He bit his bottom lip and then placed the palm of his left over his right to stop the shaking.

He held his hands over the board for what seemed like an Earthly sunrise to sunset, but it was only seconds before moving them in for closer examination. He watched the movement of his right hand as he flexed it open and closed; the trembling in his pinky and ring finger finally subsided just as the lights in his pod dimmed slightly—a sign someone was about to enter. Within seconds, he heard the familiar swoosh of the doors.

Ensign Avril Xia entered the room and stood at attention as she waited for Nereus to acknowledge her, but Nereus's attention was on his next move.

"Ahem," she cleared her throat.

Without looking up, Nereus replied, "Yes?"

"Sorry to bother you, sir. Remember how you asked me to check into the ECLSS to look for other malfunctions? Well, I found one."

The ECLSS, Environmental Control and Life Support System, was becoming the bane of Nereus's existence lately. They had only recently decoded the manual for this particular system, which, as it turns out, was relatively close to that on a human ship but not exactly. There were variances in air quality and food production, which made sense, but the engine operating systems, including booster engines used the same type of fuel.

"Let me guess. The toilets are overflowing in section three again?" He rubbed his chin.

Ensign Xia's normally perky smile flattened. The color drained from her face. "Not quite." She looked down at the board. "Who are you playing, sir?" she asked.

"A very worthy opponent."

She looked around the room and shrugged. "Eh, sir? There's no one else in the room, is there?"

He chuckled. "Do you see anyone else in the room?" He pushed away from the small table, stood, and retrieved the tablet from her. He noticed she hesitated a moment before releasing the device and felt the ever so slight static electric shock as his fingers brushed against hers.

She must have noticed it, too, as she blinked several times, and her cheeks reddened.

"Everything alright?" he asked with a teasing tone. "And, by the way, since I'm not military—I'm a civilian scientist—you don't have to call me sir. Don't salute me, don't yes-sir me. Understood?"

She nodded quickly. "Yes, sir."

"Seriously?"

She shrugged. "Sorry, sir. It's bred into us."

He twisted his lips and examined the tablet. "This can't be right," he said, moving the pages up and down as he looked at the latest scans. "You double checked this?"

She nodded again before adding, "Triple checked. I thought it was odd, too. After several crew members reported snow falling in the Magical Machine Room—"

Nereus cringed. The mere thought that an educated crew member would refer to it as a *magical* room made him ill. There was nothing magical about it. It was science. Why couldn't they just accept the science?

She corrected herself. "—sorry. The MMR. Well, as it turns out, they were right."

"It was snowing. In the MMR. Snow. In a confiscated Swarm ship in the middle of the... where are we now? The Triangulation Galaxy?"

"Yes."

"Yes, what? Yes, to our location or yes to the fact it was snowing?"

"Yes, to both?" she raised her eyebrows and rocked back on her feet.

"The temperature in the room would have to have been zero degrees Celsius or less. And, were there ski jackets involved?" he added with a touch of sarcasm.

She smiled as she tucked a loose strand of hair behind her ear.

"Wait a minute," he repeated three times. "Hypothermia would set in if body temperatures were at or below thirty-five degrees Celsius." He shook his head. "So, this wasn't typical snow."

"No, sir. It wasn't. Though, if you think about it—when was the last time any of us have seen actual snow?" She took a few steps around the room. "I like what you've done to the place."

She mumbled, running her fingers along the counter cluttered with books, some open to dogeared pages. A few books had handwritten notes in the margins. She picked up an old Quantum Physics book, flipped through a few pages, and set it back down.

"You know, they've had these on digital files for almost a thousand years now. No need for this," she said, picking up another hard cover book titled, *Intergalactic Particle Physics and the Expanding Universe*. She sighed and moved closer to the table. "I always liked the training courses that replicated what was once on Earth. You know, the sand dunes, the snow falls. How about you?"

"Hmm. Yes," he replied, not really listening to her.

She picked a pawn from the chessboard and tossed it back and forth between her hands as she continued. "And if you were from what was once Florida before the sea levels rose on Earth, you might not have ever seen it. Snow, that is. But our history books tell us what it is. In training, we were given the simulations. A little frozen water, crisp air, and you can recreate it. It was kind of fun training in snow."

He looked up from the tablet and creased his eyebrows. "I'm in the middle of a game." His piercing blue eyes bore into her as if she had committed a capital crime.

"Sorry, sir." She plopped the figure back on the board.

Nereus let out a breath, quickly straightened the pawn on the square so it was centered, and examined the pages on the tablet again.

"The snow in training was pretty delightful. I can see why one would request it in the mag—er, MMR," she continued.

"For training," he scoffed. "How the Intergalactic Consortium ever decided that recreating snow as part of a military astronaut's training would be helpful is beyond me. Have you ever seen snow on any planet we've visited? Don't answer that."

He enlarged the chemical formula on the tablet. "Is this... sodium—"

"—polyacrylate?" she finished his sentence for him. "Yes, it is. A very hygroscopic substance that absorbs water and can do it 200 to 300 times its mass."

Nereus sat back down. "Well, I'll be damned. So, whatever yahoo desired a white Christmas got just what they imagined."

"Precisely. Though I doubt they were thinking of fat, jolly men in red suits. Once the sodium polyacrylate absorbs water from the room, it swells up and produces flakes that resemble snow. It was more likely a sexual thing, sir."

He studied her for a minute. Her seriousness was almost frightening. But he admired her matter-of-fact attitude. In fact, he'd often thought of asking her out if she weren't a subordinate on loan from the military to his department. Not that he'd let that stop him before, but there was something different about Ensign Avril Xia. She wasn't just all military gung ho, but a biochemist and a damn good one at that. He didn't want just a quick roll with her. Nereus wanted to seduce her slowly and get to know her. He brushed the feeling aside.

"Okay, what else you got for me? There's got to be more, otherwise the alarm systems wouldn't be going off."

"Right. About that—"

"What is it?"

He caught her scent as she leaned over his shoulder. Her jet-black hair, normally taut in a bun secured at the nape of her neck, hung loose today.

"May I?" she asked, before using her fingers to move the tablet screen. "See this?"

But Nereus was watching her. He noticed how flawless her milky-white skin was and that her eyes were a deep forest green with tiny flecks of gold. He swallowed and turned his attention back to the tablet.

"So, Avril, do you play?" He nodded to the board.

"You wouldn't want to play me, sir. Please, let me bring your attention to this. See these levels?" She enlarged the chart and took a step back.

Nereus mumbled as he studied the charts. "This isn't right."

"Oh, I assure you—it is."

Setting the tablet down, he put his hand on his forehead and closed his eyes. He needed to think. What he really needed was an aspirin or a pleasant pill to take the edge off. He picked up the tablet again.

"Alright. Thanks for the thorough report on this. You can go."

Avril clicked her heels, standing at attention, and turned. Before leaving, she looked back over her shoulder. "What are you going to do?"

Nereus sighed. "Well... that's a good question. One I don't have an answer for—yet."

"Have a pleasant afternoon, sir." She pushed the exit button on the wall. With the swish of the door came the sounds of activity from the crew in the corridor. It amazed Nereus how quiet these rooms were once the doors were sealed.

"Avril? Hang on a second."

She turned back and leaned against the doorway. The light from the corridor silhouetted her shape.

Nereus swallowed back the urge to pull her into his arms. "Let's meet in the mess in ten minutes. We're going to brainstorm a way out of this *before* I go to the captain."

"Before? Is that wise? Shouldn't she be notified?"

"Cosima will be. But I want to make sure we have a plan first. Something viable."

"But, sir—" she objected.

"It's been like this since we boarded this vessel, right? A few more minutes won't make much of a difference at this point.

Unless we're heading straight into a meteor shower or a solar flare, let's keep this quiet. But get Harwood and Shankman. Let's put their overpaid asses to work."

"What about Dileo or Wandri?"

Nereus sneered. "Dileo's an agriculturist. And Wandri? No, not yet—just the four of us for now."

"But Wandri studies planetary effects of various environments. Though he's a naturalist, he has a degree in bio-chem. He even wrote a paper on the atmospheric negligence of MuDuhRu when they—"

The way her eyes lit up, Nereus got the feeling the young ensign had a thing for the bewitching Wandri; His thoughts of being with her just shrank tenfold. "No! Just the four of us. Go. I need a few minutes to think."

He turned back to his chessboard when Avril left the room. The intercom in Nereus's room buzzed, and a voice immediately started talking. "Nereus, this is Fatima from Doc Sanderson's office. He'd like to remind you about your appointment. Hello— are you there?"

Nereus ignored the communication.

The intercom crackled again. "Nereus, if you're in there, and the system logistics tells me you are, Doc Sanderson says to tell you it's important you show up. He said not to blow him off, again. Physicians' bay; out."

Nereus rolled his eyes. Within a few minutes, the intercom crackled again.

"Nereus, this is Doc Sanderson. Listen. We need to talk. It's about your tests. Stay put. I'm heading to your room now. Over."

Nereus slammed his fist on the table, scattering a few chess pieces to scatter to the floor. He pushed his hand on the door panel and left the room.

$$H(t)|\psi(t)\rangle = i\hbar\frac{\partial}{\partial t}|\psi(t)\rangle$$

Ten minutes later, Avril, Harwood, and Shankman were sitting at a table in the far corner of the mess hall. Nereus hoped that Chris Harwood and Anthony Shankman were as smart as they claimed to be. Before this mission on the Swarm ship, Nereus and Anthony were stationed together on another interspace cruiser, but that had been a cakewalk compared to this ship with its colored walls, rooms that made people's desires come true, and its cynical AI system which Nereus still didn't trust. They had brought Harwood on at the last minute as a systems engineer. Nereus had done a little research before accepting him as part of his crew, and the guy seemed like he had all his nuts and bolts in place. But you never really know until you work with someone. Harwood had a reputation of thinking outside of the box, and when you're traveling light years away from your home planet, you've got to be able to do just that.

"Come on... just go out with me... one date. That's all I'm asking. Why do you gotta be this way?" Harwood pleaded, reaching across the table to Avril's hand.

She pulled away. "I told you. I don't date crew members."

"Am I interrupting something?" Nereus said, plopping down next to Avril. When no one answered, he continued. "Good. Did Ensign Xia tell you what I needed?"

Harwood ran his hands through his unkempt blond hair. "All she said was you needed us for a special job. Hey man, I know you outrank us and all, but I ain't unclogging the toilets—"

"Let me stop you right there. I need you to shut the hell up and listen. And then, we will decide if you'll be pumping shit through the system or whether you'll be doing something else. I want to run something by you before I take it to the captain. I need you to keep it to yourself. Understood?" Nereus looked both men firmly in the eyes.

"Jeez, Nereus, what's up?" Anthony asked.

Anthony Shankman, though human, was raised on Mars. His parents were both engineers and part of the expansion team for *Galactic Studies and Relations*. His and Nereus's family had been friends for generations. It was Nereus's father—before he became incapacitated from complications from multiple sclerosis had called in a favor to get Anthony and Nereus stationed together right out of training. Hundreds of years traveling the heavens, finding new planets and civilizations, and not one has found a cure for MS yet. Go figure.

"I think it's better if I just show you and let you draw your own conclusions." Nereus pushed copies of the schematics he worked out towards the men and also gave a copy to Avril. He thought she batted her eyelashes at him as he pushed the stack of papers towards her. But then again, it was probably wishful thinking.

After a few minutes of reading, it was Harwood who spoke first. "How?" He looked up, wide eyed, rubbing his perpetual five o'clock shadow.

"How what? The excessive amounts of NH_4 or how we're going to get it the hell off this ship?" Nereus answered.

"Let's start with the ammonium. I always thought it smelled like cat pee in certain places on this ship. I thought I was just hallucinating," Harwood replied.

"And, you're sure..." Anthony looked up from his packet. "It's bonding with the nitrates?"

Avril, Harwood, and Anthony all looked to Nereus. "I'm sure." He folded his hands on the table. "And as it bonds... it's literally making a bomb. In the front hull of the ship," Nereus said solemnly.

"So, that means with any small spark or abruption in the panels where the ammonium is, we could..." Avril's voice trailed off.

"Holy crap. We're literally a floating bomb in the middle of space." Harwood drained his cup. "I need a pleasant pill, like now."

"Don't we all," scoffed Anthony.

Nereus explained how ammonium was like oxygen to the Swarm. The atmosphere on their home planet differed greatly from what the humans were used to breathing. Rather than oxygen, their life source was pure ammonium. It made sense they stored it in the confines. When the crew stole the ship, the AI system, light-years ahead of what the humans had, read the biometric needs of the current passengers. The system then vacuumed the NH_4 from the air and replaced it with air rich in oxygen. But a small leak in the system near the front starboard side of the ship allowed nitrates to leak into the chambers where the ammonium was being stored. It then bonded with the nitrates and formed a highly explosive compound.

"Why wasn't the ammonium just released into the vacuum of space when we boarded and the AI system switched out the air?" Anthony asked.

"Why do you think?" Avril responded quickly.

"Ah," said Anthony.

"Ah, what?" Harwood asked, still confused.

Avril looked to Nereus, who nodded to her to explain.

"Well, in case the Swarm get the ship back. Which they've been trying to do. They'll need to—"

"—breathe," everyone answered at the same time.

"Very good. Guess that expensive education wasn't a waste of your time," Nereus commented. "Looking at this—what are our next steps? I have an idea in mind, but I want to see if you come to the same."

"Give the damn ship back?" Harwood joked.

"Not in a million years," Anthony retorted. "So, we extract the ammonium, which I'm assuming based on this..." He flipped to the next page. "... is in a gaseous state and release it outside the ship."

"Well, we have to be careful there. Remember, outer space is hardly empty. It's a deep vacuum made up of low-density particles—" Avril said.

"—not to mention the plasma of hydrogen and helium," Anthony added. "And with all that hydrogen in the plasma between the galaxies... which makes up about half of the baryonic material... we're pretty much in deep shit."

Avril sighed. "What are we missing? What other barriers are there to stop us?"

"Oh, not much. Just the electromagnetic radiation, magnetic fields, neutrinos, dust, and cosmic rays," Nereus paused. When no one responded he continued. "Also, it's negative 270 degrees Centigrade outside, possibly lower—and who knows what stability or instability at those temps this will cause to the ammonium. The hazard assessment by the RAD team is good—at least there are no airborne release of cesium isotopes. No gamma or neutron radiation readings. But..."

"Big question is, who's doing the EVA?" Harwood asked.

"That's the big question?" Anthony replied. "You're worried you won't get chosen to do the EVA?"

"No, but—"

"Big question," Nereus interjected, "is how to convince the captain. It's no secret that we're not exactly friends."

"Well, if you didn't try to overthrow her—" Avril suddenly stopped herself and looked down. "I'm sorry, sir. That wasn't fair."

"I didn't try to *overthrow* her. But I also didn't choose her as my captain after Maxwell died. Either way, I'll speak with *Captain* Cosima Sabine."

"You think she'll go for it? Let's face it, Nereus, she doesn't trust you," Anthony added.

"Why not? I mean, you're one of the most brilliant scientists on this tin can. Really, you could be captain with all your experience and knowledge of booster systems, galactic relationships, and other... captain-y stuff. Not to mention all those Physics books you keep on hand."

Nereus noted a bit of admiration in Avril's voice. Maybe she *did* like him. He'd love to contemplate that, but he had a ship to keep from blowing up.

"And, you're wrong about that," Nereus replied. "It's not that she doesn't trust me. She doesn't *like* me—vast difference. Well, maybe she doesn't trust me either but even she knows I'm a damn good scientist."

The trio nodded.

"Okay. I'll get with Cosima. Ensign Xia, I want you on the EVA with me. Anthony and Harwood, I want you two on the inside. Harwood, man the camera footage and temperature probes that Anthony is going to hook up. And then, Anthony, I want you to monitor the systems. Watch for the movement of the gases and any phase changes." Nereus let out a breath.

"How are we going to fix the leak?" Harwood asked.

Nereus pulled something from his pocket. "With this."

"Is that duct tape?" Anthony asked.

"No, it looks like it, but it's a super adhesive that has a charge that will neutralize the ammonium from further bonding. Ensign Xia already located the leak, here." He pointed to the map on page three. "Once we remove the outside panels and pull the hose unit, we'll apply the adhesive and hope to whatever gods are out there that it sticks, because once those outside temperatures hit it—it may all be a moot point. Then, we'll scrape out the ammonium nitrate crystals and place it into these." He pulled out a silver-colored bag that resembled a thin foil heat blanket and placed it on the table.

They each took turns fingering the material as Nereus spoke. "These will not only keep the temp at bay, but should be able to safely house the explosive properties of the ammonium nitrate. I figure a dozen of these bags, based on the numbers, ought to do it."

"Yeah, fine, but then what do you do with it? Once you pump that ammonium nitrate into these, you've now got gigantic bags of fertilizer explosives. Still just as unstable," Anthony pointed out.

"And dangerous," Harwood added. "We can still blow at any minute given the hydrogen from the flares that have been detected the last several days. One small spark and..." Harwood let the thought of being blown into a million tiny bits hang in the air.

"Escape pod."

"What? Xia, are you crazy? You want to shove this into an escape pod? And do what?" Harwood asked.

"Why the hell not?" she replied.

"Wait—she's got a point, right? We've been wanting to outrun the Swarm that's been on our ass for the past couple of days, right? Well, we can use the momentum from the blast to push us further away from them," Anthony added excitedly. "It kills two birds with one stone."

"Can we not say *kill*, please?" Avril added.

Anthony shrugged.

"I think you're onto something," Nereus said, picking up his paper. He flipped through the pages. "If we launch the escape pod right at the Swarm—"

"—make what looks like an aggressive move towards them," Anthony added.

"They'll have to respond, right? They'll send a warning first and then they'll aim their lasers when we don't respond," Nereus said and then grinned.

"So, the blast will cause the electromagnetic waves to help boost our ship's momentum, and we just might outrun them. Hit hyper speed—" Anthony added excitedly.

"—and we're off to the next galaxy. Minus the ammonium, of course," Avril added brightly.

"Hate to be the plunger in somebody's toilet," Harwood said. "But, aren't you forgetting something? Who's going to man the escape pod? It sure as heck ain't going to be me. I ain't dying for this. At least not on purpose."

"Won't have to. Anthony can do a manual override from inside with the computer system and direct it into position using the program he created when we first took the ship. No one has to be in the escape pod in order for it to go somewhere. We just have to estimate where the Swarm ship will most likely be in the process and program the launch for their estimated position," Nereus said.

"Oh, that's all, huh?" Harwood said, dryly. "And if this doesn't work?"

"Then we all die," Avril whispered.

Nereus looked at Avril. "I won't allow that to happen."

"When's this all go down?" Anthony asked.

Nereus stood. "Six hours. I'm heading to the bridge to speak with Cosima. I need you guys in place and ready to go. Anthony, get to that computer room and start overriding the pod's system and set its destination to the Swarm. Keep your monitors on in case I need to reach out, but I'd like to use a more secure channel. When Cosima gives us the go-ahead, she will not want to advertise to the entire crew that we're a ticking time bomb."

"If she's okay with it, why the channel switch for coms?" Harwood asked.

"Because she'll also try to do it *her* way and she's a freaking mathematician, not a physicist."

"So basically, you're just informing her as a courtesy? I'm not sure I'm okay with this. We go way back, Ner, but let's not push that friendship into getting me thrown in the brig," Anthony replied.

Nereus leaned over the table and lowered his voice. "Look guys, what I'm asking will not be easy. But it's the right thing to do. You're all scientists first, right?"

Harwood sat up and said brightly, "And if we save everyone's ass on this ship—it could mean more chicks."

"You disgust me," Avril sneered.

Harwood winked at her.

"What if the Swarm moves between now and then?" Anthony asked.

"Triangulate various positions with the velocities from the current speed and position," Nereus answered.

"And, if Cosima says no way? Thinks you're trying to bullshit her?" Harwood asked.

But Nereus was looking at Avril, her forehead crinkled with worry lines. He turned his attention back to Harwood.

"Hopefully she hates dying more than she hates me." And with that, Nereus left the mess hall in search of Captain Sabine.

$$H(t)|\psi(t)\rangle = i\hbar\frac{\partial}{\partial t}|\psi(t)\rangle$$

Nereus was about to enter the bridge when he overheard Cosima talking to her second mate.

"How long do we have before the fallout from the flare hits?" Cosima asked, leaning over the second mate's shoulder.

Nereus inched into the room. From his vantage point, he saw the monitor which showed the release of a solar flare in the last few minutes. *Dammit.* That level of high-energy subatomic particles would penetrate the hull. They would need to haul ass.

As he attempted to back out of the room, Cosima spun on her heels. "What are you doing here?"

"I had an issue with the ECLSS. I wanted to run it by you," Nereus answered, hoping the perspiration gathering above his brow wasn't acting as his tell.

"I'm a bit busy. Is it something you can handle on your own?" she turned back to the monitor.

"Yep. I can take it from here. Thanks." He headed towards the door.

As he left the room, he heard Cosima say to her first mate, "Probably another toilet overflow."

Nereus radioed Ensign Xia, Harwood, and Shankman informing them the timeline was now moved up, to get into position, and that he had the approval of Captain Sabine. She asked if it was something that he could handle himself, right?

Fully suited up for the EVA, Nereus paused for a moment and then handed Avril her helmet. She didn't notice his hands tremble as he held her helmet in his hands, or maybe she did and chalked it up to nerves. He didn't know what was worse: Avril thinking he was nervous or Avril knowing the truth behind the tremors he was experiencing. Was she even aware of the excruciating headaches and the chronic fatigue? It was only a matter of time before everyone aboard this god forsaken ship would know.

"Nereus?" Avril asked. "Are you alright?" She tilted her head to one side and smiled. "It'll work. I have faith."

Nereus nodded and pulled on his helmet.

Within seconds, Harwood's voice came over the helmet intercom. "Okay, boss, we're all set."

"I need a temp check, both inside and out," Nereus barked.

"Outside temperature is a balmy negative 235.4 degrees

Celsius. Inside the hull is twenty-seven. Once you get that panel off, you've only got minutes to spare," Harwood replied. "Hope you work fast."

"That's why Ensign Xia will make the repairs while I scrape the inside hull from debris from the bonds," Nereus answered. "She'll help me finish up once the leak is repaired. Anthony, you finish overriding that system?"

"Not yet—hang on a minute," he replied.

Nereus tapped his foot.

"Okay. We're good to go."

"We're exiting the craft." Nereus turned to Avril. "You ready for this?"

She nodded. He clipped a high-density carabiner to her suit. "When we get outside, immediately clip yourself to the ship. Got that?"

"Roger that." She pushed a large red button near the door which sealed off the entry from the other side so no one could enter. A red flashing light blinked as the AI system reported the airlock was secure.

"We're clipped and ready to move into position. Harwood, anything I need to be aware of?" Nereus asked as he dragged himself along the wire and floated toward the front of the ship.

"Looks good from here. You've got about ten more meters to the panel," Harwood replied. "I'm sure it's nothing, but I'm noticing an inside temperature increase. Anomaly, maybe?"

"Keep me updated," Nereus shot back. "Anthony, I'm going to need that pod soon."

"Roger that. Working on it. I have to override the system in the output bay and make it look like it's still there."

When they reached the designated spot, Nereus turned and looked at the dark expanse before him. Between the soft glow of the ship's lights and the eerie silence, it had an almost ethereal effect. Nebulas light years away left a hazy glow as their light traveled along the waves of space. Nereus let his mind wander for only an instance to take it all in. It was a breathtaking sight. As if he was there before the face of God. He felt the tug on the cord that connected him to the ship. It was Avril alerting him she was ready for him to move in.

Her repairs were relatively simple. Once she pulled the unit out of its compartment, she released the remaining gas which would dissipate into the surrounding expanse. She then quickly patched the leak and shoved it back inside.

Avril and Nereus worked quickly to resolve the issue and were already on their second bag when Nereus's helmet crackled. "Pod should arrive your way in three, two, one." The escape pod appeared as it wrapped around the front of the ship and stopped a few meters from where they were working.

"Yep, it's here. Opening pod door now." Nereus nodded to Avril to open the pod door.

"Hey, Nereus?" Harwood's voice crackled over the com. "There's another fifteen-degree increase. Almost like..." his voice trailed off.

Nereus spoke to Avril. "I'll fill the bags; you seal zip them and place them towards the back end of the pod."

He handed her a large foil-like bag before it floated away. They continued in this manner with Nereus collecting the clumpy substance while Avril would catch the bags and place them into the escape pod. His helmet crackled again, but he couldn't understand what was being said.

"Harwood? You're breaking up. Repeat?"

"Er, Nereus? We've got trouble. Commander Sabine is here," Harwood said.

"Sorry? Almost sounded like you said Cosima was there," Nereus replied, scraping the last of the substance from the inside and scooping it into the collection bags. As he sealed each bag, he'd give them a good toss towards Avril, who was now tethered to the pod vehicle, letting the momentum of the bags carry them in a perfect projectile towards Avril. It must have appeared like a game of intergalactic catch on the cameras mounted outside of the ship.

Nereus's helmet intercom crackled again. "Thanatos, this is Captain Sabine. Want to tell me what's going on? And why you're out on an unauthorized EVA joy ride?"

Avril looked at Nereus and said, "What's going on?"

Nereus ignored Captain Sabine, but replied to Avril, "Nothing to worry about."

"So, help me god... Nereus," the intercom crackled. Nereus could tell Cosima was pissed, but he didn't care. There wasn't time to explain it to her, and he knew he was right. He just knew it in his gut.

"Sorry, Commander. We were already out the door. You told me to handle the situation myself. I'm handling it. Now put my crew member back on so I can do my job." Nereus ignored Cosima screaming obscenities into the coms and screwed the panel back in place. When he was finished he pushed himself toward Avril.

"Anthony, is the pod ready to launch? She's locked and loaded," Nereus said as he and Avril gently glided through space towards the ship's bay doors.

As they entered the bay doors, they finally heard a response from Anthony. "Negative, Nereus. Commander has shut it down. Apparently, there's a solar flare and we have to high-tail it out of here before the cosmic waves hit our navigation systems. I'm going to close and seal the bay side doors and start the decontamination process. Oh, and by the way... she's pissed. She just stormed out of the room and will probably meet you there."

"We have to stick to the plan. Anthony? Do you understand me? We have to. Did you tell Cosima what's at stake?"

"Negative. Didn't you?"

"Sort of…"

The intercom crackled again. "On my count, the bay doors will close and seal off before starting decontamination. Five… four—"

But before Anthony could finish counting down, Nereus pushed himself outside the ship which immediately closed behind him, locking closed.

The last he saw was Avril at the bay door window screaming for him. He disconnected his coms and vaulted off the side of the ship towards the pod, which was still waiting where he had left it. He pushed the access panel. The door immediately swooshed open and Nereus stepped inside. He buckled himself into the driver's seat and pushed a series of buttons. The control panel lit up like a Christmas tree.

Anthony's face appeared on the monitor in the center of the control panel. "Nereus! Are you insane? What the hell are you doing? This wasn't part of the plan."

Nereus ignored Anthony only to have Cosima's voice crackle in his helmet.

"Nereus, I command you to return to the ship at once. I'm not messing around you arrogant—"

"—sorry, Commander. I take full responsibility. Don't hold my crew responsible for this. You've got maybe minutes to high-tail it out of here and away from the flare. I've got a job to finish," Nereus replied to Cosima.

She must have already made it to the bay doors as he could hear Avril crying in the background. Within a few seconds, her face appeared on one of the monitors before him.

"Negative, Nereus. Turn that freaking pod around. *Now!*" Cosima yelled into the screen.

All the other monitors lit up on the panels before him, the anger on Cosmia's face was now joined by the worried faces of his crew.

"Captain Cosima Sabine... I know you never liked me and I never really cared who did or didn't like me. So, don't take this personally... but you can go fuck yourself. Get the ship out of here. Nereus Thanatos signing out."

He clicked off the monitors and gunned the engines; the acceleration slammed him back into his seat. The display showed the ship with his crew leaving and the Swarm ship following close behind. Nereus increased the velocity and pushed the boosters to full capacity. For a small pod, the little vehicle had quite the kick.

Nereus's last thoughts weren't of his ending his life to save his crew—though hopefully, they'd toast him later when the captain realized his sacrifice. Images of his life flashed before his eyes but they weren't of the time he was a toddler looking at stars through a home-built telescope, of his parents and siblings. No. His last thoughts were of the chess game he'd been playing earlier that day, the one he would never finish. He played the rest of the game out in his head. Queen to f5. Knight to b4. Bishop to c8 and so the game went.

Just before the pod made impact with the enemy ship, Nereus whispered, "Checkmate, you son of a bitch."

As the heavens lit up like the birth of a thousand stars in a newborn nebula, the ship where Nereus had spent the last few months was pushed forward on the cosmic waves weaving through the universe, increasing its overall acceleration towards their final destination. Home.

SPACE SHARKS CAN'T STOP
(MARCHING BRAND IDENTITY)

ELVIRA CANAVERAL

We were told a trillion times
Of all the troubles in our way
Mind we grow a little greater
Little better every day
But if We created a trillion mirrors
And We swam a trillion parsecs
Then We'd still be where We started
Cells eating each other for a while
Well We are a trillion mirrors
All across the Milky Way
But We never saw our space
Reflected in any way
Now they say your cells are telling you
Be a superstar
But We tell you just be who you are
Stay right who you are
Keep ourselves alive, yeah
Keep ourselves alive
Ooh, it'll take you through time and space
Together we'll survive

Ohm

Well We've lived a trillion cycles
In a stellar purple haze
And We ate a trillion lesser
Beings part of our forever day
Give us everything We need
To feed our body and our soul
And we'll grow a little bigger
Maybe that can be our goal
We were told a trillion times
Of all the darkness in our way
How We had to keep on moving
Our life linked to our day
But if We created a trillion mirrors
And We rode a trillion parsecs
Then We'd still be where We started
Same as when We started
Keep ourselves alive
Reflecting New Hearts
Divided together We thrive

THE END?

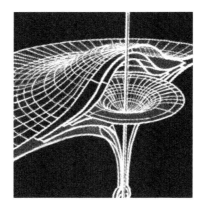

APPENDICES

APPENDIX I
ENSIGN PENNY'S PHARMACOPEIA
JEREMY NELSON

Notes compiled by Ensign Weatherly regarding the chemical substances used by the crew during their time aboard the Ship

COFFEE *(aka "the bean," "terra insomnia," "genuine joe"), see also: CAFFEINE*

Active ingredient: caffeine. Remains the most widely used stimulant in human populations, but true-brewed coffee is now an uncommon luxury given the plant's reluctance to fruit in low-g environments. Considered generally safe, though abuse is common. Side effects may include tremors, tachycardia, insomnia. Note: Often used as a signal in evening mating rituals, possibly due to the implications of shared insomnia.

HAVRIUM *(aka "nebula dust")*

Psychotropic substance more commonly found in Swarm-occupied territories. Low dosages have subtle, often therapeutic effects, encouraging openness to new experiences and a high tolerance for social interactions. In higher dosages, Havrium's effects are unpredictable, ranging from tranquil euphoria to bouts of physical violence. Little stock exists on the ship, but use of the drug is surprisingly pervasive, given results of routine tests.

KP-382-T (*aka "Pleasant Pills"), see also: UPAMC LOADOUT*

Standard-issue anxiety alleviation ration. Tested for use in moderate dosages over a combat tour. Recommended dose 0.5 to 1 mcg/kg/day, not to exceed 5 mcg/kg/day.

Precise pharmacology is ambiguous, as the analysis terminal onboard the ship is limited to molecular composition. Initial findings indicate that multiple active ingredients are likely present. Tolerance and resulting dependence is an issue among the crew. So long as supplies are available, the Pills keep the peace as we contend with a voyage none of us signed on for. Substitute compounds synthesized by replicator appear to satisfy demand.

Extraordinary opportunity to observe behavioral changes when compound is aerosolized. Emergent effects from collective dissolution of social norms are dramatic, including but not limited to relaxing of social hierarchies, egalitarian courtship and mating behaviors, and a fundamental alteration of how self and society relate. However, the crew seems less capable of operating the ship at full efficiency.

VENUSIAN COFFEE, *see also: VRS*

A blend of stimulants named for the planet orbited by the brew's originating station. Primary ingredients are caffeine and Venusian Refractory Silicate, a potent synthetic bearing similarities in effect to natural stimulants like nicotine. These parallels extend to the substances' synergistic effects, and the cocktail is a staple on UPA vessels for maintaining an alert crew. Risk of addiction is noted.

Abuse at high dosages renders one susceptible to paranoia and antisocial behavior. Altered perceptions and potential hallucinations have been reported. Empirical observation suggests users may be goaded to extreme violence.

THROUGHOUT THIS RECREATION OF 22IST-CENTURY MEDIA, WE have included translations of Union Reports, Memos, and Union Service Announcements. These have been translated and distilled down to 2 Dimensions from their original 7 Dimensional forms. There has been an attempt to translate both the language, reference, and terminology into a form that would be "appropriate" if it were to be "published" (Submitted with a Gatekeepers Permission) on Earth's Human Age of 22021, a unique age where printing things on dead trees gave way to printing things with electricity. Thus the original memos have been stripped of their music, their light show, Virtual Reality, Dance Moves, Commentary Tracks, Glossary, Index, and Library Location.

"Library" is the best way to describe the operation of 8th-dimensional "Librarian Marine" Vladimir Heyduke as he and his compatriots the "Original 88" who navigate an endless library, with books of every possibility, Vladimir descending into lower realities was due to his lucking into a book with a story, a copy of which you are now reading a translation of. Not a true copy because these 7th-dimensional "ShudderBooks" limit themselves to 23 characters a period and space. While many "Flat-timers" will scoff at the limitations of such a character set, they have no idea how expressive it is to have a light show and dance numbers alone let alone being connected to all of Space+Time*.

That said, there have been Good Will attempts to translate the work not literally, but to the best-intended meaning. Humans have a long history of fighting over how literal to take their "Gospel" (Allowing a book to replace thinking) and we are doing our best to prevent another Literal Plague. Another side effect is that words won't always rhyme.

These 2d slices will appear between pieces, dropping the words we need to get by, TOGETHER.

Elvira Canaveral
    Funk Union Historian
    High Medium Low Fi

APPENDIX III

EARTH NEWS NETWORK ARCHIVES

EMILY ANSELL

>*TRANSCRIPTS*
>>*FILE NUMBER: 3147-738596302-D*
>>>*FIND: LOCATION 1:47:39*
>>>>>*OPEN FILE*

ANCHOR PETER LORENZ: WELCOME BACK TO OUR COVERAGE OF THE HISTORIC ARMISTICE DAY CELE-BRATIONS HERE ON THE FOREST MOON OF SILUS, ORBITING THE PLANET PIRX IN THE SOLARIS SYSTEM. IT IS ABOUT TEN STANDARD MINUTES TO NOON, LOCAL TIME, AND THE CHRONDITE DELEGA-TION HAS NOW COMPLETED THEIR FORMAL ENTRY MARCH AND HAVE BEEN SEATED. IF YOU ARE JUST JOINING US, WE WILL BE SWITCHING OVER TO THE MEMORIAL SITE MOMENTARILY FOR THE UNVEILING OF THE TERRAN-CHRONDITE UNITY PROJECT THAT HAS BEEN IN THE WORKS FOR SOME TIME. WE DON'T KNOW MUCH ABOUT IT YET, ONLY THAT IT'S BEEN DUBBED THE 'LANSQUENET-

IMMANUEL PROJECT' IN HONOR OF THE TWO
SCIENTISTS SPEARHEADING ITS DEVELOPMENT.
JUST A REMINDER THAT WE WILL HAVE POST-
REVEAL INTERVIEWS WITH BOTH DR. LANSQUENET
AND DR. IMMANUEL LATER ON THIS AFTERNOON
AFTER THE CONCLUSION OF THE REMEMBRANCE
CEREMONY.

ALRIGHT, WE ARE GOING NOW TO THE SOLARIS
MEMORIAL CEMETERY, AS IT LOOKS LIKE THINGS
ARE READY TO BEGIN ON THE GROUND. IT WAS 60
STANDARD YEARS AGO TODAY THAT THE FORMAL
TREATY WAS SIGNED BETWEEN THE HUMAN AND
CHRONDITES SPECIES AND ENDING THE LONG-
STANDING HOSTILITIES THAT HAD SPARKED WARS,
BOTH HOT AND COLD, BETWEEN THE TWO SPECIES.
AS YOU CAN SEE, THE TWO SCIENTISTS HAVE
REACHED THE PODIUM FOR OPENING REMARKS.

DR. LANSQUENET: GOOD MORNING, AND THANK
YOU ALL FOR JOINING US HERE ON THIS HISTORIC
DAY. TODAY MARKS THE 60TH ANNIVERSARY OF
PEACE BETWEEN HUMAN AND CHRONDITE, AS WE
REMEMBER THE LIVES LOST IN THE STRUGGLE TO
REACH THAT PEACE.

DR. IMMANUEL: IT IS IN THE SPIRIT OF THAT
PEACE THAT WE INTRODUCE TO YOU THE COMPLE-
TION OF A LONG-RUNNING PROJECT BY DR.
LANSQUENET AND I, AMONG MANY OTHERS, THAT
AFFIRMS THE COMMITMENT OF OUR PEOPLES TO
CONTINUED PEACE. WE SOUGHT VOLUNTEERS,
NINETY-NINE OF THEM, THAT BEST REPRESENT THE
IDEALS AND EMOBODY THE COMMON EXPERI-
ENCES THAT WE SHARE. THE THOUGHTS AND
MEMORIES OF THOSE HONORED NINETY-NINE

WERE COMBINED TO FORM ONE, A BEING THAT IS THE CULMINATION OF THE HUMAN AND CHRONDITE EXPERIENCE. ALLOW US TO INTRODUCE TO YOU, AND TO THE UNIVERSE, LANSQUENET IMMANUEL.

LANSQUENET IMMANUEL: HELLO, BONJOUR, ASALAAM ALAIKUM, ANYOUNG HASEYO,

>SKIP TO 12:15:02

LANSQUENET IMMANUEL: ...ZDRAVSTVUYTE. IT IS MY HONOR TO INTRODUCE MYSELF TO THE UNIVERSE ON AN HISTORIC DAY SUCH AS THIS. IT IS MY HOPE THAT AS AN ICON OF PEACE BETWEEN THE TWO PEOPLES I AM CREATED IN THE IMAGE OF, THAT I CAN PLAY SOME PART IN BUILDING A FUTURE OF GREATNESS IN THE UNIVERSE. THOUGH THERE ARE MANY OBSTACLES AND THERE WILL ALWAYS BE THOSE THAT SEEK TO DIVIDE US, THOSE THAT ARE A PART OF ME HAVE MADE ME CONFIDENT THAT IF WE FACE THEM TOGETHER, WE CAN OVERCOME. THANK YOU ALL.

ANCHOR PETER LORENZ: TRULY AN HISTORIC DAY. WE HAVE BEEN GIVEN A LITTLE BIT MORE INFORMATION ON THIS NEW BEING THAT WE WILL SHARE WITH YOU AS WE WAIT FOR THE NEXT SPEAKER. LANSQUENET IMMANUEL IS AN ANDROID, AND AS THEY SAID, CONTAINS THE MEMORIES AND EXPERIENCE OF NEARLY A HUNDRED HUMAN AND CHRONDITE VOLUNTEERS. WE ARE TOLD THEY WERE SEVERAL YEARS IN THE MAKING, AS THEIR CEREBRAL CORTEX ALONE REQUIRED A NUMBER OF INNOVATIONS TO BRING TO FRUITION. THIS IS A STUNNING ACHIEVEMENT FOR THE SCIENTISTS AND THEIR TEAMS AND WE HOPE TO

LEARN MORE IN OUR SCHEDULED INTERVIEWS WITH
THEM THIS AFTERNOON, LOCAL TIME.
WE NOW RETURN TO THE CEMETARY WHERE THE
MEMORIAL CELEBRATIONS

>PAUSE
>>CLOSE FILE

APPENDIX IV

THE HISTORY OF THE UPA, BY BEATRICE APPLEBY

DARIUS BEARGUARD–ART BY MAGGIE B. RUBIN

The history of
the United

Planetary
Alliance

by Beatrice
Appleby

The year was 2094 EPT. It was the best of times it was the werst of times. The Earth the berfpalice of humans was at war over important living stuff. Not willing to share there Food and watter the countriees Faught and earth was berned real bad.

The people that remained started lota gangs and the Earth got real bad. But a group af space scientiss From NASA, CNSA, and ROSCOSMOS werked in secret to save Earth. They made the first ever on

the Earth Faster Than Light
drive. I call it the

SPACE RIPPER
9000!

The **SPACE RIPPER 9000!** took the
First people out of the soul
System and into real outer space.
It did not take them long to
meet the First aliens, the
Octopus Aliens! They were
pretty cool, and can rip peoples
faces right off with
there tenticles!

The Octopus Aliens said
Where to find important living
stuff, and that there were more
aliens!

In 2287 Earth got more full
so they ~~told~~ grew stuff
on a second planet called
Gally-5 however the Thunder
Face Aliens were not to
happy and they Attacked!
EARTH DEFENSE FORCES
tried to stop the attack
but lots of people got blowed
up. Earth could not defend
itself alone so they decided
to make a super Frends teem
to protect everybody!

The United Planetary Alliance was born in 2329 and they kicked lost of BUT! Even the Thunder Faces joined after they got there buts kicked so bad. Over the next 800 years the UPA grew through the whole galaxy and they made asked lots of aliens to be part of the UPA super Friends.

But all of a sudden in the year 3122 the SWARM the big meany Face evil space bugs berned whole planets like Doctor Buggington from the Captain Justice cartoons on

Nimmert Corp TV! The UPA
has lost lots of planets to
those EVIL space bugs, but
with help from our Friend
Uncle Karl Nimmert we can
defeat them and save the
Univarse!

— As always, I applaud Bea's immagination
and creativity, but it is NOT appreciated by
some to call the Vilerai "Thunder Faces" or
the Harukei "Octopus Aliens!" Perhaps we can
work on her vocabulary and more appropriate
word choices after the Alliance Day holidays?
In the future if Bea could limit her color
choice to one or two, this will help her grades
significantly in the coming year.

I wish her entry the best! — Mr. V

An alphabetical list of individuals encountered by the Ship, either in physical reality or through the analysis of crew member's psychic emanations, as recovered from her core data-core after her return to Kepler 452B in Real Space.

Ado (unknown, he/him)—*Navigator*. Navigator aboard the *The Bonny Ann*. Jagged teeth, family of 16 back on Jupiter Two, will do anything for a solid paycheck.

Alpha 3, Triangle "TATE" (Kern, he/they/it)—*Chief Warrant Officer Alpha-3*. Hive mind species. Eventually goes by "TATE." Becomes acting captain after Captain Savory's death.

Angelin, Angevin (Islii, xe/xer)—*Linguist & ethnographer*. Assigned to the mission in order to communicate with the ship, xe has a secret mission of vengeance.

Baniti (simulation, he/him)—Deceased spouse of Lazlo Brizbane.

Brizbane, Lazlo (Human, he/his)—*Widower, tourist*. Space tourist on a tour of the stars to honor his recently deceased husband.

Bryjal (Haruki, they/them)—*Staff Sergeant, Security.* A member of an octopus-like alien species. Head of security aboard the Ship.

Dangaley, Changa (Human/alien, she/her)—*Lieutenant, Medic.* Half alien (non-defined) half human, but passes as fully human.

Deandre, Altera (Human, she/her)—*1st Lieutenant, Special Operations.* Dangerous, possibly psychotic. Sexually voracious and deadly with knives.

Deron, Broggs (Weslian, he/him)—*Private.* Empath humanoid overwhelmed by his "insight" into his fellow crewmates.

Dileo, Logan (Human, he/him)—*2nd Lieutenant, pilot.* Native to Mars, very loyal to UPA with an unrelenting hatred of the Swarm.

Ellerbee, Cassandra (Human, she/her)—Found unconscious on an asteroid. Dead sexy and hiding something in her pocket.

Everest, Riker P. (Human, he/him)—Refugees from a version of reality where most humans are dead. Helps uncover the UPA/Corp conspiracy.

Figlimente, Sveltetha (Human/Saphir, she/her)—*Private.* Shape-shifter.

Gennero, Alexa (Human/Swarm, she/her)—*Counselor.* Cheerful, bubbly. Doesn't know she's half Swarm.

Glub (Cribalan, it/they/them)—Nonbinary shapeshifter who takes on the form of Penny Weatherly.

Grey, Alan (Human, he/him)—*1st Lieutenant.* Trans man determined to prove himself as a marine.

Harwood, Rockwell (Human, he/him)—*Physicist*

Hayduke, Vladimir (Human, he/him)—*2nd Lieutenant.* Clone/hive personality of Hayduke Prime. Accomplished funk musician.

Immanuel, Lansquenet (Android they/them)— Android programmed with the memory of 99 humans and Chrondites.

Iona (Human, she/her)—*Galactic Missioner.* A genetic engineer who renounces her work in faith conversion.

Jenkins, Chris (Human, he/him)—*Private First Class.* Grunt, ethnocentric, addiction problems, refuses to believe the ship can talk to people and thinks they're all going crazy.

Jerico, Marcia (Human, she/her)—*1st Lieutenant.* Enhanced human. Navigator.

Kift, Dylan Morgan (Human, he/him)—*Stow-away.* Twelve-year-old boy who disguised himself in a marine exoskeleton to stowaway on the mission. His parents were killed in a Swarm attack on his home planet of Kepler 452B. Develops a strong psychic link to the Ship.

Kitty (Spaceship, she/her*)*—Nickname given to the ship by *Dylan Krift.*

Latifah, Queen (Human, she/her)—*AI Simulation.* A virtual simulation of the rapper, actress, and activist Dana Elaine Owens. The guiding voice for Dr. Changa Dangaley as she interfaces with the ship regarding the pleasant pill effects.

Lowrie, Suzanne (Human, she/her)—*Sergeant.* Ran away to escape her evangelical family on Kepler 452B. Has a special connection to *Dylan Krift.* Devoted to the philosophy of rationalism.

MuDuhRu Hunter, unnamed (MuDuhRu, unknown)–– Found dead in outer corridors by Altera Deandre. No-one can explain why it is aboard, how it was killed, nor why the Ship has no record of its presence.

Morgan, Callie (Human, she/her)—*Space pirate.* Found by crew in an escape craft moored to a cluster of asteroids.

Ortega, Rosealin (Human, she/her)—*2nd Lieutenant, Operations.* An undercover counter intelligence officer assigned to the mission. Life-long marine who follows orders.

Owensby, Paul (Human, he/him)—*Private First Class.* Grunt, laid back, down to indulge but maintains self control. Works daily shifts maintaining a supply room. Steals small amounts of VRS for personal use. Goes on the mission to the water planet to harvest stuff for pleasant pill production.

Ren, Servan (Linnean, she/her/they)—*Linnean Intendant.* A liaison from the Linnean government, serving in the role of Intendant.

Renner, Kevin (Human, he/him)—*Sergeant.* Former merchant marine turned UPA marine. Enlisted for practical, rather than patriotic, reasons.

Rock, Chris (Human, he/him)—*AI Simulation.* A virtual simulation of 90's comedian Chris Rock.

Rolan (Venusian, they/them)—*First Mate.* Callie's second in command, lover and mutineer aboard *The Bonny Anne.*

Sabine, Cosmia (Human, she/her)—*Scientific attaché.* Part of the scientific team embedded with the Marines whose mission is to study the ship.

Sanderson, Harold (Human, he/him)—*Xenobiologist.* Former marine turned civilian doctor. Specializes in xenobiology.

Savory, Maxwell (Human, he/him)—*Captain, Mission Command.* Captain and Mission Commander.

Seren (Human, she/her)—*Safe Cracker.* Crewmate on Callie's *The Bonny Anne.* Fourteen, moody, wears lots of color. Candy-shaded hair.

Shankman, Anthony (Human, he/him)—*Computer specialist.* Works with Nereus to dispose of the explosives. Overrides the AI system on the escape pod.

Takach, Unah (Human, she/her)—*Private, engineer.* Family was involved in a plot to overthrow UPA.

Thief, unnamed (Unknown/Human-presenting, he/him)—sneaks aboard Ship with stolen MuDuhRu technology to interface with the ship. Wants an orb from the Glow Room.

Thanatos, Nereus (Human, he/him)—*Warrant Officer, engine specialist.* Physicist and booster engine specialist. Has a serious problem with authority.

Wandri, Johannes (Human, he/him)—*Naturalist.* Scientist living in the long shadow of his grandfather's fame.

Weatherly, Penny (Human, she/her)—*Ensign.* Ensign. Mostly makes coffee. Copied and replaced for a time by Glub.

West (Human, he/him)—Riker's brother. Has Down syndrome.

Xia, Avril (Human, she/her)—*Ensign.* Biochemist and Ensign in the military who helps Nereus discover excess amounts of ammonium in the ship's hull.

Yawson, Mackenzie (Human, she/her). *Soldier.* Assistant to Dr. Changa Dangaley.

AN ALPHABETICAL LIST OF LOCATIONS, ALIEN SPECIES, CHEMICALS, AND concepts encountered by the Ship, either in physical reality or through her travel through sixth-dimensional quantum theoretical modulation, before, during, or after the events of this book.

AA—An abbreviation for *After the Alliance*, it is the standardized time-keeping calendar system for the members of the *UPA*. At the start of the book, the year is 832 AA.

AB-5427—The mining asteroid where the crew discovers Cassandra Ellerbee.

ACRE—Advanced Crop Regeneration Emphyteusis. A UPA funded program that cloned genetically modified fruits and vegetables to grow in almost any environment, ideal for trade between colonies and new species.

"After the Alliance"—See *AA*

Alchimis 8—A vial containing transmutable compounds that reflect natural chemicals found on earth. Curious minds inserted Alchimis 8 into learning tablets in order to study Old World flora and fauna.

Aneas 3—*Marcia Jerico*'s home planet. Colonized by psychic humans and ruled by a monarchy.

Asteroids, Various—Any of the millions of small celestial objects revolving around a star, often irregularly shaped and having a great range in size, from as small as 6 feet (1.8 meters) across to about 620 miles (998 kilometers) across. A favorite location for mysteriously enticing women hiding dangerous secrets to hang about.

Blast Neutrino Salvation Treatments—A process for resuscitating dying stars. Pioneered by Thomas Wandri, the grandfather of *Johannes Wandri*.

Bonny Anne, The—Callie Morgan's space ship.

"Bootsy"—The nickname given to The Ship's offspring.

Chrondites—An alien race. Ninety-nine Chrondite and human minds are merged together in an artificial body to make *Lansquenet Immanuel*.

Church of the Neo-Cyber Christ. A techno-evangelical sect of Christianity. Its theology is essentially Manichean, teaching that the flesh and all physical reality are fallen and sinful, and that the only path to salvation is through Virtual Reality. *Suzanne Lowrie* was raised in the *CNCC*, but abandoned her family over its rigid and homophobic world-view.

Cluster X—Officially designated on UPA star maps as *Cluster X109IR3*. A small asteroid cluster where the crew finds Callie Morgan.

Cluster X109IR3—See *Cluster X*.

CNCC—See *Church of the Neo Cyber Christ*.

Colins, Bootsy—William Earl "Bootsy" Collins is an American musician, singer and songwriter. Rising to prominence with James Brown in the early 1970s, and later with Parliament-Funkadelic, Collins's driving bass-lines and humorous vocals established him as one of the leading names in funk.

"Color Time"—The time keeping system aboard the Ship

based on the color fluctuation of the internal walls, which fluxuate regularly over a 24-hour period. The crew begin to use these colors in lieu of hours. For example "I'll meet you in the galley at lilac..." "OMG, is it yellow already? I have a shift."

Cribalia—An uninhabited planet surrounded by the ring city to *Tadegah*. Also the name of the start around which the planet Cribalia orbits.

Cribalians—Non-binary shape-shifting aliens made of light who live in the ring city of *Tadegah* orbiting planet *Cribala*.

Dagona—A long lost civilization about which hardly anything is known. One of the few relics the UPA has encountered is one of their massive abandoned ships. See: *Unknown Alien Ship, Husk of.*

Devil's Mist—A highly toxic mist formed when the powdery soil of *HFC987* becomes airborne. The soil contains an incredibly deadly microbe, and in this aerosol form it can kill through inhalation or merely contact with the skin.

Devil's Sphere—Officially designated on UPA star maps as *HFC987*. Icy planet with a powdery white soil that's a deadly microbe. Forms *Devil's Mist*.

"Earth Common Era"—See *ECE*

ECE—Short for *Earth Common Era*, it is the current term to refer to the calendar system used by Earth before the creation of the UPA. Largely abandoned in favor of the new AA system, but still in use by a few holdout planets. Years in ECE are equivalent to those in the even older nomenclature of CE ("Common Era") and "AD" (Anno Domini). At the start of the year, it is 3152 ECE, or 832 AA.

ECLSS—Stands for "Environmental Control and Life Support Systems." (Pronounced e-cliss). It's the basis for all oxygen, water, and everything else needed in order to survive on a ship.

Elkar-2—Angevin's home planet. An *Islii* colony with super-light gravity.

Erm—Unit of time, comparable to Earth minutes.

FerRahKun VII—Planet in the FerRahK system. Location of a secret MuDuhRu Research & Development outpost. Recently destroyed in suspicious circumstances.

Funk—Funk music is dance music that mixes rhythm and blues music with soul music. Funk bands use many rhythm instruments, such as electric guitar, bass guitar, drums, and keyboard instruments, mainly synthesizers and electronic organs. It also is the key to understanding the six-dimensions of hyper-space-time reality.

Glow Room, The—In the heart of the ship there's a chamber whose function is unclear. It appears to be part of the ship's bioprocess. The chamber is full of softly pulsing floating orbs of light. It becomes a popular spot for couples seeking a romantic location to steal a few moments together.

Great Cosmic Mind—System of belief among *Weselians* that all things in the universe are part of the Great Cosmic Mind, like neurons in a brain, and are thus connected. Each individual's life adds to and enriches the Cosmic Mind's Experience. Some seek to bring the various groups in the universe into Harmony, believing that having all parts of the Cosmic Mind working in conjunction (instead of the opposition often seen) will bring about a Nirvana-esque situation where the Cosmic Mind, and all that are part of it, will ascend to some greater understanding.

Haruki—An octopus like alien species without gender or sex differentiation. (They arbitrarily, as far as the humans know, pick a sexuality to mate once every three decades.) Their culture forbids the use of any addictive substances. The Haruki were the first non-human civilization encountered by humans in 2094 ECE after the development of FTL technology. After centuries of conflict, the Haruki were eventually one of the original members of the UPA at its founding in 2329 ECE.

Havrium—Psychotropic substance more commonly found in Swarm-occupied territories. For more details, see: *Appendix I, Ensign Penny's Pharmacopeia.*

Hayduke Prime—A human in hyper sleep who has sent countless clone iterations out as backups into the galaxy. The iteration aboard the Ship is *Vladimir Hayduke.*

Hessern—A species of highly intelligent quantum-beings native to a far-flung region of the galaxy undiscovered by the UPA. They have long been enslaved by the Swarm and used as military space ships. Because of this, the UPA believes Hessern to merely be bio-organic vessels and are unaware they are actually sentient. Among the Hessern's natural abilities is the ability to manipulate their physical form at will, transport themselves and others occupants to any point across six-dimensional space and quantum reality, and communicate psychically with other sentient beings.

HD156668b—A planet 78.5 light years away from Earth, orbiting the star HD156668.

HFC987—See *Devil's Sphere.*

Host, The—The collective term for a subset of the crew receiving strange visitations from apparitions of the dead.

Hwang-Cruz, Leona—One of the very few survivors of the attack on Theta 32, Hwang-Cruz was a journalist who managed to capture much of the attack using a hand-held holocam. She later edited the footage and released it as the now classic documentary, *A First Hand Account of the Massacre of Theta 32-D.*

Islii—An alien population originating from a super-light gravity world. They use personal force-fields outside of their home planet to compensate for the difference in gravity. Completely asexual, they reproduce through a complex mitosis and each individual carries genetic memories from its predecessors back to their line's progenitor.

JXMS—The Journal of Xeno-Medical Sciences.

Kaju Delta Force—A popular cartoon on Kepler 452B.

Kepler 452—A G-Type main sequence star located 1830 light years from Old Earth.

Kepler 452B—A rocky, Earth-type planet in orbit around Kepler 452. Its orbital period is 385 days long. There are four other planets in the system—two small, rocky planets that orbit closer to the star and two large, gaseous giants further from the star. Kepler 452 B has two moons, one roughly the size of Earth's and one small rocky moon, most likely a captured asteroid. Home planet to *Dylan Krift* and *Suzanne Lowrie*. The UPA mission to capture the Swarm Ship originates in 452B's low-orbit.

Kern—A sentient insect-like collective species with a hive-mind, that has access to the knowledge and advice of the whole Kern Collective, and can communicate telepathically with the entire species.

Kitty—*Dylan Kift's* name for the Ship. He insists it's the closest he can come to approximating the name she uses for herself in her native language.

KP-382-T—Commonly known as *Pleasant Pills*. Standard-issue anxiety alleviation ration. Tested for use in moderate doses over a combat tour. Recommended dose 0.5 to 1 mcg/kg/day, not to exceed 5 mcg/kg/day.

Linnean—A humanoid alien people. Stereotyped as conniving and untrustworthy, perhaps due to their short horns above each eye and forked tongue.

L-Tablet—A learning tablet capable of projecting objects above and upon its surface that allowed the user to feel, see, and even smell what the actual object would have presented.

Magical Machine Room—Often shortened to *MMR*. A

room within the Ship that can create holographic projections from inner-most desires, one person at a time. Appears the ship AI stores and can project their subconscious musings as well. Experiences in the room have caused many aboard the ship to doubt what they thought they understood. The scientifically minded in the crew dislike the use of the adjective "magical," but the name sticks.

Medbay—The automated medical facilities aboard the Ship. Capable of modifying care to any bio organism. Produces the anti-anxiety medicine known as *Pleasant Pills*.

MMR—See *Magical Machine Room*.

mRNA Insertion—A process by which messages are inserted into an organism, instructing the cells in the organism to make proteins or modify biology. See *Transference*.

MuDuhRu Territory—A large swatch of the galaxy, spanning several star-systems, controlled by the *MuDuhRu* empire.

MuDuhRu—A quadrupedal species present in the *Cribala* system, although that is not their system of origin. They have a multi-star "empire" though the extent of it is as of yet unknown. Their heads are small compared to their bodies; many wear large, opaque helmets for the purpose of appearing more intimidating in battle or when interacting with other species.

Mycorrhizal Networks—A fungal network that allows living systems on a planet to communicate.

Nebula, Sentient (Untitled)—A nebula that displays indications of actually being a sentient being. Its actual interaction with the crew and Ship remain mysterious.

New Hominy—The home planet of *Logan Dielo*.

Nimmert Corp—A mega-corporation from Earth that is presently the chief supplier of arms and armament for the UPA.

"Orphan Planet" (Untitled)—A planet sized object freely traveling through the galaxy, not orbiting any star. Encountered in the same star system as the planet *Cribalia*.

Pleasant Pills—See *KP-382-T*.

Pop Drops—The name given by the crew to informational collections of "mindsets" of large populations found aboard the Ship. Used by the Swarm for colonization, the "pop drops" are self replicating to exponentially increase chance of reseeding.

Rationalism—*Suzanne Lowrie*'s nascent religion/cult based on objectivity and logic. Suzanne develops it based on her reading of various philosophies, life-experience, and largely in reaction to her upbringing in the *CNCC* cult.

Reslyk—UPA member planet near Venus. Inhabited by a species of ambulatory creatures resembling amoebae.

Sapharr—Peaceful seeming humanoids who use the same components as we do for Venusian Coffee. One crew member described their encounter with the Sapharr thus: "They are captivating... Gazes that pierce the soul, yet calm and generally silent. My every word was devoured within their intellect, leaving me to feel uncertain that my words were worthy of inhabiting their cranial space. I felt... lost, but I must meet with them again."

Scruggs, Elion—Author of the definitive account of the attack on Theta 32, *Death from the Darkness*. The book is based on interviews with the very few survivors, as well as exhaustive research using the sensors and cam-footage that was recovered by UPA forces.

Sensory Enhancing Suits—Uniforms created by the Ship and customized to the wearer. They enhance strength or 1-2 of the 5 senses, with the drawbacks being but the wearer will not know *what* will be enhanced, and the effect is unique to the wearer, meaning two individuals will experience the uniform differently. Some known modifications are: breathing comfortably in nearly any environment and resistance to extreme temperatures.

Shepherds—An alien people capable of transporting matter over large distances. The Shepherds have used stars to guide their exploration of various planets and galactic spaces. They seek enlightenment, as well as true understanding—whatever that may be. They abide by the belief that everyone has something to teach and all have something to learn.

Ship, The—The sentient, bio-organic vessel the crew steals at the start of the book. In truth she is not a ship at all, but a member of a highly intelligent species, the *Hessern*, who have long been enslaved by the Swarm and used as military vessels. Although she has an actual name in her own language, most of the crew are unaware of that and generally refer to her as "The Ship." (*Dylan Kift* nicknames her "Kitty" in an attempt to approximate the phonetic pronunciation.) At the start of the book the Ship is pregnant, and begins using the crew as part of her plan to liberate herself and her offspring. She develops a special connection to Dylan and eventually gives birth to her child, nicknamed "Bootsy."

Space Sharks—They're sharks. In space. They're goddamn space sharks! And they like to eat space crystals and can be trained to attack! If they don't have lasers mounted on their heads, they should. SPACE SHARKS!

The Space Ripper 9000—The name of the first faster-than-light vessel developed by humans in 2094 ECE.

Swarm—A non humanoid alien species that has been at war with sectors of the UPA for generations. It is nearly impossible to describe them, as each individual's impression of them is subjective and based on their own subconscious expectations of what the Swarm will look like. In the three decades of *The Swarm Wars*, the UPA has been unable to determine a motive or even truly communicate with the Swarm. Their technology is largely bio-organic and operates on highly-advanced scientific principles unknown to the UPA. They enslave the species that the Ship belongs to for use for transportation and combat purposes.

Swarm Pods—Pods used by Swarm to invade planets, used during the first wave of attack. The pod is made of a living tissue that wraps around the body and features an advanced pilot system that can be controlled with the user's eyes.

Swarm Wars—The common name for the series of nearly endless battles fought between the UPA and The Swarm over the last thirty years. The conflict began with an unprovoked attack against a mining colony on *Theta 32* in 802 AA, which also was the first time the UPA was even aware of the Swarm's existence.

Tachyon Pulsar—A pulsar star emanating plumes of tachyons, rather than high-energy radiation, from either pole. The effect is stunningly gorgeous, though it wrecks havoc with reality.

Tadegah—Ring city that encircles the planet *Cribalia*. Home to sentient light beings, the *Cribalians.*

Theta 32—A mining colony infamous for being the site of the first known attack by the *Swarm* on a *UPA* outpost in 802 A.A.

Transference—The process of modifying non-human organisms to incorporate human characteristics. Fostered by the UPA as a means to facilitate communication with non-human societies. See *mRNA Insertion.*

United Planetary Alliance—The major intergalactic governing body. Formed in 2329 ECE early in Old Earth's third-century of interstellar exploration. Currently, most civilizations are members of the UPA, with the notable exception of the *Swarm*, whom the UPA has been at war with for three decades.

Unknown Alien Ship, Husk of—A abandoned wreck of a massive interstellar vessel left over by the long-lost Dagona civilization.

UPA—See *United Planetary Alliance.*

UPA Evac Transport—A special emergency transport used to ferry survivors from colonies destroyed by the Swarm to refugee camps or other safe zones.

UPAMC—*United Planetary Alliance Marine Corp.*

Venus—A rocky planet in the Old Earth Solar System. Terraformed centuries ago, it is also the origin of that wonderfully addictive brew, *Venusian Coffee.*

Venusian Refractory Silicate—The active ingredient in *Venusian Coffee.* A potent synthetic bearing similarities in effect to natural stimulants like nicotine. For more details, see: *Appendix I, Ensign Penny's Pharmacopeia.*

Venusian Coffee—A beverage made by infusing traditional coffee with the chemical *VRS.* The result is a drink that gives you a jolt of caffeine along with just a little something extra. That something extra being a mildly hallucinogenic effect. Somewhat addictive.

VRS—See *Venusian Refractory Silicate.*

"Water Planet" (Untitled)—A planet entirely covered in an ocean of salinated water. Located in the Cribalian system. Home to a wide variety of aquatic life, as well as the minerals needed to make Venusian Refractory Silicate (VRS), the primary ingredient in Venusian Coffee.

Weslian—A highly empathic humanoid species from a planet in one of Earth's neighboring solar systems often prided for their careers in social work and mediations.

Yolan, Phlan—The popular netvid actor, best known to younger audiences as the narrator for Galactic Media's holo-vid series, *Immersive History.*

Zoetrope Room, The—A cabin where crew communicate directly with the Ship through tropes, stories, or metaphors.

ACKNOWLEDGMENTS

When a project involves this many people, it's impossible to acknowledge everyone who helped make it possible. But the staff of Skullgate Media would like to thank the following:

All the writers who have spent the last four months fleshing out the crew, the Ship, and the strange corners of the galaxy we found ourselves in. It is an honor to have authors and artists trust us with their creative pieces.

Aaron Hockett, our resident cartographer and illustrator. When we asked if he'd be willing to do maps for this book, we had no idea how stunning they would be. Then he asked if he could do a miniature graphic novel...

Phandy, the illustrator who did our fantastic cover. We came across him randomly on Fiverr when working on Achten Tan, and he continues to impress us with his ability to capture our weird worlds with ease. And when I asked "hey, could you add some sharks?" he didn't bat an eye.

Maggie B. Rubin, for providing the wonderful illustrations to to "Appendix IV: The History of the UPA." Thanks, Maggie!

Our Kickstarter backers, who ensured we had the finances needed to commission a cover and do all the cool, professional level things we wanted to do with this book. You all get a shout-out in a few pages, but just know we were blown away by the love and support.

Our guest editors, as without them we would still be working on editing and proofreading. None of them were paid, and all worked incredibly hard to get this book ship-shape: B.K. Bass, Jayme Bean, Alain Davis, A.R.K. Horton, Allison N. Moore, Jeremy Nelson, Sarah Parker, Sarah Remy, Lanie Storiz, and (only last due the alphabetical order) Kelly Washington.

Special thanks to Avery Alder and her game *The Quiet Year*, which inspired our world-building game. That said, *Tales From the Year Between* is not associated with Avery Alder's *The Quiet Year* in any official capacity. Her game was used as a prompt to generate ideas, but none of the text of her game is included in the final product, and while she approved of the project, she has no connection to the stories and content of the anthology. *Tales From the Year Between* is not an extension, expansion, or in any way part of *The Quiet Year* game or any of Avery Alder's projects. So don't blame her. Instead, go buy a copy and play it yourself. Maybe you'll wind up with a book.

Thanks to the #WritingCommunity on Twitter. Most of the people involved in Under New Suns met via that platform, so when someone tells you that social media is nothing but a cesspool of negativity, know that there's at least one corner where cool writers hang out and support each other.

Finally, thanks to the reviewers who agreed to look at advanced copies and shared their impressions with the world. While the UPA does not approve of stowaways, we're glad that, like Dylan, you smuggled yourself aboard. Thanks for braving the Swarm and the sixth-dimensional funk! I was hoping to thank you in print, but unfortunately we went to press before our reviewers were lined up. And while time may be an illusion (and lunch time, of course, doubly so), print deadlines are not.

KICKSTARTER BACKERS

The following people helped make *Under New Suns* possible through their financial support. Many generously added donations over and above these standard backing levels, but whether they contributed $4 or $300, we are eternally grateful to each and every person who helped fund this book.

eBook Fan
   Jedediah Berry
   Sebastian H.
   Erin R. Hoffer
   Nils Thingvall

Digital 2 Pack
   Andrew Heidgerken
   Chuck Robinson
   Duane Warnecke

Paperback Print Fan
   Winstolf
   Jayme Bean

Jonathan Beck
Chris Durston
Dan Fitzgerald
Josh Goldfein
Pat Griffith
Vincent LaBate

Print & Digital Book Lover

Guges
Jonathan
Jack Houck
Stephanie Rizzo
Daniel Berison

Signed & Numbered Print Edition

JustKickitt
Tyson Arzt
Roger Kristian Jones
Kevin M.
Renee Schnebelin

Creative Chaos VIP

Anonymous
Anonymous
Jim G. Black
Adrienne Bross
Matthew Dombroski
Michael Durham
Emily F.
John Hogan
Sarah Remy
Mary Van Dyke

Ultra-Backer Chaos VIP Extraordinaire!

Steve & Andrea Katchur

Kate Kift

Michael Mudgett

Paul Renner

Erica Shannon

ABOUT "TALES FROM THE YEAR BETWEEN"

TALES FROM THE YEAR BETWEEN IS THE FLAGSHIP PUBLICATION OF Skullgate Media, an indie-publishing company dedicated to changing the way authors collaborate and publish.

Part literary magazine, part writing club, part cult, and all creativity, *Tales From the Year Between* is a semi-annual speculative fiction anthology with a unique premise. Each volume gathers a disparate group of authors from all across the globe to collaborate in shared world-building and creative writing. Using a modified version of Avery Alder's fabulous game *The Quiet Year* as a massive writing prompt, each volume of *The Year Between* begins with nothing more than a simple premise ("a desert fantasy world, like D&D's *Dark Sun*" or "a crew lost in space aboard a sentient ship"). Contributors participate in a week-long "game" to create a shared canon of people, places, events, and themes. From this chaotic melange of ideas, each participant then creates their own stories, poems, letters, and even recipes, all set in the world they created together. Intrigued? Sound like fun? See our website on how you could help us make our next world...

CONTRIBUTORS

Laila Amado spends her days teaching, writing, never quite catching up on her own research agenda, and trying to get a teenage kid through a global pandemic. In her free time, she can be found staring at the Mediterranean Sea. Occasionally, the sea stares back. She is on Twitter @onbonbon7.

Emily Ansell is an SFF writer hailing from the cold, wind-swept prairies of Manitoba, Canada, where she lives with one husband, two kids, and two cats. You can find her latest writing endeavors, cosplays, and other nerdy things on Twitter and Instagram, as well as her rarely-updated website, emilyaansell.wordpress.com

Gabrielle Awe is the writer of the podcasts Finding Satan and Stories in the Dark, which she also narrates. She has published a collection of stories from the podcast titled "Stores in the Dark: The Horror" as well as "Empire of Sky," a YA Fantasy. Read more at GabrielleAwe.com. *(Vol. 1 alum)*

B. K. Bass is the author of over a dozen books of science fiction, fantasy, and horror inspired by pulp fiction magazines and classic speculative fiction. He is also an avid worldbuilder, a blender of genres, and a student of history. More about B.K. can be found on his website, bkbass.com *(Guest Editor)*

Steven Bayer is a drama teacher by day and a daydreamer in his spare time. He is thrilled to debut with Skullgate and hopes to share more of the wild and fantastical thoughts swirling in his mind in the years to come. You can follow him on Twitter as @sylphenwood.

Jayme Bean is a multi-genre author hailing from the sunny state of Florida. As a semi-retired zookeeper and full-time Mom, Jayme spends the little bit of free time she has telling stories. Her debut adventure novel, *Untouched*, will hit the shelves in early 2021. You can follow her on twitter @JaymeBeanAuthor. *(Guest Editor)*

Born in British Columbia Canada, **Darius Bearguard** grew up in a town caught between a village and a city nestled within acres of mountain and backwoods. He started his writing journey writing fan-fiction for the Duke Nukem games, and has been enamored with writing since. @OSTBear *(Vol. 1 alum)*

Jonathan Beck is a singer & writer from Northern Ireland who loves cats, whiskey and traveling; in the absence of the latter is hitting the other two pretty hard. When he's not running or watching Star Trek, he's can be found in coastal cafes, writing odd tweet-sized stories under the name @diminufiction *(Vol. 1 alum)*

A sincere satirist (sintire.com), **Elvira Canaveral** is the creator of GameOfDepth.com as well as Pincombo.com. Go to Word-Crimes.com for work or dial HAHACOMICS for Rep Ryan Richards r@sintire.com . *(Vol. 1 alum)*

Zackery Cuevas worked in scholarly publishing and children's publishing before switching gears to write about gaming and tech. When he is not talking about, praising, or complaining about video games, he can be found performing around New York City.

Chris "Terry" Durston in holding down the Skullgate fort this time out doing editing and stuff. Unlike D, he lives in England, where he subsists on cider and 'taters. His first novel, *Each Little Universe*, was released in April 2020. chrisdurston.com or on Twitter @overthinkery1 . *(Vol. 1 alum, Skullgate Staff, Editor)*

While not a contributor this time, **Diana Gagliardi** acted as the Game Master for Volume 2's world building game. She herded many cats and is now Den Mother to over two dozen sci-fi authors. She & her (actual) child enjoy singing in harmony & quoting Monty Python in and around Philadelphia. *(Vol. 1 alum, Skullgate Staff, GM)*

Aaron Hockett is a New York City based architect, illustrator, amateur cartographer, and aspiring cartoonist. His previous work includes the maps for Volume 1 of *Tales from the Year Between*. Aaron's comic work can be found on Instagram at @hockett.aaron. *(Vol. 1 alum)*

E. R. Hoffer writes about envirofuturism and post-fossil fuel worlds in the hope that positive imaginings might slap humanity hard enough to change things. She tweets as

@erhoffer and posts on her website, lxnishimoto.
wixsite.com/mysite. *(Vol. 1 alum)*

A. R. K. Horton writes blogs about myths, fairytales, and folk-tales. She is also a fantasy author currently working on The Telverin Trilogy. When she isn't writing, she's building websites and managing a family of five in her Florida home. You can find her blog and links to her books at <u>arkhorton.com</u>.

Debbie Iancu-Haddad is currently querying a couple of YA SFF novels, participating in three different anthologies, writing vss on Twitter & buying way too much stuff on Aliexpress. For her day job she gives lectures on humor and serves as a personal chauffeur for her two teenagers. Resides in Meitar, Israel. Follow @debbieiancu or at Debbieiancu.com. *(Vol. 1 alum, Skull-gate Staff)*

Daniel James is an aspiring writer originally from London, looking to publish stories in the fantasy and science fiction genres. He is a recovering activist and a vocal defender of LGBTQ rights, fellow disabled people and social welfare. You can find him on Twitter (@danjameswrites) and danjameswrites.wordpress.com.

Allison N. Moore is a stay-at-home mom who lives in MN. She may look sweet and innocent, but her characters know better. She is querying her first adult fantasy novel, which you can find out more about at her website: authorallisonmoore.com. Her Twittter is @MooreWriting89 . *(Vol. 1 alum, Guest Editor))*

Jeremy Nelson is a recent transplant to Edinburgh whose after-images linger in Hong Kong and Portland, Oregon. His preoccupations include accordions, photography, and outdated methods of putting words to paper. Follow him on Twitter as @jpaknelson. *(Guest Editor)*

S. L. Parker, world builder, wonderer & as a result, writer. Plays well with words & others. Prior publications in poetic & academic veins. WIP exploring creation of civilization & what if stepsisters of the divided ruling family were Fear and True Love. Tweets via @isparkit .*(Vol. 1 alum, Guest Editor)*

Sarah Remy/Alex Hall is a nonbinary, animal-loving, proud gamer Geek. Their work can be found in a variety of cool places, including *HarperVoyager*, *EDGE* and *NineStar Press*. Find them online at SarahRemy.com or on twitter at @sarahremywrites . *(Vol. 1 alum, Guest Editor)*

A. A. Rubin surfs the cosmos on waves of dark energy. His work has appeared recently in anthologies from Flying Ketchup Press and Kyanite Publishing, and in journals such as Cowboy Jamboree and Bards Annual. Follow him as @TheSurrealAri in Twitter, Facebook , and Instagram, or through his website, aarubin.wordpress.com.

Maggie B. Rubin is a 7-year old artist. This is her first published work.

CD Storiz loves to escape by reading and writing Science Fiction and Fantasy. Her previously published novelette, *Relevant,* can be found at Kyanite Press. As @LeChatGris3, she tweets samples of her writing and rants about her cat. *(Vol. 1 alum, Skullgate Staff, Editor)*

A third-generation soldier, **Kelly Washington's** writing has appeared in Pulp House Fiction Magazine, Kaleidotrope, Heart's

Kiss, and various Fiction River Anthologies. You can find her on the web at Kellywashington.com She tweets as @kellywash-writes (*Vol. 1 alum, Guest Editor*)

Chris Vandyke is back as a contributor because, in his words: "I started it, dammit. I get to be in it!" He is also the Editor-in-Chief of TFYB and founding president of Skullgate Media. You can see things he writes at cvandyke.com and follow him at @aboutrunning . (*Vol. 1 alum, Skullgate Staff, Editor-In-Chief, Grand Hierophant, et cetera*)

Phebe Yawson loves to write poetry and short stories. Author of *She Cried Wolf*, Phebe, spends her days homeschooling her 3.5 children and cooking for her husband. Well, anyone who's hungry. Her nights are for her pen. Writings available at phebeyawson.com.

A NOTE ON THE FONT

ATHELAS IS A MODERN FONT FAMILY DESIGNED SPECIFICALLY FOR books, with balanced lines and subtle serifs that work equally on screen and in print. Developed by TypeTogether, a type founder founded in 2006 by Veronika Burian and José Scaglione, Athelas helps the contemporary type-setter avoid the classic pitfalls and endless troubles presented by more classic serif fonts.

More notably, when crushed Athelas gives off a sweet and pungent fragrance and has great virtues, as the Men of the West who brought it to Middle-earth knew well. As the old Gondo-rian rhyme says:

When the Black Breath blows
and death's shadow grows
and all lights pass,
come athelas! Come athelas!
Life to the dying
In the king's hand lying!

14 Tales of
Madness & Horror

Skullgate Media Presents

LOATHSOME
VOYAGES

An Anthology of Weird Fiction
EDITED BY C.D. STORIZ & CHRIS DURSTON

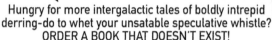

Printed in Great Britain
by Amazon